I0537131

The Killer
in You

Dean Jéan-Pierre

© 2018 Dean Jéan-Pierre

All rights reserved.

CalmWaters Entertainment Group,
Inc. presents
The Killer in You
Dean Jéan-Pierre

© 2018 by Dean Jéan-Pierre

All rights reserved. No part of this book may be reproduced or utilized in any form or by any means, electronic or mechanical, including photocopying, recording, or by any information storage or retrieval system, without permission in writing from the Publisher. Inquiries should be addressed to: CalmWaters Entertainment Group, Inc.

Library of Congress Cataloging-in-Publication Data
Dean Jéan-Pierre
ISBN: 978-0-9968835-2-8
This is a work of fiction

THE KILLER IN YOU
© 2018 by Dean Jéan-Pierre
CalmWaters Entertainment Group, Inc.

Dean Jéan-Pierre

www.deanjeanpierre.com

Book Design: Cynthia M. Colbert

Dean Jéan-Pierre

Table of Contents

IF YOU HURT ME

I told you what would happen if you hurt me. You laughed and *promised* you were different from other men. You said I had nothing to worry about. Every man always says that when they are courting you. That should have been my first clue, but I wanted to believe you. I was ready to open my heart, one more time, before I closed it permanently. I was tired of all games and lies. You said you weren't about the games. You had been around the world, sowed your oats and was ready to settle down with a real woman. When a man says he is ready for a real woman that should always be a red flag. What were the ones before me? Weren't they real also? You said all the right things. You were patient with me. You didn't ask me to do anything I was uncomfortable with. I appreciated that more than you can ever know, even now, after everything, I appreciated that the most about you. You healed that wound in me. The deepest cut a woman can ever feel—you healed me. You kissed my wounds with words, empathy, a shoulder, laughter, delicious lovemaking and patience. You did that. I was a phoenix reborn in the image that lived inside of me. I was a brand new woman. The pain I thought would follow me to my grave, slowly lifted. You lifted me from the darkness and shone your light on my heart. Spring lived in my heart. The winter had slowly thawed away and everything was now possible with you by my side. Everyone knew about you. I felt safe to dream again, to plan for a future, a family. We were making plans for our life together. And then, you just left. No goodbyes. No emails. Texts. Phone calls. You just left without saying a word. You just left me. I told you what would happen if you hurt me.

It was May 5th, the day of our sixth month anniversary. It was such a beautiful sunny day. I played that song by The Carpenters, *Why Do Birds Sing*. Corny, I know. But that's the effect you had on me. I was open, wide open. Bad things are not supposed to happen on perfect spring days. Women remember details like that. It makes it real to us. Men usually don't remember, but you did. You sent me a dozen red roses and tickets for Sade. I cried at my desk, not because you sent me flowers or the tickets, but because you remembered. It meant that it was real to you also. It meant that I mattered to you. I wanted to do something special for you, for us. I had my nails and feet done with that red polish you love. I hate Brazilians and having someone down there doing that, but you loved it, so I did it. There wasn't anything I would not do for you, the love of my life.

I ordered dinner from that Ethiopian restaurant you love down on U Street. *Dukem.* I ordered chicken samosas for appetizers and the vegetarian platter with fried fish that you love. The waitress complimented me on my smile. She was the third person that day who felt my aura of happiness. I couldn't imagine being happier. Everything was right with the universe. I had finally found a man who was what he claimed to be, a man. Not even the traffic on the highway could dampen my mood. Horns were blowing. Angry voices screamed at each other as I drove by a minor accident. The smile on my face could not be removed. I was a woman in love.

Everything had to be perfect. I wanted to look back on this night twenty years from now and be overwhelmed with happy tears as we recounted it to our friends and children over drinks and dinner. You would be over in two hours. More than enough time for me to do my womanly maintenance to get beautiful for you. An hour and a glass of wine later, I stepped out of my bathtub, silky smooth and soaking wet. I gazed at my reflection in the floor length mirror in my bedroom. You had inspired me to get back into the gym. I loved how you would stare at my naked body, drinking in all my curves and placing soft kisses in places that set me on fire. Just thinking about it, naked in my room, made me blush. All I wanted to do was just skip dinner and wait for you naked in my bed. We could have dinner after you had me for dessert. I giggled to myself at the thoughts I was having. You made me happy. You made me feel things again.

I slipped the sexy, form-fitting black dress I had bought especially for this occasion over my head and it glided down my glowing chocolate skin. I have always been conscious of being darker than most of my friends and family. It made no sense for this to be a thing with me, but it was. I was an accomplished woman. College grad. I owned my home. I was way past the age where these things should matter. But all of us have body issues and insecurities. Age is not a precursor to us accepting who we are. But with you, these things faded into the background. I bloomed. You made love to my skin, before you made love to me. Your lips told me my chocolate skin was beautiful. They praised its darkness like a god worshipping his queen. That man had me whipped like a slave and begging for more. You were too good to be true, but I wanted to believe that we were real. I deserved it, after all the losers I had been through. I deserved to be treated like a queen. I had treated every man I had ever loved like a King. None of them deserved it. They didn't know what to do with a woman like me. This time, things would be different.

I stared at my reflection in the mirror. I saw myself and imagined how you saw me through your eyes. My freshly red tinted dreadlocks swayed gently behind my back. You said the way my behind swayed along with my dreads left you mesmerized. I smiled at the reflection in the mirror. I touched the laugh lines around my eyes and along the curve of my mouth, and licked my lips. Aging wasn't that bad when you have someone who gets you. My passion had found a home. A well to empty every single emotion inside of and knowing it wouldn't spill over or break. The alarm chimed downstairs. Right on time. You were here. Even after six months of dating, my hands would still get moist knowing you were close by. I took one last look in the mirror, applied lip gloss to my lips and hurried downstairs. My man was here.

"Come here, sweet chocolate."

I love how you turned something viewed as negative by society into a positive. I wish I could change my name on my birth certificate to Chocolate.

"You're right on time as always."

Before you could respond, I jumped into your arms, wrapped my legs around your back and our tongues danced a sensual erotica tango. My wet sex pressed into your body and we moaned simultaneously. It had only been two days since we last made love, but it felt like forever, it was that good. That's how it always was with us. We went from zero to a hundred with a touch, a kiss, a look, and I became an inferno of passion.

You murmured my name on your lips and I kissed and swallowed every syllable. I never knew I was so thirsty for love and affection, until you. It was a wonderful evening. We laughed. Talked. Ate. Drank wine. We had created our own world within the walls of my home. Nothing was allowed to penetrate our sanctuary. We had agreed on always turning off all electronic communications to the world. A throwback to the times when people weren't expected to get back to you in a few seconds because of a text message. The only way to communicate was with our words and the way we touched each other. And oh how I loved how your fingers danced across the smoothness of my dark skin. My breath would escape in shallow gasps of amazement. A voice I had never heard in my forty plus years of living would beg you to please never stop, and you always obliged my desires. You seemingly placed my pleasure before yours, and that was a first for me. Men always guarantee the promise of pleasure before they reward you. The reward hardly ever merits the effort you placed in serving their needs. But you, you understood the delicate dance of allowing a woman to fulfill her deepest desires without gloating over it, as if you were the god of cunnilingus and all things orgasmic.

That evening before you left, I watched as you used your long fingers to pry the pulpy flesh from the fish. After every hearty swallow, you licked the sauce from your fingertips. It gave me pleasure to watch you eat so ravenously, because I knew in a few minutes, it would be my turn. The thought made me shiver. You instinctively knew what I was thinking as you looked up at me and winked devilishly. And of course I blushed because my thoughts were so obvious. You were a beautiful man. Dark, mysterious eyes which bore into me, leaving me naked, even when clothed. There was a strength about you that came not from your physical presence, but more so in the way you commanded attention wherever you were. I loved that. A black man, sure of his place in this world and not requiring validation from anyone but himself. Why did you have to do this to me? Why me?

We made love that evening. In the kitchen. On the stairs going up to my bedroom. On the carpet. In my bed. In the shower. You were trying to fuck the strength out of me. I didn't see it then, how could I? You were saying goodbye and hoping to leave your imprint on me, so I could miss you forever. How selfish and narcissistic is that? It made me wonder how many other women you had branded like this. But these thoughts wouldn't occur to me until later. For now, I was basking in the adulation of your lips, hands, tongue and your manhood. I was afloat now, bouncing on a trampoline, but soon, the crash would leave me reeling and questioning everything I once believed in.

We lay in bed, naked and drenched, exhausted from another round of lovemaking. The pitter patter of raindrops fell against the glass window behind the bed. I casually mentioned that I had a taste for some rum raisin ice cream, but had forgotten to buy some. You devilishly asked what I would do to get some now. *Anything you want,* I responded. You tickled me and kissed my neck. My body responded to your touch. You wrapped me up in your arms and kissed me deeply and stole my breath. Your kisses tasted like love. Your touch felt like heaven. You pulled away slowly, stared at me and exclaimed a lady should have what she desires. I didn't want you to leave, but I was craving some rum raisin desperately. Wegmans was only five minutes away. You would be back in twenty minutes you promised. I remember watching you as you dressed, unable to take my eyes off you. The hue of your dark skin made me want to lick you like an ice cream cone. I planned on surprising you when you returned. You would be my own personal chocolate ice cream cone. You dressed slowly that evening. You were meticulous as you put on your t-shirt and white shirt, placing it inside your black shorts, then sliding your legs into your brown slacks and buckling your pants. We stared at each other when you were fully dressed. You seemed torn, almost sad to leave. As I laid on the bed, I spread my legs and the message was clear, *hurry back.* The alarm chimed downstairs. The headlights of your car flooded the bedroom for a moment, before darkening again. And then you were gone, forever.

I must have dozed off that night, exhausted from too many orgasms. When I woke up an hour later, you had not returned. Texts and calls to your cellphone were unreturned. Worried and thinking the worse, I quickly got dressed and drove to Wegmans. I remember thinking and hoping that you hadn't gotten into an accident. I was relieved that the drive didn't reveal an accident had taken place. I drove around the mostly empty parking lot, looking for your car and even went inside, searching in the ice cream aisle for you. My taste for rum raisin had long since disappeared. Maybe your cellphone had died and you were at the house waiting for me. Yes, that had to be it. I sped through a yellow light. Drove 45 in a 25mph zone. You hadn't returned when I pulled into my parking space. Casual worry turned to panic. I called your cellphone numerous times. This time it didn't ring and went straight to voicemail. A once promising event to celebrate our love had turned into a nightmare. I couldn't go to the police. They require a person to be missing for twenty-four hours. I have always found this to be a stupid rule. It seems to me that most people are killed within the first few hours and waiting twenty-four hours is just wasting precious time.

It finally dawned on me to reach out to your friends and family. Then the perplexing thought surfaced that I had never ever actually met any of them. You spoke of them often, but we had gotten so wrapped up in being with each other, that we never made the time to visit. Then it dawned on me that I didn't even know where you lived. We had skyped and did facetime, but it always seemed easier for you to come to my place. The inkling of a thought began to give birth in the darkest part of my psyche, but I crushed that thought. I would not allow myself to go there yet. There had to be a good explanation for this.

Twenty-four hours later, I reported you as missing to the police. The detective, an older, pot-bellied, balding white man ran your information on his computer. The look on his face made me wonder if he wanted to use the bathroom.

"Are you sure of the spelling?"

"Yes, I'm sure," my voice raised slightly. I hadn't slept in twenty-four hours. "I should know how to spell the name of the person I've been dating for six months for God's sake!"

His raised eyebrow conveyed his thoughts without him having to speak.

"I ran every variation of his name and your boyfriend doesn't exist. I'm afra-"

"What the hell you mean he doesn't exist?"

My anger reverberated throughout his tiny, cluttered office. I could feel the eyes of the other officers watching us through the glass window. I didn't care. None of this was making any sense to me, but as I looked back now, the red flags were there. I ignored them because I was happy. I had never been this happy before and I didn't want it to end. I was complicit in my deception.

The detective stood up slowly. His belly seemed too heavy for his body to carry. His brown suit looked like he had bought it from a thrift store. The icy stare of his blue eyes cut through me, but his words were warm and caring. He sipped coffee from his New York Yankees mug before speaking.

"I've seen this a thousand times and it always ends up the same. The man you knew doesn't exist. You've never been to his home. You don't know his friends or family. And now, the name he gave you is a fake. I've seen cases of women losing everything, but it seems like he didn't bankrupt you, so for that you can be thankful. I would tell you to let this go, but something tells me that you're not the kind of woman to let things go easily. He is out of your life, so you might try and do your best to move on."

"Move on? Would you move on Detective Reed if someone had done this to you?"

The detective stared out the glass window at nothing in particular. A memory seemed to be seeping into his consciousness, but he quickly dispelled it back into its locked box.

"There are no easy answers. We all have to do what we must. If anything else comes up, I will be sure to let you know and you do the same."

We shook hands and I left his office, still unsure of what had taken place. I tried your cellphone again as I walked to my car. A steady, cold rain was falling, but I was oblivious. This time a recording came on letting me know the subscriber wasn't accepting any incoming calls or texts. This was worse than you disconnecting your phone. You knew I was calling and I didn't warrant any sort of consideration in your eyes. My rage took over as I sat inside of my car and banged my fists against the steering wheel. I could still feel your lips on my skin and it made me shudder. Your words rang in my ears as you penetrated me and entered my soul, to steal anything you wanted. I had given you the key and you had made yourself at home and taken everything that was valuable to me. I cried until my eyes hurt. I cried and screamed until my throat was sore. I could see Detective Reed staring at me from across the street in the police station, but he never came outside. He had probably seen this scene a million times before. Finally, my tears stopped flowing. The anger inside of me needed to be fed. There was only one way to feed an anger this deep. *If you hurt me there will be hell to pay.* My words were spoken with a smile on my face to you because I never thought the day would come when I would have to hunt you down and let the weight of words exact vengeance. My taste for Rum Raisin had returned. I stopped at Wegmans, then drove home. It was time to show you that you don't make love to a woman, steal her heart, and leave without so much as a goodbye. That's just rude and inconsiderate.

I felt stupid as I tried to devise a way of finding you. Your name was fake, so that was a dead end. I typed it into Google image search. A number of faces popped up, but none belonged to you. You were a ghost.

I visited a few restaurants, bars and other stores we had frequented, showed your picture to the clerks and waitresses. I made up some story about losing your address, but the look that many of the women gave me, told me that they knew I had been duped. Most were nice enough not to say so, but a few of them told me to get on with my life. The hostess at *The Blue Note* in Bowie gave me the *it could have been worse smile*, the kind of smile you give people when you want to smack them for being so stupid. How could it be worse, I wanted to ask her. I thought I had found the man of my dreams and we would grow old together, only to find out the whole thing was a vicious lie, concocted by a black devil with a devilishly sexy smile and lovemaking skills that made me forget my name. There was only one thing worse than that.

For the next few days I called in sick and did everything possible to find you. Every lead was a dead end. Every memory of a conversation that might lead me closer to you turned out to be a lie. The gym you said you frequented had been closed for two years. A bookstore had opened in its place. It wouldn't be long until it closed down also.

One day I thought I spotted you at the carwash next to Midas on Central Avenue. Your Lexus disappeared into the carwash and I waited on the other end, hands on my hips, armed with the words I had been memorizing to scream at you. Your car eased out of the carwash and I strode angrily towards you. A few feet away, my anger boiling, I waited to confront you. The car door opened and the head that popped out wasn't yours. I stood there hyperventilating and unable to move. An older gentleman, dressed in a black suit and a Bible in his hand helped me back to my car. Only when he was certain I was going to be okay, did he walk back to his car. This is what you had turned me into, a crazy woman stalking innocent men at carwashes.

I needed to get control of myself before I did something I could not undo.

I wanted revenge. I needed to hurt you as much as you had hurt me. Hating you was consuming me. I needed to release all this extra energy I had, so I took up boxing, starting running long distance again. I drove myself to exhaustion. You were never too far away from my mind. Tormenting me at every corner. Every stoplight. Every aisle I turned into, I looked for you. Nothing could make me forget you. Dating was out of the question. It would be unfair to date any man and still be consumed with you. You had managed to ruin my life and you walked away unscathed. How the hell is that even fair?

A year later and not a word from you. I had exhausted myself searching for you and finally gave up. Giving up my search was necessary for my peace of mind or at least what I had left of it. I needed to somehow move on to the next phase of life without you.

On a beautiful summer day, I drove down to Eastern Shore to visit some friends. For the next few hours we laughed, drank and I felt like my old self again. Maybe there could be life after you. On the mid-afternoon drive back home, I pulled into a gas station. The sun felt good against my skin. It had been a long time since I felt so relaxed as I filled my tank and watched the traffic drive by. A red Jeep Cherokee stopped at the red light blasting Prince. I miss Prince and sang along to *Kiss*. The car behind the Jeep wasn't paying attention and hit the bumper. Both drivers exited their cars to assess the damage. And then like something out of a movie, you stepped out of the red Jeep. You were wearing shades, a white wife beater, tan shorts and sandals. You looked relaxed, unshaven, as if you had just stepped off the covers of a magazine. After all this time thinking about what I would do if I ever laid eyes on you again, I was speechless, unable to move. I screamed and pointed at you, but no words came out. You inspected the bumper, determined there wasn't any damage and shook hands with the grateful driver. Seeing you again like this had me shook. Of all the places I imagined seeing you again—this wasn't one of them. You put your sunglasses back on and seemed to be staring in my direction. Sunlight bounced off your skin. A shiver ran through me as my body remembered your touch. I watched in horror as you slowly pulled away. Quickly, I holstered the gas nozzle and jumped into my car. There was no way I was going to lose you. I swerved into the middle lane without signaling, ignored the angry horns cursing at me. I needed to get over if you exited. Your Jeep was about a quarter mile in front of me. My hands trembled against the steering wheel. I was so close to you now. After all this time, I would finally see you face to face. I had a lot to say. You were going to listen to every word in my heart.

You took a left on Route 50, then a left on Washington Street. Traffic had dwindled down on this stretch. We were now in farmland country. Large areas of land grew nothing but corn. It's a beautiful sight to see nature in full bloom, but I didn't care about nature right now. One car, a gray Cherokee Jeep was between us.

You finally turned down a quiet lazy street with large homes and the Cherokee and I followed. I parked on the other side of the street and watched you. You were oblivious to being followed. I watched as you took out grocery bags, two in each hand and you turned casually in my direction. You froze, squinted when you saw me leaning against my car. You turned too quickly look at your house and I followed your gaze to the second floor. A woman with blonde hair held a blonde baby in her arms. They smiled and waved at you. You smiled at them and then faced me again. You had no place to hide. You were trapped between your deceit and your vows. Your wife and your ex-mistress. I didn't even know I had been a mistress. Your shoulders slumped and you took a step to walk towards me, but something distracted you. Someone, a woman screamed your name, a name I did not recognize. You had another alias.

This woman strode towards you with purpose. Dressed in tight-fitting jeans, black boots and an orange breast-hugging blouse, she screamed your name again and said something in a foreign language. Her eyes never wavered from you and a gust of wind wrapped her auburn hair around her face. Even before she drew her gun from the holster on her hip, I knew she had one on her. A woman striding with so much anger in her body came with only one result in mind, to bring death.

The gun, pointed straight at your head, never wavered. This was not a woman pretending and wanting to scare her lover. Murder was on her mind. Our eyes met as she continued walking and in that moment, I saw a reflection of myself and what I was capable of doing. We had been wronged and the only way to right a wrong is to exact revenge. Your bill was due and only one payment would be accepted.

Your wife banged her fists furiously against the window and screamed your name.

Your son stared out the window and waved at the woman with the gun.

You tried backpedaling as you begged for your miserable life, but fell backwards. The sound of breaking bottles could be heard and the contents spilled against the hot sidewalk.

I stood there, motionless, waiting for the ending.

Your lover stood over you. Rays of sunlight glinted through strands of her auburn hair. You said something inaudible with your hands stretched towards her. I could guess what you were saying.

She shook her head, looked at me again, and then pumped four bullets into your head. Blood oozed against the pavement. The fifth one exploded in your groin area and a circle of blood quickly colored your tan shorts. Your lover buried the muzzle in her mouth, turned to me and pulled the trigger. Her body crumbled against yours, and for a moment I had a vision of both of you naked in bed, smiling during better times.

The screaming sounds of sirens filled the once quiet neighborhood. Your wife was inconsolable. She loved the man she thought you were. She was a victim just like me and his dead lover. A few days later I would find out her name and everything else about her. Things I didn't need to know, but all her secrets were revealed for the world to see. The internet keeps no secrets.

She was me. I was her.

A few months ago, if I had found you, I would have killed you too. A part of me still wished that I had been the one to exact revenge. It would have meant relinquishing my freedom and maybe my life. No man is worth that much for something I would eventually get over one day soon. That day would not come for a long time. Every man after you would pay for a betrayal they had not participated in. Such is the way of life and love. The man who follows you will never get the best of me. You have already stolen that part of me, forever.

SOME PEOPLE DESERVE TO DIE

A story like this never ends well, at least for one person. Your guess is as good as mine who it will be. Charlotte Young knew she was being followed when she stepped off the 2 train on 241st Street in the Bronx. You always have to be aware riding the trains in New York City, especially as a woman. She never put headphones on or closed her eyes to catch a quick nap. That's all a predator needs these days to get the upper hand. You can do everything right and still be a victim. She had been victimized before, a few years ago, and promised herself that no matter what, it would never happen again. Her friends would laugh at her when she texted them that some random guy was looking at her with evil intentions, and up until now, she had always been wrong. Guys on the trains are just creepy and will look at anything in a skirt. This time, she just knew she was right. There was an aura of evil breathing from his body, even though he had been sitting a few seats in front of her, with his back facing her. She could just feel that something about him wasn't right. He hadn't moved a muscle for the entire ride. Thirty-five minutes he had sat completely motionless. A black hoody covered his head and it felt like he had eyes under them, staring at her, undressing her, waiting for her to get off the train. She looked around at the other passengers but some were fast asleep, others stared off into space and a few were on their phones. One lady was visibly into an erotica novel, so they were all oblivious to the imminent evil in their midst.

The conductor announced the last stop and Charlotte quickly stepped out of the subway car as soon as the doors slid open. An immediate gush of summer heat slapped her across her face and she wanted to turn around and take refuge back inside the cold subway car. The hooded stranger was still seated, unmoving and for a brief moment she thought he might be dead. There was a story a few months ago about a passenger being dead and riding on a train for the entire day and no one noticed. It was a sad commentary on the city of New York. Folks keep their heads down, go to work and just try to make it to another day.

A police officer nodded at Charlotte as she descended the stairs and through the turnstiles. She thought briefly about alerting him about her suspicions. But what exactly would she say? *Officer, there is a black man wearing a hoodie and I believe he will either try to kill or rape me?* For many people that would be justification enough for any kind of fear, but as fearful as she was now, it wasn't a door she wanted to ever open. Too many black men were losing their lives because of irrational fear of their blackness. For her to do that now as a black woman, would be a betrayal of the silent promise that black women make to themselves to nurture and protect their black men, even when some are not deserving of this special privilege.

"Have a beautiful evening, Charlotte," Mike said from behind the glass booth through the loudspeaker. His voice was heavy with innuendo. She had made the mistake of telling him her name a few months ago when her Metro card wasn't working and he had allowed her through the gates without paying. She was only being nice by telling him her name, but he had mistaken her niceness as an invitation to flirt with her. He was a nice guy, but just not her type. She waved at him, smiled and continued walking. Maybe the stranger from the train had found other prey and stalked off elsewhere. The thought made Charlotte shudder to think that, even though she wouldn't wish that on anyone, but at least it would keep her safe. The law of the jungle.

Usually there are a few gypsy cabs on the corner waiting for late night passengers. Maybe it was the heat, hovering around the century mark that was keeping them away in their air-conditioned homes and apartment. Charlotte contemplated calling an Uber, but it seemed wasteful. On foot, her apartment was only fifteen minutes away on Busby Avenue. The crowd from the train had dwindled down. Her watch read twenty minutes to eleven. Maybe she had been wrong again about the man on the train. Watching too many of those detective shows on television had stimulated her already over active imagination. Still on the alert, she began walking briskly home.

From the shadows across the street, the hooded stranger stood under a broken streetlight, watching Charlotte Young as she descended the wooden stairs of the train station. It had been a slow night riding the train back and forth from Brooklyn to the Bronx, looking for the perfect victim. He had found minor flaws with all of them. One had seemed promising at the Utica Avenue train stop, but upon closer inspection, he had found too many things wrong with her. Fake eyelashes. Her breasts appeared to be fake and he could imagine what else was fake. It was a turn off for him. He liked his women, *well victims*, more natural like the leggy bitch he was eyeballing. He had liked the professional, versatile look about her. She could be comfortable in a pair of jeans or the orange dress she was wearing now. It was the dress that had drawn his attention to her when she boarded the train at 96th Street. The spotlight always shines on women who look like her, even when they are just trying to blend in. She had boarded the train, sat away from the door and focused her attention on everything around her. Her actions were that of a woman who had encountered danger before. Women like her usually don't go down without a fight. It aroused him to think of her struggling to fight back. He watched her reflection through the window next to him and closed his eyes to imprint her image on his mind. Five-Eight. Slim. Dark Cinnamon complexion. Full black woman lips. Orange dress. Nice Hips. Well-endowed. Curly, shoulder length black hair. She was more sexy than pretty. Conceited bitches made him want to kill them. He wanted to kill all of them, but the conceited ones brought out his rage even more. The way she walked, as if a breeze was swaying through her hips reminded him of his ex-girlfriend. His pulse had raced and he gripped the edge of his seat tightly to keep from smashing his fist through the window. How can someone after seven years tell you that they no longer love you and maybe you're better off as friends? If he wanted a friend, he would get a fucking dog. A month later he found out she had gotten married. It was like he never existed or mattered. Before the night was over, they would all find out just how much he mattered. This one had a striking resemblance to his ex and she would pay for her sins, just like the rest of them.

The policeman had been too busy on his cellphone as he walked up the stairs to notice the crazed look in the hooded stranger's eyes under his black hoodie. If he had been paying attention instead of surfing Instagram for hot chicks, maybe he would have scared him off and saved Charlotte Young's life on this hot summer night. Tomorrow morning, when the police officer hears about the brutal killing in the Bronx on his beat, he will wonder if he had come in contact with any of the people involved. It would only be a momentary thought, as short as a yawn, and he would go on to read Mike Lupica's column in *The Daily News* about the crappy Knicks as he enjoyed his second cup of coffee.

Maybe the gods were on his side this time, the hooded stranger thought to himself as he stalked his prey from across the street. He sidestepped dog excrement and kept on walking. There were usually dollar cabs at busy stations like this one. He thought she might call an Uber and that would have ended his night, but when she started walking, it felt like someone was watching over him, whomever that was. Even killers have to get lucky sometimes.

The golden arch of McDonald's loomed over him as he walked by the parking lot. A few vehicles were in line at the drive thru window. One car was blasting the newest Jay Z song, oblivious to the lateness of the evening. People like that driver and his friends deserved to die, just for being rude and inconsiderate. The stranger in the black hoodie stopped and stared at the four men in the vehicle who were a few feet away and considered walking over there, slicing their throats open and then bashing their brains into tiny burger pieces. The sudden thirst for blood aroused him and it wouldn't take more than a few minutes to kill all four of them. Guys like them talked tough, but they were all as soft as marshmallows.

Even though his prey was walking at a brisk pace, he wouldn't have any problem crossing the street and catching up to her. He had the element of surprise on his side. He stood motionless under the arch debating which urge to satisfy first. A few days ago at his anger management class some fat dimwit cunt had interrupted him by coughing. The image of her cowering and shielding her face as he leapt from his chair to scream at her made him smile now. It would have been too obvious to kill her, so when the counselor, Susan Mitchell, scolded him later, he thanked her for her advice and concern. He had waited in the backseat of Susan's car to have a word with her. Well maybe not a word, but a final conversation. Her car reflected her appearance. Unkempt. Old. Neglected. And needing to be put out of its misery at the nearest junkyard. He was a big man at six-three, two hundred forty pounds, so hiding in the backseat took some doing. While he waited he sharpened a piece of twig with his penknife, until the point resembled a sharpened pencil. He waited until she had strapped on her seatbelt, tuned her radio to a Quiet Storm station that was in the middle of a Luther Vandross triple play. *Since I Lost My Baby* was playing and as she sang, she had a beautiful voice, he plunged the sharpened twig into her throat. "I love that song," he whispered in her ear as she choked on her saliva and blood. He wanted her to know who had taken her life. What's the sense of killing someone, if they don't know it's you?

The music had gotten louder. He could feel the bass rattling his teeth. They had to be taught a lesson. He quickly cast an eye toward his prey. She was about half a block away. It was still within his kill range. His fists were clenched at his side. His face cloaked under his black hoodie. He started walking quickly towards the car to teach them some manners. Parents were trying to sleep after a long day of work. Kids were in bed resting for school tomorrow. A few feet away from the car, the pimply male passenger turned his head and recognized death was fast approaching. He screamed like a little bitch, honked the horn madly and the driver stepped on the gas. The tires screeched loudly as the car careened out of the driveway. Halfway down the block, the scared little pimply boy stepped out the car, grabbed his crotch and gave him the finger. Stopping had been a mistake. The license plate was illuminated in a blue light and he was able to memorize it. After he caught his prey, he would find them and settle the score. You can find anything on the internet, no one is safe. It's a killer's buffet that keeps on giving out treats. They had barely escaped his grasp and now his lust for blood had increased. The woman would be made to suffer even more now. He walked back through the parking lot and noticed a pile of burgers, French fries and shakes where the car had been, strewn all over the ground. They had been so scared, they had left their food behind.

The screeching of tires made Charlotte Young turn around quickly, but the street behind her was empty. The dark street had an ominous presence. Overhanging branches on the sidewalk cast shadows around her. The branches looked like crazy long arms engulfing her body. A dog barked in the distance. Soca music danced on the wind. A plane flew overhead, sending a stiff breeze cascading through the leaves. The noise overhead rattled her. A few minutes into her walk she cursed herself softly. It was too late and dark for a woman to walk alone. It wasn't a dangerous neighborhood, but danger is always as close as a man who believes he has a right to invade a woman's space. There had been a few minor incidents with men who hung around the block, but only words were exchanged and they had left her alone. She knew it was just a matter of time before one of them tested her and when they did, she would be ready.

The bus station usually had one or two people loitering late at night. There was no one there this evening. The twenty-four-hour laundromat was also empty, even though there was one dryer spinning. No one was following her, so she allowed herself to exhale. It had been a fun Friday evening out with a few girlfriends from work. They had watched the new *Wonder Woman* movie over on 86th street and Lexington Avenue. This updated version wasn't as campy as the original version. Maybe in the next installment, Lynda Carter will be given a cameo. After the movie, the four of them had taken an Uber to 42nd street to walk around and have a few drinks. Charlotte was the only one who abstained. Being impaired on a Friday night and taking the train home alone was a recipe for disaster, especially in New York. She needed to be fully alert, just in case.

The last time she had allowed herself to be caught unaware was a few years ago when she was a senior at Lincoln University in Pennsylvania. It was in the parking lot of a well-known department store during the middle of the day. She had been busy talking on her phone to a girlfriend when he attacked her from behind, slamming her face against the car. The suddenness of the attack made her panic and unable to scream right away. He pressed what felt like a gun into her side and told her to get into her car or else he would kill her right there. Her survival instinct kicked in and she knew that if she got into the car with him—she was a dead woman, right after he raped her. She kicked and screamed, waved her hands wildly and fought for her life. The commotion drew the attention of a few shoppers in the parking lot. One older man in a wheelchair came to her defense. Her would be rapist growled in her ear, *next time you won't be so lucky, bitch.* A beat up old blue van had pulled up alongside her and they sped away. The encounter had left Charlotte so traumatized, she dropped out of school and became a recluse. It took her an entire year to get herself together, finish school and reclaim her life. Her self-defense instructor had commended her for her dedication to the class. He told her that he had never seen such focused rage in all his years of teaching the class. She hoped there would not be a next time, but if there was, she would not give up, until her very last breath. She had promised herself that she would never be that vulnerable to another man, ever again.

A car filled with loud males honked at her as they drove by.

Charlotte's body tensed, waiting for the inevitable as they stopped at the stoplight ahead. She slowed down her pace, giving them a chance to drive away. Her hand was in her purse, ready. At the train station she had changed from six-inch-high heels into a more comfortable pair of sneakers. If she had to run, she would. If she had to stay and fight, she would. Once upon a time she had been scared for her life. She was still scared, but the difference now was that she would be able to defend herself. There is no worse feeling in the world than being defenseless as someone else holds the power of life and death over you.

The light turned green. Something must have spooked them because they took off as if they had seen a ghost. Charlotte looked behind her. Then looked across the street. No one was there. The hooded stranger drifted across her mind. With his dark clothes, he could easily blend into the darkness and camouflage his presence. She turned around, gave her eyes a moment to adjust to the darkness on both sides of the street and waited. Her eyes darted back and forth, looking for something, anything. Just when she was about to turn around and keep walking, a street light which had been dark, flickered and beamed down an orange spotlight. A dark, hooded figure emerged from behind the street light and even from half a block away, his stare made Charlotte tremble with fear. She would be stupid not to be scared. It was late at night on an empty street, and she was staring into the imposing face of a man who had the aura of death. He pointed at her dramatically as if he were playing to invisible cameras and started walking towards her.

He had hoped to catch her by surprise and watch as she struggled for a little bit, until she realized it was pointless to resist her inevitable fate. Maybe he would have said a few soothing words to lull her into being hopeful. Giving someone hope just before they die is a wonderful sign of compassion. And just as she exhaled, he would crack her larynx between his calloused hands like a walnut. He wasn't sure which one was more satisfying, the hunt or the kill. This one might prove equally satisfying on both fronts.

Now that she knew he was in pursuit and she was the prey; the stakes had gone up. He no longer had the element of surprise on his side. You never know what women are carrying in their purses these days. It's more than just makeup or a change of underwear. They now carry mace, maybe even a small pocketknife, a Taser and a lot of them are strapped with a gun. Guys like him have to be more careful or else they're the ones who will end up dead. He wasn't ready to die yet, not that he was scared to, but he had lots of other women he had to kill before he died. He stalked her from the other side of the street, never looking directly at her. From his peripheral vision, he kept an eye on her. It was surprising she hadn't taken off running yet. Women usually panic in these kinds of situations. It made him more wary of her. Even though she had increased her pace, she wasn't running for her life.

The day of his ex-girlfriend's Laura's wedding he stood across the street, hiding like a bitch and watching another man take what was his. Maybe he had always suspected she wasn't in love with him and was only hanging around until someone better came along. But unless someone actually says the words to you, *I don't love you*, then you will believe what your heart wants to believe. She looked happier than he had ever seen her before. Seven years with someone and they leave you suddenly, makes you question everything about them. He wondered how many times had she tried to leave him? How many times had she faked an orgasm and then proclaimed her love for him? These thoughts tormented him and that's when the voices began to whisper in his ears. He had lost everything, so he saw no reason to resist the evil lurking inside of him. Brandon, her new husband for all of eight hours was the first person he ever killed. With a pretentious name like that he deserved to fucking die.

He hadn't decided to kill her new husband, until he saw them standing at the limousine, kissing and taking pictures. That's when he saw the bastard grab her ass and the rage that was now consuming him bubbled over. She might be his wife now, but that was no reason to disrespect her in front of everyone by squeezing her ass like a goddamn cantaloupe. Everyone laughed. She laughed. But he knew, *he just knew*, that she was embarrassed by the whole thing. When they were together she had never been much for showing any kind of public display of affection. They would laugh at other couples holding hands and kissing in public, so he knew that this just couldn't be something she was cool with it.

So, it was on a whim he decided to follow them all the way to the Poconos. The winding roads made it easy to remain undetected. They were probably in the front seat being all lovey dovey and shit and probably wouldn't have heard a fire engine behind them. He had always promised to take her there, but something always came up. Work. Weather. Being broke. Finally, she just stopped asking. He thought maybe she had forgotten, but it hurt him now to know that this asshole he had never met had given her something she always wanted.

It was pitch black by the time they got to the cabin. He watched as they drove up the dirt road. He remained parked at the bottom of the hill. Being in the woods so late creeped him out, but hate is a powerful antidote to fear. He followed the light from the cabin, being careful not to be detected, and waited in the woods about fifty feet away.

Patience had never been his strong point, but he was determined to get what he came for, the life of his ex-girlfriend's husband. He couldn't allow them to have the life they never had. It wasn't his fault that everything he tried to do always failed. It was as if the world had conspired against him and her marrying another man was like receiving the proverbial middle finger. He was tired of getting the middle finger and never a pat on the back.

The darkness was alive all around him. Strange noises near and far almost made him head back down the hill to his car. Just when he thought he would never get his chance at revenge, the shadowy figure of a man exited from the back door of the cottage. A few seconds later, the scent of cigarette smoke or something stronger, wafted through the air. It was like receiving a gift from God that the man he wanted to kill was so close. His back was turned to him. Slowly he crawled on his hands and knees so as not to make a sound. When he was close enough to spring on him without being detected, he nonchalantly walked up to the man who had stolen his woman.

"Hey buddy, have an extra cigarette?"

"What the fuck!" Laura's husband staggered backwards, while still holding his cigarette between his lips. "Where did you come from?"

"The cabin across the street. Heard you pulling in and needed a cigarette. Us smokers have to stick together, right? I'm Owen, by the way."

Owen hoped saying his name would grab his attention, but there wasn't any sign of recognition. It made him angrier to know that his ex-girlfriend didn't have the decency to mention his existence to her husband, or even show him a picture. She had tried to erase him from her life.

"Brandon."

He continued eyeing the stranger suspiciously as he handed him a cigarette. Something in his gut told him that danger was near, but he couldn't imagine anything horrible happening to him on his wedding day. He inhaled deeply and took a quick peek and saw the shadow of his wife behind the closed curtains. Owen followed his eyes and recognized the look of sexual hunger coming to life.

"Nothing like wedding night sex, eh," Owen said jokingly as he inhaled deeply and watched rings of smoke disappear into the air. Make sure she does anything you want. It's the one night she probably will."

"Excuse me. That's my wife you're talking about."

"She was mine before she was yours, *Brandon.*"

"Yours? I'm going to have to ask you to leave. I don't know what the hell you're talking about."

The animosity in Owen's voice was obvious to Brandon. His instinct had been right about this stranger being slightly off. He was obviously delusional.

"Laura, right, that's her name—right? Tattoo on the back of her right shoulder. Left shoulder sensitive when kissed."

Brandon tried backing up as he spoke. "Who the fuck are you?" Before he could get too far, the stranger reached behind his back and pulled out a gun. Anxious to get away, he tripped over his own feet and was now flat on his back, staring into an instrument of possible death and fear.

"Please, I just got married. If it's money you want, we have lots of cash from the wedding. Don't hurt me," Brandon begged. Without even realizing it, he was crying. The idea of dying on his wedding night filled him with dread and sadness.

"The only thing you have I want is your wife. My ex-girlfriend. My soulmate. She dumped me like a bad habit a few months ago and moved on to you. Not your fault she didn't tell you about me, but you have to be careful who you marry and their past. Too bad you won't have a second chance to get it right."

Before Brandon could say another word, Owen pointed the gun at his face and pulled the trigger. Then he pulled it five more times. He stood back and admired his handiwork. His face was nearly unrecognizable. It looked like a highway filled with potholes. In a few seconds he knew Laura would be running downstairs in this direction. He wanted to kill her with his bare hands, while staring into her eyes. Maybe with her asshole husband dead and out of the way, there was still a chance at a reconciliation. Stranger things have happened. He watched from the shadows of the woods as she knelt before his lifeless body and screamed. He smiled, closed his eyes and let the joy of her pain envelop him. Now maybe she would understand the real depths of his pain when the person you love is just taken away from you, for no good reason.

Charlotte made a left turn and contemplated knocking on one of the doors of the houses. She reasoned it was late at night. They might take forever to open the door, and the likelihood of someone opening their door for a stranger, at this time of night in New York, in the Bronx, wasn't that good. She picked up the pace, praying maybe the hooded stranger had decided that stalking her wasn't worth it. She turned her head slightly to see if he was still there as she kept walking. He was about a block behind her and gaining. Casually walking as if he didn't have a care in the world. Something about seeing him nonchalantly stalking her like an animal angered her. What had she done to draw his attention? With people like him it didn't matter. It was always some sick reason that left you shaking your head at the evil residing in the world.

The street was deathly quiet now. Night held its breath, waiting. Leaves rustled overhead ominously and branches cast long shadows as she walked under a row of them. Death was coming and she had to find some way to outrun its grasp. This wasn't how she pictured her night ending. It had been a long day. She had planned on unwinding with a glass of wine, taking a bubble bath and possibly watching the latest episode of *Insecure*. Issa and Molly were working her last nerve. Maybe because they reminded her of herself at that age, which was only a few years ago. She had to find a way to outmaneuver her stalker. He was underestimating her and viewed her death as a foregone conclusion. Men had been underestimating her all her life. Pretty women are viewed as accessories. Something to be pulled out from the trophy case and trotted out. Her intellect was just as fierce as her body. Dying was not an option. She had shit to do.

It was probably a stupid thing to do, she knew that. But when the odds are stacked against you, then you have to do something to change the outcome. Charlotte stopped in the middle of the street. The street light flickered off and on as it made a buzzing sound. A few seconds passed.

Her palms were clammy. Her heart threatened to leap viciously from her chest. But as she turned around to face down her stalker, she was the picture of calm. He stopped too, as if unsure how to proceed. Her stalker was momentarily unbalanced. Charlotte had

THE KILLER IN YOU

shown her hand. She wasn't afraid. It was his turn.

It was too dark and she was too far away to see his arousal, forming a tent around his crotch. Killing was his Viagra. The thought of taking another life did things to him that a naked woman had never been able to do. It was an elusive high, which could only be satisfied only one way. Blood had to be spilled, or else his night would be incomplete, a failure.

Dramatically on cue, the hooded stranger removed his hoodie to reveal his face. There wasn't an ounce of fear in him of being caught. The woman facing him a block away would be taking her last breath shortly. Dead women can't scream for help. He tried not to smile, but a tiny smirk twitched across his dry lips. He strode towards her and watched gleefully as the bitch turned and ran away.

The bastard was only toying with her. Charlotte knew this. Her choices were few now. Help was not coming to save her this evening. This wasn't a television movie or a fictional novel, where at the last minute, a hero swoops in to save the damsel in distress. They would kiss, make love and live happily ever after. No, this was real life and she would have to handle this on her own. Her apartment was two blocks away. There were two locks on the front door. Then another door to get into the house. Charlotte's mind whirled as she tried to calculate the odds of making it inside her home, before this crazy motherfucker strangled or raped her. Her life had always been about taking chances. They didn't always work out, but she had always done things her way. She veered left, on to a side street she had never walked before. No movement. Not a soul on the street. It was as if the entire neighborhood had retreated in fear from this monster.

Charlotte's pace increased. She made another quick left, almost tripping over a tree root bursting through the concrete sidewalk. He would be out of sight for a few seconds and she took off in a sprint, hoping to put more distance between them and make it to safety. Unaccustomed to sprinting, her legs burned, sweat poured down her face, and her chest felt like it was about to explode. Knowing the alternative, she forgot about the pain and continued running into the night.

The second she turned the corner, he knew what she had in mind for him. A predator always tries to anticipate his prey's actions, even before they know what they will do. He assumed she wouldn't lead him to her home. If she got away, he would know where she lived. Smart. Even under duress, she was thinking logically. Even though he remained confident, that his night would end with the desired result, underestimating this one wasn't something he was about to do,

His boots pounded the pavement as he rounded the corner. The sound echoed throughout the quiet street. Somewhere in the distance, a car alarm went off. A momentary flash of her orange dress gave away her position. She was faster than he had thought. Maybe she had been a runner back in school. Her stride was graceful. It reminded him of that runner from the Olympics, Allyson Felix. He always wondered what it would feel like to caress her legs and feel the power in them. This one would have to do. Once he killed her, he would take a moment to admire the finely tuned muscles which allowed her to take graceful flight. Half a dozen steps later, he was gaining on her. He sniffed the air and smiled. Her perfume lingered in the air and invigorated him.

Even with a momentary lead, Charlotte knew that the hooded monster would catch her. She would not be able to outrun him. The thought of what he would do to her made her shiver with fear and it infused her with an added adrenaline rush. The specter of death and its horrors can do that. A block away was an abandoned building. Maybe she could somehow lose him in there and double back for help. It was the only shot she had at remaining alive or catching him by surprise. She had one more card to play. It was her intention to send this monster back to hell where he could make his permanent home and resting place.

The building used to be one of those chain grocery stores, which had closed a few months ago. The chain on the front had been broken, probably by looters hoping to find anything worth selling left behind. Her eyes quickly adjusted to the darkened space. Dust covered the floor like a heavy rug. There were empty boxes and carts littered throughout the store. Rows of white empty shelves were everywhere. An industrious looter would probably be able to sell it for something. The air was stale and filled with the scent of a mixture of body odor and rotten fruit. It almost made her puke, but she was able to gather herself and move forward, trying to find a place to hide. Just before she heard him step through the front door and broken glass crunching under his boots, Charlotte ducked behind the deli counter. A few feet away from her were three fat rats, munching on something that was once some kind of meat. They were seemingly oblivious to her presence, but for how long. Between the animal stalking her and these three steroid grown rats, Charlotte reached into her purse and got ready to defend herself.

"Fi fi fo fum, I smell the perfume of a dead woman. Now that's poetry," Charlotte's stalker shouted and laughed as he entered the deserted supermarket. "I have more. Would you like to hear it? I can't hear you! I will serenade you as your life slowly slips away between my hands and death welcomes you home."

His head was covered again. Cloaking his evil in darkness. His steps were slow, deliberate as he turned around in circles, just in case she was planning a sneak attack, which would be stupid. Desperate people do desperate things. He should know. He had followed his ex-girlfriend on her wedding day and killed her husband. It wasn't the best plan to win her back, but you never know how these things worked out sometimes. The hooded stalker dropped to his knees, eyes closed and listened. People in fear for their life, unconsciously make sounds to give away their position. Nothing. His eyes flickered opened and a scowl tattooed his face, but then he smiled. In front of him were her footprints imprinted in the dust. He stood up and peered into the distance, tracking the footsteps to behind the deli counter. Then he took off running.

Charlotte looked around her, while keeping an eye on the frisky rats a few feet away and saw her footprint trail in the dust. Panic set in. Instinctively she knew he would find her and took off running down aisle five, where the canned foods were once kept. He was hot on her trail as she flew down the aisle, avoiding cans of fruit strewn all over the dusty floor. He was about halfway down the aisle from her, screaming obscenities and vile things he had planned for her. Charlotte reached into the shelves as she ran by, grabbing a few cans and threw them behind her. Hoping maybe that he would step on one of them and break his stupid ankles. That was too much to hope for because he dodged each of them as if he was a linebacker sidestepping a tackle.

At the end of the row, Charlotte turned around and saw him barreling towards her. His head was uncovered. Hoodie flapping behind of him. Sweat poured down his face. Hate radiated in his black eyes. His long face reminded her of a horse and his shaggy braids looked like a dirty black mane. Summoning every ounce of strength in her tiny body, she grabbed the metal column of the shelves and tried to bring it down on him before he could reach her. It wobbled, but did not fall. He grinned at her, aware of what she was trying to do. His big horse toothed grin made her angrier.

With about twenty feet between them, she reached deeper. This time, fueled by anger and fear, the shelves about twelve feet high, toppled over. Leftover cans and bottles came tumbling down on him. The noise was deafening as everything came crashing down on him. The last image she saw of him was with his hands up and being buried under an avalanche of falling bottles of ketchup, mayonnaise and pickles.

A few seconds of silence ensued. Maybe he was dead. Shocked and trying to catch her breath, Charlotte stared at the heap in front of her. From somewhere buried deep inside the rubble, she heard movement and someone groaning. She backed up a few steps, not believing this monster was still alive. That's the thing with monsters, they don't die. You have to kill them and watch as the life drains from their body, just to be sure they have left this world. She gasped when she saw a hand, covered in what looked like blood, make its way through a gap in the fallen shelves. Then his other hand came through and finally his face. He looked up and stared at her. Red tears streamed down his face and was matted in his hair.

"Taste like ketchup," he sneered at her as he licked his lips. "But I rather have your blood on my hands as you beg for mercy."

Something inside of Charlotte snapped. Men like him felt entitled to a woman's body. Something made for their pleasure and easily discarded after they've had their fun. She whipped out her licensed pistol, safety off and walked briskly towards her defenseless stalker. After what happened to her in college, she had promised herself to never be a victim ever again.

Charlotte was an expert shooter and could have stood where she was and hit him right between the eyes. Standing over him, she leaned over, still pointing the gun at him. She wanted to watch the life drain from his eyes, to make sure he would never hurt another woman.

"You got the wrong one, motherfucker. I don't beg."

"You can't kill me. Even if I die, there is another man like me, waiting in the shadows, watching your every movement. The minute you let your guard down is when we pounce on you. We are like cockroaches, eager to feed on your exposed weaknesses."

Her finger curled slowly around the trigger as she stared into the eyes of evil. He was already dead, but still among the living. He wanted to die. A flash of pain glided across his face. A memory was fighting its way to the surface, but he quickly drowned it and reclaimed his evil sneer. Killing a defenseless man would haunt her, even if his was death was justifiable and a kindness to the world.

Charlotte stood up, whipped out her cell phone and dialed 911. She explained the situation and gave the dispatcher the address.

"There will be a stench in here, like feces," she said to the dispatcher will looking at her stalker, "but it's only the piece of shit lying here like a bitch, waiting to be arrested. Take out the garbage when you get here. Thank you."

"This ain't over yet, bitch," Charlotte's stalker said to her as she walked away, the same way she came in.

"That's what they all say, at least the impotent ones."

Owen stared up at the woman who had become his nemesis and temporarily she had the upper hand. Rage sparked in his eyes, but beneath that, hidden, was a grudging respect. A cornered animal who fights his way through a trap has a deeper purpose than just to escape. An animal like that, a person like that, is what guys like him crave to kill. It's more than just a kill. It's the killing of hopes and dreams, just like his had been killed by that bitch of an ex-girlfriend.

Charlotte took one more look at the beast who would probably be haunting her dreams for the next few weeks and walked away, pistol still in hand. A woman has to always be prepared. When she stepped outside, away from his view, she leaned against the wall, wiped tears from her eyes as her hands shook. She gathered herself and a few minutes later, walked across the street and took a short-cut through a children's park complete with swings, slides and a merry go round. It was eerily silent now. She imagined all the noise during the day with kids running around and was thankful for the silence.

Her ordeal had taken a toll on her. Even though she wanted to get home, take a bath, maybe have a glass of wine before going to bed, she sat down on the park bench to calm herself down. Adrenaline was still flowing. The possibility of the worst-case scenario flashed before her eyes. It was an image of her raped and disfigured with the rapist beast staring down at her. It could have easily turned out that way, as it had for many other women.

Charlotte stared up into the sky, looking for a star. Stars in a New York skyline are almost non-existent. But it gave her a feeling of floating away, momentarily forgetting the ordeal she had just experienced. The backfiring of a muffler brought her back to reality. She blinked a few times at what she was seeing. It was him. Standing in the middle of the street, even though she couldn't see his face, now covered. She could feel his eyes on her defiling her body. How the hell did he get out from under that mountain of shelves piled on top of him? Charlotte knew the answer. Evil always finds a way to survive. The only way to end this, was for one of them to die.

He lumbered towards her, swaying like a tree caught in the wind. This time moving slower than he had earlier. Charlotte froze on the bench. She knew she had to do something, but she was unable to move. The image of her being raped and brutalized earlier came back to her in a hurry. That same feeling of being powerless was on the cusp of overwhelming her again. Just when it seemed she would just sit there and allow him the pleasure of doing as he pleased, she bolted and ran blindly. Unsure of where she was going or what to do now, her instincts for survival took over. In front of her was a tall slide. The echoes of children laughing as they slid down its winding structure was now a whisper on a breeze. The night was thick with fear and it held its breath, waiting. It seemed like a good place to hide or to just get away from this monster, until help arrived.

Perched now at the apex of the slide, twenty feet above ground, Charlotte looked down at the surrounding darkness. A few streetlights dotted the surrounding eerily quiet neighborhood. In the apartment buildings across the street, a few lights were on, one by one, they were all turned off, as if sensing danger was near. No one was coming to save her. The reality dawned on Charlotte that she was all alone. There would be no cavalry. No last second reprieve by some handsome hero. No riding off together into the sunset. Either she would have to stand up to defend herself or allow another man to determine her future, which would be nonexistent.

Absorbed in the moment, Charlotte hadn't realized the sky had opened. Raindrops splattered around her, drenching her clothes and streaming down her face, temporarily obstructing her vision. At the bottom of the slide stood the monster with the grin of death plastered on his face. He finally had her cornered, or so he thought. He motioned to her with one finger from both hands and arms wide open, for her to come on down. There was nowhere else to run to. With her bag clutched to her chest, knees up, Charlotte pushed her body down the wet slide. She hadn't anticipated her descent would be that quick, as her body zigzagged out of control. Her left knee banged against the side of the railing and she screamed in pain. Finally, halfway down the slide, Charlotte regained control of her body and prepared herself for the inevitable.

Owen's ugly face contorted into what appeared to be a smile. Anyone looking at him right now, would probably run away screaming at the top of their lungs. Arms wide open, rain pounding on his body, he was anxious to feel the euphoric feeling of crushing her to death in his arms. He wanted to look into her eyes as life left her body and the last face she would see, would be his. He clenched his fists, bared his teeth for extra effect, hunched over and got ready to receive his gift.

Charlotte couldn't afford to feel fear right now. Fear makes you indecisive. With her life on the line, she didn't have time to be indecisive. There would be enough time for that later. A smile crossed her face because she was planning for a future beyond this moment.

The rain picked up its assault and the sound of raindrops pounding against the metallic frame reverberated in Charlotte's ears. It was time to face the monster. She brought her head up from between her knees, and with her purse dangling around her neck, Charlotte stood up straight like a surfer riding the waves on the rain slickened metal surface. *Nowhere to run this time, bitch*, the monster mouthed the words through a hail of rain. Her eyes conveyed what she was thinking. *Your time is up.*

Knowing that she had the element of surprise on her side, Charlotte knew she had to wait just until the last moment to give herself every chance of coming out of this alive. Demons don't die easily. They have a lifeline directly to hell. With no time left and the demon staring right at her, Charlotte refused to look away. It was just the diversion she needed. She reached into her purse and slid her finger around the trigger like a key, a perfect fit. In one smooth motion, she flung her bag over the side of the slide and with two hands on the trigger, aimed and fired.

The look of smugness quickly turned to shock when he realized what had transpired.

The first shot crackled through the rainy night and pierced his left ankle, staggering him backwards. The second one found a home in his right ankle and Owen screamed into the rainy night sky as he fell hard to his knees. The third shot ripped through his chest and put him on his back. The sky looked like it was falling down on him. He struggled to get up, but his body would not cooperate.

The three shots she fired seemed to propel Charlotte forward even faster. She skated down the last few feet as if gliding on ice. Her gun now lowered, she landed with both feet on his chest and he screamed a profane greeting of disgust.

"I'm going to kill you, bitch!" he roared through gritted teeth.

"Hard for a dead man to kill anyone."

Charlotte stood over him, rain dripping down her face and arms. A few strands of wet hair stuck to her face, but she refused to brush them aside or take her eyes off him. Her finger still on the trigger, she was ready to use one more bullet to put him to sleep, permanently.

"Go ahead, call the cops. I will do my time, be out in a few years and I will come looking for you to finish this dance."

Charlotte stared down at the monster who would be haunting her dreams for the next few weeks, possibly longer. Men like him never go away. They feel entitled to your life and keep coming back like radioactive cockroaches. She had lived that life before, in fear and constantly looking over her shoulders. There was no way she would revert to being that scared little girl.

"Thank you for telling me what I already knew. It makes this easier."

A look of shock dawned on his face when he realized he had signed his own death warrant. He had underestimated this one's fortitude. She had appeared to be like all the others and he assumed she would back down when things got tough, like they always did. He opened his mouth to get in one more taunt, but he had already spoken his last words.

One minute he was alive, and the next, he was dead.

Charlotte stared at the hole in his skull and forced herself to take his pulse. She had to make sure he was dead. It was amazing to her, that someone who looked so menacing, was now so still. Death can be so swift and occur before you even take your next breath. It was over. She dropped to her knees in a pool of water, gun still clutched in her hands and sobbed.

Tomorrow morning, she would search the papers, listen to the news to find out if the police had any suspects or leads. She would go on with her life, maybe go out dancing with friends and pretend that this night never happened. She would not allow this monster to have any power over her from his grave. She stood up, took one more look at him and wished him well on his first-class trip to hell as she walked away and never looked back. The rain felt cleansing. Tomorrow was a new day.

GILBERT TUESDAY COMES HOME EARLY

The scent of a cologne he hadn't worn in years, taunted the nostrils of Gilbert Tuesday as he entered his home. A sneezing eruption was on the cusp, but as quickly as the sensation came, it disappeared. He had only been gone a few days on a business trip, but this time his house felt different, almost as if he were a stranger entering it for the first time. He set his carry-on bag next to the front door, took off his winter coat and gently closed the door behind him. The heat was turned on high which he never liked, but Karina needed it that way, so it was that way. The floor-board under the burgundy rug always creaked, so he avoided step-ping on it as he turned towards the kitchen. He wanted to surprise his wife, so he had come back a day early. Gilbert smiled as he remembered the earnestness in his wife's voice last night as she told him how much she missed him. It was the idea of her being lonely, that prompted him to cut his trip a day short. There wasn't any-thing he couldn't do in person that he could not do on his phone or via Skype. Modern technology had taken away many obstacles to business trips. In the kitchen, Gilbert looked for his favorite coffee mug he had bought at a street fair fifteen years on their first date. It wasn't in its usual place next to the Keurig. Maybe his wife had missed him so much and using his mug was her way of feeling con-nected to him. The thought made him smile as he tiptoed up the stairs to surprise her.

At the top of the stairs, red roses in hand, Gilbert Tuesday froze when he heard screaming coming from down the hall in their bed-room. His first thought was that an intruder had somehow gotten into their home and was now defiling his beautiful wife. The loud piercing sound filled the upstairs part of the house, but as he ran towards the bedroom, the screaming turned into passionate moans and squeals of pleasure. Gilbert stopped in mid-run and listened again, this time as a man and not a husband. Just that short burst of speed left him winded. For years he had been promising Karina to get into better shape and join her at the gym, but he just didn't have the motivation anymore. The male voice, which sounded like that of a large man, ordered his wife to get on her knees. There was still a part of Gilbert Tuesday that wanted to believe that some stranger was raping his wife. The alternative would be too much to handle.

Not sure why he was tip-toeing on the carpet, Gilbert walked slowly towards his bedroom door, which was slightly ajar. His hands were sweating. His heart rate had increased to a dangerous level and as he peeped into his bedroom, he made a mental note to take his heart medication later on, if he still needed it. The scene in front of Gilbert Tuesday's horrified eyes made him clench his fists as the blood rushed to his chubby face and his entire body trembled in anger. His wife, blindfolded, was on her knees doing something that she claimed was disgusting whenever he asked her to do it, but here she was, doing it to a dark-skinned tattooed male with great zeal. Her mouth wasn't made to do such filthy things she had told him and he had understood, even though he craved it from her. Over time, he had learned to do without it. But from the pleasurable moans escaping her mouth it had all been a lie. It sounded as if she had been starving for it and now that she was being fed, the idea of stopping didn't occur to her. Watching another man receive oral sex, something his wife only did on special occasions filled Gilbert with jealousy and rage. The seed of hatred was planted, but would need more water to bloom.

Sweat poured down the rippled back of the man doing filthy things to his wife. Distracted by the man's physique, Gilbert marveled at how broad and muscular this man was in comparison to himself, and how his buttocks kept perfect rhythm as he thrust forward. He had never been concerned about things like that, but in that moment, he wondered about his own physical appearance. His pot belly suddenly made him self-conscious, even though no one was looking at him. After numerous pelvic thrusts into the waiting gap between his wife's lips, the man ordered his wife to stand up. Still on her knees, his wife removed the blindfold, stared up into his face and declined. As quickly as she refused, his right hand descended from the air and made contact with her face. The crackling sound ricocheted in his bedroom and Gilbert stood there, shocked at the sudden violence. He was even more shocked, when his wife stood up and with a devilish glint in her eyes, asked for more slaps, *please*. The naked, sweaty man obliged her, and with every slap, Gilbert watched the woman he knew, transform into someone he had no clue about. His wife of fifteen years was a stranger, and yet, for some strange reason, he loved her more than he ever had in his life. The idea of not knowing that something so primal and savage lived inside of her, made him sad. She had been hiding this part of herself from him. Either she was unwilling to share it or didn't think he deserved to know. He couldn't decide which one was worse.

The open sliver in the door allowed Gilbert a full view of their queen-sized bed and he was able to see about half of the dresser on his side, which was always the right side. Sitting on the dresser was his coffee mug, and from about twenty-feet away, he could see steam rising from it. He inhaled the scent of freshly brewed coffee and also the scent of the cologne he no longer wore assaulted his senses like an insult that knows your vulnerable spots. He watched as the naked stranger walked over to his dresser, still fully aroused and sipped from his coffee mug. He closed his eyes and seemed to be enjoying the taste of the hot liquid. Gilbert wondered if he took any sugar or cream with his coffee, or like him, drank it black, no dilution.

Gilbert remained perfectly still outside the door, barely breathing and wondered how long this affair had been going on. This man was in his bed. Comfortable enough to be drinking from his mug, as if he had paid for it. It didn't feel like something casual. There has to be a degree of familiarity for him to treat his wife in such a savage way. Until this moment, Gilbert hadn't been aware of his own arousal. It repulsed and confused him that his body was reacting in such a perverted way. He was about to burst in and re-claim his shattered manhood, even though he was almost certain that his wife's lover would beat him to a pulp, but before he could, the pelvic thruster spoke. His voice boomed across the room and seemed to slip through the crack in the door and strip him naked. Even hidden, he felt naked and weak.

"This mug, where did Gilbert buy it from?"

Hearing his name spoken from this intruder's lips, filled Gilbert with renewed rage. He spoke as if he knew him, even though they had never met. And until fifteen minutes ago, Gilbert had no idea that this man existed. This man knew of him, didn't care that he was defiling his wife in his bed and drinking from his mug.

"He bought it from some street vendor for twenty dollars."

"Can you buy me the exact same one?"

"He bought it fifteen years ago."

The naked stranger stared intently at Karina. Her body visibly trembled under his gaze as he continued to sip coffee. Gilbert watched this strange dynamic of arousal. Without saying a word, this man was doing things to his wife, almost willing her body to comply with his demands.

"Take it." Gilbert assumed that his wife was referring to her body, again. She had never been this insatiable with him. "I will just tell him it broke." The casualness in which she said it stung him. "He never doubts me." His wife laughed. It was the kind of laugh filled with a history of many lies she had told him over the years. One lie makes you wonder how many others were told.

"Leave it here for next time. A man has few possessions in this world he can call his own. It might be just a stupid mug to you, but to Gilbert, it's a time stamp of a memory of who he was before he became the person he is today."

As if experiencing some sort of telepathy, Gilbert's wife expressed his thoughts to her lover.

"You got all of that from drinking from his mug?"

"You can find out a lot about a man by how he drinks his coffee."

"You're just full of surprises today. What do you have planned next for me?"

The brief affinity Gilbert felt for his wife's lover quickly vanished. He became the enemy again as he flipped her over on the bed. He gripped her around the waist and stole what was already promised to another man in front of God and family. A man who has no regard for the sacred vows of marriage is obviously a man who cannot be trusted. Gilbert watched as this stranger used each one of my wife's orifices for his pleasure, and by the moans she exhibited, hers too. He took a few steps back away from the door and caught a view of himself in the hallway mirror. For the first time, he saw himself as his wife probably saw him. An overweight middle-aged man who probably wasn't going to lose any weight or get back all the hair that had been lost. If he was being honest, he could understand how a woman like his wife, still youthful looking, in good shape and fairly attractive would go looking for some excitement. If he were married to himself, he might be in the bedroom of a stranger right now.

Gilbert made sure to retrace his steps so as not to leave any evidence he had been in his own home. He put his coat back on and buttoned it over his ample stomach, put the alarm on silent and turned it on before leaving. In one hand he held the red roses which seemed less red now and in the other, his carry-on bag. Once outside he exhaled, but didn't allow his emotions to overcome him. And as quietly as he came, he left the same way.

There was only on entrance into his neighborhood. So Gilbert Tuesday waited across the street, parked under a tree and texted his wife that he was on his way home. While he waited, he logged into the app on his phone to watch the images from the camera on his front door. It wasn't something he ever checked. It was more for his wife's safety and his peace of mind whenever he traveled. She hadn't wanted the surveillance system, but for once, he had insisted. Now he understood why. He watched as his front door swung open and they embraced, then kissed as a few cars drove by. Gilbert wondered how many of his neighbors knew and had never said anything. Would he have said anything if Veronica the next door was stepping out on her husband, Steve? He probably would have just minded his business as he always did. He didn't like to meddle in the affairs of others and expected the same. Twenty minutes later, a black Ford Explorer being driven by her lover cruised down his street, and turned left towards the highway without signaling.

Gilbert wasn't sure how to tail someone, but he had seen it enough time on television to have a basic idea of how it worked. Stay behind a few cars. Remain inconspicuous. He could that. His entire life had been built on not being seen. At the office, managers would regularly walk right by him or interrupt him without apology. He was the kind of man who people did not remember and were often surprised to have met him when Gilbert tried to prompt their memory of a past encounter. It never made him feel bad. It was just who he was.

About twenty minutes later, the Jeep pulled off the highway and then onto a side street. Gilbert lingered about half a block behind and watched as his wife's lover parked, crossed the street and disappeared into a bar. It wasn't a neighborhood he was familiar with, but it didn't seem any more dangerous than any neighborhood in Maryland. Safety anywhere is a lie people tell themselves so they can make it through the day. The lies people tell themselves sometimes is the only comfort they have against an ugly, unforgiving world. Maybe his marriage had always been a lie, but up until about an hour ago, it was a lie he didn't know he was living.

Parked across the street, he wasn't able to see inside the bar or tell what the stranger was doing. He could only assume he was having a drink. A police vehicle crawled down the street and the officer on the passenger side, stared at him. It was a stare to recall his features later on, if it were warranted. Gilbert completely out of character met the glare of the blue-eyed officer and a knowing thought passed between them. He had no doubt they would be back for a second look.

The heat in his vehicle had quickly disappeared. He didn't want to idle the engine while he waited, so Gilbert stepped out his car and quickly crossed the street. He paused at the door, unsure now if he should enter. He wondered if his wife's lover knew his face. Before he could change his mind, he turned the knob and entered the bar.

A few people sat at the bar. The lighting was low, obscuring the faces of anyone who shouldn't be there. A couple sat at one of the tables engrossed in their world. His eyes adjusted to the dim lighting as he searched for the stranger. Finding courage he didn't know he possessed, Gilbert walked deliberately to the bar and sat down next to the man who had just fucked his wife. A stool separated them. It would be kind of weird to see two strangers sitting down next to each other at a bar. A little separation is always needed. It's an unspoken bar rule.

"What's your poison?" The muscled bartender asked. He seemed oblivious to the fact it was cold outside and was wearing a black wife-beater t-shirt. A long snake tattoo wrapped around his right arm, but the left one was bare.

"Hit me off with a Corona to start." Feeling braver than he looked, Gilbert turned his attention to his wife's lover and said, "give this man another of whatever he's having."

The stranger, bleary-eyed and obviously already had a few to drink, lifted his head from his cellphone and turned slowly to look at Gilbert.

"Do we know each other? This ain't no queer bar, friend."

Gilbert instantly disliked him even more than he already had.

"Just being friendly. I had a hard day and wanted to do something nice."

The stranger seemed satisfied with that response and signaled to the bartender that it was okay. Gilbert took a cursory look at the dark-skinned man and then stared straight ahead. The man wasn't overly handsome, but he seemed to possess an air of confidence which probably had drawn his wife to him. He had an Afro and a goatee which reminded Gilbert of someone from the seventies.

The bartender bought them their drinks. A Corona for him and a shot of Tequila for the stranger. They raised their drinks at each other and the man with the Afro went back to staring at his cell phone. Something on his phone made him laugh out loud and then without warning, he turned to Gilbert and slid his phone over to him. "Look at this. I can't believe the things she lets me do to her." His speech was already slurred and he was on a fast track to getting wasted.

Gilbert stared at the image on the phone in front of him. The cold beer felt hot going down his throat.

"Press play," the stranger almost demanded.

Gilbert did as he was told. Something already told him what he might see, but knowing and seeing are two different things. He needed to see it. He pressed *play* and the image of his bedroom came into focus, before settling on his wife's face. The camera zoomed in on her face and despite being in her mid-forties, a few years younger than him, there was a youthfulness in her face. Her eyes sparkled as the voice behind the camera engaged her and she blushed.

"Why do you let me fuck you in the same bed you share with your husband?" The voice probed her. He seemed to already know the answer, but needed to capture it on film, maybe so he could watch it again later and have a good laugh.

"It helps me sleep at night knowing your warmth is close by, even though you're not here. The memory makes me smile until next time."

The camera panned around the bedroom as if searching for something that only the camera's eye could detect. It settled on Gilbert's mug, which was a dark blue color with hints of sky blue and a half moon painted on it. Gilbert watched as the camera followed the hand of the cameraman and his fingertip glided around the rim of the mug.

"You seem enthralled with that mug, Kurt. Just take it with you when you leave."

All Kurts are assholes Gilbert thought as he continued watching. He finally had a name for the stranger, *Kurt*. He looked like a Kurt. Kurt is the kind of guy who will fuck your wife and drink out of a mug that isn't his. The stranger aka his wife's lover and now known as Kurt turned the camera back to his wife without answering her question. Gilbert would have loved to hear his answer to the unanswered question.

"Why don't you just leave him? There's nothing here for you anymore. How long have we been together? A year? A year and a half?"

The camera held steady on her face, waiting for an answer.

"He needs me. If I leave he will have nothing left."

"I need you," anger rose in Kurt's voice, but quickly disappeared when he spoke again. "You deserve so much more."

"You don't want me, Kurt," Karina sighed. "You only want me because I won't leave him."

"From everything you've said, your husband is a loser. I don't understand how he snagged you."

"It's a long story and you *really* don't want to hear it."

As if in answer to what she had just said, the camera panned down her naked breasts and rested between her closed thighs. Gilbert continued to watch as his wife laid down on her back, spread her legs and beckoned her lover to put the camera away.

"Say it again and I will give you what you want."

"I love you, daddy."

The words felt like a rusty knife being simultaneously plunged into his heart and back by the woman he loved. He studied her eyes as she said it and watched her lips. They curled around the word *love* as she spoke it. Her features softened even more as she made the declaration. Her heart was on full display for him to see. How had she managed to hide being in love with another man? How had he missed it? He hadn't been paying attention as she slowly slipped away from his grasp, into the arms of someone named Kurt. He wanted to puke, but swallowed the bile back down when he felt it about to erupt through his throat.

"She's something else, isn't she?" Kurt bragged as if he were the luckiest man in the world.

Gilbert watched the frozen smile of his wife on her lover's phone one last time, before sliding it back down to him. He motioned to the bartender that he wanted something stronger and pointed to what Kurt was drinking.

"Too bad she won't leave her husband for you," Gilbert stared at Kurt as he swallowed his drink in one gulp and motioned for two more. One for him and Kurt. His words were meant to taunt him. He wanted to exact some sort of pain on this man who had taken the most precious thing in the world to him.

"If I *really* wanted her—I would just take her. Women like her are yearning to be seen, to be loved and if you can give them anything that remotely resembles love, they will do anything you want. I have the videos to prove it."

"Why would you share something so private with a stranger?"

Gilbert sounded calmer than he felt. He wasn't a drinker, but whenever he had a drink, a certain clarity came to his thoughts. It felt almost like some sort of superpower, even though he knew that was ridiculous. Alcohol was a shortcut to the truth.

"Are you offended? Most men wouldn't be. Especially if it's a beautiful woman."

"Well, I'm not most men."

"My apologies for offending you," Kurt responded sarcastically. His eyes were drooping and he seemed almost ready to pass out, but came to just before his face crashed against the wooden bar. "As I was saying," he continued undeterred, "it's not like I showed you a video of us fucking. Now that would be disrespectful. Gotta shake the snake," he said abruptly without even looking at Gilbert. He walked away, leaving his cell phone on the bar and walked unsteadily to the bathroom.

The bartender watched him and waited until the bathroom door closed behind him. His voice didn't match his muscular frame and demeanor as he spoke to Gilbert. It was the voice of man speaking quietly in a library, so as not to disturb anyone. Gilbert thought maybe the alcohol had impaired his hearing, but the bartender smiled as if understanding his dilemma.

"I get that all the time," said the bartender.

"Sorry. That was rude."

"Just a warning, that dude is bad news. I wouldn't go getting all friendly with him. He can be a mean drunk after a few shots and by the looks of him, the ugliness is about to come out soon. My shift is over, so let's square away your tab before I leave. Kurt has a running tab here, so he's straight."

"Good looking out." The words sounded strange coming from his mouth. The quizzical look on the bartender's face confirmed Gilbert's suspicion. Men who looked like him couldn't pull off that phrase.

The couple who had been in the corner when Gilbert walked in stood up to leave. The guy, a rather suspicious looking man shot daggers at Gilbert and he turned back to sip on his drink. Kurt's unattended cellphone vibrated against the wooden counter and then stopped. A few seconds later, it vibrated again. The bartender was busy tabulating the day's receipts and not paying attention to Gilbert. He grabbed the phone and was surprised to find it unlocked. The messages were from his wife. There were an assortment of naked pictures in various sexual poses and each picture was accompanied by a text, telling her lover, Kurt, what she wanted done to her. Gilbert glanced in the direction of the restroom and continued scrolling through the phone. The texts went back at least a year. Not even caring if anyone saw him, Gilbert scrolled through the messages of his wife proclaiming her love for this man. The time stamps were all throughout the day, even times when he was home working or sleeping. She was texting this man and telling him how much she loved him. Words he had never entertained about his wife leapt into his mind now. He saw it clearly now. It wasn't Kurt who had broken up his home. It wasn't Kurt who had broken his vows. His wife had a duty to him and she had failed. There are consequences for every action. Sometimes they are immediate. Sometimes when least expected, they have to be paid, long after you have forgotten about your debt. He had been a giving, loving and always respectful husband. He wasn't a handsome man. He wasn't exciting. The things about him that were good were not sexy. He was a good provider. Loyal. Loving. He was a good man. Good men don't deserved to be fucked over by assholes like Kurt. Guys like Kurt were always shitting over guys like him, because guys like him let the Kurts of the world do as they pleased, as if the world was their toilet and they could shit anywhere they damn well pleased.

Gilbert stood up, unsteady at first but then he got his bearings. He swallowed the last of his drink and walked with purpose towards the restroom. Right now he didn't know who he was. He just knew he didn't want to be the guy who took shit from other people for the rest of his life and said thank you. Gilbert turned the brass knob of the restroom door and held on to it for a fraction longer than necessary. The moment dictated he become someone he wasn't. Who he was hadn't been good enough for his wife, so he would try on this new persona and see if it suited him better. It could be the new suit he needed and would finally get.

The stale stench of vomit mixed with the fresh farts of a grown man who had eaten some bad food greeted Gilbert's nostrils. He ignored the offensive odor and found Kurt standing at the urinal, his pants and underwear around his ankles and shoes, a puddle of piss surrounding him and fast asleep.

The image of his wife impaled with Kurt's manhood in all her orifices, her screams of pleasure tortured Gilbert and the final stab to his heart, was hearing her say she loved another man. A guttural, foreign roar spewed from his mouth as his anger rose to the surface to claim its rightful place of being disrespected and used. Standing directly behind Kurt's exposed buttocks, Gilbert had a fleeting evil thought, but he quickly dispelled it. He wrapped his big hands around the thick, dark neck of the taller man and in one fluid motion, bashed his head against the ceramic wall in front of him. The blow shook loose the cobwebs and Kurt placed both hands against the wall to regain his balance. Disoriented and in an inebriated haze, he didn't know what was happening to him. He tried turning around to face his assailant, but Gilbert still had his hands wrapped around his neck and was squeezing his throat tightly. Gasping for air, Kurt swung his left elbow into Gilbert's pillowy stomach. The blow caught him by surprise and stole his breath momentarily, but he held his position and bashed Kurt's face into the wall again, this time with more force. The heavy thud of flesh meeting immovable object made Kurt grunt loudly, but not in pain. The alcohol had dulled his senses. Pain wasn't really registering in his mind. It felt more like a hard slap to the front of his face, than his face crashing into a wall. He steadied himself and quickly turned around and came face to face with Gilbert. Blood oozed down his forehead. His nose appeared to be bent now and shaped like the letter c. Two of his bottom teeth hung loosely from his bloodied mouth, but for a man who looked like he had gotten his ass kicked in a street brawl, Kurt was surprisingly upbeat.

"You. You finally grew some balls, Gilbert."

Hearing his name from the bloodied mouth of his wife's lover caught Gilbert by surprise. He didn't recall ever mentioning his name or introducing himself during their conversation. He tried to look directly at him, but it was difficult to focus with his dick swinging freely as he spoke.

"How do you know my name?"

"I know everything about you, Gilbert. Right down to the last time you tried to fuck my woman and couldn't rise to the occasion. Don't worry after you left that morning, I came over and handled her for you. No need to thank me. She thanked me in ways I never imagined."

Kurt winked at Gilbert and held his dick in his right hand. He pointed the dark projectile at Gilbert's shoes, and a stream of dark, yellow urine jetted forward, drenching his brown shoes in the warm liquid. With urine that color, Gilbert was sure it wouldn't be long until Kurt's kidneys malfunctioned. He stared down at his stained shoes and took a step towards his offender. A quick slap to the left side of his face rocked him backward and Kurt's derisive laughter rang in his ears.

"How did a fat, out of shape loser like you get a fine woman like Karina? Did you blackmail her or was it just pity she felt for you? I know for sure she doesn't love you. She never did. I'm sure you scrolled through my phone I left behind and read all the texts, saw more videos and now understand the pathetic truth of your life. It's all been a lie. I feel bad for you. You're a hardworking man, honest and by everything Karina told me as we laid in your bed, you have never once mistreated her. Maybe that's the problem. Sometimes a woman needs to be mistreated to keep her in line. Treat her right all the time and she begins to take you for granted. Your wife was bored with you and came looking for me. It didn't have to be me. It could have been anyone. I just happened to be at the right place and caught her at her most vulnerable. Men like me can smell vulnerability on a woman like the newest perfume. Their skin is bathed in the scent and all I had to do was sniff it a few times and she was lapping on my nuts like a bitch in heat. If I hadn't known better, I would have sworn she was a virgin. She was embarrassed at how many orgasms she had. Can you imagine a married woman only having an orgasm through masturbation?"

Kurt's brain suddenly remembered he was drunk and his mouth suddenly stopped moving.

Gilbert had just stood there, absorbing the verbal insults of the man who seemed to know his wife better than him. He had kept quiet and allowed him to speak, to learn as much as he possibly could. What he heard had brought tears to his eyes. He hadn't even realized he was crying, until he tasted the salty liquid on his lips. The continuous body blows to his ego would be permanent. A man does not recover from hearing his wife of fifteen years never experienced an orgasm when they made love. Every word spewed from Kurt's bloodied mouth was true, because even if Gilbert would never admit it to anyone else, he had always known his wife had never loved him. He had always known she had settled for him. He had been the rebound boyfriend and had caught her at a vulnerable time in her life after a disastrous breakup. He had held out hope that she would eventually fall in love with him, the way some arranged married couples often do. But as the years had passed, they had always been civil. No fights. No passion. Nothing. He had managed to somehow convince himself that he didn't need love. That having her companionship would be enough to sustain him. He had seen her around her friends and family, how warm and loving she always was with them. But when it came to him, there was a barrier, one she couldn't seem to cross to extend herself to him. He ached for some of the warmth she freely gave to others. Asking her why she didn't love him after everything he had done for her would embarrass him and her, so the question went unasked.

If the situation hadn't been so unbelievable, Gilbert would have broken down in laughter as he looked around the dingy restroom. Here he was with piss stained shoes standing in front of man with his shorts and pants down to his ankles and surrounded by urine. The smug look of dismissal on Kurt's face was the last straw for Gilbert as he charged a surprised Kurt, who swung too late at Gilbert's head and only connected with air. Gilbert used his head as a battering ramp and barreled into Kurt's chest, pushing him backwards against the urinal. His head snapped back and Gilbert used the five fingers of his right hand to palm his face like a basketball and bang the back of his head repeatedly against the wall. He was no longer Gilbert, the loving and trusting husband and friend to everyone. He was an angry husband hell bent on revenge and exacting physical and emotional pain. The sound of bones crushing vibrated in his fingers and trails of blood splattered and oozed against the ceramic white tiles. Being inebriated slowed down Kurt's response to defend himself. If he were sober, Gilbert knew he wouldn't have been able to manhandle the bigger and stronger man.

Kurt's body slumped to the urine stained restroom floor. His eyes were closed, and his arms hung loosely at his side. He groaned softly. His penis hung limply between his legs and didn't seem all that powerful anymore. Breathing heavily and sweating, Gilbert stood over Kurt, unzipped his pants and released the contents of three beers and four shots of Tequila all over his face. The urine bath brought Kurt back to his senses as his eyelids fluttered open but closed again, weighed down by a steady stream of piss. "Now you know what it feels like to piss all over a man's life." Gilbert zipped up his pants, took a look at his disheveled appearance in the bathroom mirror and what looked like a smile shadowed his face. From the corner of his left eye, he saw the image of Kurt lumbering towards him. Adrenaline still flowing through his body, Gilbert spun around and for the first time in his life landed a punch, directly to the throat of Kurt. The throat punch made him sway side to side as he skated in his own urine. He somehow spun around like a ballerina, still clutching his throat and before he could regain his balance, he fell forward and cracked his forehead against the bowl of the urinal. His body went limp. Gilbert stood there, frozen, waiting for him to get back up. A few seconds passed which felt like an eternity and he was still motionless. Slowly Gilbert walked back to him, bent over and felt for a pulse. Nothing. He tried two more times with the same result. He straightened up abruptly and took a few steps backwards to the door. This wasn't supposed to happen. He couldn't be dead. The realization of what he had done dawned on Gilbert. His immediate emotion should be shock and guilt, but instead, he felt calm. He knew it was wrong to take a man's life, even it was by accident, but men like Kurt had been taking him for granted all his life, and for the first time, he had the upper hand and wasn't going to waste it by feeling a useless emotion like guilt.

No one looked in Gilbert's direction as he walked through the bar. The first bartender was gone. His replacement, a short, blonde woman had her back turned to him and on her cell phone. The front door closed behind him as he slipped back on his coat. The cold air felt good against his skin as he walked briskly towards his car. Parked a few feet away from the bar was Kurt's black Ford Explorer. The driver's window was halfway down and in the driver's seat, was his mug. Gilbert stared at the mug, looking at it as if it were some sort of mirage. It felt like a sign that he had done the right thing. This man had come into his home, defiled his wife and then taken his favorite mug he had paid twenty dollars for. He reached into the window and cradled it delicately between his hands.

Back in his car, Gilbert checked his cell phone. It had been hours since he told his wife he would be home, but there were no messages from her concerned about his whereabouts. It made him sad that even at the most basic human level, she didn't care enough about him to make sure he was okay. The anger he felt for Kurt resurfaced. He cranked the engine, took a quick detour to his job to shower off the blood and change clothes, and then headed home to see his wife.

In his driveway, he reached into his front pocket and pulled out Kurt's phone, which had been vibrating, unlike his silent cell. He didn't bother to read the recent texts from his wife to her now deceased lover. Instead he typed a message that read:

Found this phone and read all the messages. You're the last number called. Your man dead. Somebody beat his ass to death. The cops are on the way. I hope your husband never finds out or he will beat your ass. If it were me, I would break every fucking bone in your body. Enjoy the pictures of your dead lover.

Gilbert scrolled through the apps on his phone and activated the camera in their bedroom, but she wasn't there. He then tried the living room, nothing and then finally he found her crying in the kitchen. She had fallen to the floor and was staring at her phone, as if trying to will away the images of her lover, Kurt. He watched the feed, impassively as his wife grieved for another man. He wondered if Kurt had somehow managed to kill him, would she be as grief stricken as she was right now. He already knew the answer. She would probably have Kurt moved into his home before his body was even cold and buried six feet under. The asshole would probably make himself at home in his man cave and help himself to his wine fridge. The idea of Kurt drinking his wine infuriated Gilbert. He was at least thankful that it would never happen now. He had seen to that.

Thirty minutes later Gilbert entered his home. The stereo was playing a jazz tune he didn't recognize. The saxophone cried a tune of lost love. He listened for a moment and turned it off. He kept his coat on and carried his bag upstairs to their bedroom. The lingering scent of another man's cologne lived in the air. If he listened closely enough, he could almost hear the sounds of their fervent lovemaking. He stood in the doorway of their bedroom, almost in the same spot he had stood a few hours ago, watching them make love. She was curled in a fetal position, her back turned to him and naked on top of the sheets. It had been weeks since he had seen her naked. The last time was by accident. She hadn't been aware he was home and came into the bedroom, whistling a happy tune. Seeing him on the bed had startled her and she almost ran back into the bathroom as if he were an intruder in his own home. She had apologized later for her behavior, but it was an apology empty of meaning.

Her shoulders were heaving slightly and he could hear sniffling every few seconds. Gilbert quietly rested his bag next to his stand and tossed his coat on the bed. He sat on the bed, with his back against the headboard and watched her. Her tear-stained face was now turned to him, looking at him, but not really seeing him.

"What's wrong?" He finally asked her. He assumed his face registered the correct level of concern and his voice followed suit.

Without Gilbert asking, Karina crawled to him and rested her head on his lap. Gilbert stroked his wife's hair and stared into her eyes. They were vacant and far away. He asked her again, just in case she hadn't heard him the first time. Her eyes blinked a few times, as if registering him for the first time and being cradled in his arms, but she didn't try to move away.

"A friend of mine was killed today. I just got the news."

"Oh, I'm sorry to hear that." He continued stroking her hair, reveling in being so close to her and being allowed such intimacy. "Was it a good friend?" He could see the hesitation in her eyes before she answered.

"I loved him…as a friend."

She was telling the truth, but it was a half-truth. He wanted more from her. He deserved more.

"What was his name? Did you ever mention him to me?"

"He was a friend from years ago. We lost contact and now he's dead." She closed her eyes to let him know she didn't want to discuss it anymore, but Gilbert was in no mood for her to dictate what he did, especially now.

"How did he die?"

"Some maniac killed him in a restroom in a bar."

"A maniac? Maybe it was a disagreement. You never know about these things these days."

Her eyes shot open and a glint of anger pierced through him. He suppressed a smile and continued to stroke her hair and her shoulders. Her skin felt extra soft under his fingers. A low heat radiated from her naked body. A shadow of her right nipple peeked out and he tried to recall the last time his lips had tasted them. He couldn't. Just a few hours ago another man was tasting them as if he had free reign of a candy store. His right hand slipped lower than her shoulder and gently tried to cup her breast.

"Stop it!" His wife angrily swatted his hand away and pulled away from him. He stared at the secret between her thighs he no longer had access to and wondered what it would feel like to just take it without requiring permission. He wasn't that kind of man, but today, that's the kind of man he wanted to be. "You're defending a maniac without knowing what really happened?"

"I'm not defending anyone. I'm simply saying we don't know what really happened. Do you?"

Karina stared at Gilbert, aware that something had changed about him, but unable to tell what it was. It had been years since she had actually looked at him and wondered what he felt and thought. She needed to grieve in private. Maybe she would tell him she was going to visit her sister tomorrow just to have a few days to herself. The man she loved was dead. The man she didn't care about was still alive and still her husband. It made no sense to her, that this was her life.

"You look like you could use some tea," Gilbert offered with a smile on his face.

"That would be nice. Green tea. No sugar."

"Of course." He was already off the bed and striding towards the bedroom door to go downstairs to the kitchen.

The blue flames leapt to life under the tea kettle as Gilbert waited for the water to boil for her tea. One day he was sure that a study would come out that boiling water in your microwave caused cancer and a host of all other ailments. There were enough things killing us in this world, without doing it to ourselves willingly. While he waited for the water to boil, he washed and scrubbed his mug, hoping to remove all traces that Kurt had touched it. But knowing he had put his lips on it would always be in his mind. Using a man's favorite mug is like wearing his shorts. It's an unforgiveable betrayal of male etiquette.

He made her tea just as she liked it, no deviation. Just the slightest change and her taste buds could tell. One time he had added just a tiny bit more sugar than the one teaspoon she required and without saying a word, she had looked at him and poured out the entire cup in the sink. By her reaction, you would think that he had tried to poison her. After making her Green tea, he used two pods of Colombian Medium Roast to make a cup of coffee using the Keurig. Before going back upstairs, Gilbert opened the front door, stepped outside and looked up and down the block. Nothing seemed out of the ordinary. He nodded at his neighbor, Steve who was wheeling two trash cans to the front of his house. Before Steve could walk over and engage him in conversation, Gilbert stepped back inside and locked the door.

Karina had gotten up and was now wearing a blue robe in bed. Her face was buried under a pillow. Gilbert rested his mug on his night stand, sat back down in his same position on his bed and tapped his wife on her shoulder. She sat up in bed and took her mug between two hands. Gilbert watched as she drank slowly and clouds of heat rose from her mug. Her eyes were puffy from crying and strands of hair clung to her face. He wanted to embrace her as they drank together, but he knew the moment they shared earlier had already passed. Without looking he reached for his favorite mug with his left hand, then switched it to his right and sipped his coffee. It was the best cup of coffee he had ever made and he wondered if he would be allowed to keep his mug in prison. He didn't imagine so, but it never hurt to ask. When his wife had drank about half of her cup, she finally looked up, not to look at him, but to stretch her neck. She froze in mid-stretch and then stared at the mug in her husband's right hand. Her cup shook between hers and a few drops of tea spilled against the sheets. Karina looked at her husband, smiling and sipping on his tea.

"You should not have given Kurt my favorite mug," Gilbert said calmly as he continued drinking the best cup of coffee he had ever had. Not even her screams could take away from the taste of it as he drank it to its last drop. The sound of her screams, and Kurt's groans and last gasping breath would be something he would always hold on to for the dark days ahead.

THE DAY I KILLED LOVE

S ometimes you have to kill the love you feel, to free the person you love. I tried to kill the love you had for me with distance, silence and indifference, but it had already taken root and had a stranglehold on my heart. My emptiness only grew deeper as I watched you from the shadows of social media. It occurred to me I had made a mistake and given you your freedom for the right reasons, even though you hadn't asked for it. Had I played God with your feelings? Being without you has left me without purpose. But my pride will not allow me to call and beg you for a second or third chance. I fear this time, we have arrived at the end of the road and I only have myself to blame. How did we get here?

We were not supposed to meet or even entertain the idea of getting involved with other people. You were in the midst of an unhappy marriage. I was going through the motions in my relationship. You were a light in the midst of a storm, my north star. You were free with your feelings. I never had to guess how you felt about me. I heard it in your words and your actions. You were a woman in love. I was a man walking a fine line without committing to the whispers in my heart. I fought a losing battle, even I was the only one who knew of my inner turmoil. I led you to believe my feelings were not as deeply rooted as yours. My words were hedged when we made love. Your feelings were as clear as daylight. Mines were hidden like night. I didn't want to give you hope. Hope as a friend told me a long time ago, is comfort to a fool. We were fools in love, even if you thought you were the only one who felt this way.

A part of me maybe knew this is how it would end. Something so beautiful cannot be sustained based on a lie. The lie eventually crumbles under its own weight, drowning you in every guilty thought you have ever had. With each conversation, every time we made love, exchanged texts, I knew we were marching towards an end that only I could see, maybe you saw it too and held on tighter. You never knew I felt this way because I never mentioned it, for the obvious reasons. I would imagine a life beyond secret meetings, all too brief conversations when we could be free to love each other. You never heard it in my voice because I hid it. But I heard it in your voice every time we spoke. That need for more than just stolen moments, a quickie, a text in place of a hug and a kiss. I heard the yearning in your voice of a woman who deserved more than being relegated to second place. You were never second in my heart and mind, but the situation dictated you were second. I wanted more for us than this. Everything we did had to be planned, as if we were committing some sort of crime. It was usually unspoken between us the rules of an affair. The things we could and could not do. The times we could talk on the phone or text each other. It was all orchestrated for the most part around my schedule and my desires. You were usually accommodating, even if I knew you were upset. You would sometimes become passive aggressive, but again, I ignored it, knowing to acknowledge it would lead us down a road I did not want to travel. We had to come to an end. It was inevitable.

We have not spoken in six months. Not a phone call. A text. No exchanges on social media, even though we are still connected. You left that window into your life open for me. Maybe it's to punish me when I see you are living your life, or maybe you just don't care anymore. Pictures of you at restaurants, hanging out with your friends, trying on a new dress both taunt and infuriate me. I know it's irrational behavior. But nothing about us was rational. We burned brightly and then crashed. I analyze your photos, dissect your smiles and wish you were smiling for me. I miss the way your face would light up when I told a joke and you would laugh hysterically. You understood my sarcastic, dry humor. You got me. I didn't have to be anyone else with you, just myself. If I had met you ten years ago, before you were married, before you had kids, before I was involved, before we were on our way to being broken, we would have been happy. We were happy, but it was happiness on a schedule. It wasn't the kind of happiness that was sustainable because it lived in the shadows, unable to blossom into its full beauty without any interference. A happiness like that is not real. It cannot last because it is only lived in glimpses and the possibility of what could have been.

I miss you in a way I cannot fully articulate. In a way I cannot share with anyone else because of the obvious. It's like experiencing death on some level, but worse. Let me explain. Actual death is permanent. All you have are memories and regrets. This kind of death of love tortures you hourly, daily because the person is still living in the world, a phone call away, a car drive away is worse. You can actually reach out and speak to them, but a combination of fear and ego keeps you immobilized and unable to find the right words. At this point there doesn't seem to be any words which could bring us back to where we once were. An apology probably would not suffice. Even if you took me back, I know you, everything I did afterwards would be put under a microscope. Your mind would be in overdrive, everything becomes overanalyzed and not viewed on its own merit. You become passive aggressive. I want you back, but I don't want to deal with that side of you. I hate that side of you. It makes me feel like a child waiting for a scolding. It's the same way I felt when my mother used that method of manipulation against me. After we hang up, I am angry with myself for not calling you out. For not telling you exactly what I thought. And I wonder why I have never done this. I am not a confrontational person. I wait for things to cool down and then move on. It worked for us. The next day we would be fine, as if nothing had ever happened. Over time this is not sustainable. It hardens you. It makes you watch what you say. Something as simple as telling you I had a good weekend creates tension. I can feel it as we speak, so I never really say anything. It's the same thing for vacations. When I come back, you never ask. I understand why. It's one of the unspoken rules we have. You deserve more. I deserve more. Love should not hurt like this, but it does. It is the kind of hurt you wake up and go to sleep with. It consumes you. In the end, it obscures all the good and everything becomes tainted.

You posted your whereabouts on Instagram last night. It has been five months since we've had no communication. I am like an addict right now in need of you. I haven't heard your voice, except for the videos I have of you, even that doesn't fill me up. I need you, not a version of you on video that no longer exists. I can still conjure up the sound of your laughter in my memory, but I fear that sometime soon, even that will soon fade away. Maybe all along I needed you more than you needed me. Isn't it ironic that you're the one who made yourself vulnerable, but I protected myself and I'm the one now who seems unable to deal with a situation we mutually created? If I wasn't in so much pain, I would laugh until I cried.

I get to the restaurant before you do, parking at an angle between a few cars where I hope to be inconspicuous. I don't want to freak you out and make you think I am somehow stalking you, even though in the strictest definition of stalking, I am.

It's a Friday evening and I should be home with her watching Netflix or whatever it is couples do these days. But instead I am waiting for you to show up. An hour passes, nothing. Maybe you know I am trolling you and it's a fake out. I scroll every picture you post without ever liking any of them. I feel pathetic for indulging in this kind of juvenile behavior, but I can't help myself anymore. Finally you show up with a girlfriend. You look absolutely stunning as you stand under a light. You are wearing that red dress I love so much. It accentuates your curves. Flirty but never trashy. Black pumps, lips and toes painted a sexy red. You turn towards my direction and your friend has told a joke. You are laughing. I roll down the window a bit to catch the echoes of your laughter riding on the wind. It caresses my ears and my heart aches. I want to be the one you're laughing for. You touch your hair which is cut short by choice. I always thought you were bold for doing that and not caring about having long hair as most women seem to want these days. Did I ever tell you that? I don't think I did. I wish I had now. I know you smell delicious. It's one of the things I loved about you. Always a lady without making it seem unnatural. You were as they say a lady in the streets and a freak in the bed. Another ache courses through my body and centers on my groin. Memories of our lovemaking haunts me. It was raw, passionate and filled with love. I know this now. I see myself holding your face between my hands, kissing your lips as I looked into your eyes. I saw love in your eyes. I don't know what you saw in mine. It was love masked by coolness, a detachment maybe. It was intentional. Telling you I loved you would open a portal. Once that door was open there was no going back or taking back the words. Words come with expectations. What would happen next time we made love and I didn't say it? Would you wonder why, but not give it voice? Would you now expect more of me now that I had said the words? You cannot tell someone you love them and then go back to your life as if nothing ever happened. It's unfair to them, to you. It creates resentment. It's a promise without fulfillment. I was in position to tell you the words I felt, but didn't have the courage to once voice them to you. I know you yearned to hear the words. Many times when we made love or just some random time we were together, the words were on my lips but stayed silent.

Before stepping into the restaurant, you paused at the front door, looked around as if sensing something amiss. Maybe your mind wandered to me. Maybe you remembered you were wearing my favorite dress and wished I was escorting you to dinner. Maybe you wished many things and had grown tired of wishing and had decided to move on with your life. Wishing doesn't keep your bed warm at nights. Wishing doesn't give you orgasms. Wishing doesn't hold you tight when you've had a bad day at work. Wishing only makes you realize how lonely you are without the person you love. I waited for a little while longer, but you never came out. Going inside would be too risky, so I drove off and saw you through the restaurant window having a glass of wine and laughing with your friends. It was good to see you laughing, even if it wasn't with me. Later that night you posted that another friend had been lost to cancer. *Cancer Sucks!* Were your words. Knowing you and how much your friends and family mean to you, I felt your pain through those two words. I wanted to reach out to say something, anything. Maybe just to listen and not talk about us. Just to let you know I was there for you, but I lacked the courage to pick up the phone. I imagined the coldness in your voice when you heard my voice, the same detached indifferent tone I had heard in your voice when you spoke to your soon to be ex-husband. Hearing you speak to me that way would only break my heart.

The day we broke up, if you can call it a break up, you accused me of two things which seem stupid now. But for me it was just another sign of how you jumped to conclusions without asking me first. Maybe you realized after you said it, you should have asked, but I think we were at a point in our relationship where we were not going to apologize. I texted you last. Maybe I could have picked up the phone the next day. Maybe you could have, but we didn't. One day turned into days, then weeks and now months. Somewhere during the first week of not hearing your voice, I realized that maybe you needed to be free of me to find happiness. Happiness with me came with rules of behavior. Love should not have to abide by rules. Your spirit was free, untamed. It's one of the many things I loved about you. Did I ever tell you that? Maybe it's too late to tell you I love you. Would it make a difference at this point? We are both scarred now and hearing those words might make it worse. But it seems such a shame not to let someone know you loved them and valued their presence in your life. Everyone should know that. It lets them know their time had not been wasted. It tells them that even though it didn't work out, you knew how special they were to you. Maybe it helps them to heal a bit faster. I don't know. I just know I wished I had told you as you stared into my eyes that I love you. You would have cried. It's one of the things I loved about you, how easily you cried. You cried when we made love. You said you were so overcome with emotion. You even apologized for it. I told you never to apologize. When were together you were always free to express your deepest emotions. You were safe. *You were safe.* Those three words I meant them every time I said them, but in the end, I wasn't able to keep my word. A man who cannot keep his word to the woman who loves him doesn't deserve that woman.

You deserve the world. I could only give you a taste of love's infinite beauty and that wasn't enough, it shouldn't be. You will never know it, but I miss us, what we could have been. Maybe you can be that person with someone else and I will have to watch you from the shadows as you lay our love to rest and rise like a phoenix from the ashes. Ashes that have renewed your resolve. Ashes that once held you back, but you've shaken it off and grown wings to soar again. You will never know for the first time I was unselfish and thought of you and not myself. I killed your love because I was undeserving of it. Maybe one day I will be, but by then it will probably too late. I will be a memory of a love past that no longer makes you cry. I will leave you with these words. *You. You were my first breath in the morning and my last prayer at night. You are my fondest memory who touched the deepest part of my soul. Perhaps we will meet again in another life, before others cloud our judgment and time withers our spirit. We will then be able to fully experience all that love and life have to offer. Until...*

SUNSHINE ON A CLOUDY DAY

M issy knew that her neighbor, Dan, hated her cat, Sunshine. She never imagined he would have gone that far to kill her, until she scrolled through the video feed of her front yard a few days later and saw how her beloved cat had actually died. Her favorite coffee mug fell from between her trembling hands as she stared at the horrific image. There was Dan, on his knees in a few feet of snow, strangling Sunshine. It was a cloudy the day Sunshine was murdered. She had clawed at his gloved hands and hissed angrily when he approached her, then fought bravely for her life. They had a contentious relationship even before Dan had screamed at her for temporarily parking in his space as she unloaded her groceries from Wegmans.

"You cannot just park anywhere you want to," he had said angrily to her. "There are rules in place for people like you. The HOA will hear about this at the next meeting."

She had stared at him incredulously that he was being such a dick. This is how some men get when you reject their advances. He was a perfectly decent looking man, but she was just coming out of a ten year relationship that had left her mentally and physically drained. There wasn't any space in her life for a man right now. The only man she wanted in her life was Sunshine. Her friends had teased her that naming a male cat Sunshine might turn him gay, which was just stupid but she hadn't cared. The name suited him because he was the only person that had brought sunshine into her life.

"Dan, I will only be a minute. Someone is parked in my spot. I can't believe you're being like this."

"Not my problem," the man child had responded.

His hands were crossed in front of his chest. His lips pouty like a female. She had thought he had nice lips the first day she moved in a few months ago. He was short, muscled and was holding on to scraps of hair, that should have already been given a funeral. At five-ten, she had towered over him and could almost see the reflection of her face in his bald spot. None of that had been the reasons for rejecting him, but she was sure he had taken it that way. Men like him always do. Ever since that day, he had been curt with her and acted like a spoiled child. Maybe she should have given him a chance. Maybe he was a good guy. Then it made her angry that she was trying to rationalize her decision. She shouldn't have to appease a man's ego, just to keep the peace.

Now, he had murdered her cat in cold blood in the snow.

Her surveillance system was only a week old, so Missy was pretty sure he was unaware his heinous act of cat killing had been caught on camera. The worst thing was that he had left Sunshine buried in the snow for a few days. By the time she had walked over to his frozen white coffin, his furry white little body was frozen harder than chicken legs in a butcher's market. Seeing her beloved Sunshine encased in a block of ice brought tears to Missy's eyes which instantly froze against the slick, icy surface. Not knowing what else to do, she lifted Sunshine with her bare hands. For some reason, she remembered *The Christmas Story* movie when that kid's tongue stuck to the pole. Every time that scene played, she had laughed like crazy. Now all she wanted to do was cry for her murdered cat.

There were a few dirty dishes in the sink. Missy quickly cleared them away and placed the block of ice in the sink and wondered what to do next. Maybe she should google it, but that seemed kind of stupid. What do you do with a dead cat in a block of ice? It seemed callous to just leave her beloved Sunshine in the sink, defrosting, like frozen fish. Sunshine's life had been difficult. She had rescued him from a shelter. For weeks after she brought him home, he had sulked, and hissed at her anytime she came within a few feet of him. Missy felt like an intruder in her own home. She would tiptoe over his sprawled body in the hallway and stairs. Pick up his cat fur from her bed and couch. Empty his litter box daily or else the entire house would smell of cat shit. It was almost as bad as living with an untidy man. Everything changed the day Dan knocked on her door and asked her out on a date.

THE DELIVERY PERSON had mistakenly left a large, heavy box from Amazon on his doorstep. So Missy was grateful when he brought it to her and carried it inside of her house, into the kitchen. She thanked him, but he lingered, making idle conversation about the election, the Obamas leaving and how many degrees he had obtained. She hadn't wanted to be curt, because it's always beneficial to be on good terms with your neighbors. You never know when they might come to your aid, or their nosiness might stop someone from burglarizing your home. But then there are neighbors like Dan Rivers who just don't know when to leave or quit while they are ahead. Guys like him need to sell you on their accomplishments instead of their character. In the span of five minutes, she knew he had three degrees, drove a Lexus, made over 150k a year, and basically that she would be lucky to date someone like him.

"So…"

"Soooo, what?" Missy asked.

"You want to have dinner with me? A sort of welcome to the neighborhood."

His invitation sounded like a statement. His smile was forced and his teeth overly whitened. Missy wondered if she could see them glowing in the dark.

"Are any of the other neighbors going to be there?"

It was meant as a joke. She knew what he meant and was trying to let him down easily. She had a date with a pint of Rum Raisin Ice Cream and season two of *Unbreakable Kimmy Schmidt.*

"What do you mean? I am not paying for anyone else."

Right then and there, Missy knew this guy had no sense of humor and if she disregarded the warning signals blaring in her mind, she would have no one to blame but herself.

"Listen Dan, I appreciate you bringing my box over," Missy started walking to the door, hoping he would follow her dutifully like a pet, "I don't want to lead you on. I'm not really interested in dating anyone right now. Just got out of a long relationship, so I need some alone time. You know how women are," she said jokingly.

Missy hoped he would get the message.

"It's not a date. Just trying to get to know you, but if this is how you treat men who ask you out—no wonder you got dumped."

His statement shocked her. She wanted to strike back, but they were in a narrow hallway of her home, and she didn't know this guy well enough to know what he might be capable of doing. And she didn't want to find out.

Missy opened the front door and waited for him to catch up. He stopped in front of her, hands at his side, with a scowl on his face. When he looked up at her, there was a silent threat in his eyes. The energy in the hallway shifted. Her keychain with mace hung on the wall behind her. She calculated how long it would take her to reach it and spray him. He took a step towards her, but before he could take another, Sunshine came dashing from the living room and screeched to a hissing stop between them. His teeth were bared. Tail straight up in the air like an antenna. He was her protector. Maybe Sunshine didn't like her, but he wasn't going to allow anyone to enter his home and hurt the person who fed him and picked up his shit.

"Keep that beast away from me," Dan growled. His growl lacked the necessary bass. It seemed ironic he was calling her cat a beast.

"You need to leave now."

Missy didn't want to further escalate matters by threatening to call the cops. This guy was her neighbor. It would be uncomfortable living next to him once she did that. He left without any more words being exchanged. Her hands were shaking as she clutched the doorknob. She waited for at least thirty seconds, contemplating what could have happened. The realization made her sob loudly. Sunshine stared up at her, never making a sound, waiting for her to gather herself.

He followed her into the bathroom for the first time.

Waited with her in the kitchen as she got ice cream.

When Missy plopped down on the couch, covering her lower body with a blanket and turned on the television, he stared up at her. They locked eyes and came to an understanding. For the first time he meowed and leaped onto the couch. She tickled his belly and he didn't scratch her. From that day on they became buddies. Now he was dead.

THERE WAS A cat killer in her neighborhood. Missy wondered if he had done something like this before. People like him usually have a long history of this sadistic kind of behavior. She googled missing cats in her zip code but nothing came up. Then she tried missing dogs. There were about ten for the Upper Marlboro area. Maybe cats are more expendable and dogs are better companions, so they aren't reported missing. She needed to do something to avenge Sunshine or at least get him justice. How do you get justice for a cat? She could call the cops. She had the video to prove she wasn't crazy. Telling the cops that your neighbor strangled your cat without any video proof…well, would just sound as if she were a crazy cat lady. Would killing a cat be a misdemeanor, a fine or just a reprimand? She needed to focus on something else, so she tuned in to Pandora to listen to the eighties station. The first song that came on made her cry. It felt like Sunshine was urging her from the spirit world to get justice for him. *Walking on Sunshine* by Katrina and the Waves blared from her ear buds and without thinking, she started dancing. Dancing was her stress release. It allowed her to vent and think. There was no way she was going to let this asshole get away with murdering her cat.

Missy checked on Sunshine again in the sink. He still hadn't thawed out. She needed to use the sink to defrost and season some fish. She turned on the hot water and a few minutes later, the ice had completely melted. Missy almost expected him to look up and meow at her. But he remained still and dead. His white fur streaked with leaves and a few pieces of ice were embedded into it. She stroked his wet fur, tickled his stomach one last time, before placing his body inside an old towel and heavy duty trash bag. Tomorrow was trash day. She could either bury him in the yard or dump him in the trash. Stray dogs, foxes and possums sometimes wandered into the yard. She didn't want them to dig him up and have them use him as a toy, or worse, food.

One of the things she hated about being single was wheeling out the heavy trash can from the backyard to the front, especially in the snow. The wheels stuck in the snow and would sometimes tip over. She had to use all her strength to pull it. Even before she arrived at the front of the complex, she saw Dan pulling into his parking space next to hers and blasting a Prince song, *I Wanna Be Your Lover.* Anyone who plays Prince can't be all that bad, but then she remembered he was still a murderer of cats.

The snow had turned grey and dirty. A few patches of ice were still on the sidewalk. Missy bent over to pick up an empty water bottle buried in the snow and dumped it in her trash. Dan stepped out his car, music still blasting and stared at her from behind his shades.

"Did you find your cat yet?"

His tone was mocking, almost gleeful. She wanted to leap on him, and bury his stupid face in the snow and watch as he choked on dirty snowballs.

"Not yet," she lied.

Missy wasn't sure how she was going to play this yet. She didn't want to show her hand too early. She needed a plan. She attended church every few months, but wasn't a Bible thumper. She didn't believe in the notion that evil people get their comeuppance in the next life. She would prefer them to receive its blessings in this life, where she could enjoy them being punished.

"Well, if there's anything I can do for you, let me know."

He opened the back door of his black Ford Explorer and took out a small bag of gourmet dog food from Wegmans. She heard Barack his two year old Chow Chow barking from inside his house. Dogs know when their owners are near. Dan's face lit up when he heard his dog barking. His face had transformed from a vindictive, hateful person into something human. If she hadn't seen what he was capable of doing, she would have been fooled. Behind that smile lurked a monster she wanted to expose.

"He's never been gone this long, especially in this weather."

"Did you try putting up flyers, knocking on your neighbors' doors?

"I did all that. No leads."

"You didn't knock on my door."

The murderer was flirting with her. Unbelievable. He had strangled her fucking cat and now believed he could cozy up to her by being nice. Sunshine must be turning over in the garbage can she had in her hands.

"Well, since you offered, I could use your help walking around the complex to look for him."

"Whatever you need. Give me a second let me put this bag away."

His smile turned her stomach. He turned away and walked to his house. Missy wanted to throat punch him, but she didn't want to give herself away. The safer you make someone feel, the more likely they are to give themselves away. Barack jumped on him as the front door swung open and the killer's demeanor changed. His face softened into a human smile as the dog licked his face. It's not something she had seen many black people do, letting dogs lick their faces. When you love someone or something, you will let them do almost anything to you.

"You love your dog," Missy said to him as he rejoined her.

She wasn't sure, but it looked like he was blushing, which she found weird.

"Barack has been a good companion. More loyal than most of my friends."

That's the kind of statement that demanded a follow up question, but she didn't care to know anything else about him. Next thing she knew, she would start to feel sorry for him...see him as a person and forget that he was a cat killer.

For the next hour they walked around the complex calling out Sunshine's name. They barely spoke to each other, but she could feel his eyes on her. Dan even went in between the houses, looked into a few yards, searched through trees looking for Sunshine, knowing that he had wrapped his hands around my cat's throat and strangled him. What kind of person pretends to be concerned and waste an hour, looking for an animal they killed? A sociopath is who does that.

"Either your cat froze to death or someone took him."

We had circled back to my house and were only a few feet away from where he had kneeled down and strangled Sunshine. The wind had picked up. Some loose debris flew past us and disappeared into another yard.

"Or maybe someone killed him," Missy said without a hint of emotion in her voice.

He stared up at her, more like through her as he formulated his thoughts. His hands were shoved into his coat pockets and clouds of cold air drifted from his chapped lips as he spoke.

"Anyone who would kill an innocent, defenseless cat would have to be a sick demented bastard, wouldn't you say?"

"Yes, I would say that. I would think that if someone did that, then they would have to be a pathetic, sick excuse for a human being."

He walked a few paces closer to her house and stood directly in the spot where she had found Sunshine, frozen and looking like an oversized drumstick. He cast his eyes down to his feet, then stared directly into the video camera above her second floor window and then stared at her. His eyes were dead. Missy stepped back, scared he was about to attack her, but then, just as just quickly, he smiled.

"You never know what someone like that is capable of doing. I would be very careful. They could snap at any moment. I wouldn't want to see you get hurt, Missy. You're my favorite neighbor," he smirked as he said this. "Anyway, Barack needs to be fed."

The cold air swirled around her body, but the chill that ran through her body under her winter coat wasn't from the cold. She had stared evil in the eyes, granted it was from a short guy, but evil doesn't care how short you are when it inhabits your body. His words were laced with threats as deadly as a joint laced with Xanax. The chances of her leaving one asshole, controlling boyfriend to move next door to a sociopath were astronomical, but here she was and she didn't know whether to call the cops or move out.

The moisture in the air had caused her front door to swell a bit. Opening it was sometimes difficult as Missy pushed it open and closed it quickly behind her. For a brief moment she waited for Sunshine to come around the corner, meowing a greeting and rubbing against her leg. The house remained quiet. In that moment, Missy knew she couldn't back down from Dan. Guys like him had been intimidating her all her life. Her last boyfriend had belittled her for years, until her friends had stepped in and made her leave him. This time she would handle this on her own. A person has to know that when there is no one left to depend on, they can depend on themselves.

For the next few hours Missy tried to come up with something to get justice for Sunshine and hurt Dan in the process. She did her best thinking over a cup of black coffee, no sugar and dilution. She paced up and down throughout her house and the only thing she accomplished after three cups of coffee was adding ten thousand steps to her Fitbit. Exhausted from thinking, Missy set the house alarm and it chirped into active mode. Hearing the chirping alarm gave Missy an idea, she would sleep on, and the next morning she would put it into action. But for now, she would mull it over before acting impetuously. Impulsive behavior had gotten her into the last relationship. After one date, she told all her friends she was in love and had met her future husband. He turned out to be her future nightmare for ten years. She would not make that mistake again. This time, she would make sure she wasn't the one on the other side feeling pain.

FROM HER BEDROOM window the next morning, behind drawn curtains, Missy watched as Dan pulled out of his parking spot. She waited to make sure he wasn't coming back. Her mind was made up about moving forward with her plan. All she had to do was make sure she wasn't caught. Getting caught might get her the Sunshine treatment. First things first, she had to call her manager and give an excuse for not coming in to work. When she got his voicemail, she coughed a few times and left a message saying she was not feeling well. Now, it was time to put her plan into action.

"911 Operator, what is your emergency?" The voice on the other end sounded exhausted and had probably been at work longer than eight hours.

"I would like to report a possible gas leak. It smells like it's coming from the house next door.

"Is the scent faint? Are you having trouble breathing?"

"I'm okay for now, I think."

Missy gave the operator Dan's address and any other information she needed.

Ten minutes later, two fire trucks with their horns blaring came roaring down their street.

Already fully dressed, Missy stepped outside in the cold and watched as eight firemen dismounted two fire trucks and raced towards the house. All of them looked like bodybuilders and could be part of some exotic dance crew. She needed to remain focused and not allow a muscled body to distract her.

She watched from her doorstep as one of them forcefully banged on her neighbor's front door. No response. She waited for what was supposed to happen next. They banged a few more times and shouted his name. Two of them went around the back. Finally they used a crowbar and something else she didn't recognize to pry the door open. Within a few minutes they were inside the house and searching for the reported gas leak. The front door was broken and wide open. Missy waited breathlessly to see if her desperate plan would work. She would have to act quickly for everything to go as planned.

Barack appeared in the doorway, stopped and sniffed the cold air. He appeared confused, unsure of stepping outside without his owner. Missy clapped her hands softly to get his action and waved him to her. He didn't budge. She was prepared for this. She reached into her coat pocket and produced a handful of beef flavored doggie snacks. Barack scampered towards her and Missy dropped to her knees in the snow to greet him. The dog lapped at her hand and she quickly got up, created a trail of the doggy treats to her front door. She made sure none of the firefighters had seen her and hastily closed the front door behind her.

Her pulse had quickened. Her hands were shaking as she leaned against the closed door, trying to catch her breath. She had never done anything like this before in her life, like kidnapping the neighbor's dog. No one else in the complex had placed cameras around their homes, so there would be evidence of her crime. Stealing a dog. Who does that and actually goes to jail for it, she wondered.

Barack stared up at her, tongue out and eyes on her pocket. Being in a strange home didn't seem to bother him. All he wanted was more treats to remain quiet. She continued to bait him with dog treats as she descended into the basement, where his barking would less likely be heard. He would be only there for a few hours at best. She made sure that Barack was comfortable with an assortment of toys and treats, and she turned on the television. She recalled reading somewhere that dogs love to watch television. It was tuned in to *Cesar 911*, hosted by Cesar Millan.

Loud voices could be heard coming from outside when Missy went back upstairs. It was Dan. The firefighters had found no evidence of a gas leak. One of them apologized for breaking in the door, but it was protocol. Dan the asshole didn't want to hear that.

"Listen, you break down my fucking door and now you tell me you didn't find anything?"

"Yes, that's what we're telling you. Better a broken door than a fire, which could have taken down your entire block."

The fireman's tone was measured. He was used to dealing with ungrateful residents like Dan. He handed Dan a business card and turned to leave.

"Don't you turn your back on me. I'm not done with you yet, fireman Jim."

The tone in Dan's voice stopped the beefy fireman in his tracks. His other firemen buddies stopped what they were doing and waited, as if they had seen this scene before. His broad shoulders swiveled through the cold air as he turned around to face Dan. His unshaven dark face shielded by his fireman's hat made him look imposing. Missy stayed hidden behind the curtain, but had a clear view of the action a few feet away from her house. Maybe she would have to call the cops also if things went awry.

The fireman removed his gloves from his hands and stepped quickly towards the loudmouth. The suddenness of his steps caught Dan by surprise, and he almost tripped on the ice as he took two steps backwards.

"Guys like you talk a lot of shit. Because you believe you are safe from guys like me because we have on the uniform. I've had to put a few motherfuckers like you in their lowly place over the years and I have no problem doing it again. Understand?"

The unexpected response caught Dan off-guard. He assumed the fireman would have taken his shit because he was on the job. He realized too late, he had tried the wrong guy today. He was used to bullying people, especially women, and now he was the one shrinking away.

Before Dan could fashion a response, the other firemen stepped forward and cautioned their co-worker on harming him. He glared at Dan and then smiled at him. The smile said everything. *Next time there won't be anyone to save your bitch ass.*

Dan looked around as the two fire trucks pulled out of the complex. No one had seen him reduced in stature. Something dawned on him and he quickly turned and ran into his house. He had finally remembered Barack. Missy imagined him looking everywhere in his house and calling the dog's name and then panicking. He came running out the house, almost sliding down his front steps and calling out the dog's name. She could hear his voice, but couldn't see him. When he finally returned, sweat poured down his worried face. She almost felt sorry for him, but then remembered what he had done to Sunshine. Whatever she could do to him was justified.

An expected knock on her door found them face to face.

Panic raised in his voice. "Have you seen, Barack? Stupid firefighters left the door open and he must have ran off. Did you hear him barking? He's not used to being on his own."

The worry in his voice gave me great delight. It struck me as being ironic that he could care so much for his pet, but didn't give a crap about killing mine. I wanted to put the fear of God in him.

"The temperature is supposed to drop tonight. I hope you find him before night falls."

"My poor baby. He is not an outdoors kind of dog. He won't know what to do."

She gave him a little hope by saying, "Maybe someone will find him and bring him to a shelter."

"You think that's possible?" his face perked up.

Missy had him right where she wanted him, on an emotional elevator ride. At any second, she could toss him overboard and watch his feelings splatter against the ice beneath his feet.

"I loved Sunshine. I know if I saw a dog like Barack roaming the complex I would take him in or call a shelter. I've never understood how anyone can mistreat an animal with malice."

Her eyes were squarely on his. She watched, waiting for something, anything that looked like remorse for him killing my Sunshine. Nothing. He was incapable of caring about anything except himself and his feelings.

"What happened to your cat was tragic. It's a tragic world. Shit happens," he said as coldly as the air between them.

"Sunshine wasn't a stupid cat. I still don't understand how he died in the snow."

"Animals are curious creatures. They can do such random things. Maybe he was just tired of living," he smiled without laughing.

"Are you trying to say that my cat committed suicide?" Missy asked him incredulously.

Before he could respond, she slammed the door in his face. Any doubts she had previously about kidnapping Barack were now gone. She waited for him to drive off. Made sure the coast was clear and quickly loaded Barack into her car and drove off. Three hours later, she was at a kennel on the Eastern Shore of Maryland.

"YOU'RE SUCH A good boy," the young lady at the kennel said as she hugged and kissed Barack, who was a stranger a few seconds ago. Tattoos adorned her arms. One peeked out from behind her neck, but was covered by her red hair.

The smell of dog wasn't overpowering but it was obvious. Loud barking ricocheted throughout the kennel, but it reminded Missy of dogs running around and happy. Rock music blared in the background. She had brought Barack to the right place.

"He seems to like you," Missy offered to the young woman who was still kneeling and playing with Barack.

"Dogs feel my soul. They know mommy loves them," she smiled a gap-toothed smile as she stood up. There was something nurturing about her, even though she looked to be in her mid-twenties. "So you said the owner died suddenly and you found him wandering the streets?"

"Yes. I didn't know the owner too well, but I wanted to make sure that his dog found a good home."

"Well, lucky for-"

"Barack."

"Lucky for Barack, I have a family that's looking for a dog that fits his description. He seems well-behaved. Friendly. No obvious bruises or sickness. We will run some tests on him to make sure, then try to place him. But I don't foresee a problem getting him a home."

"That makes me happy."

Missy bent over a little to ruffle his fur. He barked at her and darted towards the sound of the other barking dogs. She wondered how long it would take before Barack forgot about her and his owner. The idea of erasing Dan from Barack's memory made her smile as she exited the kennel. The first part of her plan was complete, it was now time to up the ante. She was going to make that sonofabitch feel what she felt when she found her Sunshine dead and frozen. Just thinking about it was enough to bring Missy to tears as she pulled into her parking spot three hours later.

The soft tapping of knuckles on her car window made Missy jerk away from the steering wheel. Seeing it was Dan, she quickly wiped away her tears and stepped out her car.

"Don't cry. Barack will come back."

"What?"

"I miss him too."

Missy stared at him, dumbfounded, that he would think she was crying over *his* dog. Infuriated, she launched into the second phase of her plan.

"There was an accident a few blocks away on Addison Road."

"I don't care about no damn accident," Dan said impatiently as he turned to walk away.

"Barack was involved in the accident."

"What?" How do you know?

"When I drove by the accident, I saw his bloody body under the front wheel. It looked like the tire of the eighteen wheeler rolled forward and backwards on his entire body. It was a mess."

She watched him as her graphic words sank in and his face contorted into unimaginable pain. His eyes brimmed with tears and he furiously tried to wipe them away, but they were coming fast and furious. His body collapsed against her car and folded like a cheap lawn chair. She wasn't done yet. She wanted people like Dan to feel the full vengeance of pain they have caused other people. It's the only way to make things right and balance the universe.

"I wasn't sure it was Barack, even though it looked like him."

Dan lifted his head from the hood of the car and stood up straight. A glimmer of hope registered in his eyes. Missy twisted her face to avoid smiling. She had him right where she wanted him. A sliver of hope gleamed in his eyes. In a few moments, despair would take its rightful place.

"So maybe it was a dog that looked like him?"

Missy almost felt sorry for what she was about to do to him. Regret might come later, but in that moment, she would revel digging the dagger deep into his cat murdering heart.

She reached into her purse, pulled out her cellphone and paused dramatically before handing it to him. Late last night she had gotten one of her graphic artist friends to Photoshop a picture of Barack, bloodied and crushed under the wheel of an eighteen wheeler. It was impossible to tell it was a fake. Her graphic friend had even added an extra touch of having Barack's dog tag dipped in blood under his paw. The letters BA and K could be seen. The rest was covered in blood. Seeing his beloved Chow Chow looking like road kill, broke Dan down. He dropped to his knees, cupped his face in his palms, then looked up dramatically into the night sky and wailed like a tortured animal, "why God!" He paused in between sobbing and heaving his chest, as if waiting for an answer. The only thing they heard, was the barking of a dog in the park down the street.

Missy finally allowed herself to smile as she pressed the lock button on the key chain to her car. There was only one more thing to do before leaving him out in the cold. She bent over, her keys jingling and whispered into Dan's ear, "I know what you did to my Sunshine. I have it all on tape." He looked up at her, tears still in his eyes and couldn't find the words to respond. "Now you know how it feels to lose someone you love, even if it's just a stupid dog." And with that, she strolled away whistling a tune and never turned back.

I DIDN'T MEAN TO KILL MY NEIGHBOR

E ven though he was an asshole, I really hadn't planned on killing my neighbor. Things just got out of control and before the rational side of my brain could assert itself, my neighbor was dead. I had no ill feelings towards him one way or the other. God rest his ugly soul. I blame social media. If it wasn't for social media, I wouldn't have known what he said about me, and my neighbor would still be alive. Forgive me, I have gone too far into the story. I know you're lost and I'm leading you into a tunnel without a flashlight, so let me backtrack and catch you up on exactly what happened, then you will understand that I had no choice—I had to do it. People always say you have a choice, as if that's an answer for everything. Sometimes, your choices are taken away from you, and all you have left is your self-respect. If you don't have that, then what do you have? A man has to be able to hold his head up at work, home and while walking down the street. You have to walk the walk. If you can't look your wife and kid in the eye and see that they respect you, instead of thinking you're some sort of nerd weakling—then what's the fucking point. Sorry. I didn't mean to use profanity. It's just that I am so angry that Joe made me kill him. Anyway, let me tell you what happened and I will allow you to be my judge and jury.

It was early February and the first snowstorm of 2016. We had gotten up to twenty inches in Upper Marlboro, with another ten in the forecast for the next day, Sunday. I had cash on hand because I was sure that the kids in the neighborhood would be knocking at my front door trying to make some extra spending money. Not one kid came by or was outside playing in the snow. They were all probably indoors playing video games and having snowball fights on a goddamn app. This generation has seriously gone to shit, but that's another story.

So I spent the next five hours shoveling snow, along with my neighbors on the block. The news reported that seven percent of men suffer heart attacks shoveling snow, which is a pretty high number when you really think about it. Men don't want to admit they need a break, especially when they are other men and women around. It makes you look weak, womanly, so we push past the point of what we would normally do. Why? To impress others, to show we can shovel snow at a faster rate? It's ridiculous to be lying down in a bed of white, clutching your heart and about to die from a heart attack. It's such a silly way to die. It's not heroic. It's embarrassing for your friends and family when they recount your demise and print your obituary. I have a tendency to ramble, so forgive me. It's just that I'm so angry as I write this in my personal blog. It will soon be time to go to bed, so let me get on with it, before the lights go out.

"You can't let that asshole get away with it again," my wife Sara urged me. I looked in the rearview mirror and saw the smirk on my thirteen-year-old son's face, even though it was buried in a video game. We had just driven back from Costco and Wegmans to pick up some food, snacks, another shovel, and of course, wine. Being stuck in a house with your wife and kid for five days can be a test of your patience, love and your commitment not to take a life. We had enjoyed getting out the house, until now.

"I've asked you not to use those words in front of our son."

"Dad, they say that word on regular television now. I hear words worse than that from kids at school. I'm not a child."

Rudy still hadn't looked up to give us his attention. His video game had him captivated. I had lost my son a long time ago to fighting robots and aliens. A child who doesn't see the world around him and who is constantly lost in a world of make believe, when it matters, will he be able to survive when it matters?

"Fuck that shit! I'm tired of Joe Asshole pushing you around and you being his bitch!"

I bristled at my wife's characterization of me. My son snickered again, but kept his head down. I wondered if he agreed with her. My wife has a filthy mouth. So does her entire family. Sometimes, I wanted to slap her, but of course, it will get nasty. Cops will become involved. Jail time. Just too messy. Instead, I absorbed her tongue lashing and pulled alongside the parking space in front of our home. It was now occupied with Joe's truck.

"I'm sure he just parked there until we got back," I tell her with a tight smile on my face. My lips were dry. No matter how much chapstick I put on them, they were perpetually cracked. "Stay here, I'll be right back."

I left the engine running and the new Rihanna song with Drake, *Work*, was blasting on the radio. I am in my mid-forties, but I try to keep with what's current, even though my son won't talk to me. But the day he does, he will be surprised how much his old man knows. The temperature was dropping rapidly with more snow in the forecast, so I walked carefully to my neighbor's house. The last thing a man wants to do is slip on ice while his wife and kid are watching him.

I adjusted my glasses, zipped up my coat, stared up momentarily at the camera pointing down at me and waited nervously for someone to answer the doorbell. I am not a man who enjoys confrontation. You saw what happened with my wife in the car. I have violent thoughts, but as they say, I would never harm a fly. My thoughts are cathartic. If I didn't have them, I shudder to think of what I might actually do. Everyone around you is a ticking time bomb. All that's needed is the perfect storm to light that fuse and watch them go *kaboom*. I believe everyone in this world has the capacity to kill another human being. There is a killer inside of everyone. It just takes the right circumstances to push you to the edge of your patience and then watch as all hell breaks loose.

The front door swung open and the scent of chicken, pizza and popcorn filled the doorway. Music was coming from the basement along with the loud voices of teenagers. Standing in front of me was Joe's oldest, Zachary, a junior at Largo High School. He had bully written all over his pimply face and jail was definitely in his future. With some kids you just know where they will end up or their career vocation. His steroid enhanced muscles bulged out of his red muscle shirt and black basketball shorts. Scrawled across his t-shirt was the word N*G*E*R. It didn't make any sense to me why someone would willingly wear such an offensive word on their clothing, as if it were some sort of fashion statement. Don't the kids today know the history of that word? How much our people suffered and were devalued by it? I balled my fists in the pockets of my jacket and reminded myself that the future jailbird was in his house and he had parents. I wasn't there to be his parent. I was there to reclaim my parking spot and my family's respect.

Before I could say anything, Zack sneered at me and tried to intimidate me with his beady mongoose eyes. "What do you want, *Leslie*?"

The kid had no respect for his elders. I'm sure it came from his father, but being addressed by my first name, instead of Mr. Barnes didn't sit well with me. I should have straightened him out. Let the little punk have it, but I had to be the adult.

"Is your dad home, Zack?"

"The name isn't Zack."

I stare at him momentarily confused. I thought I had confused him with his older brother.

"You can call me Mr. Zack."

I shifted uncomfortably. The kid was fucking with me. My brain didn't work fast enough to come up with sarcastic stuff to say. Then the kid broke out into a hysterical fit of laughter, clutching his stomach, with tears streaming down his stupid face.

"Yo, you shoulda seen your face. That shit was hilarious. I wish I had my phone to record you and put it on Snapchat. My dad was right about you."

Of course I had to ask the obligatory question because I would wonder what his dad said, and needing to know if I was a topic of conversation over dinner. "What did he say?" I asked casually, or it seemed casual to me.

"He said that Leslie is such a pussy. I bet his hot wife is the one who fucks him."

"That's enough young man. I'm sure your dad would never say anything like that." I knew the kid was being truthful.

"I'm only messing with you, Mr. Barnes." Even the way he said my name was filled with sarcasm and disrespect. It's what we teenagers do these days. "Let me get my dad for you. Please don't tell him what I said, okay?" I couldn't tell if he was being serious or daring me to repeat the vile words he had just uttered. They would probably have a good laugh about it later at my expense. I nodded and he jogged off screaming for his father.

I waited on the stairs, outside. The least he could have done was invited me inside from the cold. My neighbors definitely weren't neighborly. As I waited, I heard the door to my vehicle slam shut. My wife and son had decided they had waited long enough. She mouthed to me as she climbed the stairs to our home, *handle your business or I will.* My son stared at me blankly as if I were a stranger and he was deciding whether or not to call the cops on me.

"What can I do for you, neighbor?"

I had to look up to meet Joe's smirking eyes. He was also wearing basketball shorts with no underwear and a white t-shirt. Nothing a straight guy hates than when another man's bulge is daring him to stare at it. You don't want to stare, but it's right there, like a blinking red light, hypnotizing you and you cannot look away. It's a natural curiosity that every man has, even if we don't want to admit it. It's like wanting to know how much money somebody makes at their job, same thing. He was an incarnation of Terry Crews, minus the personality. Large hoop earrings adorned his ears. His goatee threatened to swallow his large lips. He stood at least six-three, two hundred plus pounds. I don't have to tell you, this sonofabitch could crush me into powder if he wanted to. It's a sad thing when both parties know they can kick your ass and there's not a damn thing you can do about it. I could hear my screams making their way through the neighborhood like a bad horror movie if Joe decided to pummel me into the snow. Needless to say, Joe Wills scared the shit out of me.

"Listen, Joe," my practiced smile slid over my almost frozen face, "I'm sure you forgot to remove your vehicle from the spot I shoveled. No harm, no foul. Do you mind moving your truck now? My wife is busting my balls over it." Any man who invokes his wife for sympathy is a goddamn pussy. I *am* a pussy. If my wife hadn't made such a stink about it, I wouldn't be here on my neighbor's doorstep begging him to give me back something that was mine.

"If I move my truck—then where do you suggest I park, *Leslie*?"

You should shovel out your space asshole is what I said in my mind, but of course, the words couldn't find their way out of my throat and to my lips. Three years this guy has been my neighbor. The only nice one in the family is his wife, Isabelle. For the life of me, I don't know what she sees in that Neanderthal prick. The first week they moved into the neighborhood, we had them over for lunch. I fired up the grill, but Joe proceeded to take over and began telling me how I've been grilling the wrong way. He proceeded to show me how it's done in front of our families. I felt like a child being schooled by his parent. I chalked it up to him just being the new guy and wanting to impress me. Later that evening, I entered the bathroom right after he used it. The asshole had pissed all over the toilet seat and on the floor, as if marking his territory in my goddamn house. Now of course, I can't go up to him and say, "would you mind lifting the toilet seat and not pissing on my goddamn floor next time?" He watched me as I exited the toilet and said, "nice bathroom." He was daring me to confront him, but of course

I didn't, and this sets up our relationship for the next three years. *The Bully* vs. *The Nerd.*

I looked up and down the block and the only space that's not shoveled is his. There isn't any assigned parking in the complex, so you can basically park anywhere. Common courtesy says not to park in front of someone's home or to steal their parking space after a snowstorm. What are we animals? This is what's wrong with society these days. The lack of respect we show each other is appalling. When common courtesy isn't valued. Communication is met with tension. What is the alternative? What is a sane, rational person to do when he is accosted with someone who is intractable and just plain rude?

"I'm not sure where you should park, Joe. But-"

"But nothing, Leslie. I am teaching you a valuable lesson. Next time you move your vehicle, at least put something there to let people know it's taken. It's the neighborly thing to do."

"The mere fact that I shoveled the spot and it's in front of my house, shouldn't that tell someone that it's taken?"

That's the most smartass comment I've ever said to Joe—and it felt good. His black face turned a deeper shade of black, if that's even possible. He clenched his fists and his forearms bulged in anticipation of being put to use. I think I peed myself just a little and it froze between my legs. If I was sure no one was watching, I would have turned away and ran home. But then from out of nowhere, a soft, angelic voice broke the tension.

"Is that you, Leslie?" It was Joe's wife, Isabelle.

My balls crawled out of my asshole and I exhaled a trembling breath. My face wouldn't be smashed in today, and I wouldn't be needing false teeth or any facial reconstruction surgery.

"Yes, it's me."

Joe's big body blocked the entire doorway. Isabelle nudged him aside and stood in front of her giant husband. A blue robe was wrapped around her body. Her auburn hair cascaded down past her shoulders. Her skin seemed paler than usual, but her brown eyes were alert as she stared at me.

"How did you guys make out with all the snow?" Her voice was soft, with barely a hint of her Spanish accent.

"Not too bad. More snow is on the way."

"We're ready for it." Joe had placed his big mitts gently on her shoulders. The same hands that only seconds ago were ready to pummel me into the snow. "I saw you shoveling earlier. You were out there for hours."

She peered towards my parking spot and a quizzical look came over her face. She turned around and looked up at her husband. I tried not to look down, but her robe was fitted tightly around her ass. I think in Spanish an ass is known as *culo*. I will have to google it later to be sure.

"Joseph, why are you parked in Leslie's spot?" The softness in her voice was gone now. There was an edge to it now. "I hope you weren't intending on keeping his spot after he spent hours shoveling snow, while you were watching football."

Joe stammered. His balls were in his wife's delicate hands. He finally mumbled something about forgetting it wasn't his spot. I wanted to jump up and cheer, but instead I remained quiet.

"Leslie, I am really sorry about this. Joseph will be right out to give you back your spot and shovel out his own parking space. Won't you, Joseph?" She had turned around to face me and the softness in her voice had returned.

"No problem, Leslie. Just let me toss some clothes on." His voice was friendly, but his eyes radiated death. I might have won this small battle, but something told me that it wouldn't be worth it in the long haul. Joe would be plotting to go all WWF on me.

"Tell Gina I said hello. When this storm is over, we will have you guys over for lunch."

I smiled at her and then she was gone. Joe waited until she went back up the stairs, closed the bedroom door and then stepped towards me.

"You're going to regret this you little pussy." Then he slammed the door in my face like a man-child who hadn't gotten his way. I tried not to smile as I walked back home, but this was what it felt like to finally win one. Even though, in all honesty, if it wasn't for Isabelle, it would have turned out differently. A win is a win.

After taking off my boots at the door, Gina didn't allow shoes on the wooden floor and hanging up my coat; I half-expected my wife to greet her champion at the door to applaud my victory. Instead, she was seated in the living room, feet up, sipping on a glass of red wine and reading one of those rah rah-rah-girlfriend-neck twisting-eyes rolling cliché books that I detested. Readers dictated the market and that's what they were reading, so it's what writers were pushing out. Sometimes, I questioned how smart readers really are. The consumer is always right, right? Luckily I am not a writer, or else I would be pissed to see the kind of crap that folks are going crazy for and the really good, deep, insightful stuff is going unread and ending up at thrift stores in ninety-nine cents bins. The whole damn world is crazy. The same can be said for television and music. Shit is supposed to sink, instead of rising to the top of the heap and sitting there to be consumed.

I poured myself a glass of wine and made a mental note that a glass wasn't there waiting for me. In a marriage you pick your fights, even if I never picked any. Gina is the kind of person that wrong or right, she had to have the last word. An argument with her is always pointless and just wore me down.

"Did you get that asshole to move his truck?" She kept on reading and sipping without looking up at me.

She had undressed and was now wearing just some red panties and one of my long-sleeved white shirts and no bra. My wife is a beautiful woman—and she knows it. Behind my back, I know people refer to us as Beauty and the Beast. I know they want to know how some ordinary nerd got the hot girl. I still haven't figured it out myself. Maybe she had grown tired of the losers she dated before me who cared more about their rims than buying a home and taking vacations. Maybe she had gotten tired of always being broke. Maybe she wanted to know what it felt like to have someone love her more than she loved them.

"Yes, I reasoned with him and he decided that I was right."

"Oh." She looked up briefly and her long eyelashes fluttered and a slight smile danced in her eyes. "Isabelle called and invited us over for dinner next week. She apologized for her husband's behavior." She continued to stare at me and beneath my shirt she was wearing, I could see her nipples pushing hard against the cotton material. I felt powerful for the first time in a long time, and I wanted to spread her brown legs and delve into her secret treasure. We were already at her imposed sex quota for the month. It was once a month and that was three weeks ago. I tried to negotiate, but she wouldn't budge. I'm the one paying all the bills, and yet, I am powerless in my own home.

She knew I was lying and was waiting for me to admit that Isabelle had come to my rescue. I wasn't about to give her that satisfaction. My wife is a wonderful woman, but sometimes, she can be a real cunt. She likes to let me know in her own subtle ways that I am lucky to have her. She respects my ability to make a good living, but she doesn't respect me as a man or a lover. Whenever we go out, which is hardly ever, she walks ahead of me and the message is clear. *I don't need you.* One day I will put her to the test and see how far she really is willing to go with her disrespectful ways. It wouldn't hurt her to be reminded that she is lucky to have me also. In my own way, I am a catch.

"He moved his truck and that's the important thing."

She opened her mouth to say something sarcastic, but thought better of it. Instead she said, "Good for you, honey." I stood up and the bulge in my pants announced my intentions. My wife cast a glance at my crotch and went back to reading. Her meaning was clear. I would have to handle my pleasure on my own. My right hand and penis are best friends. They never go a day without saying hello to each other.

On my way upstairs, I peeked into my son's bedroom. Headphones were on his head and he was busy typing away on his laptop from his bed. There's a parental lock on his laptop, but kids these days are too smart. I'm sure there is an app to bypass these safeguards. Even in your own home, you cannot protect your children. The internet owns their minds.

The combined visual of seeing my wife almost naked and Isabelle's sexy little ass had me feeling frisky. Don't get me wrong, I am not a man who goes around desiring other men's wives, but Isabelle has always been so sweet to me. I have a natural fondness for her. I share a bathroom with my son. My wife said she needs her privacy to do her business. Privacy for what, I don't know. I conceded again and let her have the master bathroom in our bedroom all to herself.

I locked the door behind me and turned my cell phone to my Pandora reggae station. When I use the bathroom, I like to be unencumbered, completely naked. It's about the only time I feel free in my own home. Naked, I stared into the mirror that stretched from the sink to the toilet bowl. Have you ever stared at yourself and examined your body from the front and back? Bent over and spread your ass, just to see what it looks like? It's your body and you should be familiar with everything it does and how it looks. I am an average looking man with a below average body and penis. I squeezed the pouch around my stomach and wondered when did it get to be this size. It's not huge, but it's surely not attractive to me. I am sure my wife doesn't find it attractive either. I try to work out, eat decently, but it's a hard thing to do once you've hit that forty plus mark. My wife works out like a demon and has the body and clothes to prove it. She doesn't work, so she can afford to work out all day. She claims to be working on a book. A book I have never seen her working on yet. Being a writer is the new hustle. No credentials needed. Upload to Amazon and just like that—you're a writer.

Even though I tried not to think about it, I reached into the cabinet for my Vaseline. Images of Isabelle slipping off her robe right in front of her husband and bending over for me in her doorway aroused me. In my mind, I was taunting Joe as I fucked his wife in front of him and he was unable to stop me. Before I could stop myself, my hand was gliding over my erection and the raw power of it filled my right hand. I came so violently that I grabbed the edge of the sink to steady myself. I felt weak, as if I was about to pass out. An orgasm is the best stress release to clear out all the cobwebs from your mind. My little mental indiscretion wasn't hurting anyone. Imagine if people knew who was masturbating to their naked image, they would be shocked at the things being done to them, all in the name of sexual gratification. It's a good thing the imagination of a person is free and able to roam anywhere it wants to without permission. It's one of the last things we humans truly own. Everything else comes with a price. Anything with a price cannot truly be owned.

On the toilet was where I did some of my best thinking. I bet you if you asked entrepreneurs and scholars where their good ideas gave birth, they would tell you it's while sitting on the toilet. The world seemed to slow down as you opened your bowels and expunged all the filth accumulating in your body and mind. It's the best one two punch for thinkers, an orgasm and taking a dump. I have been known to sit on the toilet for an hour or more, just staring at the yellow wall in front of me or sometimes surfing the internet on my cell phone. It's my sanctuary. I know my wife won't disturb me. She has an aversion to certain scents that assault her delicate sensibilities. You should see how she reacts when she walks past my bathroom and I'm in the middle of doing my business. The door is closed, but she makes these sounds as if she is gasping for breath and being attacked by the defecation demons. It's the funniest thing. Sometimes I just wanted to drop a stink bomb to infuriate her. How can you get mad at someone for something like that? It's not like they are choosing to stink up the damn bathroom. Some things just cannot be helped. Anyway, that's my wife, the woman whose shit doesn't stink. She probably thinks hers should be bottled up as perfume.

I didn't remember falling asleep. It must have been all that sho-veling snow that wore me out. I woke up two hours later in darkness, unsure of where I was, with my left hand in my pants and drool on my face. My cell phone read five minutes after nine. My wife doesn't cook on Saturdays. It's usually fast food. A diet of that can quickly pack on the pounds. For a man my age, those pounds become part of you, no matter how much you exercise. I struggled to get off the couch in the basement and finally rose unsteadily to my feet. The television was tuned to *Big Bang Theory*. My wife hates it. She doesn't find it funny at all. She prefers slapstick funny stuff like *Martin* and *The King of Queens*. We enjoy different things, and as a result, we hardly spend time together as a couple. Unless we go shopping, meeting friends for dinner or a school function for our son. A couple that doesn't bond, the branch that holds them toge-ther will soon die. I love my wife, so I continue to try, even when she is unwilling to meet me halfway. I think most marriages fail, not because people fall out of love or cheat, but simply because people just stop caring about the other person's feelings. If you care about someone's feelings, you will go the extra mile to sometimes appease them, even when you don't feel up to it. That's marriage. That's compromise. Iyanla should teach my wife a lot about that.

A few months ago, I ran across this Facebook page called *Men Talking Shit*. To my surprise it was started by Joe my asshole neigh-bor along with a few other administrators. I never commented, just read all the statuses and comments. Usually it was just men blowing off steam about their jobs and wives, and of course sports. Today's status caught my eye. It was posted by Joe.

What do you do when your neighbor is a whiny, nerdy asshole? My wife wants me to be friends with my neighbor, Leslie. What kind of man is called Leslie? Should I be friends with him—or kick his ass?

The comments came flying, fast and furious. Men who didn't even know me were encouraging Joe to beat me up and teach me a lesson. A lesson about what, I did not know. The anonymity of social media emboldens even the meekest person with courage they don't have. It's like giving a coward a gun. All of a sudden, he's a cowboy, ready to ride out on the fucking range and be John Wayne. Joe chimed in and said vile things about my wife. Things I cannot repeat here. Things of a sexual nature. I wasn't even aware he was looking at my wife in that way. I typed furiously and called him eve-ry filthy name I could imagine, but when it came time to post my comment, I decided to delete it. Arguments are never won on social media. The fire just continues to spread as people without anything invested in the outcome, egg you on because they want to see you destroyed. It's like the Animal Kingdom on social media these days. Decorum is a nasty word.

I was so upset, no *pissed off,* that I took two shots of Tequila and followed it up with a glass of wine. Luckily because of the snowstorm, the federal government would be closed for at least the next two days. That's the thing about this area, DMV (Washington DC, Maryland and Virginia) a little snow and people lose their minds. The stores are filled with everyone buying shovels, salt and things they don't even need. They are more scared of snow than of violence on the streets. I suppose when you see or hear something daily you become desensitized to its impact. Now snow, that's some scary shit.

I wanted to bang on Joe's door and give him a piece of my mind, but I wasn't that drunk or tipsy enough not to know how it would end up. The house was quiet and I stared out the front window, looking at the snow falling again. A few inches had already fallen. The vehicles were under a blanket of white. I didn't want to wait until another ten inches fell to shovel again. The experts say to shovel every three inches or so. It's less strain on your heart. Dying isn't on my agenda right now, even if I am not the healthiest person.

After tossing on the full ensemble of winter clothes plus my boots, I stepped outside to complete silence. No one was outside. Snow fell silently, but it felt like I could hear it, you know what I mean? It was my own private concert of falling snowflakes. My boots were covered in snow by the time I got to my vehicle. I opened the trunk to retrieve my shovel. It was one the newer models with the metallic blade at the end. It helped to scrape away all the snow before it turned to ice.

My mind was still on the Facebook post as I began to shovel snow from the sidewalk and then work my way to my vehicle. The more I thought about it, the angrier I got. I work hard. Pay my bills. Try to treat everyone with respect and people who don't even know my character were mocking me on the internet, all because my asshole neighbor stirred them up. People are literally followers being led down a one-way street with an idiot as their leader. Not one person came to my defense. They just fell in line and piled it on without questioning the validity of what Joe was saying. It's easier to go along than to stand on your own and be vilified online. I suppose I can understand the desire of wanting to be accepted by a group, but when you're the one who's getting verbally smacked around by strangers, it's quite unsettling.

The quiet of the evening was shattered by a noise, some sort of clattering sound. I couldn't quite ascertain what it was. It sounded like the muffler of a car backfiring, but there weren't any vehicles on the road. The highway was too far away for the sound to be so clear. I stopped shoveling my sidewalk and listened intently and walked towards the disturbance. It was coming from Joe's truck. I stood by the door on the driver's side and the noise was definitely coming from inside his truck. I looked around to see if anyone was around and then brushed away the snow which had accumulated on the window. The noise was Joe snoring. It was deafening. His cell phone was on the dashboard, still logged on to the Facebook page, *Men Talking Shit*. He must have come outside to shovel snow, gotten inside his vehicle to keep warm and just fell asleep. He hadn't done much because my legs were halfway buried and it was still piled high on the hood of his truck. His face rested against the window and his lips vibrated every time he snored. For a moment, I contemplated letting him sleep, but the engine was off, and the bastard might freeze to death overnight. The temperature was steadily dropping and in the next few hours, it would be in the single digits. I tapped lightly on the window, but snorers are almost half dead when they are in that zone of deep sleep and dancing with death. I rapped on the window again, this time harder with my gloved right hand. I had rested the shovel against the door. He blinked his eyes a few times, unsure of where he was and then he stared up at me. He looked at me, trying to decide if he was dreaming or having a nightmare. Slowly he peeled his face away from the frosty window and wound down the window. Snowflakes flew into the open window and melted across his face.

"What the fuck do you want?"

"Just being neighborly and making sure you're alright, Joe."

My two hands were on the handle of the shovel as I stared down at his slumped body. His eyes were bloodshot and his lips were dry. His black jacket was open, exposing his muscled, veined neck and white t-shirt. It was a mistake trying to do the right thing and making sure the asshole was okay.

"Now you want to be neighborly. You had to go blab to my wife like a gossiping bitch that I stole your parking spot. Just for that, she will be on my ass all week, asshole."

"I didn't mean for that to happen, Joe. I apologize."

"Fuck your apology and the horse you rode in on."

I wanted to ask him what horse, but it would only make him angrier.

"No need for foul language, Joe."

I gripped the shovel so hard my fingers were hurting me. Snow had completely covered me now. I looked like a white snowman in blackface. I needed to finish up and get back inside. The last thing I wanted to do was get sick. Getting sick meant taking nasty ass cough medicine. I hate medicine. I would rather be verbally abused by my wife than drink it, well maybe that's too extreme, but you understand now how much I hate it. I turned to walk away and leave Joe to his thoughts, but he continued to verbally abuse me when I turned halfway around.

"How does a nerd like you get such a hot wife like Gina? You surely don't know how to handle that fine ass woman. Such a fucking shame. She must go to bed every night frustrated and wondering why she married your lame ass. It must be for the financial bene-fits— it couldn't be for anything else."

I turned around to look at him. The shovel head was buried in the snow. He was taunting me, hoping to make me react to his insults. He was embarrassed that his wife had dressed him down in front of me. In his mind, she had taken away his power. All she had done was make him do the right thing. Bullies never like to be shown up in front of their victims. He had to regain his power and emasculate me.

"I'm sorry you feel that way, Joe. I won't stoop to your level of insults."

"Of course you won't—cause you're a pussy. I know you're on my Facebook page, *Men Talking Shit* and you didn't say shit earlier. Stalking me like a bitch. A real man would have talked some shit and taken his balls out his mouth. Not you, *Leslie*. Our wives are more of a man than you. Your son is more of a man than you and he seems to have some tendencies."

The more he spoke the angrier I got. My body was trembling under my coat, not from the cold, but from anger. The heat radiating from my body seemingly melted the snow from my coat and hat. Joe was smirking at me. His mouth still moving a mile a minute. Everything he said was true. My wife and son didn't res-pect me. I had doubts about why she was with me all these years later. But here's the thing, a man should never tell another man disrespectful stuff like what Joe had spewed at me. Think it, yes, but don't say that shit. Men have feelings too. We hurt. Besides it's the man code. Joe had crossed the line. I couldn't imagine this asshole being my neighbor for the next five, ten—twenty years. Something deep inside of me snapped. When asked later to articulate the feeling, I would smile and recollect the moment in graphic detail to my psychiatrist. They called it a psychotic break, which is a temporary break from reality, like a mini-vacation. My anger was fueling me now and I couldn't stop myself from what I was about to do next.

I lifted the shovel from the snow. Snowflakes fluttered all around me like a mist of water falling from a showerhead. I brought it back to the side of my face, as if I were about to swing it like a pickaxe. His face didn't quite register what was coming. It was his hubris to believe that I was incapable of doing what I was about to do, which would be his ultimate undoing. The shovel head was turned upside down as it hurtled towards his neck. In retrospect, I didn't quite know what I was thinking would happen as the blade of the shovel sliced open Joe's neck and blood spurted all over his white t-shirt and on the steering wheel of his truck. His eyes sprung open. Shock registered on his stupid face as he brought his two hands around his neck. He looked down at his bloody hands and the realization of what had happened dawned on him. My anger hadn't arrived at its apex yet. It was still rising as I exacted my payback. The newspapers and social media would call it premeditated murder. I would come to be known as The Snow Shovel Killer of Upper Marlboro. The memes would be flying fast and furious. Especially in the next few snowy months, people would use a meme of me to scare their neighbors. But all of that hadn't happened as yet. I was still an anonymous person. Zack and Isabelle were fast asleep, unaware that their beloved Joe, I used that term loosely, was being shoveled to death. Gina and my son didn't know that their mild-mannered Leslie had reached his breaking point.

Words tried valiantly to escape his mouth. Instead, the only sound that came out was him was gasping for air. I imagined if he could find the words, he would try to apologize and beg for his life. The thought of Joe Asshole apologizing to me made me smile as I plunged the bloodied blade of the shovel deeper into his neck, over and over again. A sizeable gash had opened around his neck now. Crimson red soaked his white t-shirt and his ten fingers seemed to disappear into the open gash. I was surprised his head didn't topple over like a Jack-O-Lantern. His eyes pleaded with me to stop and save him. I wanted to, but I couldn't bring myself to do it. It would be like admitting I had done something wrong and needed his forgiveness. I would find out later from my lawyer that there were fifty-five gashes with the shovel around his neck. It's a miracle his head didn't topple over onto the steering wheel and blow the horn.

Exhausted from the exertion, I eased the shovel out of the window and it was dripping with blood. Red dots of blood splashed on the freshly fallen snow and formed random patterns around my feet. Joe's hands slowly slid down his neck, exposing the deep wounds around his neck. His fate was sealed and he continued to stare at me, wondering where it had all gone wrong. He was probably wondering how he had managed to underestimate the nerd. I wanted to say something to ease his mind, to ease him into the afterlife, wherever his destination might be.

"You were a real asshole to me, Joe. I didn't want any of this. We could have been friends or at least cordial neighbors because our wives like each other. Speaking of wives, I know you're thinking this will be hard on Isabelle. But I have to tell you since you were honest with me about my wife's hotness that she can do better than you. Your death will free her to maybe start dating at an appropriate time, maybe six months. In the spirit of more honesty since you will be dead in a few minutes, I have always wanted to fuck your wife. Truth be told, I think she has a soft spot for me. But don't worry, Joe. I won't try and fuck your wife—but I am sure if you had killed me, you wouldn't show me the same respect. I am a married man, and I love my wife. That's all I wanted from you, Joe. Respect. I'm sure you respect me now, don't you, Joe? Why does it take violence to gain respect and not basic communication? This didn't have to happen, Joe. You made me do this. This is all your fault, you fucking asshole."

I was rambling and hadn't even noticed that I had lost my audience. Joe was dead. It felt surreal to me standing there in the snow, that I had killed a man. It hadn't been a conscious decision. I didn't like Joe, but never once had I thought about killing the asshole. Maybe it was the psychotic break, but feelings of remorse and guilt hadn't as yet surfaced. What I felt, as I recounted the incident to my shrink was a feeling of being powerful, an adrenaline rush of excitement which would continue when I slipped into my bed. It was a foreign feeling to me of being in control, and I wanted to hold on to it for as long as I could.

The blood stains around my feet had already disappeared and painted over by a fresh coat of white snow. Since this was my first killing, I wasn't quite sure what to do, so I reached inside the window and wound it almost all the way up. I avoided looking at Joe's neck and face. Stuff like that gives me nightmares. The District Attorney would show them to me at my trial. I had insisted on testifying on my behalf which would turn out to be a mistake. Joe's hubris must have somehow transferred to me as he lay dying in the front seat of his truck. The jury came back in ten minutes and I was sentenced to life in prison without the possibility of parole. My beautiful wife had decided not to attend. She was on vacation in the Virgin Islands, spending my money. The next day I was served with divorce papers. Women don't waste any time when they are motivated.

I placed the bloody shovel back in the trunk of my truck and casually walked up the stairs to my house. I paused at the top step, stared into the surveillance camera to the left of the door and smiled like it was a selfie for Facebook. That video would become one of the state's best pieces of evidence against me. I have to admit that if I was on that jury, I would have found myself guilty too. Maybe not for the actual killing, but because I looked happy as I stared into the camera. I couldn't explain to the jury that it wasn't happiness, but a sense of reclaiming my manhood, my dignity. Rational people don't reclaim their manhood by killing their neighbor, so I kept that explanation to myself.

My wife was still fast asleep when I stepped back into our bedroom. I kind of expected her to be awake after this monumental thing I had done. Her naked body was partially covered with a sheet and she snored gently like a lullaby. Adrenaline was still pumping in my veins like a jackhammer. I undressed in one full motion and my erection stiff with the rush of conquest saluted her beautiful chocolate nakedness as she slept on her stomach. The powerful scent of sweat pulsated from my body, but taking a shower was the last thing on my mind. My wife must have smelled me the moment before I laid down on her back and entered her swiftly. She groaned at the unexpected penetration. I had never taken her like this. I always had to ask, as if I was a child in my own home, my own bedroom.

"What the fuck do you think you're doing?" She managed to say as I stroked her again, this time harder in an effort to shut her up. She moaned this time, even if it was against her will because it felt good to be handled like this. When we first started dating, she had confided in me that she liked to be dominated. It was how she got off, but the first few times we tried it, it didn't feel natural. It felt disrespectful, as if I was hurting her, when I tried to slap her and she laughed. We never tried it again.

I didn't need to answer her. She knew what I was doing. This time I didn't care about her feelings. It was all about me. Sweat dripped from my body as I entered her over and over and pummeled her relentlessly. I had never heard my wife moan and whimper so many times. I turned her over to see her face. I needed to see the pleasure registering in her eyes. I needed to see and hear her moan for me.

"What's gotten into you, Leslie?"

Her voice was low, a little scared. I could tell she was turned on by this new me.

I slapped her twice and the sound of flesh meeting flesh resounded through the quiet bedroom. Anger flared in her face and she opened her mouth to say something. Before she could, I slapped her again and entered her swiftly and pinned her two hands behind her head with my left hand. She gasped, but met my deep thrusts with enthusiasm and hunger.

"So you're the man now, huh?" She taunted me.

I glared at her and wrapped my two hands around her throat and continued to pound her. Her eyes flew open and she gasped for breath. This is what she loved, the idea of being helpless and pleasured. My grip tightened around her throat. Her eyes flickered open and closed, while her nipples grew in size. Her arousal fueled me with even more adrenaline. This is what our marriage had been missing all these years. A wife has to respect her husband. If she doesn't, everything else suffers in the household. It was a lesson I had learned too late. It took killing Joe to teach me that lesson. The irony made me want to laugh out loud and then cry.

"What's my name?" I demanded.

Her confusion at my question kept her quiet. I asked her again. This time applying more pressure to her throat as I bent over and bit her nipples. It was as if her body had been electrocuted as spasms ran up and down her legs. I stared down at her again, sweat running down my face. Again I asked her the question. This time she knew the answer.

"Master."

I removed my hands from around her throat and she gasped when I squeezed both nipples. She begged and pleaded for me stop as she gripped the sheets. The meek me would have stopped because she seemed to be in pain. This me hopped up on adrenaline knew that this is what she craved to feel. Her body thrashed back and forth and she came so hard that she remained still and moaning for a few minutes. I remained in the same position observing her and trying to memorize every detail of this moment so I could play it like a movie in my mind in the years to come. For a few minutes, I had the respect of my wife. I had shown her that I knew how to take control and be the man she had always wanted me to be. There was a smile on her face when she opened her eyes and kissed me passionately. That was incredible she said before falling asleep in my arms. A memory like that, a man holds on to until his dying day.

The next morning, the cops knocked on the door, read me my rights in front of my wife and son. The entire incident had been caught on the various video cameras that my neighbors had installed on their porches. Ironically, I was the one who spearheaded the campaign last year because of a rash of break-ins in the neighborhood. Unknowingly, I had sealed my own fate. The entire neighborhood was outside, pretending that they were doing something else. Isabelle screamed at me and spit in my face. I wanted to tell her it was for the best and that I had done her a favor, but she was grieving. Maybe in a few years she would visit me and say thank you. But for now, her grief was raw and understandable.

Snow was still falling as the nice police officers helped me into the back of the squad car. I opened my mouth, closed my eyes and allowed a few drops of snow to fall on my tongue before entering the squad car. My son stood quietly on the stairs, taking the whole scene in. It was the last lesson I could teach him. Don't take shit from anyone. I hoped he was paying attention.

The cops were in the front seat arguing about the football game, talking about their wives and kids. I sat back and listened to their conversation for the entire ride until I fell asleep. I was exhausted. I had had a busy night and missed out on my normal eight hours of rest. The memory of making love to my wife put a smile on my face as I replayed it again for the first of many more times to come. The radio in the squad car was tuned to WHUR. *Respect* by Aretha was playing. Maybe God did understand and this was his way of giving me the thumps up.

OUR FIRST KISS

You look beautiful dead. I didn't have the pleasure of talking to you face to face, until now, when I can tell you the things on my heart. You changed my life and made me feel things no one ever has done before. There I was, just going about my life, minding my own business and then, like a tsunami, you upended everything I believed in and forced me to see the world through new eyes. You had a power over me that sometimes left me paralyzed, unable to function. I forgot who I was and became who you wanted me to be. Maybe I deserved it since I allowed you into my life. I let you in to rummage through my life and discover all my secrets and weaknesses. Truth is, I created you from a need I did not know I had — a need to be heard, seen, loved, and validated. You gave me all of that and used your power to break me down, leaving me vulnerable for others like you. But you underestimated my courage. You took for granted I was a shell after you discarded me. Your words haunted me. Even as you manipulated me, a part of me knew you were too good to be true, but I needed you to be everything you claimed. The world had disappointed me for too long. I needed some magic. I needed a match to ignite my flame and you threw gasoline on my life. You made me feel alive when I was just merely existing, sleepwalking through my life. You did that. You brought me back to life, and then you took it all away.

One day you did not exist. You were out there somewhere in the world unknown to me. And the next day, you walked into my life, well, you dropped into my inbox. You were unassuming, not pushy like most men who are easily distracted by the physical and neglect everything else about a woman. In retrospect, I can see now how you got past my defenses. You saw me as a person and not as an object of desire. You spoke to my mind and not to my libido. You celebrated my ideas and that made me feel beautiful, seen. This was revolutionary to me, but to you it was all part of the con to reel me in like a prize-winning catch. You targeted and profiled me. I still cannot figure how you knew I would be susceptible to someone like you. You knew the trigger words to get me to react, to anger me into action. You knew what would soothe me and the things that would make me smile when the world was trying to tear me down. You were a welcome diversion into my world of monotony. A daily rush of excitement that made me feel alive. On those occasional days when I would find my inbox empty of any correspondence from you, I would sink into an immediate depression. I felt abandoned. Useless. I recognized the irrationality of feeling like this, but I was unable to stop myself. I was addicted to someone I had never met, but your words made me feel as if I knew you, as if you knew me. It made me feel as if your heart was beating through my screen. I could touch you in our world where no one else existed. It was beautiful. You were a secret I kept to myself. I didn't want anyone else to have you. There is too much oversharing in today's social media world. Everyone knows everything. Nothing is private or sacred. Nothing is special. I wanted us to stay special so the magic would continue to enrapture me.

I am staring at your dead face now, a face I don't even recognize as I imagine you typing words to me. Words that made my soul smile and leap for joy. When your name would appear in my inbox, I would caress the screen with my fingertips, making circles around each letter of your name and absorb your energy. It felt as if you were penetrating me with each rapid fire message to my inbox. You were there with me touching my skin and illuminating my mind. I was breathing in your aura, pure and uncut like a drug. I drank you in and became a disciple. I gave you everything and you gave me the illusion of freedom and a belief that even though the world did not value my presence, you saw beyond the exterior. You saw the person I was too scared to share with the world for fear of being rejected again. You were sunlight and I became the flower that bloomed from your light. Our connection was never sexual, even though we shared intimate thoughts and photos. It wasn't the foundation for what we became. You made the world tolerable. Every day had purpose. I found myself in the elevator, walking down the street, or in line at a coffee shop thinking about our exchanges and I would smile. I didn't care if people gave me the side eye. They didn't know what I knew. They didn't know you.

You look so peaceful now, like an angel. You were the furthest thing from an angel. You were a predator, a vulture that preyed on the kindness of strangers and their vulnerabilities. I want to tell all of these mourners who you were as they cry over you. Your family praise your virtues. It's not their fault. You were a chameleon changing like the weather and adapting to whatever people needed you to be. No one knows who I am as I stand among the mourners. They must assume we were colleagues or one of the countless people who revered you. I let them believe that because the truth would not do them any good. They are better off not knowing the monster you were. They don't need to know about the countless innocent women and men you preyed upon, disrupting their lives, seducing them, manipulating them when you did not get your way. It was all a game to you. You toyed with us like a bored cat toying with a mouse before it pounced on it and devoured it whole. This is how you entertained yourself by using everyone to pass the time. How could I not see the monster behind the smile? The manipulator behind the carefully structured words used to elicit the sought after reactions. You knew before I spoke what I was going to say. You were in my mind reading my thoughts. You were too good to be true. You were a free gift with invisible strings that would be pulled when least expected. You were the ultimate puppet master. I wonder now if your power will extend beyond death and manipulate my thoughts in the shadows. Will seedlings you secretly planted in my mind take hold and grow into something insidious? It's a horrible thought, too horrible to even contemplate. I want to shake you awake to ask you. The thought is slowly mushrooming and a smile appears to be creeping over your face. *I win*, your smile grins at me. The dead cannot win.

Then, just like that, everything changed.

I didn't see it coming. It was a Friday evening. I remember it was snowing outside. We loved the snow. I thought you were joking when your words, once used to soothe and enlighten me, took aim at the most vulnerable places in my armor. I opened myself up to you and you knew exactly where to strike with your poisonous insults. Each one felt as if you sliced a dagger into my physical being, all the way to my soul. I was left bleeding and naively hoped that you would stop, but you took great joy in my pain. Even after I confessed to you that you were hurting me, you continued your onslaught, until you felt that I was broken. You said things to me that I cannot repeat. It would reinforce how worthless it made me feel. At least when it's just thoughts in my mind I can still rationalize it. How ridiculous is that?

I begged you to stop attacking me, but you were relentless. This is what you wanted – to build me up and then tear me down. I was left naked under your relentless attacks. I had no safe place to hide. You had given me everything and, then in one calculated evening of verbal mayhem, you set out to destroy me. When your mission was accomplished, you simply logged off and disappeared into the black hole of the internet. You left me down in that rabbit hole of self-pity and I didn't have the carrots of dignity to entice you to empathize for me. I logged on every day hoping that that day would be the day you forgave me and returned the light to my life. I didn't know exactly what I had done that warranted your forgiveness, but whatever it was, I wanted to atone for it. As the days dragged on, every second of every day was spent thinking about you and wondering what you were doing. Had you found someone more interesting, someone with the prowess to match your wit? Had you grown weary of your ways and sought redemption? But I knew you hadn't. You had simply grown tired of me and moved on to your next victim. You had simply used me like toilet paper, flushed me down the toilet, and washed your hands of my existence. Slowly my neediness for you turned into frustration, and then anger — the kind of anger that consumes your thoughts. The dueling emotions of anger and love for you flowed furiously through my veins. I needed to confront you, to ask you the questions burning in my mind and heavy on my heart, but there was nowhere to turn. You were a ghost. It was as if you were a recurring dream I had for months and then I woke up. I wanted the life we shared. I wanted you.

I scoured the internet looking for signs of you, looking for a trace that would lead me to you. I set up social media accounts using aliases as bait. We shared similar tastes in music and books, so I started there, joining hundreds of pages, searching through thousands of profiles trying to hunt you down. I figured someone like you would get comfortable and begin to feel invincible. I was counting on you believing that I was too weak and broken to come after you. Arrogant prick.

One day, I commented on a post and noticed that someone immediately responded to my comment. *I knew it was you.* You were using an alias, just like me, but I recognized the flow of your words. Every writer has a signature, a tell. Yours had been imprinted on my heart. I waited, knowing you would not be able to resist contacting me. My hands were shaking. I imagined that you were scrolling through my profile trying to dissect me and find my weak points. I left a few exposed spots of my neck for you to sink your teeth into. Predators like you get a mental erection when they find a way into their next victim's life. I was turning the tables, giving you what you wanted to get what I wanted. You didn't know it yet, but you were the prey and I was the predator.

Back to your old tricks, you entered my inbox once again. This time I knew your method of attack. How you used self-deprecating humor as a Trojan horse to enter your victim's life. I was ready for you and gave you just enough to make you believe you'd hooked another victim. You probed my perceived weaknesses with misleading questions and answers designed to get me talking. I smiled as I sipped on a glass of red wine, matching you stroke for stroke. You never know how strong you are until you have to be. I had anger-induced adrenaline and steroids pumping through my steely veins. I was on a mission to destroy you, the same way you had destroyed me.

The mourners begin to disperse from the church. An older woman, her face covered with a black veil announced that the repass would take place at your mother's house after the grave-side burial. Maybe I will attend if only to pay my respects to your family's perceived notion of you. The thought makes me want to laugh out loud. I bet you still can't believe you're dead. You never saw it coming. The grasshopper had trumped the master.

You were too cocky after that first conversation with my alias. You sent me photos of your McMansion and cars and the places you had visited all over the world. You even provided tales of philanthropy and photo-ops as a bonus. I laughed. They were all lies. Lies. Lies. And more lies. A quick search on Google revealed that all of your photos were photo-shopped and belonged to someone else. Your lies would be your undoing. I was able to track your IP address that led me right to your doorstep. *Jackpot!* You lived within five miles of me in a modest one family house — with your mother. Go figure that, a man of the world living with his momma. I stalked your mom's Facebook page. She was way too open with her life. She posted everything from what she watched on TV, to the places she went for dinner. When I saw that she posted she was away on vacation in the Caribbean, I knew it was time to make my move. You would never see me coming. I was cloaked in the darkness of anonymity. I didn't exist to you. I was nothing. Soon you would regret the day you charmed your way into my nothingness.

It wasn't that hard to figure out the four-digit alarm code to your house. I found your mom's spare key taped under the flower pot next to the front door, of course. According to her postings, she loved to garden, so it would stand to reason she would hide a key there. I knew that I only had forty seconds to turn of the alarm but if I didn't, I would just give up and run away. The cops never responded quickly in this neighborhood. But I had guessed right.

Zero. Nine. Two. Five. Your mom's birthday.

Just like that, I was inside your home, your life; the same way you had infiltrated mine. Turnaround was fair play. I just wanted to get some answers. I should have known it would not make me feel better. Maybe I knew how this would end, but you pushed me too far to care. You have no one to blame but yourself.

Fifteen minutes later, I heard the front door chime and alarm beep to disarm. You were home. There hadn't been enough time to thoroughly dissect your life from inside your lair. But from what I found – meticulously kept logs that included photos and biographical info of your victims and the dates you infiltrated their lives, hundreds of your aliases, and sophisticated computer equipment – I was able to discern that you had been victimizing people for many years. I made sure to delete any trace of me from your records. Maybe one day you would discover it was missing, but the thought of how you traumatized me after reading your crib-notes on our communications had pissed me off.

There was no time to leave the house undetected, so I hid in your bedroom closet, waiting for you to come upstairs. There was something off about your room, I didn't remember seeing any of your personal effects, just computer equipment. Maybe the adrenaline pumping through my veins made it impossible to focus. This was a bad idea, but it was too late now. Things had been set in motion.

You entered your bedroom and stopped in the middle of the room. I couldn't see you but you had stopped walking, as if sensing a foreign presence. Had I forgotten to turn off your laptop? Did I leave your desk in disarray? Maybe I was breathing too loudly. I slowly began to panic and reached around into my backpack still strapped to my back. My fingers touched the cold steel of the gun I had bought at a gun show last year. I was surprised how easy it was to acquire something that could kill someone. I wanted you to know how it felt to be vulnerable – I was only going to scare you. I pushed open the closet door, stumbled out holding the gun in my outstretched hands, and stood there face-to-face with *you*. Something was wrong. This wasn't the person I recognized from our doomed online relationship. Had someone other than you entered your house? The gun shook between my hands as I pointed it at you, a young woman. My mind was spinning trying to make sense of everything. You were a girl. Maybe you had a sister I thought to myself, but no, I knew I had the right room. Then it dawned on me. You didn't ask who I was and looked at me with recognition. You didn't even seem scared. I was the one holding a gun, yet I was the one in fear.

The pieces were beginning to fit together. All the clothes in your closet were for a female. The picture on your profile was of a man, though we had never spoken or video-chatted, just emailed and IM'd. You said you were shy. You said you wanted me to know the real you and not the physical. You had an answer for everything and I was addicted to you so I believed you. Your deception was even more sinister than I could ever imagine.

You said my name. Even with a gun pointed at you, you had no fear in your voice. It felt like you were toying with me. Again. Your voice was girly, flirty even, but evil twinkled in your eyes. You said my name again and smiled at me. There was a taunt in your smile. You still believed, even after everything you had done to me, that you could control me. Put the gun down, you said. Your voice remained calm, but your directive was clear. You were in control, or so you thought.

You're not the boss of me, I said childishly.

You grinned.

I was still in shock to discover I had been talking to a girl all these months. You were pretty - no, beautiful. You had a face that made men say stupid things. You told me again to put the gun away. I refused. Then the real you came out. The angry version whose abuse I was oh so familiar with. You laughed. Called me pathetic. Your words cut me. I thought I was bleeding, but it was only tears streaming down my face.

I loved you, I screamed.

You're not the first, you responded.

You were smug, a bit too cavalier about my feelings. Then it just happened. People say that all the time, but that's the truth. I squeezed the trigger to scare you, to make you shut up. One shot to your chest – your heart, ironically. Your eyes were open in shock as you fell to the floor. You never saw it coming. My hands were still shaking but I collected myself, wiped down everything I touched, and retraced my footsteps through the front door, making sure to turn on the alarm.

That was a week ago. The police had no leads. They found your dirty laundry and assumed, correctly, that one of your many victims had gotten revenge but unsure of which one. My name was nowhere to be found. I didn't exist in your world. I didn't mean to kill you, but if I am to be truthful, I didn't feel any remorse. You played God with the emotions of innocent people. You got what was coming to you. A violent death was always in your future.

You look beautiful dead. No one is paying attention to me, so I walk up to your casket and place my hand on your chest, by your heart, where I shot you. It's only then that I cry for you. My love. My tormenter. My stalker. Someone whispers in my ear that it's okay, you deserved to die. I turn around, but there is no one there. Maybe it was my conscience whispering words of solace to my heart.

I lean in closer to your body, until our faces are almost touching. And, for the first time, I kiss you.

THE SEDUCING WHISPERS OF MELANCHOLY

I wanted it all to end. The pain. The tears. The constant feeling of uselessness and detachment from everything around me. I was tired and just wanted to sleep, without ever waking up. The end felt so close, but every time I reached for its eternal embrace, all I felt was rejection, not even death wanted me. Cue corny sitcom laugh track.

I wasn't always this person obsessed with ending my life. There must have been a time when I was happy and had happy thoughts like regular people. It was getting harder and harder to recall such thoughts, as if they had just all suddenly disappeared and left a hole in my memory. A part of me knew feeling like this wasn't normal, but I had worn the dark suit of melancholy for so long now, it felt like my permanent wardrobe. I had grown used to the fit and didn't mind it anymore. As strange as it sounds, it felt like a friend coming to visit me every day. There wasn't much in my life I could count on, but I knew like clockwork when my depressed sidekick was on its way. It felt like a rising wave, pulling me under without any resistance. When I was fully submerged, it was the only time I felt free, like myself. I felt understood and didn't have to smile or hide my feelings. I could just be myself. Do you know how hard that is? I felt as if everyone was constantly judging me and waiting for me to crash and burn. I kept fighting off the inevitable, but I know the day will come when I am too tired to fight off the demons. I feel them lurking like a shadow, feeding on my insecurities. And the harder I fight, the more I feed them chunks of my soul and spirit. So I want to let go, drift slowly away like a wayward leaf floating on the ocean's belly, until Mother Nature does what it does and consumes me, until I am no more.

You don't know how hard I have tried to resist this feeling, this urge to harm myself. I know it's unnatural. I know it's a sickness, but when you are sick, all you want is peace, even when peace means not knowing you are at peace. I see people like you happy, seemingly free of worry. I wonder how do you do it? I want to ask you about your secret to combat the seducing whispers of melancholy. My greatest fear is that there is no secret, but simply a choice to live life to its fullest, while understanding bad things happen and there is nothing you can do about it. A choice? Could it be that simple? We choose to do battle with the demons that know our secrets and weaknesses and if we win more than we lose, then it's a successful life. So this morning I decided to wake up and choose a happy mindset and keep the darkness at bay.

It was a Saturday morning. I sat outside on the porch drinking coffee, enjoying the quiet of the early morning island sea breeze. The neighborhood was quiet. A few birds were in the mango tree having breakfast and enjoying a spirited conversation. My restlessness was asleep. It felt good not to be worried about anything, just living in the moment and enjoying life. I wanted this feeling to last. I wanted to be someone who is capable of being happy. From my porch, I could smell the ocean air. It was only a ten minute walk away from my home. It's not something I would have normally done on a Saturday, but I wanted to keep my happy momentum going. Five minutes from my home is Sandy Point. It's where they shot the final scene of *Shawshank Redemption* starring Tim Robbins and Morgan Freeman. You know the scene where Red is walking on the sand towards the fishing boat that Andy is working on. That scene always kills me. It's a happy scene, but somehow always just fills me with sadness.

The road to the beach had been a dirt road when I was growing up. My parents used to take us there every Saturday. Now it's only me. Dad would fry Snapper and Jack Fish he had bought from a fisherman named Prince. We had to call him Mr. Prince. He was always parked in the same spot by the fish market. The boat was always on the shore, but submerged halfway in the water. I remember how clear the water used to be when I stepped in it and my feet would sink into the warm sand. My father would hold my hand as he bought fish and chatted with Prince about baseball and local island politics. Tiny fish of all colors of the rainbow would circle around my feet, but I was never scared because my father was holding my hand. It was like living inside of my own personal fish tank. I remember my father used to lift me up and run with me in the water. My tiny feet would skim the surface as I shrieked with joy as water splashed everywhere. It felt like I was walking on water. I miss those days. Maybe that's when the whispers started.

Even at eleven in the morning, the white sands at Sandy Point was already hot. For miles and miles in both directions not a soul was in sight. It felt like I was the only person in the world at the moment. The water was varying shades of blue and had a very steep drop off. A park ranger told me once that parts of the drop off was at least eight thousand feet deep, which is as deep as the Grand Canyon. It was like stepping off the edge of a cliff and falling through space. The water was still, but I could feel the waves rising again inside of me. My mind raced ahead trying to think of good thoughts to stall the inevitable. I didn't want to drown anymore. I wanted to surf above the water and walk on it like I did with my father as a child.

My bare feet was hot against the sand. I walked closer to the shore into the wet sand to cool off my feet. The sun beamed down against my body, but my feet were now submerged in the cool water. A school of tiny reddish fish swam around my feet. It made me smile. I missed my father. My mother. My brother. The innocence of my youth before the darkness made its first appearance. Memories of my father was many years ago, but it stills feels like yesterday to me.

My feet kept moving through the water. The shades of blue darkened. Waves were coming at me from every direction. My mind felt like a swirling tornado in the midst of an ocean swell. The water had risen above my waist. I could no longer see any fish around my feet. The water was cold, but I didn't feel cold. I was with my father splashing around in the water. Everything was easy. The future was bright as the sun beamed down on my body. I was a happy child, and then I was not. How does that happen? How do some children survive tragedy and come out the rabbit hole in relatively good shape? Why didn't I? Was there something deficient in my DNA that robbed me from being resilient? I did try, for a short time anyway. Medication. Meditation. Prayer. Therapy. I even tried hypnosis. Obviously nothing took. Maybe every step I took was always leading me here. Maybe this was always my fate and I was fighting a losing battle. Once your footprints are cast, there is no changing it.

I turned to look back, but my body kept propelling forward as if unable to stop. It has somewhere to be, a schedule to keep. The shore looked shimmery, out of focus. Sandy Point is a protected habitat for turtles, but I didn't see any. There is nothing here for me. My legs took over and my mind and body followed. The blue water ahead is so dark it looked ominous. I wanted to turn back, but I can't. I want to be happy, but I can't. I am tired. I want to rest. To sleep. To dream. I want to see my father again. I want to recapture that feeling of being happy, without even thinking about it.

A gust of wind makes the water around me ripple and for a moment, the breeze sings a familiar whisper I have heard all my life. Maybe it's a sign I am doing the right thing. Who sends us these signs I wonder, but the thought doesn't go beyond that. I step off a cliff and I am freefalling. I wondered if this is what Tom Petty's song was about. It feels like I am floating through space or skydiving, without a parachute. My eyes are open, but the bottom of the ocean is invisible, it's like it doesn't exist and could go on forever. I can't see myself floating, but I imagine it looks like the first cover of *Life After God* with the baby floating or the cover of that Nirvana CD. These are things I shouldn't be thinking about considering where I am and what's about to happen, but it's how my mind has always worked, a bit askew.

From somewhere I don't know where, a deeply buried memory resurfaces. Maybe it's not a memory, but a feeling, but it feels real. My mother is smiling at me. My face between her hands. They feel warm and feel like love. I start to cry and suddenly the waves in my mind disappear and I want to head back to shore to finish my coffee on the porch and listen to the end of the birds' conversation. I continue to sink. It feels like my body is weighted. I cannot swim. Seems ironically funny now that I was born on an island and raised five minutes away from the sea and never learned to swim. It never dawned on me to learn, until now. I keep my eyes closed because at least in my mind, I can create my own reality. I am safe there, finally.

JAY Z KILLED ME

Morning rush hour into Washington, DC is always a beast. With nothing else to do, I downloaded the new Jay Z CD through Sprint. I had to sign up for a free six month subscription through Tidal in order to hear it. I added a note on my Google calendar to delete it a few days before the paid subscription kicked in. I miss the old days of going to Tower Records or The Wiz and buying a CD. Something tangible in my hand, so I can read the linear notes, the lyrics. Now everything is downloads. Sometimes I can't even find the damn thing on my phone to listen to it.

Hearing that song 4:44 got me killed. I should have known the minute that that fucking CD dropped that my life was in danger and I should have packed my bags and just left everything behind. *Fucking Jay Z. Why couldn't you keep your mouth shut about cheating on Beyoncé?* That's your private business, man. Why you had to get all Kanye Heartless on us and get all sensitive thug and shit. Weren't you the one who said *sensitive thugs, you all need hugs?* Now you're the one who sounds like you're about to have an emotional breakdown and the world has a first class seat to your pain. Not cool bro. Not cool at all. The streets aren't loving you right now, *Sean.*

I had my phone on shuffle and the first song was *4:44.* When I heard the singer wailing like Patti LaBelle and she sang the first few lines—I just fucking knew you, *Jay Z,* had gotten me into some deep marriage shit. *Do I find it so hard, when I know in my heart, I'm letting you down every day, letting you down every day, why do I keep on running away?* I had to rewind that shit when I heard it. Those words, man, you just don't understand—that's exactly how I felt *every single fucking day.* I'm not the man Briana deserves. She *upgraded* my status when I married the baddest chick in the game, well on my block—but it's the same shit. I didn't feel like I was good enough for her. I don't make enough money, so I can't buy her the things she deserves or take her on vacations. We are always having to juggle bills. That shit depresses and stresses me out. A *Queen* shouldn't live like a pauper. My baby always tries to comfort me, tells me she doesn't need these things. All she needs is me. The words sound good, but they are empty. Our future is bright she always says. When she smiles at me and holds me in her arms, I want to cry, but I can't. I only cry in the shower. There is a limit to how sensitive a man should be in front of his woman. You want to be sensitive enough that she knows you can relate to her emotions, but not so sensitive she gives you the side eye if you start bawling uncontrollably. A woman hates a man who cries too much, just as much as a man hates a woman who just won't shut the fuck up.

So I'm in my car, stuck in traffic. It's not too hot yet, but the weatherman god said it's going to be close to the century mark. When it gets hot in DC, it feels like your brain is on fire. Do you remember that drug commercial with the fried egg and they say, *this is your brain on drugs*? That's how the heat feels down here. I look around at the cars surrounding me. Luckily, I am not claustrophobic or else I would be losing my shit now. Some people are on their phones, others are listening to music and then there are those who are spacing out. One dude in the next lane was having a full blown conversation with himself. He looked at me from behind his window, smiled and then waved. I looked away. *Crazy motherfucker.* There are sirens up ahead. A fire truck behind. A serious accident had taken place and I would probably be stuck here for a minute. I texted my manager, Steve, and he responded with "k." A grown person who cannot spell out a simple word irks me. Not even okay, or ok—just responding with *k*. That kind of means you don't care if I come in or not.

The heat was rising outside. I cranked up my A/C and got back to my Jay Z download. What I heard next perplexed me even more and I gripped the steering wheel tightly. That nigga was apologizing like a bitch, not once, but *seven motherfucking times*. That shit had gotten real for me. It felt as if there was a gun to my head, but it's only the words piercing my guilt. Stuff like this has ramifications for regular dudes like me. What the fuck was Hova thinking about? You cheat on the baddest chick in the game and then you admit that shit to the world? Either he's really stupid or just gangsta enough to know, he has Beyoncé on lock and his metaphor game is superior enough to earn him forgiveness. I almost expected Beyoncé to start singing background, *to the left, to the left.* I can only imagine that Briana is in her feelings right about now at home, listening to this confessional rap shit. She hasn't called yet. No texts yet, so I know she is dissecting every lyric and when I get home, I'm the one who will be interrogated like an episode of *Law & Order.* Jay Z apologizing, crying, admitting he sucks at love and even going to therapy—therapy—do you understand how deep that shit is? Black people, *black men* don't go to therapy. We talk shit with our boys, get stupid drunk, listen to rap music or smoke some weed to get our head right, then get back to life—that's our therapy. We are not into that Dr. Phil, *Iyanla Fix My Life* bullshit. *Big Pimpin'* done gone soft and probably *can't bust a grape in a fruit fight* now.

Traffic around me slowly began to inch forward. A red truck pulled alongside me, windows down, the driver was sweating from the heat and his music was cranked up. He looked at me, buck-toothed, in need of a shave and his eyes were reddish. He pointed at the steering wheel, but actually he's directing me to listen to the music. It's the same song I'm playing. He shouts to me, "this nigga cheated on Bey and rapping 'bout that shit! That's a boss move!" Before I can respond he swerved into the next lane, still bobbing his head and had already forgotten about me.

I imagine many men like him all over the country are doing the same thing. I imagine their women are probably waiting to have a conversation with them later at home. Intentionally or unintentionally, Hova done started some shit that won't end well for a lot of people. Women are probably thinking to themselves, if this fool can cheat on the baddest chick in the game, what's stopping my raggedy ass man from thinking he can do the same thing and get away with it? Jay Z must have a helluva a prenuptial agreement to even try some shit like that. But at the end of the day, sometimes it doesn't matter how much you have to lose, you do what you want and say fuck the consequences. When it's time to pay the weight of those consequences is when that regret and guilt thing might come into play.

I thought Hova had my back. His music was the one place I could go and just vibe without feeling exposed. Steve Harvey wrote that damn book and men were left scrambling to come up with answers. That was a dark time for men. And now this shit from Hova. Another hero blindsides his male fans. I didn't expect much from this CD. Seems like Hova was on cruise control the past few years, heading out to Florida, wearing flip flops, trick or treating with Blue Ivy. He replaced his gangsta/thug cape with a suit and vacation time with the family. Nothing wrong with that. Everybody grows up. But when you grow up, it doesn't mean you throw your boys under the bus. You're leaving tire tracks all over us. We get you feel ashamed for stepping out on Bey and you feel guilty. Goes to show, even when a dude has the baddest chick in the game, he can still go Eric Benet. *Look, I apologize, often womanize.* There's no metaphor in this. No double entendre. You straight told everyone you were a dog to your Queen Bey. So when you fuck with Beyoncé, the beehive will string your black ass up faster than a police officer can draw on an unarmed black man. But more importantly— you put a fucking police helicopter spotlight on my life. Now there's no way to turn that shit off. If I survive this betrayal, there's no way I'm buying your music anymore. You will need to put a sticker on your CD to warn dudes that you're going all Keith Sweat on us.

I cannot even tell you what I did at work for the next eight hours. I was in my feelings and closed my office door to further dissect this damn CD, which could be the inspiration for my obituary. I walked around my office to make sure I had service on my cell phone. No texts or phone calls from my wife. I called her and it went straight to voicemail. She was working from home today, but I was sure we were doing the same thing. I knew she was shedding a tear or two over these lyrics. *I seen the innocence leave your eyes / I still this death and I apologize for all the stillborns / Cause I wasn't present, your body wouldn't accept it / I apologize to all the women whom I toyed with your emotions because I was emotionless.* Another punch to the gut.

I can still hear you crying from your hospital room after another miscarriage. You were inconsolable by the time I got there — three hours later. I should have been with you, instead I was with my Becky. I hadn't thought about it much until Hova spit those lyrics at me and the bass boomed in my ears through my headphones. *I apologize for all the stillborns / 'Cause I wasn't present, your body wouldn't accept it.* That shit broke me down in my office. Tears were streaming down my face. I called Briana again, no answer. I imagined both of us listening to the same lyrics at the same time. I don't know if we can listen to it together, in the same space. The energy would be too much. Words would be said that can never be taken back. We listened to the Lemonade CD together. Then Solange's CD and now this dude drops a CD with more drama than a fucking reality show. That whole family had me fucked up.

Men always say even though they might cheat, they still love their wife or significant other. Love has nothing to do with cheating. It might not have anything to do with it because I still love my wife. But if love has nothing to do with it and it's only a physical act of betrayal, how do you reconcile the deception? How do you sleep at night, next to the person you love and have them believing you are something you are not? The moments before it would happen it was an adrenaline rush, a new experience. Seconds after my body was drained of its liquids, the stranger who had been inhabiting my body would disappear back into his self-inflicted hell and I would come back to my senses. It was a one-time thing, but that didn't matter. One time is all it takes to lose everything. The first time I cheated was the same night we lost our first child. *I apologize for all the stillborns / 'Cause I wasn't present, your body wouldn't accept it.*

I didn't know how I drove home that evening. Maybe I would have been better off sleeping on the couch in my office. A night apart to digest this CD and the ramifications to our marriage would have been best, but we had decided a long time ago, that no matter what happened, we were to always sleep in the same bed. That's at least one promise I have managed to keep.

The neighborhood was quiet as I pulled into my parking space. Quiet as a cemetery. It felt like my neighbors were watching behind their closed curtains, aware that some drama was about to go down. Guilt makes you paranoid. That shit fucks with your reality. I only had one move left, to go inside and face my wife.

Even though there was still some light outside, the curtains were drawn and the house dark. I had to give my eyes a few seconds to adjust to the darkness in the hallway. That's when I heard it. The strains of the wailing from the song *4:44*, wrought from pain buried so deep and now it was rising to the surface, it needed a place to be embraced safely. I stood at the bottom of the stairs, waiting, listening, and allowing the words and music to wash over me before venturing any further. I still had time to leave. I wanted to leave. I wanted to do the right thing. The right thing won out. We had too much history together for me to walk out like this. What kind of man does that? But what kind of man cheats on his lover, friend, wife…soulmate? *What good is a ménage à trois when you have a soulmate?* My legs felt heavier as I trudged upstairs. The last thing I wanted to do was have a confrontation. It would have been nice to come home. Have a drink. Dinner. Watch *Power* to see what Ghost got himself into again. You would think that watching *Power*, I would have learned from Ghost to just stay away from the Angela Valdes' of the world? Stupid men. Stupid me.

There she was, my wife, sitting down in the middle of our bed, with her back against the headboard. Our bedroom was illuminated with the orange glow of numerous candles around the bed, on the dressers and nightstand. There was even a few in the bathroom as I walked by towards the bed. The song was on repeat on her cellphone between her thighs. The only thing she was wearing was her naked brown skin. Even after knowing her so many years and being married for a few, there were still moments when her beauty set my skin on fire. Briana was 5'5, cinnamon complexion, with just enough ass and breasts to make you hungry for more. It was the look in her eyes that hooked me. A deep sensuality flowed through her veins and we just connected. How could I have been so stupid? Everything I wanted and needed was right here in this room and I had to be a man and fuck it up. Are there any magical combinations of words you can string together so that a woman will forgive you? Can she ever get the picture out of her head about your indiscretions? Indiscretion is a world that dilutes the meaning of what you did. It seeks to wrap it up in a bed of roses and make it smell good. The weight of what I had done didn't hit me, until my wife stared at me as if I was a stranger.

"I always knew, but I didn't want to know. I wanted it to just magically go away and we could have the life you had promised."

"We can still have that life," I said stupidly. I dropped to my knees next to the bed. My hands close to her feet, but not touching them. "I can make it up to you." More clichéd words.

"You can never make it up to me. You lied to me for years and I let you lie. Does that make me your accomplice? I was everything to you, and still that wasn't enough."

"What more could I have done, Samuel?"

It's one of those questions you never answer in a situation like that. No matter what you say, it will not be enough. Silence is your best friend in that moment.

Her braids fell in front of her face, obscuring her eyes. I didn't have to see them to know she had been crying for hours. She had undoubtedly sung the lyrics to that song an infinite amount of times, and it was already probably a soundtrack to our marriage. It sang in her soul.

"I made a mistake, Briana."

"A mistake is when you get red onions instead of white. A mistake is when you get two percent milk instead of one percent. This wasn't a mistake, Samuel. It is you wanting what you want and not worrying about the consequences. It only matters now that I am confronting you and calling you on all your lies. I knew what you had done, but I ignored it. To admit it, was to admit that I had made a mistake in choosing you as my husband and father to the children we will never have. Maybe not speaking up sooner made me complicit. I blamed myself for losing our daughter. The stress I was under wasn't a healthy environment to bring a baby into this world. Maybe losing her was the best thing for her, for us. Maybe it was my punishment for not protecting my child from you."

"You will never know how sorry I am."

"Yes, I know how sorry of a man you are, Samuel."

My wife only calls me by my first name when she is disgusted with me. Our eyes meet for the first time. I am where I should be on my knees, begging like the dog I am. The soft scent of her skin reminds me of chocolate. My wife has the softest skin. I love how she moans when I touch her. The simple act of my fingers on her skin is magical. I miss that. I want to create magic now, but I don't have that right anymore. I feel her slipping away from me.

"How could he cheat on Beyoncé? He stole her innocence and gave her pain. What kind of man takes your virginity, gives you children and cheats on you in front of the world? That nigga needs to sleep with one eye open." It was the first time I've ever heard my wife use that word. The venom in her voice scared me. I believe if she could kill Jay Z for Beyoncé, she would. That first track *Kill Jay Z* would be more than just a metaphor. "We do everything for our man, and yet, it's never enough. There's always an excuse as to why men cheat. Maybe if they thought about the aftereffects, then maybe it would stop them. Or maybe not. How am I ever suppo-sed to trust you again, Samuel?"

My mind raced for an answer, but it was like traveling down a dark alley, completely blind. I had no answers. The only thing I could offer was my regret and undying promise that it would never happen again. "I love you," I managed to say.

"Didn't you love as you cheated on me?"

Her dark eyes bore into mine. Not really looking at me, but through me, as if I no longer existed. I wondered if she had already moved on without me. Her question angered me. It was a trap, but I had no right to be angry. I had given up the moral ground in this argument.

I told her I loved her again. Maybe if I said those three small words enough times, maybe it would create a balm to begin soothing her pain. Maybe from all this pain, the weeds that grew around our marriage will be reborn into flowers. Maybe.

"I need to feel safe. You stole that away from me. I don't know what I'm supposed to do now. This isn't something I had planned on going through. Most women don't. You hear of other women going through this, but you never think it's going to be you. It's like cancer or something. It happens to everyone else, but when it hits home, your whole world just collapses in front of you and there's nothing you can do, except to watch it crumble. How do you rebuild from that? How, Samuel? Where do we go from here?"

"We start from the beginning. We tear it down and build it brick by brick, until the house that we thought we had becomes a reality. We build a new foundation."

"I want what you promised me on our wedding day. I want back the man you claimed to be before God and family. Can you give me that?"

"I promise I can try."

"Take a shower. You stink. We can talk some more," she said calmly.

I nodded. Stood up and tried to kiss her, but she turned away. It was too soon. I would be in the doghouse in my house for a long time.

The face staring at me in the bathroom mirror looked like a stranger. It was my face, my eyes, but I felt disconnected from myself. The life I had been living wasn't me. This wasn't the man I wanted to be for myself, my wife and our children. *And if my children knew, I don't even know what I would do/ If they ain't look at me the same / I would prob'ly die with all the shame.* She had turned up the volume, so even behind closed doors, my wife had Jay Z talking to me. How had we come this? How do I get us back on track? These questions pounded my mind as hot water scalded my skin. I needed to be punished, but not by losing my wife. Standing under the cascading water burning my skin, I closed my eyes and saw the look in her eyes. Tears streamed down my face as the look of disappointment burned in my mind and tore at my heart. A movie reel of images of us making love, being silly and talking overwhelmed me and I crumbled to my knees. It was in that point, I realized what I had done and what I could potentially lose. I don't know why we only realize these things after the fact. On some level we always know how much pain we are capable of inflicting on the ones we love, but to see them wearing those feelings on their face is an image that has to haunt any person, long after the initial pain has subsided. As much as I wanted to make this right, there's no way you can make something like this right. What took years to build has been torn down by me. As a man you have to own that truth. The light that was in her eyes for you, might be forever dimmed. *I apologize 'cause at your best you are love / And because I fall short of what I say I'm all about / Your eyes leave with the soul that your body once housed / And you stare blankly into space.*

Even after a long hot shower, my muscles were still tight. Stress throbbed in my body. Shadows from the candlelight danced on the walls and I was pleasantly surprised to see my wife in bed, lying on her back, still naked. She reached out her hand to me and spread her legs. My towel dropped to the carpet to show her my response and accept her invitation. My body levitated over hers as our bodies touched. I ached to be inside of her and begged for her forgiveness as orgasms rained down between her thighs.

"Not like this," she murmured in my ear. I need to be in control tonight." She whispered the magic word, *Halo* and I relinquished the upper hand.

My eyes followed her when she slid out of bed and walked to the base of it. There were four restraints positioned on all sides of the bed. The leather straps were tightly secured to my ankles. Then she made sure to fasten them to my wrists. I was now at her mercy. It was not a position I was used to being in, but saying no wasn't an option right now. I didn't enjoy being this vulnerable, powerless. She traced her fingertips between my lips and my body shuddered. A slight smile, more like a smirk shadowed her face. Her favorite song was still on repeat. Jay Z on his apology tour. His words matched my deeds as he spoke for me to my wife.

"Did you tie her up like this?"

The question caught me off-guard. The obvious answer was no, even though I had. I didn't want to lie after everything we had been through. My mind quickly calculated the odds and I answered. "No."

She smirked again as she caressed my inner thighs and used the inside of her palms like a scale. "You didn't have to lie. It would have meant so much if you had been honest. After everything you've done to me, you're still lying, Samuel. I can never trust you again."

"It was just one time. I swear."

"It's never ever just one time. Every man always uses that magic number one. I just fucked her one time. I just let her suck my dick one time. The number should be zero, Samuel."

She cupped her right hand around my balls and smiled at me. A lightning bolt of pain shot through my body. I was powerless to stop her, so I tried closing my legs around her wrist, hoping it would deter her.

"Spread them open or else," the threat in her voice was real as she sat down next to me on the bed. "Try me and I will show you what I'm capable of." I spread my legs open again. She stared down at my erection and said, "good dog."

"Why are you doing this?" I pursed my lips together to keep from screaming. She was applying more pressure.

"I want you to feel some degree of the pain you have inflicted on me. Even if your balls popped like balloons right now, it still wouldn't be enough. You hurt me, Samuel. You took my love for granted, thinking you could fuck around and just come back home to wifey and everything would be okay. You had your *Becky* fun and now you want to get back to the life we had. So now I'm supposed to take care of you again, wash your clothes, cook for you, suck your dick, hide my feelings of rage and pretend that I am okay. No, Samuel, I am not okay. I will never be okay. You cannot have the life we had back again. The minute you decided to stick your dick in another woman, you gave up all rights to it and to me. What did you think, I didn't know you were dipping out on me? I knew motherfucker. But I was, maybe, too shocked and in denial to admit that you would do this to me, to us. I thought you were different. You ain't shit, Samuel. I thought you had everything at home you would ever need, but I was wrong. Women believe if they do everything for their man, then there will never a reason for them to look elsewhere. Men don't need a reason to hurt a good woman. Look at Beyoncé. Look at me."

Briana exhaled, turned away from me. Perspiration glistened on her dark skin. There were no words I could find to say right now, so for the first time in a long time, I did the right thing and kept quiet. Her shoulders moved a little. She bent her head down and I heard her sniffling.

"I will spend the rest of my life making this right. I swear."

"You don't have the rest of your life, Samuel." My wife turned around. Gone were the tears. Her eyes were hard, cold as she strode towards me and leaped on to the bed and plopped down hard on my belly, straddling me between her thighs. Her words rang in my ears like a siren. *You don't have the rest of your life.* I wanted to ask her what she meant by that, but I was scared. I had been thinking with my dick again and not my brain when I allowed her to tie me down to the bed. "You're now wondering why did I let her tie me up and what the hell did she mean. I see fear in your eyes, Samuel. Are you scared, baby?"

I shook my head no and forced a smile. It was an attempt to de-escalate a volatile situation.

"You're stupid not to be scared, Samuel. You should be petrified. I'm surprised you're not already pissing and shitting yourself." She sniffed the air for confirmation. "Maybe this will help you."

In slow motion my eyes followed her right hand as it slid under her pillow and withdrew a pistol. Her finger was already caressing the trigger, ready for the inevitable next step. My body tried to buck her off, like a mechanical body, but all those hours of exercising had made her legs strong. They remained clamped around my chest so hard, until it felt as if I could not breathe.

"Open your mouth, Samuel. Maybe the visual will bring back memories of Becky sucking your cock."

"Don't do this, Briana," my voice was in between a throaty plea and then a whiney falsetto pitch.

"You don't get to tell me what to do anymore. Before I feed this gun to you, my loving husband. I want to show you something. As you travel on your first class seat to hell, I want this to be the last image you see of me. I want you to know that you did this. That you fucked up a good thing and turned a loving, faithful wife into *this.*"

Briana released her kung-fu grip from around my testicles and pressed play on a video on her cellphone. The images were dark at first. All I could hear was loud moaning and a man's voice saying misogynistic things to a woman. And then it was all clear. The imagery was sharp and unmistakable. My boss, Steve had his dick buried inside my wife, doggy style. She was staring into the camera, lips quivering, moaning with pleasure and pain, until she finally screamed. "This is what you did to us," she whispered into the camera. "This asshole doesn't deserve this sweet, tight pussy. You gave it to him. You allowed another man to fuck your wife. You did this, Samuel." Just when I thought I couldn't take anymore, she turned around and took him in her mouth. And as she pleasured him orally, her eyes never left the camera. His moans of ecstasy filled the room and he whimpered when she swallowed him. The camera then slowly panned to Steve, lying in my bed. This motherfucker had been in my house—fucking my wife. No wonder he didn't care if I was late or not. He was too busy banging my wife. A primal scream escaped my lips and I strained with all my might against the restraints, but they would not give. The last thing I heard on the video before it ended was my wife saying to my boss, "maybe if you are a good boy, I will let you slide that dick up my ass. I'm still a virgin back there." Then she winked into the camera and it went dark.

"How could you do this? How could you let another man defile your body like that? Have you no shame?"

"You gave me away. You didn't want me."

"I didn't give you away."

"That's what it felt like. You didn't want me, but Steve gave me what I needed, while you were busy elsewhere, giving away what was mine."

Briana picked up the gun again. "Open your mouth."

I refused to do as she asked and kept it clamped shut.

"I was hoping you wouldn't make this easy for me."

Before I could respond, she held the gun between her two hands, lifted it above her head. My eyes opened wide in disbelief and she rammed the butt of it into my mouth. The breaking of teeth filled the room as Jay Z apologized for the hundredth time. Blood gushed from my mouth.

"Are you fucking cra-"

The last word remained stuck in my throat as my lips encircled around muzzle of the gun, buried inside my mouth. My eyes pleaded with her not to do something she would regret for the rest of my life.

"I won't regret it," my wife answered, reading my mind. "I regret marrying you. I regret falling in love with you. I regret the abortions you convinced me to have because you said we weren't ready. I was always ready to be a mother. You were the one not ready to be a husband and a father. I have many regrets, Samuel, but this I will not regret."

How had it come to this? Me naked, tied down with a gun in my mouth and watching another man bang my wife. Sad truth was that I had no one to blame but myself. I had everything a man could need and still I wanted more. How much is enough? When do you know you've had enough and it's time to be satisfied with your life? The last thing I heard before my wife pulled the trigger was *like the men before me, I cut off my nose to spite my face / I suck at love, I think I need a do-over*. I don't remember anything else after that because I was dead.

Chunks of brain flesh and a river of blood from my husband stained the white pillow cases and splattered across the headboard. I watched lines of blood stream down the wooden headboard and pieces of his brain clung to the wood. You don't realize until you actually see it for yourself just how peaceful a dead person's face can be, even seconds after being murdered. You would think that after enduring something so traumatic, it would somehow register on Samuel's face, leaving some kind of evidence behind as to his last thoughts. But there was nothing. He looked as if he didn't have a care in the world, except for me blowing a hole through the back of his head. What other choice did I have but to kill him? If I let him live, then he would move on with his life, get remarried, have the kids we should have had and in a few years, he would want to be friends and act as if none of this ever happened. That shit wasn't happening on my watch. Men can do that. Women can't. I took vows. I made promises. 'Til death do us part. Death has arrived and one of us has departed this earth.

Before calling the cops, I needed to get my story straight and give the performance of my life. But before doing anything, I logged onto Facebook and resigned from my position as Head Beyhive Keeper for Beyoncé. I love Beyoncé, but after listening to all of her empowering feminists lyrics through the years and knowing that Jay Z did dirt on her and she still didn't leave him. I cannot listen to her music anymore and swallow her bullshit. Maybe I will try to lead a group supporting Rihanna. At least with her, what you see is what you get. Maybe that's all any of us needs is to see people as they are and decide for ourselves if we are willing to support them.

DON'T TRUST THE QUIET GUY
(EXTENDED FROM ORIGINAL STORY)

Ted Boils gripped the armrest of his chair so tightly, his fingers went numb. Sitting across from him, yelling at him, as if he were some fucking intern or a child, was his boss, Jeff Keels. He pounded his fat fists against his desk. His keyboard jumped into the air with each fist pound and paper that littered his desk fell to the floor. He pointed his fat fingers directly at Ted's face. For a brief insane moment, Ted wanted to jump up from his chair, grab his hand, and bite off each finger, one by one. Instead, he remained seated and waited for his boss' volcanic temper to subside. It wasn't the first time he had been used as a verbal piñata whenever there was a client complaint. He remained calm with a smile on his face. He was employing the method used by George Costanzia's father on *Seinfeld.* Whenever the character felt as if he was about to get angry, he would say *serenity now* to calm himself. It felt like it was working, but he couldn't be sure. He waited patiently as his boss reached into his desk, popped open a bottle of pills, tilted his head back and swallowed one without drinking any water. Ted recognized them as being heart medication. His doctor recommended he take them a few years ago, but Ted had refused. They would have been too costly and there weren't any guaranteed benefits to taking them.

"And one more thing before you leave my office."

"What's that, Mr. Keels?"

"I cancelled your vacation—I hope you don't mind."

Jeff Keels stared at Ted, almost daring him to question his authority. His eyes narrowed so much, it looked like they were being sucked into his fat face. He wanted his kiss ass employee to challenge his authority so he could rip him a deeper asshole. He knew that it was Ted's annual summer leave for the past twenty years. No one ever knew where he went. There were never any pictures or stories, not that anyone cared or even asked. Whenever Ted came back after his two weeks, his co-workers would look curiously at him, as if unsure if they had seen him the day before or a few weeks ago. No one ever asked. No one ever missed him.

"Well, it's my annual leave, sir, but I can cancel it," Ted Boils said with that same smile on his face.

Jeff Keels wished he could just get up, slap the shit out of the spineless little bastard and kick him out his damn office. The last thing he needed was a lawsuit. He had a boss too, his wife, and two kids in college. He had too much to lose.

"You're a boil on my ass, Boils," Mr. Keels waited for the usual self-deprecating laugh every time he told that joke, and his employee did not disappoint him. On cue, Ted Boils guffawed and slapped his knees, like George McFly's character in *Back to the Future* before he located his balls to stand up to the bully, Biff Tannen. There didn't seem to be any chance of that happening with Ted Boils.

Ted Boils unclenched his fingers from around the armrest and stood up. His cheap tan suit, one size too large, hung loosely on his body. Even now in the summer, he still wore his suit. Whenever he sat down, his pants always seemed to get caught up in the crack of his ass. He tried being discreet, hoping that a shake of his legs or moving his body around would dislodge it. The only thing he succeeded in doing was looking stupid to his co-workers, who already thought he was a loser.

"You've wasted enough of my time," Mr. Keels shooed Ted away with a dismissive wave. He had already turned his back to Ted, facing the window view of the park and began speaking to someone on his cell phone. Ted Boils did not exist to him anymore.

Sunlight bathed the office and Ted watched as it made a path through the balding remnants of his boss' blonde hair. There was something sad and beautiful about it all at the same time. It made Ted want to stretch his hands over the black desk and just pet it—then punch his boss in his face and throw him out the tenth floor window. That's what he should do and wanted to do, instead he turned around, bent down, picked up some of the paperwork which had blown off his desk. He placed them neatly on the desk and walked out the open door of the office.

His co-workers pretended to be on their phones, checking emails and generally looking busy, but everyone overheard Mr. Keels emasculating him. The only thing missing from the office was popcorn as they listened to another episode of Ted Boils getting chewed out.

Ted Boils trudged through the office, head down, staring at his brown shoes which were badly in need of a shoeshine. It always seemed wrong to him, to sit down like a freaking king and have someone shine his shoes. It was an honest day's work, but people who shined shoes and performed other jobs that required servitude, like him, were forgettable people.

Ted Boils is the kind of man that no one remembers. He has done unremarkably ordinary things in his life. He could get lost in a crowd and no one would remember seeing him, even if he smiled at them, opened the door when their arms were filled with groceries, or said good morning. People don't remember you unless you have done something special. The world does not acknowledge mediocrity. Average is that in between number easily forgotten like the middle child. He had given thought, plotted and even googled ways to kill his boss. It's astonishingly easy to kill someone when you're motivated. It's like anything in life once you apply yourself to the task at hand, you can accomplish it with reasonable certainty. You approach it methodically as you would, say, a job interview: You do the research on the company to find out their strengths and weaknesses. If possible, you might want to call up a few past employees to see why they left. Get familiar with your surroundings before the interview. Know the locale. Don't be hasty in accepting. If it feels wrong, then walk away. These same principles can be applied in killing someone. Surprisingly, skill sets are transferable. You just need to find out what your strengths are and sharpen them to perfection. It is more important to know your weaknesses when you decide to become a killer. Your strengths will only get stronger as you become more accomplished. There are just some things that not even a killer has a stomach for. Pinpoint your weaknesses and make sure that it doesn't come back to haunt you. Ted Boils had all these thoughts, like any other normal human being who hated his job and boss. Confrontations and stress always made him want to use the bathroom. Ever since he was a child, it was something that started when he would witness his parents fighting. His father would scream at him until little Teddy peed his Six Million Dollar Man pajamas. In a drunken stupor, his father would laugh at him, until Teddy cried and ran away humiliated. Years later it still haunted him in times of crisis.

Ted lifted his head as he walked through the long hallway on the way to the bathroom and tried to form a smile as one of his female co-workers walked by. His attempt at a smile went unnoticed. The person on the other end of her cell phone was probably relaying some important information, so it made it impossible for her to acknowledge his presence.

The four stall bathroom was empty as he washed his hands before using the urinal. Ted Boils kept his head down as he methodically washed his hands. At the urinal he dabbed the tip of his penis with a tissue to wipe away extra seepage. It had been his experience that shaking three times was not enough, but blotting his penis several times stopped any unsightly urine stains around the crotch area. About six months ago, he had briefly flirted with the idea of trying to market some sort of man wipe for men to use at work. He googled the idea a few times and nothing popped up. Then he considered all the work, time, money and research that would go into getting something like that from planning, developing, financing and getting it into stores. Slowly, he talked himself out of the idea. He worked hard for others, but he couldn't sum up the energy and passion to get it done for himself.

Ted washed his hands again, making sure to scrub in between his fingers as the sign in front of the urinals suggested. Grown men shouldn't need a sign telling them to wash their hands, but many times he had seen them walk out without doing exactly that. He tried focusing on the hot water cascading over his hands, which were quite soft and without any calluses for a man, but finally he raised his eyes slightly to look at himself. His glasses were too big for his face and seemed to enhance his receding hairline. Black men couldn't do the comb over bit, so either he walked around looking like *this* or he went bald. Both weren't options that would put him in a better light. His lips were unusually thin, which gave him a fishlike quality. His eyes were sad and it made him seem as if he was always on the verge of tears. The tan suits he wore didn't do anything to enhance his appearance, but he kept on wearing them. He hoped one day it would somehow take and give him some sort of magical swagger. Ted touched his shaved face and it felt good to be touched by someone. He had read somewhere that a shaven face in the workplace makes a man seem more approachable. The only time he ever grew facial hair was on his two week vacation, which would not be happening this year. Darkness grew in Ted Boil's eyes and he clenched his fists again. He exhaled and quickly

his practiced smile returned to his face. It was a smile he had perfected over the years. There were different variations of it: one for
his boss, co-workers, cleaning people, strangers at stoplights and
the wait staff at restaurants. He was always smiling, even though he
was never happy.

He watched as the water drained from the sink, until there was-
n't any left. For some reason this struck him as being strange. One
second it was filled and then the next, it was completely empty, like
life. Here one minute and gone the next. A few drops of water had
splashed across the mirror, so he leaned forward to wipe it away.
When he stepped back the entire crotch area of his pants was wet.
He'd forgotten that water pools on the surface of the sink. He
couldn't walk back to his cubicle looking like this. Before he could
decide what to do, loud voices from outside the bathroom made
him panic, and Ted Boils ran into one of the empty stalls to hide.

"You should have seen his face when I told him his vacation was
cancelled."

"Do the face again. I love it—it's fucking classic." The second
voice belonged to Paul Stearns, a Data Analyst Specialist.

Ted Boils sat down on the toilet bowl, elbows on his knees and
bent forward. It was bad enough hearing them talk about him. It
would be worse to get caught and have to explain himself. Both
men were standing in front of his bathroom stall talking, urinating
and laughing.

"I still don't know how they hired that fucking loser. He has
seniority, but has never been offered a management position in IT.
He is still just a grunt. You know what he did in my office?"

"What?"

"He picked up my papers from the floor and placed them neatly
on my desk right after I ripped him a new asshole. Can you believe
that shit?"

"Damn. Poor guy. So when are you going to tell him? The guy's
been here forever. This job is his life. It will destroy him."

Both men peed like horses, loud and splashy.

"I promised my wife that I would give her sister a job. She
won't let me hear the end of it, so I'm going to have Boils train her
doing Helpdesk stuff as an intern, then in one week, lay his ass off.
Guys like him take this sort of stuff in stride. They kind of expect
the world to fuck them over, so when it happens, they are already
prepared for it. So in a way I'm just giving him what he expects."

"You're such an asshole," Paul Stearns said as he shook once and tucked his penis away.

"I would rather be an asshole than have an unhappy wife at home."

"I don't trust quiet guys like Boils. At some point you dump enough shit on them and they might snap. You never know what's going on inside their minds."

"Boils is stuck in a time warp. He's scared of authority. He might even thank me for laying him off so he can go seek new opportunities. Pussies like Boils never amount to anything."

Ted Boils wanted to rise from the toilet bowl, kick open the stall door, put on his angry face and let his boss have a piece of his mind. He imagined the entire scene in his mind. Mr. Keels would see him as a man to be reckoned with and apologize for wanting to lay him off. They would shake hands, after he washed his hands of course. But Ted remained seated and waited until both men left the bathroom.

One week. He was nearing fifty in a few months. In twenty years with the company, he had never taken a sick day and would often donate his leftover vacation days anonymously to other co-workers who had family abroad or had health issues. Ted Boils was the kind of employee that employers said they wanted, and yet he was often overlooked, forgotten. Maybe if he was more outgoing, went out for drinks after work and spoke up at company meetings, then it might make a difference. A few years ago he tried going out for drinks, but no one showed up as a prank on him. Another time he stood up at a monthly meeting, but his mike didn't work, so he stood there shouting, and then magically, the mike came on. The entire room broke out into hysterical laughter. Ted tried, but his efforts had been in vain. *One week.*

Ted stood in front of the elevator lost in thought. His reflection in the elevator doors made him look shorter and fatter than what he was. Years of eating takeout and drinking sodas had added some weight to his short frame, but he wouldn't say he was fat—more stocky than fat. The crotch area of his pants had dried out while he listened to his co-workers demean him. It was almost lunchtime now and no matter the season, Ted Boils always ate alone in the park, three blocks away from his job. He enjoyed the solace of it, especially during the winter because most people stayed indoors. And on a hot and humid day like today, it would probably be uninhabited except for probably the homeless who called the park home.

The elevator door slid open and standing against the wall was a woman Ted Boils hadn't seen before in the building. Dressed casually in a white skirt and pink blouse, he refused to allow his mind to venture beyond what his eyes could see. He hesitated before stepping in, mumbled a quiet hello without making any eye contact. She stared ahead stoically without saying anything. The doors closed and the scent of her perfume washed over Ted Boils. The scent of her in his nostrils gave the illusion of intimacy and he embraced it, gulping loudly a few times before the door opened, and she disappeared forever.

"Are you inhaling my scent?"

The tall brunette turned to face Ted Boils. Indignation rose in her voice as she waited for a response from him.

"No—no," Ted quickly responded. His elevator smile automatically surfaced to convince the tall brunette that he was not a threat.

"I can take care of myself if you try anything funny."

Ted noticed she had discreetly placed her right hand inside her purse. He stepped away from her, and the elevator plummeted to the first floor without any further conversation.

He wondered as she walked briskly in front of him, if there was something about him, an odor, a look, a vibe that gave people the impression that he was not a man to be reckoned with. His pace slowed down as she pushed her way through the revolving door of the building, put on her sunglasses and merged into the lunch hour crowd. Ted Boils watched her from inside the waiting area, making sure she would not circle back and make a complaint of harassment against him to the building security.

The humidity hit him like a wall when he stepped outside. A few steps later sweat drenched his t-shirt, and this time when he swallowed his throat was dry. Halfway up the block, on his way to the park, he realized he had forgotten to take his lunch with him: tuna fish sandwich, an apple and a can of Coke. Bringing his breakfast and lunch to work every day, Ted Boils had saved four thousand a year for twenty years, and with accrued interest, he was sitting pretty. He was a man who lived within his means. While everyone else splurged on their fancy Starbucks coffee at work, he was content to drink the generic version served in the cafeteria. When you piss, it comes out the same, his father used to say. He had died of prostate cancer.

Instead of buying bottled water from a street vendor, Ted Boils stopped at Subway on the corner, helped himself to a large plastic cup and filled it with water from the soda fountain. He lingered inside of Subway for a few minutes to allow the cool air to get inside his suit. A slight shiver ran through his body as he watched the long line of customers waiting to throw away their money on a sandwich they could easily make at home.

The park was empty except for a few homeless people and a young white couple sun tanning on the scorched grass. Ted Boils sat down on his customary bench and surveyed the park before closing his eyes. The sun felt good on his skin, but he could see no reason to sit in it all day. What didn't make sense to him, made sense to someone else, so Ted Boils didn't waste too much time wondering about the motives of others. Human beings have their own rational for doing things their way, and as long as it made perfect sense to them, then the opinions of others didn't matter. He didn't understand why, after twenty years, he had not received a promotion. He had trained Jeff Keels and countless others, and they had all been promoted ahead of him, without so much as an explanation from his manager. He hadn't wanted to make waves, so he kept quiet and continued doing his job, hoping that his work ethic would eventually pay off. He had overestimated his value to the company and exactly how far having a work ethic can carry you in the corporate world.

Sweat dripped down his neck and armpits, and his toes felt squishy inside his socks, but he remained calmly seated. The park felt like an oasis in a city filled with chaos. He relished the quiet time he spent there. It focused his mind and helped him to get through the rest of his day. Small things like this gave him hope and he would go back to the office feeling refreshed, but of course nothing changed once he got back. He was still Ted Boils. No one noticed if he was there or not. He wondered when he died would anyone even miss him or say kind words about him, not as an employee, but as a human being.

The sounds of the couple laughing on the grass made him open his eyes to observe them. They were oblivious to his stares and continued flirting and kissing each other. The display of public affection embarrassed Ted, but he could not turn away from the spectacle. Female companionship was not something he had in his life right now. They didn't really seem to gravitate to him, for whatever reason. He had tried talking to a woman at work a few years ago, they had even gone out for coffee, his treat, but the next day at work she ignored his inter-office texts and walked right by him later on in the day without speaking. He documented everything he had said and done with her, and for the life of him, he couldn't figure out what he had done to turn her off. So as usual, he didn't push it and went about his life, as if the entire incident had never happened. A few months later she got married and most of his co-workers were invited, but he wasn't. Ted Boils, ever the gentleman sent the couple a wedding present. It wasn't much, but it's the thought that counted. He assumed his thank you note was probably lost in the mail.

"Hello, Mr. Boils."

Ted looked away from the couple and stared up at the man looking down at him. He didn't have to look to know who it was. The unwashed scent of the homeless person announced his presence with one whiff. It was Ishmael, a homeless man he had befriended a few months ago. They had something in common, and it made Ted stop one day after work to strike up a conversation. Ishmael always referred to him as Mr. Boils, even though Ted told him to use his first name, but today it felt good to be addressed with a modicum of respect.

"Ishmael," Ted Boils rose to greet his friend. "Where have you been?" Concern weighed in his tone.

"You know how it is, Mr. Boils. Stores around here don't want the homeless messing with their clientele, so they shoo us away every chance they get. But I've been around."

"Must be rough."

"It's not all bad. They don't mean no harm. I try and stay out their way. You know, make myself invisible."

Ishmael laughed wryly at his own joke. Ted Boils did not join in the laughter. Both men sat down and stared at a flock of birds a few feet in front of them eating bird seeds. One of the larger birds bullied its way through the flock and started pecking at one of the smaller birds. The small bird flapped its wings and backed away, seemingly content to give up its portion of the seeds. Ted and Ishmael watched, transfixed at the scene. The small bird made its way through the circle and when it was almost clear of the flock, suddenly turned around and charged the larger bird. A furious battle ensued. Feathers flew through the air, loud angry chirps disturbed the tranquility of the park, and when the last feather floated back to the concrete—Tweety Bird had slain Big Bird. If it were a sporting event, Ted and Ishmael would have jumped up from their seats, thrown their fists into the air and embraced awkwardly. Both men innately knew what they had seen was a metaphor for their lives. Ishmael had more pressing matters on his mind: food, shelter and trying to remain positive in a world that wished he were invisible. Ted Boils would replay that simple act of courage over and over in his mind, until he could almost feel the thoughts of the bird he had renamed Tweety. In that span of maybe thirty seconds, he saw himself, always walking away and never putting up a fight. As he sat there on the bench with Ishmael, he replayed scenes from his life, and for the first time, he stared unflinchingly at who he was.

Ted Boils was a coward.

Ted Boils was a boy who did not know how to be a man.

Ted Boils never stood up for himself.

Ted Boils had existed for almost fifty years and had never truly lived, one day.

This revelation was so cathartic that he placed his face in his hands and began to sob quietly. Ishmael placed his dirty right hand on Ted's shoulder and patted it. It was a scene that seemed out of place and not within the natural order of things. But what is more natural than another human being trying to comfort someone in distress.

"It's okay, brother. Life can catch you off guard sometimes when you think you have it all figured out."

Ted Boils wiped his face, embarrassed. It was the first time he had cried in front of anyone ever since he was a child. He stared into the kind grey eyes of Ishmael and wondered in what kind of perverse universe, can someone like Ishmael suffer the indignities of being homeless and a terrible human being like Jeff Keels thrive, without a care in the world. It made him angry. His body shook slightly, as if the remnants of winter were shaking loose in his bones.

"Don't you get angry?" Ted asked and waited for the obvious answer. He stared at the bald spot in the middle of Ishmael's afro, and wondered if he would be completely bald in a few years. Ishmael was badly in need of dental care. His teeth had grown a few rows deep and were now pushing against each other, struggling to find enough space to co-exist.

"Anger is a poison, man. It gets in your blood and makes you feel entitled to things you have not earned. Yeah, I get angry sometimes, but then I put my headphones on my head and turn on my Walkman. Stevie Wonder takes me away, man. Keeps me sane. What keeps you sane, Mr. Boils?"

Ted had never given the question any thought before. He assumed he was sane and it wasn't something he would ever have to worry about. He had defined his sanity and life by getting up every morning, putting in eight hours of work, and then going home. That was his life. There was no separation between the two. Within that narrow box, he had managed to keep his sanity and keep the world at bay. But maybe he had not taken an honest look at himself in the mirror all along, until now.

"So I just keep listening to my music, keeping out of my people's way and doing the job hunting thing, man. It's hard out here, but every now and then, I get an odd job to put a few dollars in my pocket. It ain't much, but I'm thankful, you know what I mean?"

Ted Boils nodded his head absently. Ishmael's mouth was moving. His face was smiling and hands moving everywhere as if directing traffic. It became obvious to Ted that the hard truth about people like Ishmael, who fell through the cracks and were stepped on every day, is society would rather forget about them, than to give them a helping hand. Ishmael would probably die in the streets and whatever family he had would not know that he had passed. A John Doe in the morgue. A corpse in an unmarked wooden box in a shallow grave. It depressed the hell out of Ted Boils to have these thoughts. And yet, Ishmael had probably done more living than he had done. The line *get busy living or get busy dying* immortalized by Andy Dufresne in *The Shawshank Redemption* popped into Ted Boils' mind. He bolted to his feet so fast, that Ishmael shrunk back and threw his hands in front of his face, unsure of what he might do next.

"Sorry. Didn't mean to scare you, Ishmael."

"No problem, brother. Out in the streets you have to always be ready to defend yourself. You would be surprised at how many people want to use the homeless as punching bags."

"Human beings can be such assholes."

Ishmael stood up. It was the first time he had heard Ted Boils use any kind of profanity. He was an odd man, but not in a bad way. He seemed like the kind of person that anything could be true about them; the kind of person that no one knew, until it was too late. When Ted approached Ishmael a few months ago, at first he was wary of a well-dressed, successful businessman stopping and talking to him on the streets as commuters hustled back and forth to get home to their families. Ishmael was so grateful for the human contact that his wariness quickly faded away. There had been times when he had gone days, sometimes weeks without anyone ever saying hello to him. They saw him, but pretended that he was not there. He looked forward to seeing his friend during his lunch hour and sometimes after work. Their conversations were never too heavy, but it made him feel like a person, that he mattered, even if it was for just a few minutes. Articulating it would probably embarrass both of them. Bantering allowed them to mask their need for something to keep them going to the next day.

"Did you eat today?"

The eventual question always made Ishmael blush. It was a strange rush of emotion for him to know someone actually cared enough to ask. The growling in his stomach was so loud, he could feel it doing waves if he pressed his palm against it.

"Not yet."

He always looked away whenever he answered. Another flock of birds had descended in the park, on the grass.

Ted realized that Ishmael always looked away to hide his embarrassment. He did not want to assume that he had eaten, so he had to ask. He reached inside his coat jacket and handed Ishmael a crumpled ten dollar bill. It was the cost of a lunch and breakfast for him. He would find somewhere in his budget to recoup it.

Ishmael stared at the money in his palm, closed it and deposited it into the front pocket of his oversized jeans.

"You're a good brother. I appreciate your kindness."

The heartfelt words made Ted Boils smile. It was only a few months ago that he started carrying cash on him because of Ishmael.

"You're welcome. Stay safe out there." They shook hands and walked away in opposite directions.

Ishmael stopped at the stoplight on Pennsylvania and 19th and turned around to find his friend. He seemed to be walking faster, instead of his usual slow, deliberate walk. There was now purpose in his stride. He wasn't sure what had transpired, but whatever it was; it felt good to know that it took place when he was around. In a small way, he felt responsible for this possible rebirth. From his peripheral vision, he noticed a pedestrian slowly moving away from him. Ishmael kept his head straight, held on tightly to the two duffel bags he had on each shoulder and started walking before the pedestrian traffic light gave him permission to cross the street.

The humidity didn't bother Ted Boils as he made his way back to the office. His mind was working overtime now. There were not thoughts about ways to improve on the job and getting people to like him. He wanted to teach Jeff Keels a lesson. He had allowed this man to emasculate and treat him like an imbecile over the years. Ted knew that he had purposely left his office door open, so that everyone on the floor could hear him talking down to him. It gave him power he did not deserve, at the expense of another person's self-respect. The only thing a bully responds to is a show of strength. A physical altercation was out of the question for Ted Boils. The mere thought of fighting the obese Jeff Keels scared him. In his almost half-century of living, he had never been in a fight. He had been picked on, but had never been the instigator. With someone like his boss, Ted knew he would have to methodically eviscerate him, layer by layer, until he had nowhere to hide and was completely vulnerable. Only then are bullies forced to look at themselves as the weaklings they truly are. These revelations were not new to him, but it was the first time he had analyzed it for his benefit.

"It's a beautiful day, isn't it?" Ted said to a white man about his age as they waited at the stoplight. The man responded with a tight smile and a nod. Ted was oblivious and continued walking. He gulped the last swallow of his bottled water before depositing it in the trash and entering his building.

The cold air cooled his hot skin as Ted stood alone at the elevator soaking it in. Marilyn Miller, an eccentric older woman, from Human Resources sidled alongside him as he waited. She collected stray cats and a loose hair or two could always be found on her clothing.

"Hello, Ted. I like your suit," Marilyn complimented him as they entered the elevator. They were almost the same age, but time had weathered her appearance. Most people assumed she was in her mid-sixties with her greying auburn hair and harsh lines around her eyes and mouth. The light in her blue eyes had dimmed, but every once in a while there was a sparkle.

"Thank you for noticing, Marilyn."

"I heard what that asshole Keels did to you today. It's just plain wrong. It's an abuse of his power that should not be tolerated."

"It's okay. I can handle Jeff."

"Well you're not doing a good job of it right now, Ted. People like him only understand one thing." Marilyn talked tough, but she was a softie. "You can't let these sons of bitches treat you like that. You're a nice guy." Marilyn blushed at her excited utterance in

Ted's defense. Hearing someone come to his defense so effusively made Ted Boils smile. Marilyn would never be mistaken for a catch, but she was a sweet woman.

"Don't you worry about me anymore, Marilyn." There was a twinkle in Ted Boils' eyes as he spoke. It made Marilyn tingle and cross her arms in front of her chest. She knew Ted did not make idle conversation with just anyone. She wondered why a smart, well-dressed man like Ted did not have someone in his life. He was up to something but she did not know what, yet.

"Hmmm. Just be careful. It wouldn't be the same without you here."

The elevator door slid open to let them out. "I plan on being here, at least until I retire." They chatted for a few more minutes, and Marilyn tried in vain to pawn off a cat on Ted. He politely told her again he was allergic, which was the truth. They parted ways and walked back to the sanctuary of their cubicles.

Ted Boils slid his cubicle door close and stood behind his chair, staring intently at the dark screens of his two monitors. Once he started down this road there was no turning back. His only hope of surviving a work skirmish with his boss was a total annihilation. He had the resources right in front of him, being in the IT department. There was information he knew about every employee: their search histories, the sites they visited, passwords they used to access their online banking, and emails they sent using their work emails. People foolishly believe that no one is watching, even in 2018. Someone is always watching. If they are not watching, then the information is being catalogued, to be used later for leverage.

All around him, the other Helpdesk specialists were busy on the phones helping clients. Their voices bordered on being condescending because they could answer every question without using any brain power. Hayden Wilson, who sat on the other side of Ted's cubicle, placed his client on loudspeaker so everyone could listen and mock his lack of computer savvy. After a few minutes, the joke wore thin and they moved on.

Ted hung his jacket in his mini closet, checked to see if his Philodendron plant above his cubicle needed watering and finally sat down. It was time to get to work. He was about to rip Jeff Keels' life wide open and drop a bomb on it with a few keystrokes. He would connect the dots and pull the loose strings from every corner of his life, until it formed a perfect picture of the man who was trying to mess with his life.

Ted Boils led a meticulous life. There was an order to every-thing he did. He did not deviate from his lifestyle. He woke up the same time every morning. Read a verse or two from his Bible. He wasn't a church going man, but he believed in something bigger than himself. This morning he had read Exodus Chapter 21, which now seemed prophetic. It had to be a sign. God's way of telling him not to let anyone walk over him and keep giving him shit. The thought made Ted smile as he hummed along to Carole King playing in the background on his Pandora station. The first place to start researching anyone's life these days is on social media. Bread crumbs are sprinkled everywhere, and people unknowingly give you the keys to enter their lives. You can poke around through their most intimate thoughts and photos, without ever meeting them. Someone with enough time on their hands can make your life a living hell, if they are so inclined.

Ted quickly found Jeff's profile on Facebook, but decided not to send him a friend request, which would probably be denied. He combed through his Friends list and found a Collector. A Collector on social media is someone who accepts friend requests from ran-dom people they don't even know. The more friends they collect, the more popular they supposedly are. A Collector also will post numerous Selfies, give constant updates about their life and become overly involved in conversations on their page and every other page. Ted found the perfect person to use as a Trojan horse and backdoor his way into Jeff Keels' life. It was Jeff's not too com-puter savvy mother-in-law, who allowed Ted access into her son's life. She would never know that accepting a friend request from someone with a cat as a profile picture would be the catalyst for the eventual demise of her son-in-law.

Now that he had the key, Ted Boils slowly clicked through the folders on his boss' Facebook page. Pictures of his family, friends, vacations and all the pages he liked were in front of him. Ted studied the picture of Jeff's sister-in-law, the woman who would be taking his job. There wasn't anything sinister about her that he could see in her pictures. Maybe she wasn't aware of what her brother-in-law had planned to get her employment. Ted studied one particular picture. A family portrait, she stood off the side, seemingly uncomfortable and staring off when the picture was taken. She wasn't a classic beauty by any stretch of the imagination. Her face was pretty, but not beautiful. There was something about her that made Ted's eyes linger over her green eyes and auburn hair.

He had never had the opportunity to be with a woman like Tammy Russo. They made him uncomfortable, and he always found himself getting tongue-tied and feeling unworthy. For some reason, he never felt that way around Marilyn. There wasn't any pressure to be anyone but himself.

Ted jotted down a few notes, and saved the links and pictures of women that Jeff liked and commented on. He was surprised by some of the overtly sexual comments that were time stamped during the work day. His boss was getting his jollies on during working hours. He wondered what else he might be doing that would be frowned upon by management. A quick search of an internet database gave Ted what he was searching for.

"Hello."

"Good afternoon Ms. Russo. I'm calling from Prenax," Ted said pleasantly. He was hoping she would not ask his name. "I am just calling to welcome you aboard and ask you a few preliminary questions before you start. Is that okay with you?"

"No problem. I'm just happy to get to work again."

"We are happy to have enthusiastic new employees. "So," Ted got right down to it, "How did you hear about the job?"

"Well, Jeff...I mean Mr. Jeff Keels recommended that I apply for an available position in the IT department."

"Okay. We are always looking for younger employees."

"Yes, that's what Mr. Keels told me," Tammy Russo volunteered. "He said that a new infusion of youth was needed in the company. The lifers were just hanging on and waiting to retire." Tammy Russo was a regular motor mouth. Ted sat back and listened to her.

"You sound like just the kind of employee this company needs. A go getter," Ted stroked her ego. He could feel the wide smile on Tammy Russo's face over the telephone.

"I have tons of new ideas," she gushed, hoping to impress whoever it was on the other end of the conversation. "Hopefully I can move up quickly and make some changes. I'm a go getter. No one is going to stand in my way."

Ted had heard all he needed to hear. There was an air of entitlement in her tone. Maybe Jeff had promised her certain things. This woman would not only get his job, but would likely be promoted in less than a year. He banged his closed fists against his desk and wanted to punch a hole through both his computer screens.

"Hey Ted! You going all Incredible Hulk over there again?" One of his co-workers snickered. Someone else mimicked the green behemoth signature sound to perfection and laughter engulfed the surrounding cubicles. "You won't like Ted when he is angry." More laughter. He blocked it out by focusing on the task at hand and silently mouthing the lyrics to *Take The Long Way Home* by Roger Hodgson, while he ate his lunch.

Checking the company's intranet system verified his boss was away from his desk and at lunch. Ted quickly logged into the system under Jeff's profile and into his Outlook email. He deleted all of his upcoming meetings from his calendar which made him chuckle as he took another bite of his tuna fish sandwich and chewed slowly. He would need exactly twenty-five chews before he could swallow. It helped his digestive system and gave him wonderful bowel movements. It was something his late mother had instilled in him every night at the dinner table. *You are not an animal. Stop wolfing down your dinner*, she would always chastise him. The words of his parents came to him at some of the oddest times. It had been over ten years since their untimely deaths. Ted often wondered if there was anything he could have done differently. Thoughts like that depressed him, so he focused on something he could control, making sure his boss understood that messing with someone's life just wasn't a nice thing to do.

Ted read a few more emails and deleted new messages which required a response from his boss. A couple of them were marked urgent. There would be a few angry phone calls he would have to field from angry clients and the CEO of the company. He wished he could be an ant on the wall as a confused Jeff Keels tried explaining why he hadn't responded to numerous emails. He would soon be back from lunch so Ted began to log out, but an alert to send an email popped up. The subject line of the email said: *Termination of Ted Boils*. It was addressed to the head of Human Resources.

Mrs. Jacques,

This Friday will be Ted Boils' last day as a member of my team. After much consideration and prayer, I have decided for the good of my team to replace Ted. He has been an adequate, yet ineffective employee. He lacks the necessary leadership that is required for someone of his tenure. I don't make this decision easily, but I am sure that I can find someone to step in immediately and replace him. Please prepare the necessary paperwork to expedite his termination. I will be interviewing a very talented candidate to fill his position immediately. Thank you.

Today was Tuesday. The bastard planned on terminating him in less than three days. Ted picked up his silver coffee cup, but his hands were shaking so badly; he had to put it back down. Everything had suddenly changed. His mind was spinning out of control. He suddenly felt dizzy. His entire adult life he had been employed. His job gave him purpose. Security. A place to go every day. Having children and a wife were never in the cards for him, so he had let his job become his companion. He didn't have any close friends, except for Ishmael. Without his job, he wouldn't have anything. Anxiety surrounded him like a wall of fire and he felt submerged, drowning in water, which was his most feared way of dying. The other two ways were underground in the metro station and choking to death home alone.

He had work to do, but he would be unable to concentrate and get anything done today, or for the next three days. Ted stood up, and paced back and forth in circles inside his cubicle. He had two problems. The immediate one was his boss. Trying to speak to him man to man would not work. A man only listens to another man if he respects him. Ted already knew that his boss did not respect him. Tammy Russo was the other problem. Her paperwork was probably already being fast tracked by Human Resources at Jeff Keels' request. He knew what he had to do.

Ted walked briskly to his boss' office, aware that eyes were turning to look at him. They were anticipating another dress down, but he was keen on not letting that happen again. He pretended to knock timidly on his boss' open door, while faking a slight cough.

"What now, Boils? Don't you have work to do instead of disturbing me?"

"I'm sorry, Mr. Keels. I suddenly feel very ill. Would you mind if I left early today? I will catch up on my work tomorrow." Ted Boils used the sort of subservient voice that made people like his boss feel in control. It played to his over-inflated ego, which wasn't lagging too far behind his swollen stomach that appeared to be resting on the edge of his desk.

"Stay where you are, Boils. Whatever you have I don't want to catch it. Take the rest of the day off, or a few days if necessary. I want you healthy and not spreading your germs around the office."

Jeff Keels thought he had seized upon the perfect opportunity to appear magnanimous. Having Ted Boils out of the office for a few days would play nicely into his plans of getting rid of him. The faster he could get his wife off his ass about her sister, the quicker he could go back to his regular life and she left him alone. They were at that point in their marriage that the only things they discussed were the bills, kids and which unlucky relative's house they would go to for the holidays. They had come to a silent understanding over the years that they would probably be married forever, but each person could do as they pleased, as long as whatever secret lives they led did not show up on social media or at their front steps. It was for that reason that Jeff Keels had no problem taking an axe to Ted Boils' life and letting him bleed slowly. Every man for himself was his motto. He didn't owe Ted Boils a goddamn thing.

"Thank you, Boss. Very generous of you," Ted Boils genuflected. He was finding it hard to hide the smirk lurking around the corner of this mouth. He turned away and strode off, just as it took hold of his face. Necessity or more like survival was bringing to the surface the other side of himself he had not encountered and barely knew it existed. He had never had to call on the other Ted Boils, until now. As he waited for the elevator, it made sense to him now, how a person could be two different people without even knowing it. The Ted Boils everyone knew at work could not be called upon to handle this situation. He needed the other Ted Boils, lurking beneath the surface. The angry one, who was always taken for granted, slighted, spoken to in a manner that an almost middle-aged man should never be spoken to. Even though he was livid inside, he needed to channel the Ted Boils who was always passed up for promotions, but continued to smile. He believed in living his life a certain way. In doing so, the universe would eventually reward good behavior, sort of like creating good karma. All his life he had done that. Doing the right thing by the people around him—even when he hadn't wanted to sometimes, he had dug deep to find the Ted Boils he wanted to be. He knew now that the Ted Boils he had created for the world was viewed as nothing more than a doormat. He knew that he was viewed as a loser. A non-essential employee who was never missed, even when he took his yearly two weeks' vacation. His co-workers never feigned interest at his whereabouts or even asked to see pictures. The elaborate stories he had concocted while he sat at home for two weeks were not even necessary. Nobody cared. He was a nobody in this world. In a world of trends, he was not even a dot on anybody's radar. He knew what he was, or at least how the world viewed him. Until now, he had been fairly okay with it, but *hearing* his boss and Paul

Stearns discussing him in the men's bathroom earlier had begun to stir the Ted Boils that had been asleep all these years. It's one thing to assume to know what people think about you, but then to actually hear them giving those thoughts a voice with such glee and disrespect, well, any man who takes that in stride deserves their scorn.

The elevator ride down was solitary. He didn't have to fake a smile or carry on some insipid conversation about the weather or sports. Generally, those are the two accepted and safe topics of conversation in an elevator. No one ever really remembers your answers. It's just something to say to fill up that quiet block of time until the elevator doors fly open, and you are free to go on with your life forgetting that person you met in the elevator. .You might see them again in a few days and have the same inane conversation without ever recalling having met them a few days ago. No one really pays attention anymore. Our minds are simultaneously recording so many unimportant things at one time, that we are unable to fully grasp the moment as it is happening. Ted Boils did not have that problem. He was a man who noticed things that no one else paid any attention to. Being invisible allows you the anonymity of being under the radar.

It was the first time in twenty years that he had left work in the middle of the day. It almost felt like he was playing hooky. Guilt stopped him in his tracks just before he opened the front door of the building. It didn't last long when he recalled the evil smile on Jeff Keels' face when he told him to take a few days off. Ted pushed open the door, leaving the cold air behind and stepping once again into the sweltering heat of the Washington, DC afternoon.

Heat has a distinctive scent. It smells like the sun when you inhale. Even if you cannot always smell its oppressive odor, there is a scent to it that your mind associates with heat. It envelops your thoughts and makes every step almost unbearable. Today, Ted Boils felt light and liberated as he picked up the pace, walking past Potbelly, then an Indian restaurant he had been to several times. The service had been quite good, but then again, he couldn't remember ever being to an Indian restaurant and the service not being pleasant. Nordstrom on the corner of 17th was filled with women looking for a bargain in the middle of the day. The bookstore, Borders used to occupy that building. It had gone the way of the Walkman when CD and MP3 players took the nation by storm. On the other side of the street where Filenes Basement once was,

Ted saw his friend, Ishmael waving at him. If he waved back, then he would be held captive for at least thirty minutes. He pretended not to see him and took the long escalator ride down into the metro station to jump on the Red Line.

Riding the metro was the only time when there were always people around him. At home he was alone. At work he spent most of his time inside of his cubicle. Throughout the day he would hear laughter and co-workers ribbing each other, but he was never a part of it. The metro was always an adventure. A random person could sit down next to you and strike up a conversation. It could be about the most banal subject, but the opportunity to have a conversation about anything always excited Ted. He was well-versed on all almost every subject. A few years ago, he had made sure to become well acquainted with the five metro lines that connected the DMV area and various attractions around the city because at least once a week, someone needed directions.

There were a few empty seats available, so Ted took one close to the door so he could stretch his legs. The conductor warned commuters that the doors were closing and leaning against them could cause the train to immediately evacuate. It was not an idle threat. He had seen it done before. It never made any sense to him that simply leaning against a car door could cause hundreds of commuters to unload the train.

"Mind if I sit here, buddy?" Ted stared up at a friendly face and he nodded his response. The man with the white hair reminded him of the actor Mark Harmon from *NCIS*. "Thank you. Getting off in a few stops," the white haired man volunteered. He didn't seem that old to have such shocking white hair, so Ted assumed he was probably prematurely white, the same way other men went prematurely bald.

"Where are you traveling to?"

Ted had made note of the blue duffel bag with countless airline stickers. The Red Line didn't go to DCA airport, so he assumed the stranger was on his way to Union Station.

"The name's Mark, by the way." They shook hands and Ted gave his full name. "I have a yearlong pass on Amtrak. I'm just going to look at the departing board and pick a place, scroll through my phone and find a friend in the area to crash with for a few days."

"Really? People don't mind you just popping up?"

"Well, I hope they don't mind. It's a good way to catch up with old friends and students."

"So you're a teacher?"

"Retired."

"If you don't mind me asking," Ted was bolder than he usually would be, but today was turning out to be an unusual day, "you look too young to be retired already."

"That's what you get from good clean living," Mark responded with a self-deprecating laugh. "I love my job and students, but I needed a break, you know? To travel the way I did when I was younger. Life is short, my friend, and getting shorter by the day. You have to live your life and fuck tomorrow—it might never come."

"That's the best advice I've received all day," Ted responded with a genuine smile. Thank you."

The conductor announced Union Station as the next stop. Ted felt the urge to get up and follow this person into the station; hopefully they could sit down have a cup of coffee, while he waited to board his train and just talk. Something told him that if he asked, the stranger would agree. He had this laid back attitude about him that Ted wanted to know more about.

"It was nice chatting with you, Ted. Whatever you're going through, it will pass. If you ever find yourself down in St. Croix, look me up, okay? We can have a beer together."

"I would like that."

They shook hands again. Ted watched as the friendly white haired stranger strode through the crowd without a care in the world, getting lost in the mix and on the way to his next adventure. Maybe for his next vacation, he would actually travel somewhere and take the stranger up on his offer. St. Croix was as good a place as any to get busy living.

A few stops later, he disembarked from the train at Brookland. It wasn't a neighborhood he was familiar with, but he had Tammy Russo's address. A cab or bus would get him there faster, but he decided to walk. It was a typical suburban mixed neighborhood. The streets were quiet. There wasn't anyone out walking their dogs or doing yard work. The extreme heat probably had a lot to do with it. He noticed a shadow behind closed curtains of one of the homes. It was hard to tell if someone was watching him, or maybe it was just nothing more than a shadow.

It dawned on him as he stood outside the fence of Tammy Russo's house, maybe she wasn't home. It was the middle of the day after all. Maybe she had gone to the movies, shopping, or having lunch with a girlfriend. It was too late to turn back now, so Ted walked through the partially opened front gate, admired the yellow and red rows of flowers on both sides of the path. He imagined Tammy Russo on her hands and knees digging up the earth and planting them. This was not a woman afraid of hard work. Before knocking on the door, he straightened up his suit, wiped the perspiration from his face and put his glasses back on. It was a secret weapon he had read about in some book. Glasses make a black man look less threatening. People normally don't associate criminal activity with people who wear glasses.

Ted knocked on the door three times. He smiled suddenly when he recalled Sheldon from *Big Bang Theory* knocking on his neighbor's Penny's door. He would knock the same way, every time. Penny! Penny! Penny! That show cracked him up. He looked forward to watching it, along with *Mike & Molly* on CBS.

Someone was home. The floorboards on the other side of the door creaked. Ted imagined that Tammy Russo was now peering through the peephole and wondering why a well-dressed middle-aged black man wearing glasses was knocking on her front door. He exhaled and tried not to look too serious.

"Who is it?" The voice from inside the house sounded high-pitched, like on the phone earlier.

"It's Ted Boils from Prenax, Ms. Russo. We spoke earlier on the phone."

"Oh, Mr. Boils," the door flew open as she spoke, "what are you doing here, at my house?" It was a perfectly innocent question to ask. Ted had a perfectly plausible answer ready for her.

Ted lost his train of thought for a moment. Her picture had not done her justice. A stunning woman with dark, auburn hair pinned up, flirty green eyes, with freckles dotting her pale face, lips that were ruby red and a nose too perfect to be real stood before him.

"Well, Ms. Russo, Prenax is trying out a pilot program of visiting potential employees in their home before they are hired." Her green eyes didn't blink as she stared at him. Tammy Russo obviously believed because of her brother-in-law, the job was already hers. "You are under no obligation to allow me into your home, but it will be noted on my report."

A strand of hair swung lazily in front of her face, but she was oblivious to it. It distracted Ted's gaze as she tried to remain focused.

"Jeff never mentioned anything about this visit. Maybe I should call him, just to be sure it's something I should be doing."

"Mr. Keels isn't aware of this. As the person who recommended you for the position, he isn't allowed to be a part of this. It's standard company policy."

Her eyes wavered, unsure of her next step. She was probably just fresh out the shower. Her hair was still wet and she had hurriedly put on a long-sleeved white shirt and jeans. There didn't appear to be anyone else in the house as Ted waited for her response, he had played his trump card.

He took out his cell phone and got ready to dial his office number. His smile hadn't left his face. "I will inform Human Resources that I came by to finish up your paperwork, but you were busy."

"No need for that, Mr. Boils. It's wonderful that Prenax cares so much about their new employees. Come on in. Excuse the mess."

There wasn't any mess as far as Ted could see. He followed her into the living room and tried not to stare at her ample derriere which filled out her jeans. The living room was adorned with candles and artifacts from her various travels abroad, but as far as Ted could tell, no picture of a boyfriend.

A mid-size sofa, the color of sunset was fitted between two plants that looked like palm trees.

"You have a beautiful home, Ms. Russo," Ted complimented her.

"Thank you. Always something to do when you have your own home, but I love it. I watch a lot of HGTV to get ideas. Have a seat, Mr. Boils."

He liked that she called him Mr. Boils and not Ted. They sat on opposite ends of the sofa, but turned slightly to face each other.

"Thank you for letting me into your home. I won't take up too much of your time. Mr. Keels, who will be your immediate supervisor is a great boss," Ted lied. He wanted to gauge her response. "I'm sure you won't have any trouble adapting to the fast paced environment of Prenax. Has he discussed with you what your responsibilities will be?"

Tammy Russo placed both hands on her lap. Her left thumb tapped nervously, even though she wasn't nervous. "Jeff said I would be running the department once I became familiarized with the systems."

"Good. Good." Ted pretended to jot down a few notes in the mini-pad he carried in his pocket.

"It's a wonderful opportunity," Tammy continued. Her thumb had stopped tapping. "I plan on making some changes once I get to know my staff better. Jeff. I mean Mr. Keels told me that department is in need of younger blood to keep ahead of our competition."

"You seem to know Mr. Keels very well. I only say that because you called him Jeff on two occasions. If you have a prior relationship with Mr. Keels, then now would be a good time to disclose it."

"I'm not sure what you mean by relationship, Mr. Boils." Her nervous tick had returned.

Ted leaned in closer, while placing the pad and pen back into his breast pocket.

"I just meant are you and Mr. Keels having some sort of inappropriate relationship, because he is a married man."

The color drained from Tammy Russo's face. If she had been expecting this line of questioning, she would have prepared herself better. The casual ease of the question had left her defenseless.

"That's none of your business, Ted. I played your little game. I should have told Jeff you called, but I wanted to preserve what little you had left of your dignity. I felt sorry for you, but Jeff was right about you."

The gloves were off.

"What did that fat fuck have to say about me?"

Ted removed his glasses and placed it in the inside pocket of his jacket. He saw no reason to hold his tongue.

"He said what you could not accomplish in twenty years at the company, I could probably do it in a week. He said you're a fucking loser and deserve to get fired. Now, get the fuck out of my house." Tammy pulled out her cellphone from her shirt pocket and quickly flipped through her contacts to find Jeff's number.

The anger he had been sitting on all day had been ignited once again. Someone he didn't even know was discounting him and thought he was a loser. Maybe if he had an extra five seconds to calm down, he wouldn't have slapped the phone out of her hand and watched it land in her potted plant. Maybe he would have stood up, left her home, and accepted his fate. After all, that's what losers do. But he didn't have five seconds and so Ted Boils reacted. Today, Ted Boils did not feel like being a loser. He did not feel like allowing this stranger to come in and steal his job. Today, he would fight for what was his. Today he wouldn't bend over and just accept what the world gave him.

"What the fuck do you think you're doing?" Tammy Russo screamed as she tried to stand up.

Ted bolted straight up and pushed her back down into the oversized pillows of the sofa. He couldn't allow her to call Mr. Keels. He wasn't sure what his intention was for coming to her house, but now that he was here, the only logical thing was to follow his flawed decision to its conclusion.

His knees sank deep into the soft fabric of the sofa, and he fastened his ten fingers around the long neck of Tammy Russo. His sudden attack caught her by surprise and his fingers were surprisingly strong around her neck. She tried using her hands to push him off, but he narrowed the distance between their bodies, until they were almost touching. The full weight of his upper body was on hers, and the tighter he gripped her neck, the more urgently Tammy tried to break his grip.

Ted Boils stared down at the sweating and reddened face of Tammy Russo. It hadn't been his intention to do this, but once he placed his hands around her throat, it felt, *good*. He was now in control. Her eyes opened wider, the more pressure he applied to her throat. It didn't seem that he had a choice now. If he let her live, then she would call the cops and his boss. He couldn't allow that to happen. Both of them had mocked him. They had thought him to be lesser than them. He lifted his face away from hers. The scent of her shampoo penetrated his nostrils, and wet strands of hair stuck to his face. Her eyes pleaded with him to let her live. They said she would not tell anyone. Of course it was all a lie. He mouthed the words *I'm sorry*, closed his eyes, and applied more pressure. Her thrashing once wild, was now more subdued, until it stopped.

Ted Boils opened his eyes.

Hers were open and lifeless.

His hands were still clamped around her throat. It didn't feel real to him that she was now dead. A few seconds ago they were having a conversation, and now, she was a corpse. He stood up, unsure of what to do next. This wasn't something he had any experience with. Ted Boils imagined that in a situation like this, someone would call a friend for advice, but he had no one to call. He was on his own.

Her body was spread across the sofa with her legs on the floor. He lifted her two legs and placed both of them on the sofa. He stepped back to take in his surroundings. His mind was thinking too fast. He took a deep breath in order to try and calm his nerves. He hadn't touched anything when he entered the house. No fingerprints. He examined his arms and face for any scratch marks. There were none. She looked so peaceful, as if she were sleeping. He almost expected her to wake up and continue their conversation. Satisfied that he hadn't touched or left anything behind, Ted took one last look at Tammy Russo, a woman he had not met until a few minutes ago, and now she was dead. Maybe it had been his intention all along to do her harm, even though it had not been a conscious thought. His intention no longer mattered, she was dead.

He used the sleeve of his jacket to open the front door. There were no neighbors anywhere in sight as he stepped off the porch and put his glasses back on. Halfway down the steps, Ted turned around and walked back to the front door. He wasn't sure if it was necessary, but he wiped the area where he had knocked on the door. He was thinking like a criminal who didn't want to get caught. An hour ago the most pressing thing in his life was being unemployed, but now he had to worry about going to jail. Ten minutes later, unseen as he walked through Tammy Russo's neighborhood, Ted Boils boarded the Red Line train again and headed home. This time he sat by himself and no one bothered him for directions.

Later that evening in the comfort of his apartment, Ted scanned the news channels for any possible news of Tammy Russo's death. Death made it sound like an accident. Saying the word murder made him into something he didn't see himself as, a murderer. Her body hadn't been found as yet. He wanted to go to the police and explain to them what had happened. But in the real world, you don't kill someone; give an explanation and go back home to your life. Tonight he would try and get a good night's sleep. Go back to work and put this unfortunate incident behind him.

Only a ruthless killer can kill an innocent woman and sleep soundly. Ted Boils tossed and turned all night. Nightmares dogged him through all the dark alleys of his mind. Even when he woke up to relieve himself, Ted thought he saw the naked body of Tammy Russo smiling at him in his bathtub. The image so disturbed him, he was unable to get back to sleep. With nothing else to do, Ted made his usual breakfast of black coffee with a fried egg, turkey bacon and a slice of tomato on an everything bagel. He saw no sense in wasting good money buying coffee outside. Folks walking around with their Grande, Venti and Trenta Starbucks cups always struck him as being elitist, or at least pretending to be. They wanted everyone to know that they drank expensive coffee and didn't have to settle for the cheap office crap that everyone else had to drink. Sometimes he felt the urge to purposely bump into someone, making them spill their expensive coffee all over the goddamn floor and then watch to see if they would go buy another one, but of course he never did. It struck him as mildly amusing that he hadn't had the courage to do that, but had somehow managed to kill a woman. He took a quick shower and twenty minutes later, he was dressed in his customary tan suit and seated on the early morning train rumbling into the city.

Ted Boils wondered if he looked different this morning. Would someone who didn't know him be able to tell he had done something terrible? Did he look guilty? He felt guilty and wanted to confess his crime, but the few passengers on the train were scattered and either sleeping, reading or fast asleep. It would be rude to disturb them, so he leafed through a copy of the latest Walter Mosley novel, *And Sometimes I Wonder About You: A Leonid McGill Mystery*. Normally Mosley could hold his attention, but right now he was too distracted to concentrate on fiction when his real life felt like a crime novel. The soothing voice of the female conductor and the churning, rocking rhythm of the train soon had Ted Boils snoring as if he were home in bed. His eyelids fluttered rapidly as he descended into a dream.

"Ladies and Gentleman," the voice of the conductor commanded the passengers, "we have a murdering no good man in our midst."

All eyes turned to Ted. He tried to defend himself in the dream, but the words would not leave his mouth. He wanted to explain his side of the story to the strangers now staring at him with disdain.

"You took an innocent life, Ted Boils, and for this you must die."

The crowd started chanting for his death. Old ladies shook their fists at him. Babies cried in their mother's arms. Men stood up ready to defend the honor of a woman they did not know. They closed in on Ted Boils. His breathing became more labored. The conductor spurred on the agitated crowd. "Next stop, Ted Boils' Demise." Two large men approached him, the doors of the train opened and he was thrown into an open sky, screaming for mercy. Ted's eyes popped open. The train was now filled, but no one had noticed him sleeping and dreaming, or at least they were pretending not to.

"Next stop is Farragut North," the familiar voice of the train conductor alerted the passengers. "Be careful out there, today. It's going to be a hot one." She seemed to be taunting him, but no one noticed. They had other things on their minds to worry about. Their life took precedence.

The old lady standing next to him is on her way to see her dying husband of fifty years in the hospital.

The young man dressed in a new suit is on his way to an interview hasn't eaten as yet. He is broke and spent his last five dollars on transportation.

A young mother of two is on her way to her second job, sleep heavy in her eyes, smiles at Ted Boils. He smiles back and wonders if she will make it through the day as they ride up the escalator, side by side.

They will never have a conversation, but the shared experience of life has created an unseen thread that will link them together as they go their separate ways, and try to find their way in the world.

Book in hand, Ted Boils strolled down Pennsylvania Avenue, past a packed Starbucks, early morning commuters crammed into the store in need of their fix. The city is still peaceful at this time of morning. The sun is struggling to rise. Ted waits on the corner, waiting for the pedestrian traffic light to count down before crossing. Before he can cross, he turns around and heads back towards the Metro station. Today, he feels like indulging in a cup of coffee from Starbucks.

He sidesteps two women engrossed in conversation as they sip on their specialty brand of coffee and steps inside. It feels like a different world inside of the coffee shop. A buzz of conversation snakes through the long line. The various scents of coffee overpower his nose. He is a man of simple taste. "Black," he tells the barista when he finally gets to the counter. He senses momentary confusion in her expression, as if she has forgotten how to pour black coffee. Everyone who comes in these days wants something exotic. Something that separates them from everyone else. His request finally clicks in her mind. She smiles sheepishly and pours him his coffee. He doesn't have to wait for any special creation as he slips by a crowd of people, waiting impatiently for their drinks to be made to specification. He can bet that someone is posting on Facebook about the service, which seems to be pretty good to Ted, but then again, he does not have a lot of experience waiting in line for coffee.

The first few sips are way too hot. He holds the hot beverage in one hand and his book in the other. The streets are coming to life.

The sun is wide awake, and coffee drinkers are speeding past him. They are all high on caffeine. He turns the corner and jumps back as a vehicle careens into the garage. Hot coffee spills on his hands and jacket, but Ted manages to hold on to the cup. He wants to keep on walking, to enjoy his last minutes of freedom before clocking in to work. This is what he wants to do, but a rage has enveloped him now, and he quickly walks down the steep embankment to find the vehicle.

"You're lucky I didn't knock your ass down. You should be thanking me," the driver said when Ted approaches his vehicle.

It's his boss, Jeff Keels. Maybe he too has had his cup of flavored coffee and is wired.

He opens the driver's door, his suit already disheveled, suitcase and keys in hand. He seems to be bigger than Ted remembers.

"You almost killed me—you fat fuck, and I should be thanking you," Ted responds incredulously. The word *fuck* feels foreign in his mouth, but it feels good, powerful. Maybe he should say it more often.

Both men are staring each other down. The garage is still relatively empty and so their voices travel. No one is around. The color in Jeff Keels' face drains. His thin lips appear to recede inside of his mouth. Ted's outburst catches him by surprise. He has grown accustomed to him kowtowing to him. It is the expected role he has played since he became his boss.

"You fucking ingrate," Jeff finds his voice. His voice is quivering with contempt. "I should have fired your ass a long time ago. "Now, you just made it easier."

"Easier? You were going to fire me at the end of the week anyway. Right, *Boss*?"

The revelation by Ted catches Jeff off-guard, but not for long. He tries to barrel his way past Ted, and as is the custom, he expects him to step aside and let him through. Ted stands his ground. There is no going back now.

"Get the fuck out of my way, Boils—before I move you out the way."

Jeff Keels hopes that the threat in his voice and being Ted's boss will have the desired effect. This time they are on equal footing. Man to man. They are not in the work place and attempting to assert superiority only angers Ted further.

He doesn't have enough time to react, duck or move back from an object moving towards his face. The full force of the hardback

Walter Mosley book smacks Jeff so hard in his face, he tumbles backwards and trips over his feet. His suitcase goes flying into the air and lands without popping open. His keys fall on his stomach as he lies on the garage floor. His breathing has escalated. The garage is too hot and he cannot catch his breath.

"Help me, Boils. I think I'm having a heart-"

Ted Boils stands over his fallen boss and watches as he reaches into his coat pocket. In his haste, he grasped the bottle of pills containing his heart medication too hard, and it rolls away.

"Please, Boils…help…me," Jeff Keels' eyes plead.

Ted calmly kneels down, places his cup of coffee on top of his book and slowly picks up ten pills from the ground. He stares at the pills in his palm, pops open the cover of his coffee and deposits every single pill into the hot, dark liquid.

"You fucking moron," Jeff Keels tries to scream, but it comes out in a whimper. "Are you trying to kill me?"

His question doesn't need an answer. The smile on Ted Boils' face is the nail in his coffin. Ted lowers his face to his boss' left ear and whispers something to him. The dying man's eyes open wider, until he finally takes his last breath. Ted gathers up his book and coffee before standing up. He refuses to allow himself to think about what he has done. Thinking will bring on guilt. He doesn't want to feel guilt. He had taken back his power. He had stood up for himself. Guilt and remorse would not find its way into his heart today.

He exited the garage the same way he came in and walked casually to work. The sun felt good on his face. It was going to be a hot one today. Maybe he would stay indoors for lunch and read some more of his book. Two hours later as he sat inside of his cubicle drinking the company's generic coffee, he made a call to HR.

"Ted have you heard?" Marilyn said in a hushed tone.

"Heard what?"

"Mr. Keels is dead."

"Dead?" There is concern in his voice, but a smile on his lips and eyes.

"The entire block was shut down. Apparently some homeless man followed him into the garage, accosted him for money and during their altercation, Jeff had a heart attack."

"A homeless man?" Ted stood up when Marilyn said that. "How do you know this?"

"I was in the crowd when they brought him out and he was babbling all of this to the cops."

"What did this guy look like?" Ted held his breath as Marilyn described his friend, Ishmael to him. *Fuck*, Ted mouthed. What the hell was Ishmael doing in the garage? Had he followed him in there?

"Another strange thing happened also?"

"What's that?"

I just heard on the news that they found a woman named Tammy Russo dead in her home. The name sounded familiar and then I remembered that Jeff had forwarded her resume down to me. I knew he was going to fire you and hire Ms. Russo to replace you, Ted. Imagine that, both of them dead in twenty-four hours. What are the odds of that happening?"

"Quite a coincidence."

"I don't believe in coincidences."

There was silence on the other end of the phone line. Marilyn finally broke the tension.

"Why were you calling, Ted? Did you need something?"

He had called to ask her if Tammy Russo's resume was already on file. Asking now would only confirm whatever suspicions she might already have.

"The cops will figure out this whole mess. Sometimes things work themselves out for us. We won't need Ms. Russo's resume anymore and I can just delete the emails."

Ted coughed before saying anything. "Well, if you think that's best, Marilyn."

"Nothing good can come of it."

"I suppose not."

"I will see you later at the company meeting."

"Hey Marilyn, would you like to have lunch with me tomorrow?"

"I would love that Ted."

"Good. Me too. Do you have a preference?"

Marilyn paused before answering. "Anything will do."

A week later, there were still no leads on the murder of Tammy Russo. The police had released Ishmael when the cause of Jeff Keels' death was discovered to have been a heart attack.

The park was filled today with people trying to enjoy the cooler temperatures. Couples were holding hands and oblivious to their surroundings as they shared their affections. A group of women were sweating to the oldies and exercising in outfits better suited for an indoor gym. Men walked by, pretending to casually walk by, but their eyes, hidden behind sunglasses bored into the sweating, gyrating group of women. A few homeless men and women were scattered throughout the park, bothering no one, just sitting, as if contemplating where their lives had taken a wrong turn.

Ted sat on the end of one bench and a fellow human being sat on the opposite end, book open and headphones on. The international sign of *do not disturb me. I am not interested in making small talk. Thank you very much.* He didn't feel much like having a conversation either. All he wanted to do was read his book and enjoy the two slices of pepperoni pizza he had bought. These days he didn't worry so much about saving every dollar. It dawned on him sometime during the week that he could inexplicably die, and then who would get all the money he had saved? The government? So he had drawn up a will to make his wishes known, just in case.

Lost in thought, he didn't hear a voice calling out to him, until he felt someone's hand on his shoulder. Ted stared at the dirty hand on his jacket. Fingernails caked with dirt, but the fingers were long and slender. He imagined with a manicure that his hands would look beautiful. Simple things one can afford when they have money. To another person, it is the furthest thing from their mind.

"Mr. Boils, it's good to see you, man. I been worried about you. I even asked the security guard by your building if he had seen you, but the brother called the cops on me. Said I was disturbing the peace. So, you doing alright, Mr. Boils?"

The concern in Ishmael's voice touched Ted. He wondered what kind of person Ishmael would have been if life hadn't fucked him over. Would he still be this caring person, or would he have been an asshole?

The person seated on the other end of the bench abruptly got up and left. Both men watched him in silence as he sat down on a bench on the other side, already seating three people. He looked up, saw both men staring at him and quickly dropped his head to continue with his reading.

"Ishmael, please call me Ted—I insist."

Ishmael had never heard this forceful tone of voice used by Ted before. He finally relented.

"Okay, Ted." Ishmael smiled and said the name again as he sat down.

"I heard you had some trouble last week."

Ishmael met Ted's eyes and despite his best effort, he smiled. He turned off his Walkman and removed the headphones from his ears.

"Nothing I couldn't handle. I guess the cops figured out I didn't hurt that man and let me go. They questioned me for hours about why did I follow this dude into the garage. I just told them the truth."

"The truth."

"The truth is whatever you believe it to be, man. I feel bad that he died. I wish death on no man, but in this life you have to pick which side you want to be on."

"Which side are you on, Ishmael?"

"You're my friend, Ted. You always treat me with respect. Hook me up with some food and few dollars. You don't have to do any of that. You could pretend not to see me like most folks and go about your business. I appreciate that, Ted. To a person like myself who society has forgotten, that means an awful lot. So for that, I just want to thank you, Ted. You're alright in my book."

"Thank you, Ishmael, for everything."

Ted exhaled and for the first time all week, he smiled. He had already killed two people. The second had gotten easier. He imagined if he had to, that he could do it again. He handed Ishmael a slice of pizza and both men, leaned forward, stared straight ahead, watching people walking in and out the park. They were enjoying a temporary reprieve from the oppressive heat. It was a beautiful day to be outside, enjoying life. Days like this you put in your memory bank, so when the bad days come, you have something to hold on to, until the sun shines again.

"Gentleman," Ted and Ishmael looked up together into the sun's glare to find the female voice. The person stepped back, giving both men a clearer view of her, and they had the same thoughts that men have when they see a beautiful woman. She was a bit too young for Ted's taste, but Ishmael was giddy and smiling. He couldn't recall the last time a woman had addressed him in such a manner. It made him feel seen for the first time in a long time.

"The metro is two blocks this way," Ted gestured with his right hand and his mouth filled with pizza. It was generally the question most tourists asked whenever they cut through the park.

"Is your name Ted Boils?" the young woman asked, dismissing his attempt at directing her towards the Metro.

Ted Boils stood up to get a better look at the young woman who knew his name and where to find him on his lunch hour. He was a few inches taller than her, but what she lacked in height; she more than amply made up for it with her aura. There was something familiar about her, which he could not quite place. His relaxed demeanor had disappeared. A murderer can never ever fully relax. Jail was not a place on his bucket list to visit.

"Yes, I'm Ted Boils. How do you know me and how can I help you?" His voice was calm, but the events of the last twenty-four hours had him on high alert. Ishmael stood up next to his friend. He had a bad feeling in the pit of his stomach, and it wasn't because he was still hungry, even after eating his slice of pizza and three garlic knots. It felt like a storm was brewing, and he was right in the middle of it.

"I'm Detective Eva Storm, Mr. Boils. The security guard at your building saw you heading this way, and I figured I would pop by and ask you a few routine questions about your boss, Jeff Keels, if you don't mind."

"Ex-boss," Ted quietly corrected her. "I don't mind."

"Yes, your ex-boss. Good book," Eva commented when she glanced at the bench. "Mosley writes eloquently about the marginalization of the black man, especially middle-aged black men. He gives them a voice. That voice makes them no longer invisible."

Ted nodded his approval at her short review of Mosley's book. There was something formidable about her. He could tell she didn't make casual conversation. There was always a point to be made.

Now he knew where he recognized her from. She was the detective who had single-handedly taken down a syndicate of rapists and more recently had received a medal from the city for breaking up a sex slave ring in Baltimore. She was the real deal. The way she stared at him, with a smile on her face, but her eyes spoke of something different. He had covered his tracks. There was no way she could be on to him already.

"Detective Storm, I'm not sure how I can help you. I thought the case was closed."

Ishmael shifted back and forth. He wasn't sure where this was going, but it felt like a game of cat and mouse to him. He wasn't sure as yet who was who.

"The case is closed. This is more, how should I say it, off the books. I'm just doing a favor for a friend of the family."

"Okay." Ted wanted to exhale, but the air around him seemed to be getting more stifling. He swallowed the last gulp of water from his bottle and waited. "How can I help you?"

"According to Mrs. Keels, her husband was going to hire her sister, Tammy Russo to work in your department. The police didn't make the connection of Mr. Keels being Tammy Russo's brother-in-law. It's quite a coincidence that both of them were murdered on the same day. Wouldn't you say so?"

"That's a hell of a coincidence," Ishmael chimed in.

"I'm glad you agree, Mr. Bending."

"You know who I am?"

"Yes, Ishmael. I know who you are."

Eva stepped towards Ishmael and searched his eyes for dishonesty. They were the most honest eyes she had seen in a long time.

"You're beautiful," Ishmael volunteered. It's been a while since I saw a sister with red hair like yours. It reminds me of one of those Greek goddesses."

"Thank you, Ishmael. I don't recall reading in the police report that you and Mr. Boils were friends," Eva noted casually.

"Oh yeah, Ted and I are good friends. He looks out for me."

If Ishmael hadn't been so enamored with Eva, he would have noticed the frantic look on Ted's face, urging him to be quiet.

"Well, I try to help when I can," Ted stepped in front of Ishmael. A lot of people are suffering in the city."

"Very admirable of you, Ted. You don't mind if I call you, Ted?"

Ted nodded that it was okay. Talking to this detective could only get him in trouble. He had to get away and think. He had to get a handle on this and Ishmael before it spiraled completely out of control.

"I should be getting back to work now, Detective Storm. You heading down this way, Ishmael? We can pick you up another slice."

"Sounds good, brother."

"I know how to get in contact with you if I have any more questions, Ted. That goes for you too, Ishmael. Here take my card. Call me if you remember anything else," Detective Storm said to Ishmael as she handed him her card. "My number and the name of my hotel is on it."

The three of them exchanged goodbyes and parted ways. Ishmael pushed his cart in front of him and struggled to keep up with Ted, until he met him at the stoplight. He wasn't quite sure what had transpired, but he felt the difference now as his friend turned to look at him.

Eva watched both men from behind her sunglasses as they interacted at the stoplight. It was interesting dynamic of friendship of what's owed and what is given freely. There wasn't any doubt in her mind that Ted Boils had killed both Tammy Russo and Jeff Keels. Knowing is one thing, but proving it could be tricky. The entire case rested on the shoulders of Ishmael Bending.

Ted Boils heard Ishmael's voice, but his attention was focused on the Detective at the end of the street. Their eyes met. She removed her sunglasses and nodded, ever so slightly. He knew what that meant. *Game on.* Her intention was to take him down. His goal was to survive, by any means necessary. He placed his hand on Ishmael's shoulder, smiled at his friend and they crossed the street together.

Ishmael would talk at some point. Ted knew this. People like Ishmael are simple-minded. Lying isn't something that occurs to them because even though he was homeless, there was a basic decency about him that Ted admired and also pitied. Ishmael was a survivor on the streets, but in the real world, he was a sheep being led to slaughter.

"That Detective Eva was nice, huh Ted. And pretty too." Ted didn't have to look at Ishmael to know he was blushing as he spoke glowingly about the detective.

"Pretty women are trouble, Ishmael. They use their beauty to sometimes trick men like us into doing things we normally wouldn't do."

"Like what, Ted? It's good to see a female detective. Women are pretty meticulous. It's a good trait for a detective."

It was the last thing Ted Boils wanted to hear from Ishmael. His admiration for the detective would make him say something incriminating without thinking about it. Poor bastard, Ted thought to himself as they stood in front of the Ethiopian food truck, a few feet away from his office building. No one would miss him when he was gone. The sad thing was that people who knew Ishmael probably already thought he was dead. So in a way, Ted felt as if he would be helping him by putting an end to his tragic life. What kind of life was this? Living in the streets. Eating from garbage cans. Depending on pedestrians to toss you some spare change as they pitied you. The merciful thing would be to put him out of his misery. The compassionate thing for him to do as a fellow human being, would be to kill Ishmael.

"I will look for you at your usual spot later," Ted said to a smiling Ishmael as they both walked away.

"Hey Ted, if you remember can you bring me a pencil and writing pad. I need to get my thoughts down before I forget them."

"Yeah, I can do that."

Ted watched as Ishmael crossed L Street and 20th against the light. He prayed a bus would come speeding through the stoplight and kill Ishmael on impact. It would save him the trouble of doing it, but he had no such luck. He would have to do it himself. Killing him would be easier than defending himself against anything incriminating he might tell that detective. Some people just have no luck at all. First being homeless, and now dying for being in the wrong place at the wrong time. God was definitely screwing with Ishmael.

Ted said hello to the young female security guard as he walked by the security desk and towards the elevator. She stared right through him as she continued a conversation on her cellphone. She didn't even know him, and yet, she had easily dismissed him as being unimportant. Even though he was dressed in a suit and a tie, in that moment, he felt as invisible as Ishmael. People didn't see him. What was it about him that made even strangers look through him? Before the elevator door could close shut, Ted stuck his right foot between the sliding doors and contemplated walking back to the security desk and confronting her. What would he say? *Why didn't you acknowledge me?* It was a bad idea. Nothing good could come from it, so he pressed the button for his floor and rode up in silence, while staring at a distorted image of his reflection in the door.

There is a stench of guilt that some criminals wear without even knowing it. Detective Storm could smell the guilty sweat emanating from Ted Boils' out of shape body. If you could convict people by merely smelling their guilt, solving crimes would be so much easier. Solving a murder, possibly two hadn't been on her list of activities to do that day. She had wanted to visit the African American Museum a few blocks away on Constitution Avenue. Then maybe see a comedy show later to lighten the load of revisiting an ugly period in American history. Bad guys don't take days off, so Eva Storm knew she had to wrap this case up fast, before another body showed up, courtesy of Ted Boils. He didn't look like a murderer, but they never do. It's the ones you never suspect that catch you off-guard, and for a detective, that could cost them their life. She needed to rattle him and let him make a mistake. She would take the fight to his doorstep and wait for him. A photo from the crime scene had identified Marilyn Miller, a co-worker of Ted Boils. It was as good a place as any to start. An hour later, after stopping at an Indian restaurant for lunch, Detective Eva Storm stepped into the offices of Prenax. She flashed her badge and was quickly ushered to Marilyn Miller's office. On her way through the sliding doors, a map of the floor gave her Ted Boils' cubicle seating.

Being in an office setting always made her just want to strip off all her clothes and run like hell to freedom. The idea of sitting down, in an assigned area for eight hours with no windows made her wonder how many murderous thoughts were these people having, just to keep sane.

Eva scanned the cubicles as she walked by. Some of the workers had their heads down, minding their business. Others were on the phone. A few were staring off into space, pretending to be deep in thought. And there was Ted Boils. He had stood up as she walked by with an expressionless face and his eyes following her. Detective Storm nodded at him slightly, but this time no nod was forthcoming. She then stepped into Marilyn Miller's office and closed the door behind her. He was still standing up, watching. A slight smile crossed Detective Storm's face. She had accomplished her goal of rattling him. One more push closer to the ledge and he might just jump, right into her handcuffs.

"Thank you for seeing me on such short notice, Ms. Miller. I only need a few minutes of your time."

"What is this about, Detective Storm? I really don't know how I can help you."

Detective Storm quickly glanced around the office. There were pictures of cats. No kids No husband. As a detective, she had to make quick judgments of people and their character. She hated being judged as a woman, so it wasn't a part of her job she particularly enjoyed. Marilyn Miller didn't seem to care too much about her appearance. She dressed for comfort and not for compliments or to stand out. She wore a drab blue dress which was a size too big. Her hair was more grey than auburn. Her blue eyes bore into Detective Storm as she waited for an answer.

"Have you ever heard the name Tammy Russo before?"

Detective Storm was fishing, hoping that the surprise bait of hearing that name might shake Marilyn Miller. She sat down across from the head of the HR Department and waited for a response, which was taking too long in coming.

"Not that I can recall at the moment."

"Did you maybe speak to her or receive an email?"

"I receive many emails from prospective employees and companies."

Marilyn Miller's body language was uncomfortable. Crow's feet wrinkled around her eyes and she tapped her fingers nervously on her desk. She hadn't been prepared to defend herself or answer any questions about a murder.

"Do you mind checking?" Detective Storm smiled at Marilyn. "If you don't have any record of it, don't worry, I can always have our IT department check her email and have her phone dumped." The smile was still plastered on Detective Storm's face, but her voice was stern, direct. The tone of it told Marilyn Miller that she wasn't a woman to be fucked with or lied to.

"Don't you need a subpoena or something to look at our records?"

Detective Storm stood up, hands at her side and the easy smile now wiped clean from her face. "Whatever you think you're doing to help Mr. Boils don't do it. You have a chance to tell the truth and walk away from this with your life and your freedom. Now, if you piss me off and make get a warrant, then I will have no problem hauling you off to jail." Her eyes glanced over to the framed pictures of all Marilyn Miller's cats. "Who will take care of your beloved cats when you're in jail?"

Invoking her cats was the last straw. Marilyn Miller's lips quivered and she lowered her face into her palms. Detective Storm expected her to start crying, but when she lifted her head, there was a no nonsense resolve on her face. She spilled every detail she knew about the three primaries in the case, Jeff Keels, Tammy Russo and Ted Boils. Detective Storm connected the dots. It was all circumstantial, but guilty people when pushed and manipulated into a corner forget about being rational and methodical. They forget what helped them to escape detection and revert to basic instincts of survival.

"You have been very helpful, Ms. Miller. Please don't discuss this case with anyone, especially Mr. Boils."

"I understand. "I'm not in any legal trouble, am I?"

"As long as you were completely honest with me, then you will be fine."

Marilyn Miller slumped over in her chair, clutching a photo of her favorite cat, Gandalf. Gandalf needed her more than Ted ever would. Her cats were her life. She was sure Ted would understand why she couldn't abandon her cats. It really was a shame if he was involved in any of the murders. They were just starting to build a rapport. She had even scheduled a beauty parlor appointment, along with having a manicure and pedicure. Maybe she would still keep it, she thought to herself as she walked to her office door and locked it behind her.

On her way to the elevator Detective Storm made a detour to Ted Boils' cubicle. The two cubicles behind him were empty. She stopped a few feet in front of his cubicle to observe him. The distinctive scent of Brut assaulted her nose. She wasn't even aware it was still being manufactured. His two computer screens were off. His palms were resting on his desk as he stared straight ahead into the blackness of the screens. His eyes must have been closed because when he saw Detective Storm's reflection in the darkened screen, he quickly spun around in his chair and stared up at her.

"To what do I owe the pleasure of a second visit?"

"Just tying up some loose ends before I close the case."

"I thought you said the case was closed. You must love your job, Detective Storm."

"I do. But I love catching the bad guys even more."

"Why is that?"

"The bad guys think they are good guys in disguise and they are somehow ordained to make the world a better place. Know what I mean?"

"Can't say I do."

"What kind of guy would you say you are, Mr. Boils?"

"I think of myself as a quiet guy."

"You know what they always say, right?"

"What's that, Detective Storm?"

"Don't trust the quiet guy."

"Yes, I've heard that saying before. I suppose that's because they can be deadly when underestimated."

"I never underestimate an opponent. I always keep them locked in my sight, until they are behind bars."

"I'm glad for cops like you who go the extra mile for justice."

"Every victim deserves justice. I won't stop until that happens. You can count on that."

"Well, I've enjoyed the chat, but I have some work to do."

"No problem. Just wanted to let you know I spoke to your HR Director, Ms. Miller. According to her, Mr. Keels was going to hire his sister-in-law, Tammy Russo to replace you. According to Ms. Miller who can be quite chatty when persuaded, Mr. Keels hated you and would have screwed you over by firing you, instead of laying you off. Ms. Miller also went on to tell me that she told you about receiving Ms. Miller's resume and deleted it from her system. Do you recall her telling you about this?"

"Ms. Miller is an incompetent old hag. A woman who calls her cats her babies cannot be taken seriously."

"Being thought of as crazy doesn't make her a liar."

"Thank you for coming by," Ted Boils said abruptly. "I have some work to do."

"No problem. You should try and wrap up any projects you have. You never know when you might have to go away for a long time," Detective Storm said as she walked away before he could offer a response.

The bait had been cast. Now it was just a matter of time before she reeled him in. The trick to being a good fisherman is patience. You wait long enough, and eventually you will catch something. Detective Storm stepped into the elevator and smiled at the tall gentleman dressed in a black suit. His complexion matched his suit. She stood in front of him, a little to the side and kept an eye on him, just in case. She had been assaulted when she was younger and it now made her wary of being in any closed space. His reflection in the elevator towered over her and he remained still. The elevator doors opened and he arrived at the front door of the building before her. "After you," he smiled as he held it open for her. His smile was warm, practiced. The kind of man who knew how to get what he wanted from a woman. His smile was his bait. He wouldn't be catching anything today, at least not with Detective Storm. "Thank you," she responded and stepped back outside into the busy street, leaving him staring at her as she walked away.

Ted Boils knew he had to act fast. He could almost hear the handcuffs clicking shut on his wrists. The imagery frightened him. He wasn't made for jail. Maybe it was something he should have considered before murdering his boss, Jeff Keels and his sister-in-law, Tammy Russo. All his life he had prided himself on being rational, remaining unemotional. It had served him well. The one time he had allowed his emotions to override his common sense, this happened. The last nail in his coffin would be Ishmael. He must have seen what he had done to his boss, but had decided to remain quiet. Once that female detective smiled at Ishmael again, he would probably give him up without thinking twice about it. It was obvious to Ted that her coming to his office was intended to rattle him. That HR bitch couldn't keep her mouth shut. Why don't women know when to shut up and mind their own business? He glared towards her office, but the door was closed. The open door policy had been temporarily suspended. After he dealt with Detective Storm, he would have to teach Marilyn a lesson. Maybe if he played his cards right, he would still get the job he deserved. After all the years he put into the company, he deserved at least that much. First things first. Eliminating Ishmael would still leave him with a Detective Storm problem. He would have to eliminate the source of his angst. It was either him or her, and he valued his freedom more than any feelings of remorse he would have after he killed Detective Storm.

He would need two things. A gun and where she was staying. The former would be easy. Getting a weapon in Washington, DC or Virginia is as easy as finding a Redskins fan, they are everywhere. Ted decided to take the rest of the day off. It wasn't like he had a boss to check up on him. The sick joke made him smile and he temporarily forgot about his problems.

Marilyn Miller opened her office door to use the restroom and saw Ted Boils walking towards her to the elevator. She quickly slammed her door, hoping he hadn't seen her. If he had killed two people as she suspected, she didn't want to be his third. A person like that, you never think they could be a killer – it's exactly why people end up dead. It made her shudder to think what could have happened between them if their relationship had developed any further. The thought brought tears to her eyes and she slumped down to the carpeted floor of her office. Her cats had almost become orphans. They deserved a treat this evening from her for putting their well-being in jeopardy.

An hour later and three hundred dollars poorer, Ted was the owner of a 9mm pistol. The store owner in Virginia gave him a quick tutorial and he was out the door. Getting his license from the DMV had taken longer than this.

Before jumping on the Orange line train to Virginia, he had taken a walk to see Ishmael. Convincing him to give up the detective's address had been easy. In many ways he was like a child, trusting and innocent. Ted had promised to come back later to bring him the pencils and writing pad he had promised him earlier. He would decide at that time, if it was worth the effort to kill Ishmael. The bodies were beginning to pile up. Maybe he had found his calling after all these years. He didn't look like a killer, which would work to his benefit. Being anonymous might finally work in his favor.

An out of town group of teenagers and a few adults were in front of the JW Marriott when Ted arrived. He hated tourists, but realized they were a necessary evil for the economy. He shielded his face as he went through the revolving doors. Their laughter and noise followed him into the hotel. His stomach growled as he walked confidently towards the front desk. The male clerk behind the front desk smiled at him and waved him over. It wasn't much of a smile. It reminded Ted of someone who was bored with their job and just passing time, watching the world go by and hating every second of it.

"Good afternoon. How can I help you today, sir?" His voice was disinterested, but held a practiced ease of caring just enough. Ted knew men like this. He was a man like this.

"Not too bad. Quite busy today. My colleague checked in earlier. Our department forgot to book my room. Her name is Eva Storm. Can you give me the room next to her? We have a lot of work to do. I would appreciate it."

Ted Boils held his breath as the clerk lifted his droopy eyes and stared at him. Maybe his foot was on the alarm right now, alerting security that a double murderer was in their midst. A trickle of sweat leaked down the left side of his face and fell against the counter. He was ready to turn back and make a hasty escape. This had been a bad idea. He had a gun on his person and was ready to kill a police officer. This was madness.

"Oh yeah, I saw her," the clerk winked his droopy left eye at Ted Boils. He was the kind of lecherous older man that he had tried hard to avoid becoming. "I tried flirting with her, but she turned me down cold. Imagine that? Women these days don't know how to be nice to a man." Ted listened and nodded his head in agreement, waiting for the jilted Romeo to say something of importance. "I checked her into Room 1503 on the 15th floor." And there it was. It was Ted could do to avoid jumping for joy. "You ever hit that?" The clerk asked crassly. He leaned forward, a gleam in his eyes and his fat face bouncing off his chin.

"I wish," Ted grinned. "Be right back to check in. I need to make a phone call," he said as he walked away.

He watched from the seating area a few feet away. As soon as the loud group from outside approached the front desk, he made a beeline for the elevator and kept his head down. Luckily he was the only one on the elevator. He was in no mood for idle conversation with a stranger he would never see again. What's the point of that? We waste enough time in life on lines and trains. No need to waste more time talking to someone who will have no impact on your life.

An older couple was waiting at the elevator when the doors opened. They were arguing about using too much hot water and didn't even look in Ted's directions. He slipped by them and continued down the hall. Parked outside of Room 1503 was a hotel maid's cart and the door was wide open. Ted Boils couldn't believe his luck. Everything was going according to plan without much effort from him. He stood outside of the door adjacent to Detective Storm and pretended to be fiddling with the lock. The maid's back was turned to him as she walked away, leaving the door ajar. Just as it was about to close, Ted snuck in and held his breath, hoping the maid hadn't seen him. He pressed his ear against the door and heard her enter another room. The television was turned to CNN. Ted Boils nodded his head vigorously as President Trump ran down the list of his accomplishments at his first State of the Union. He would never admit this to anyone he knew, but he was in the minority of black men who had voted for Trump. Sometimes you have to look out for number one, even if no one else understands that way of thinking. It was the story of his life, being taken for granted, just like his vote had been by the Democrats. The guy after Trump would take care of the disenfranchised, but for now, he needed to look out for his own self-interests.

Her luggage was on one of the two beds, still unopened. The ironing board was flipped open and the iron was left on. She must have just ran out for a moment and was on her way back. Ted Boils scanned the room as he pulled out his 9mm from his waistband. He looked around trying to decide where would be the best place to kill her. The element of surprise was on his side. He would need to act quickly to keep her off balance. Shooting her might attract too much attention from the other guests. Some nosey person next door might hear the gunshot or her screaming and decide to be a good citizen and call the cops. The wall next to the bed would block her from seeing him when she entered, but it didn't give him enough space to maneuver. The bathroom was too small. Ted stood in the bathroom door staring at the mirror across from him and stared at the man looking back at him. Middle-aged. Overweight. Cheap suit. He pulled the gun from his waistband, felt the weight in his hand and pointed it at the mirror. A surge of adrenaline rushed through him. He felt in control, as if he mattered now. Was it really that simple? With a gun in his hand, he suddenly felt invincible. It shouldn't take a gun for a man to feel like a man. Anything can be bought these days, even confidence, though it may only be temporary. The keycard being inserted into the slot alerted him it was time to get ready. Not quite sure where to hide, he quickly decided to take cover behind the room door. When it swung open, he would be behind of it with his gun drawn, and catch her by surprise when it closed.

Detective Storm stood outside her hotel door with a bucket of ice as she inserted her keycard into the slot. It dawned on her as the door swung open that she had forgotten to turn off the iron, even though she had only walked down to the end of the hallway. The room was quiet. She always left the television on for company. The scent of something familiar drifted across her nostrils. It registered instantly with her what it was as she stepped into her room. Brut. Ted Boils had found her.

Her survival instinct kicked in when she felt a presence looming behind the door as it swung close. Her training at the academy taught her that most assailants aim high with their weapons. So without even seeing him behind her back, Detective Storm ducked down, just in time. The bullet went whizzing by her head and pierced the glass door of the balcony. The ice bucket flew from her hand, spilling cubes of ice all over the carpet. Before her assailant could squeeze off another bullet, Eva scooped up a handful of ice in both hands and like a pitcher throwing her best fastball, she aimed them at his face.

The avalanche of hardened ice cubes being pelted at his face at blinding speed made Ted flinch and he put his hands up to protect his face. He grunted loudly when a few of the ice cubes found their mark, one hit him squarely in his left eye and another one dented his forehead. Frantically he squeezed the trigger, hoping to hit something, even though he had been temporarily blinded. One bullet shattered the screen of the television and the next one put a hole in the wall next to the balcony.

His vision cleared up just in time for Ted to see a crouched woman darting straight for him. One bullet in the middle of her forehead would end all of this Ted thought frantically. Before he could squeeze off another shot, Detective Storm managed to slap the gun away from him and in the same motion, delivered a punch to his protruding stomach. Ted swung wildly and missed as she ducked under his awkward punch. It was the first punch he had thrown in his entire life. From the kneeling position, she rocketed upwards and with an open palm and drove it into his chin. The suddenness of it rocked him backwards and he crashed against the closed door. It felt like his teeth were loose marbles rolling around in his mouth and he could swallow all of them at any second. He searched frantically for his gun, but it had fallen in the bathroom. He knew he was outmatched by the smaller detective and it was probably just a matter of time before she had him in cuffs. The thought of being arrested and being in handcuffs sent him into a panic and a rush of adrenaline made him want to fight for his freedom. With his fists clenched he swung wildly and only managed to connect with air. In a moment of clarity, as Detective Storm was delivering repeated shots to his soft stomach, Ted wrapped his strong arms around her waist and arms to immobilize her. He would squeeze every breath out of her, until she was dead.

He was stronger than he looked. Detective Storm felt as if every bone in her body was being broken as she gasped for air. Her feet dangled a few inches from the floor, so she didn't have any leverage to break free. She had cast her line and dangled the bait for Ted Boils and he had bitten. When she left his office, she tracked down Ishmael and told him to give Ted Boils the address of her hotel. Next she made sure that the front desk clerk gave him her room number. Men like Ted Boils are so enamored with their own intelligence, they don't see they are being played, until it's too late. The last part of allowing him to sneak into her room was probably foolish. She didn't have any backup and was working on her own, without her department's knowledge. It wasn't the smartest decision she had ever made, but if she followed every rule and regulation, there would be a few more criminals roaming the streets.

Eva needed to think fast or else her death would be the lead story on the evening news. Being so close to him, the scent of his Brut was overpowering. She could feel his chest pounding against hers and his rancid breath on her face. She stopped struggling, allowed her body to go limp, and pulled in her shoulders to make herself smaller. It allowed her to slip a few inches out of his grasp. She brought the full weight of her right foot down on his left foot and he let out a bloodcurdling scream. Eva stumbled backwards as ice crunched between her feet and a charging and enraged Ted Boils barreled his way towards her. She took a few more steps backwards, about a foot away from the balcony glass door and purposely fell on her back. Hoping she had judged his distance correctly as laid on her back, she raised her legs halfway into the air and braced herself for impact.

Ted Boils had that *oh shit* look on his face. All his momentum was carrying him towards her and there wasn't enough time to brake himself. The curtains to the balcony was open. Off in the horizon a bird flew by and then took a dive out of sight. He felt the bottom of her shoes pressed against his upper chest and the absurdity of being somersaulted through the air by such a tiny woman would have made him laugh, if it wasn't happening to him. He was still in flight as he crashed through the glass door of the balcony. Broken glass rained down on him. Blood dripped from his face and arms. He came to an abrupt halt as he crashed into the metal railing on the porch. Down below the cars and people looked like pieces on a board game. The bird he had seen a few seconds away was circling, as if keeping an eye out for his potential lunch.

"Stay on your knees! Place your hands behind your head!" Detective Storm barked at Ted Boils.

He lifted his head, blood dripping from his cheeks and chin. She was on one knee with her weapon pointed at him. It wasn't supposed to end like this. The sounds of police sirens drifted up from the streets. This was the end of the road. He still didn't understand how he had ended up on this path. He hadn't meant to kill anyone, not his boss or the woman. It had just happened. But how do you just happen to kill someone? Maybe one, but not two. He had intended to kill the lady detective also and if necessary Ishmael would have been collateral damage.

"I didn't want to kill those people," Ted said as he stared at the detective. "They were trying to take something away from me and I couldn't have that."

"You can confess later," Detective Storm said as she slowly started walking towards him to place handcuffs on him.

Ted struggled to stand up. His body felt like dead weight.

"I said don't fucking move!"

As Ted rose to his feet and faced Detective Storm, he realized he had been outsmarted. She had cast the bait knowing he would take it, because she knew he was guilty. Ishmael. The front desk clerk. The maid. They had all been part of her plan. His arrogance had led to his demise. He shook his head with a wry smile.

"You got me."

Yeah I got you."

He would probably spend the rest of his life in jail. He would die behind bars. No one should ever live like an animal in a zoo, not even an animal. Ted Boils backed up against the railing, until he felt the metal in his upper back. If he turned around, he wouldn't have the courage to do it.

"Don't do it, Ted. Let me take you in."

"You won, Detective Storm. I lost. I just want you to know I'm not a bad person. Things got out of control, maybe I could have handled it a different way. I see that now."

Before Eva could respond, Ted, still facing her grasped the top of the railing with both hands and somehow hoisted his body to the top of it. Eva rushed forward in an effort to pull him back to safety, but he leaned back further and went over the top. The silence of the moment is what struck Ted Boils as being odd. He had pictured himself dying in many different ways, but this one had never entered his mind. Funny how life can throw you a curveball. You are going along, minding your own business your entire life, and the one time you show any backbone, you end up dead. He thought about laughing, but didn't have enough time before he was splattered all over the sidewalk. Just like that, it was over.

THE GIRL IN THE FOREST GREEN DRESS

There wasn't any reason why I should have been there on that day, but I was. Most sane human beings were inside, soaking in the air-conditioned offices and eateries. I'm sure a few people walked by or were sitting in a cool restaurant and silently laughing and judging me. If this could possibly be my last day on earth, who knows, I would rather be outside, feeling the sun on my skin, than inside, waiting for someone to serve me.

It was so hot, my sweat felt like heat seeking missiles streaking down my back looking for shade in my shorts. None of that mattered to me. I needed to be outside, away from the office, connecting to something besides my computer and social media. Maybe I just needed to disconnect or I just felt disconnected from a world that didn't make sense anymore. But what can you do when you feel this way? Take more selfies? That might make you feel better when random stranger friends stroke your ego, before moving on to the next hot pic of the day. And you are once again back where you started, in a cesspool of humanity, who cannot seem to process the world, unless it pertains to their own lives. Once in a while, it seems like every week now, an event happens, and the world galvanizes around said event, because it's what humans are supposed to do. After all, this is why we are here to be human and caring. Now that's funny. Insert LOL here. So, these humans change their social media statuses to appear more caring, rant and rave online in this fake reality, but in real life, they go about their business and hope that the politicians will make it all better, like their mommy used to when they had a tummy ache. Hope is an empty promise people make when they have nothing else to offer. I saw a commercial for a new film a few days ago and it said, "Your twenties are about hope, and your thirties are about realizing how dumb it was to hope." Those words went around and around in my mind like a machine wash cycle, until it settled in that small hidden part of my heart, where I am still able to discern truth from fiction. The world isn't hopeless, yet it's been running on fumes for years now, and soon those fumes will just disappear into the clouds, into nothingness. President Obama sold us hope, but I believe deep down, he knew he was selling us a bag of lemons. You cannot fundamentally remake a country or anything that was built on the evils of slavery and turn it into sunshine. You are bound to get burned. The fire this time is upon us. Humanity is burning, and people still believe there is time to save the planet.

Ten minutes ago, I saw a young lady smelling a dandelion at a flower stand next to the Warner Theater. Even though I was lost in thought, I noticed. I noticed how the vendor, a young man, smiled and flirted with her, and she indulged him. He was trying hard, but her body language said he didn't stand a chance. My mind really didn't register her, but more the act of what she was doing. It wasn't anything unusual, but as pedestrians milled around after the 12 o'clock lunch hour, she was oblivious to it all. I must have watched her for all of five seconds, but it was a memory I knew would stay with me. Sometime in the future, when I least expect it, the imagery of her standing there in the chaos of lunch hour in downtown DC, will come rushing back to me to offer me solace when I needed it most. The funny thing about a voyeuristic memory like that, is that she will never know it took place and go on about her life. She will never know, for a moment in the history of the earth, she and I shared something special. That's the beauty of a memory, no oversharing or explaining. It's private and it's yours, which these days goes against everything we are bombarded with in this world. The more you share, the better human being you are and the more people love you, even as you prostitute your deepest, private moments for adulation. As if letting people into your life will make you happy. The Humans will rummage through your personal things, take, prod and steal whatever they want and then exit, without so much of a thank you. They will share your personal thoughts and pictures like a MEME going viral, never once thinking they have done something wrong because everyone is doing it, so it must be right and acceptable. It has become acceptable behavior to steal what was once sacred, the essence of someone with just the click of a mouse. Somewhere inside of us, we know we are being violated hundreds of times a day, but we have now become so desensitized, because get this, we are now doing it to everyone else, and it's all perfectly legal and validates that we are one of the masses, the in crowd. We belong to the club known as Humans, even though we preach individuality, we don't always believe it. Individuality puts a scarlet letter on your face. You become different. Not one of us, an outlier. Humans take comfort in what they understand. We love routine, even if we believe it's boring. It makes us feel safe in a world that's no longer safe. So, the person who dares to put up a page on social media and doesn't share anything of themselves is immediately suspicious. This isn't normal behavior. What is normal is dictated by mass appeal and not personal choices. Normal now feels nostalgic.

If you knew someone who did not have any social media activity, no email accounts, and get this, didn't even own a fucking cellphone, what would you think? I will pause and wait for your predictable response. You may want to stand up and cheer for them like a cheesy movie, because maybe you wish you could do what they are doing. But you know what you will think of this loner, loser, and social misfit (all because they are not conforming to the societal rules of being accessible). You cannot help yourself where your mind instantly travels to and it all happens so organically. You are thankful that you're not the one so cut off from society. You are thankful you are not the one people will be mocking behind your back. It doesn't occur to you that maybe, this person has made a choice that fits their lifestyle, and they don't need the false adulation of social media or the need to feel relevant because they can be reached at the press of a button. Maybe they are enhancing their lives by getting in touch with who they are, minus all the noise that surrounds us daily. You cannot go anywhere without noise. In the elevators there is music. In the bathroom people are on Google—googling what? Can you not take a shit in quiet and listen to the soft splashing sounds of your poop drowning in the toilet bowl? It's just too fucking much. Anyone who can find the secret and somehow turn off the noise all around us, I would like to shake their hand, give them an old man grandfather hug and find out their secret for not being needy. The secret is not exercise, eating healthy, having a good job or any of that stuff. This is the secret, not giving a shit what anybody thinks and doing your own fucking thing. A good friend told me that a long time ago. Everyone says they do, because let's face it, no one wants to admit to being needy. It's weak, pathetic and that's the last thing you want to project in this social media world because anonymous assholes will bully you, until you disappear into the black hole of social media. There is no escaping neediness. It's a prerequisite to being human. All of us need something. It doesn't have to always be something good, but it makes us feel good and dulls the pain of this often times lonely world. The societal misfits of the world long to belong also because being out in the cold can get, well, cold and lonely.

The sun continued to beam down on my exposed bald head as I strolled along, oblivious to everyone walking and talking around me. I exist in the world of my mind, where I am King and create my own reality. It dawns on me that I forgot to put on sunscreen. Most bald headed black men don't wear sunscreen because it never occurs to us we are susceptible to cancer. It's not really a thing for us, but it is. You never see any commercials warning us about that, so how are we supposed to know? Commercials inform and tell us what we need in our lives. Black men look cool with our bald Michael Jordan heads shining in the sun like a bowling ball. Our bald heads are just shining beacons for the tentacles of skin cancer. Take a survey of your bald headed black friends and ask them if ever wear sunscreen or even know that they should. Their unspoken response will be only white folks do that kind of shit, then they will laugh in your face and walk away unprotected into the embrace of summer's killer heat. Another black man dead and it didn't take a bullet to accomplish the deed.

Lathering your scalp in sunscreen to avoid cancer.

Taking a finger up your ass to save yourself from prostate cancer.

Simple, yet so difficult for us to do.

I am completely exposed to the elements. A vacuum of sunlight surrounds me, darkening my skin by the hour and making me more of a threat to a society that shoots first before asking questions. Car horns are blaring everywhere, but I heard none of it. My ear buds are plugged into my ears. Chaos is silent. I self-medicate my mind with music to beautify an ever-increasing ugly world. Today my Pandora station is tuned to Yemi Alade, a Nigerian songstress. Two of my favorite tracks are *Kissing* and *Johnny*. Her music is infectious. It makes me want to be happy, even if I am not feeling happy. That in itself is powerful and an underrated power to have; the ability to override the ennui of the world. There is a secret ingredient in music that can switch the moods of its listeners and infect them with happiness. The world needs music more than it needs many other things which are more hungered for, but do less for the human condition.

My head is cast down. The sun beats down on my neck like sunshine fists. I allow the music to take over and take me to a different place. The glare bouncing off the concrete hurts my eyes. I am about to close them and drift away, but just before I do, from the corner of my right eye, the shadow of a woman approaches me. The silhouette of her frame is curvy and seems to go right through me as she approaches and walks by. I lift my head and it's her. *Dandelion Girl.* Her walk is unhurried as she strolls across the park. She stops for a moment, turns her face upwards to the sky and then continues walking. She is wearing a green dress. More like forest green and now the music in my ear buds is background music. My pulse quickens as I watch her walk away towards the stoplight. A sensation comes over me and a voice not so silent commands me to follow her. That would be like stalking, even if I am not a stalker. Every rational reason keeps me cemented on the bench, but I pride myself in being an outlier in training. I want to go against my nature before she walks out of my life, for good. A force that I cannot explain or understand makes me stand up, a bit too quickly, and it feels as if I am about to float away. I find my footing, wipe beads of possible cancerous sweat from my head and face, place my sunglasses over my eyes and follow her.

This is not something I do, so I am unsure of how to act, or even why I am doing this. I don't want to lose her, so I quicken my pace and watch her from about twenty feet away. We are separated by pedestrians lost in their own world and faces glued to their cell phones. A lady almost walks into traffic with her face buried in her phone, but another quick-thinking phone junkie pulls her back to safety. She sheepishly thanks him. The light turns green and as if hypnotized by her phone, she is on it again. It's an addiction that many don't view as one because the effects cannot be seen right away.

Across the street is The Ronald Reagan Building and Trade Center. I've been here a few times for wine tastings and other events. It's a beautiful building which also houses the EPA (Environmental Protection Agency). The irony of having the building named after a Republican president while elected Republicans are constantly trying to dismantle the EPA would be funny, if it wasn't so dangerous. The front of the building is lined with trees and benches. There is an open area where people can sit down, have lunch and just relax. When there is a big sporting event, like the Wimbledon championship, a huge screen is turned on. It's a wonderful atmosphere and an oasis in the middle of the city.

I slow down my pace. I don't want to get too close and spook her. The building is crawling with cops and security personnel. One scream and the entire place will be shut down. These days everyone is on high alert for the next threat. Everyone different is viewed as suspicious. One bench is empty and she sits down. It's more like glides down as if she is sitting down on a pillow instead of a park bench. All the other benches are taken. I can't just stand around being obvious, so I sit down on her bench. There is about five feet between us. I stare straight ahead, ear buds still in my ears, but the voice of Yemi Alade has now gone quiet. It feels like I am stalking her, but I am not, even if what I am doing is the definition of stalking. My lunch hour is almost over. I want to get up, but the force which pulled me to her won't allow me to leave. I want to continue my outlier journey.

The noise of downtown DC once kept at bay by Yemi's voice crashes through my defenses and comes at me all at once. My heart is beating too fast. My palms are sweaty. The shade offered by the tree branches overhead has stopped my head from perspiring. Through the relentless stereo of sounds and smells, I hear a voice speaking to me. It's soft, but firm. Feminine, yet in control. I hadn't imagined what her voice would sound like, but hearing it now, it sounds just like her.

"If you are going to follow me, at least introduce yourself."

I turn to face her and for the first time make eye contact and see the face of the woman I am stalking. Her eyes are piercing and I instantly know she will be able to sniff out any lies I tell her. They say the truth shall set you free. In my case, it might get me arrested. Outliers are truth tellers. The truth is foreign to most people. When we taste it on our tongue, it has a slimy foreign taste. It leaves us exposed. A lie keeps you protected as long as you don't have to confront who you are. Today was a beautiful day. I didn't want to lie.

"This will sound weird and I hope you don't get up screaming and call the cops."

"Try me, Mr. Stalker."

That name made me visibly wince, but I wanted to speak my truth and see where it took me. It would be my own personal experiment. Most of us are afraid to be ourselves anymore, constantly hiding who and what we are. The world will judge you anyway. At least let them judge you on your truth, instead of a persona created to appease people who don't give a crap about you.

"I was at the stoplight on 12th and G. Through the crowd of people, I saw you smelling a dandelion." The dandelion flower was now at her feet. "I thought to myself as I watched you, that you were experiencing something beautiful and you had probably floated to a memory in your life. It couldn't have been more than five seconds, but something happened. I felt a connection to you. I wanted to know you. Protect you. I know that sounds stupid and presumptuous. And I knew even if I never spoke to you, and unknown to you, we had shared a moment. You disappeared and I shelved away that memory into a safe place for another day. Then you walked past me and I felt a tug, like a fishing pole yanking a fish from the sea. I couldn't help myself, which I suppose is what all stalkers say when they are caught. The lure wasn't sexual, even though you are very attractive. I can't fully explain it, but I just felt as if I had to meet you by following you. I hope I am making sense."

"Your honesty is very refreshing. I wasn't expecting such honesty. Are you always this honest and do women run from you after that?"

"Well, I've never felt the desire to be this honest. Honesty is always motivated by an ulterior motive to get through someone's defenses. Even in their honesty, there is a level of being deceptive. It's a special kind of bullshit that few people possess."

"I've never heard it put quite that way before, but there is some logic to what you said. Do you possess this level of deception? For all I know, you could be doing it right now to me."

It hadn't occurred to me until she said it, that maybe my sort of easy going *the world sucks but I'm a cool guy* was indeed my con. Everyone has a con. They don't necessarily think of it as con because it's instinctual and not something we sit around planning to be.

"I don't think it's a con. This is how I always am."

"Maybe you've been doing it so long now; it's become part of who you are. And you're not able to tell the difference."

Her lower body had swung towards me and I tried not to stare at her long, shapely legs which reminded me of track star, Allyson Felix. Her gaze held my attention as if she could see through my every thought. I blushed as I tried to recover. Even when we are trying to be gentlemen, there seems to always be a part of our brain that wanders to that other side of lustful hunger.

"Maybe that's why I am so drawn to you."

She leaned in closer and waited for me to continue. I resisted my natural urges and wondered what shade of lipstick she was wearing. Her lips were full and the rich color of plum. A dark shade of red accentuated their sensual beauty. My mind was tingling, but I suppressed those hormonal emotions and tried to connect to her through verbal arousal. Physical connection can be made without any effort. It's just the act of being visual. Verbal arousal tests our skills of communication, knowing the right words to say, when to keep quiet and let the silence speak for you. It's a nuanced dance that has no leader or follower. It guarantees its participants are up for the challenge. It exposes a fraud that has nowhere to hide when their words are empty and leaves you wanting.

I searched my vocabulary, looking for the right words to articulate my thoughts. Before I could find them, a shadow crossed in front of us, temporarily obscuring the sun. The shadow remained still and both of us looked up. It was the flower guy. The one who had sold her the dandelion earlier.

"I don't mean to interrupt," he began. If he hadn't meant to interrupt, he wouldn't have stopped. His eyes fell to the flower on the grass next to her. "Something so beautiful shouldn't be on the ground." I wanted to say, *but it came from the ground, but of course I didn't.*

Up close now, he had bags under his eyes, as if he needed to sleep. Dressed in jeans, black sneakers and a red t-shirt that read, *The Beautiful End.* He appeared to be in his mid-thirties, dirty curly brown hair and average height. His face smiled, but his eyes didn't. There was a darkness lurking behind them.

"I will keep that in mind. Thank you for the flowers," she smiled back. It was the kind of smile that women give men to let them know it's time to move on. It dawned on me that I didn't even know her name. She turned back to face me. He stood there awkwardly for a few moments, until he walked away. I watched him stop at the stoplight, turn around to watch us and crossed the street before the light turned red and car horns blaring all around him.

"That was interesting."

"Glad you were here. Sometimes even when you give men a hint, they don't know how to just walk away. Anyway, where were we? Oh yes, you said you are drawn to me without knowing anything about me. My name. What I do for a living. If I'm married or single. Do I have kids? Maybe once you found out these details, that initial spark of attraction could somehow be instantly extinguished."

"If it was extinguished, then what would that mean?"

"You tell me. You're the one who stalked me."

A playful smile formed around her eyes and she suppressed a smile by pursing her lips.

The urge to suddenly kiss her overwhelmed me. I've never kissed a woman and not known her name. That sort of intimacy requires at least that basic introduction. A bold move like that would probably end one of two ways. She would either slap me or summon a nearby cop and have me arrested for unlawful kissing, or something like that. So I kept my lips to myself. There are laws against that kind of behavior, except of course if you are Donald Trump.

"It would mean that I've wasted both our time. You will probably have a good story to tell your girlfriends about this nut job, who stalked you for lunch."

"Every girl needs a nut job stalker story. It's how we know men find us attractive."

Her words were playful, but her face remained serious. It was hard to tell if she was kidding or not, but more than likely she was.

"I find you very attractive. I am drawn to you."

It was her turn to blush. Even the most confident woman needs a compliment once in a while. It reminds them of something they might already believe, that someone else sees them as they see themselves. I wondered briefly if there was someone in her life that made her blush and feel appreciated. I casually glanced at her ring finger, it was naked. President Obama was right. There is always hope.

"After saying something so sweet, you have to tell me your name."

At that moment I wished my parents had given me some fancy name with a deep meaning. I wanted when I said my name that her eyes would light up and the spark of desire would ignite on her lips. We wish for things we cannot have and hope that what we have will be enough to make us stand apart.

"Max."

"I'm Shana."

I said her name silently and tried to create her life story from her name. *Shana.* We remained silent for a few moments, looking around at people going to and fro. I'm a people watcher. I like to imagine the lives of strangers. Everyone has a story. Most never get heard. Most are never recorded for posterity. I want to stop and talk to everyone I meet. Find out about their experiences. Their loves. Their disappointments. What makes them tick. A former co-worker thought I was crazy when I would start talking to people on the elevator. Why do you do that she wanted to know. Sometimes people just want someone to acknowledge their existence had been my response. We go through our days sometimes without being seen. Everyone lost in their own little cubicle worlds. When some-one asks us a question we look like a deer caught in a headlight, startled that another human being is reaching out to us. You go long enough without human contact or communication; it makes you paranoid and suspicious when it comes your way. How sad is that?

My lunch was over, but I wasn't going anywhere. Work isn't life. I was basking in the moment, engaged in conversation and feeling alive, for the first time in a long time. I wanted my high to con-tinue. I wanted to lose myself in Shana and discover things about her that would make me smile. I wanted to have a conversation with her and not watch what I said. I wanted her to look at me and see the person that I am, flaws and all. I wanted a lot, but it's part of what being human is about. We reach for the stars. Maybe we reach it, or maybe just reach the top of the building and fall back down to earth. Either way, we try and make the effort to exceed our expectations of ourselves.

"Can I say whatever is on my mind?"

She paused and stared at me intently, as if trying to figure out if it was a good idea. It seemed like the perfect day to take chances. I wanted to at least have one conversation today, so when I am lying down in bed tonight, I could reflect on it. I needed something real. Not a conversation on the internet or text messaging. I needed to look at someone, feel their words and connect, even if it was for a brief moment. Sometimes you just need something without knowing that you need it.

"Yes, speak your truth. But, be respectful."

"It's the only way I know how to be. It would hurt and haunt me if I disrespected your kindness in any way."

"You have a way with words. Maybe you should write poetry. Maybe you already do."

I have always wanted to write poetry, but until that moment, hearing someone say that I should inspired me to. When I got back to my cubicle, I would write my first poem aptly titled, *Dandelion*.

"So, what kinds of deep, introspective questions do you have for me, Max?"

"Only if you promise to answer them honestly."

"I will. If you do the same."

We nodded in agreement.

"Are you happy?"

"You don't mess around, huh? You get right to it."

Her face didn't light up when I asked the question. Her body shifted away from me. There was a momentary flash of sadness, but it quickly disappeared. It was like a dark cloud obscuring the sun, but you blinked and the sun had returned to its brilliance. It seemed like a small thing, insignificant. But people show you who they are in flashes; you just have to be looking to notice.

"You don't have to answer that question, if you don't want to." I wanted to give her an out. After all we were virtually strangers, even though it was a simple question.

"I am most happy when I am free," she answered wistfully.

Her voice was tinged with melancholy. A woman trapped, but unwilling to give up yet. The shadow of a bird flying above our heads cast a temporary shadow on us.

"When was the last time you felt free?"

"I don't know if I have ever felt free. It's a state of mind I try to wake up with and carry with me throughout the day. Sometimes, it's all we have to get us through the day. That belief that even in the chaos of the world, we matter and care about who we are."

"What would need to happen to make you feel and believe that you are completely free and not just something you try to be?"

"Amnesia."

"Amnesia?"

"Yes. If I could forget everything I have been through, all the heartbreaks, maybe then. But who would want to forget the things that make them who they are? It's denying the path to your very existence. I like who I am, even though there are some things I would like to change I accept my flaws, my weaknesses, because it makes it uniquely me."

"Do you have someone who appreciates this unique and beautiful woman you are?"

She was staring directly into my eyes, but I willed myself to breathe evenly and not look away. The gaze of an attractive woman is a man's Achilles heel, our Kryptonite. It was ambiguous, yet comforting. I couldn't tell if she was thinking about me or her mind was far away, searching for another memory, a memory that would eclipse our connection.

"What if I said there was?"

She was teasing me now. A hint of flirtation danced in her words. I wanted to take the bait, but I knew she was only being kind. If I leaped, I would go over the cliff and there wouldn't be anyone to catch me. I was tired of falling. This time I sensed I wouldn't get up, ever again.

"If there is, then he is a lucky man. If there isn't, I would like to throw my hat into the ring."

My boldness was unlike me, especially when it came to women. But today was not a usual day. It felt like a new beginning and the universe was extending its hand to me. All I had to do was reach out and take a leap of faith.

"You don't strike me as a man who hits on strange women."

"I'm not."

"Why me then?"

"I don't know."

"Good way to sweep me off my feet by saying you don't know. Good way to make a girl feel special." She was teasing me again and I liked it.

"I do know."

"So, you were lying when you said you didn't know."

"Not exactly lying."

"When you say you don't know something but you know it. By definition that's a lie."

"Okay, sorry for lying.

"Apology accepted. So why are you flirting with me on your lunch hour, which I am sure is over by now."

"You are the possibility."

"Possibility of what?"

"The possibility of the woman I have envisioned in my mind. I don't know you, and yet, it feels like I do. Does that make any sense?"

She didn't answer, but in her silence, I knew we were on the same wavelength, heading towards the same destination.

"There was someone until a few weeks ago." I held my breath, knowing the next sentence could alter my life. "He wasn't the man he claimed to be. So, I let him be himself and stayed true to what I need in a man."

"So, to clarify, you are single?"

"Yes, Max. I am single, but I am not looking to get involved in another relationship. Relationships are hard work. It doesn't seem like men today want to put in the hard work required to make it work. They want the perks without earning it and when the hard times come, they never put in the overtime, so they don't have the necessary foundation to get to that other level that relationships require. You know what I mean?"

"I understand your heart is still full from your last relationship. It needs a vacation before allowing itself to come back home and reinvest in something else. Maybe men aren't scared of the hard work."

"What are they scared of then?"

"They might be scared of the same thing as women. They go all in and find out later it wasn't worth the effort they put into it."

"But that's life, Max. Either you leap or you stay put."

"Has anyone caught you when you took that leap?"

"I have bruises all over. Bruises you might never see, but like you, I believe in the possibility, so I continue to leap."

"You are a beautiful plagiarist."

Both of us laughed. My left arm eased around the back of the bench, without touching her. Mentally, I moved her closer to me and allowed her laughter and smile to seep into my being. This is how love begins. Someone opens the door to their heart slightly, allowing a sliver of light to shine through. If your light dances with theirs, that door opens wider and soon it will be filled with stars. This is how it begins, the connection of searching and finding someone who allows us to be ourselves and it's not a threat to who they are. A slow beginning, a jog, and the wider the door opens, it turns into a full-on sprint as your heart races to an uncertain future, but it's a future you know you must, at least, try to embrace. My arms were open. I hoped that my future was staring right at me, with eyes the color of hope and skin the hue of our beautiful struggle to find our place in this world. She had a story I wanted to hear, maybe over a bottle of wine as jazz music played in the background, and we flirted with each other. I wanted to be her safe place to fall, if that is what she needed from me. My mind was already racing to a future that was still in its infancy, but this is what Outliers do, they fashion they own reality and make it come true.

She stood up slowly and my eyes never left hers as I followed suit. Something had happened. My world had shifted to something I didn't fully recognize, but it didn't scare me. I willed myself not to say anything. I didn't want to say anything stupid that might cause her to doubt my intentions. I didn't want to be that guy.

"Thank you for the conversation, Max. It was interesting meeting you. This has been the best lunch I've had in a long time."

"It was my pleasure."

Without thinking about it, I leaned over and embraced her. The second I did, I wished I could take it back. But her body didn't recoil. Instead she embraced me, as if to seal what we had just shared. The warmth of her body radiated through her dress and the subtle scent of her perfume teased me of the possibilities. We separated slowly and I bent down to hand her the bouquet of dandelions she had bought.

"Now don't be one of those guys when I walk away."

"What guys?"

"The guys who let their eyes and imaginations linger on a woman's frame too long. You know they only have one thing on their minds."

"My mind already lingered on your smile and laughter. That is enough to keep me full for now."

"Listen to you," she laughed as she walked away. I turned to leave also. A few feet away, I heard her call my name. *Max*. It sounded like music from her lips as it kissed my ears. "Please stop at Walgreens and get some sunscreen for your head. Our black men don't realize they too are susceptible to skin cancer." It was an unusual thing to say, but it was the perfect thing to say. I nodded my head and said okay. "Good," she replied. "Same time, same place tomorrow?" It was a question filled with hope and the possibility. We both laughed, realizing our journey had begun. Tomorrow could not arrive fast enough for me as I detoured towards Walgreens to keep the first of my many promises to her.

The rest of the day I was floating on air. Funny how the day starts out and you don't expect too much to happen, and then you meet a stranger, something clicks and the same life you thought was meaningless, is now filled with infinite possibilities. From the thirteenth floor, sirens were screaming below. In downtown DC, so close to the White House, sirens are heard almost as often as car horns.

I resisted the urge to search for Shana on social media, even though I didn't know her last name. I wanted to be original and give us a chance to get to know each other without already knowing too much about each other. I didn't want to find out things about her that she hadn't told me. I didn't want to pretend. I had grown tired of that. This time, I wanted to do it right.

Heat engulfed me as I stepped out my building at 5 pm. Pedestrians were speed walking on their way to catch their trains, cabs blew their horns angrily because that's what they are supposed to do, but I was above all of that as I descended into Metro Center to catch the Orange Line to New Carrollton. I was in my own world as people swirled around me. My eighties Pandora station thumped in my ears to the music of Duran Duran. Lady luck was on my side. I never get a seat at this busy station. The cool air felt good against my skin as I sat down, closed my eyes and replayed my lunchtime meeting with Shana again. There was a smile on my face and I'm sure anyone looking at me would find it a bit weird. I don't know when it became weird to see someone smiling when they are by themselves. I didn't care. Tomorrow couldn't come fast enough so I could see her again.

Half an hour later, the train pulled into my stop. A blur of people and feet walked by me on their way home and through the turnstiles. On the way up the escalator, a young man, short and muscled, pushes by me, grabs an older woman's purse and takes off up the escalator and through the subway doors on the street level. It happened so fast that other commuters looked around stunned, but no one moved to assist. The woman is screaming, pointing at the thief, but no one makes a move to go after him. For no other reason than just instinct, not to be mistaken for bravery, I bounded up the moving escalator and took off after him. I hoped someone who witnessed the crime has the decency to alert the transit police, instead of posting it on social media. These days you just never know about the priorities of people. What you might think makes common sense to you, doesn't to most folks,

He was fast and ran like someone who was used to escaping from dangerous situations. Not once did he turn back to see if he was being followed. He dodged a few cars in traffic and disappeared into the park next to some new condominiums. Sweat poured down my face. Running wasn't something I did anymore, unless I was sprinting a short distance to catch a bus or a train. The path he had taken was a worn walkway. Branches hung over and slapped my face. A bug flew went into my mouth, I spit it out and continued, unsure if he was already too far ahead and my chase was now futile. My mind temporarily drifted back to my lunch date and wishing I could fast forward to tomorrow, so I could see Shana again. I ran into a blind corner and the rustling of leaves drew my attention too late, to a fast approaching shadow. Before I could defend myself, he was on me and I fell hard against the concrete. The ground was wet against my back. Sharp twigs and branches poked at my body. Everything was a blur as he punched me in my face and body while shouting at me. "Why the fuck you following me for?" Spit flew from his mouth. My arms were like windshield wipers trying to block it and the force of his blows at the same time. I managed to get in a few punches to his legs and arms, but nothing that seemed to cause him any pain. He was built like a truck and the gym was his home. "Stay your ass down," he warned me as he stood up, retrieved the purse and ran away.

My body was bruised as I stood up, gasping for air from all the body blows and that's when I felt it. A sharp pain in my lower back and right leg. I winced out loud, reached behind my back with my left hand and felt something embedded in my skin. My fingers closed around the neck of a glass bottle wet with my blood. Another piece was lodged in my thigh. Thick red blood streamed down my leg. I looked at my right hand and it was covered with my blood. I instinctively knew that if I tried to pull out either piece, it would be my death. I thought of calling out to the guy I had just scuffled with, but he was long gone. I doubt he would have come back to help me. He didn't strike me as being a Good Samaritan. Dizziness was beginning to set in. I fumbled in my pocket for my phone and tried dialing 911. I had no reception. Panic began to set in. Death was on its way, I was losing too much blood. There wasn't anyone around. The nearest building, I could see through the branches and leaves was about half a mile away. I tried screaming for help, but no one heard me. Playing hero might cost me my life. I took a couple more steps, the park swirled around me as if I was on a merry go round. I grabbed for something to steady me, but there was nothing there as I fell back to the cold ground. No one was coming. I stared up into the blue sky through leaves and branches, searching for something. A sign maybe, that everything was going to be alright. A plane flew by and I wondered if someone in it was maybe looking down at me. I wanted to wave, but my hands were numb now. My eyes closed, and she came to me, Shana.

"I wish we had more time, Max. We would have been good for each other."

I reached for her and touched her face, even though my arms couldn't move. She smiled and held my palm against her face. It felt warm. My body felt cold. Death was impatient for my arrival.

"I am glad I met you. I would have made you happy. Made you laugh. So many memories we would have shared."

"We are sharing one now. Be still. It will soon be over."

A tear slid down my face and then she was gone. There was nothing else.

Three days in a row, Shana had gone to the same bench and waited for her lunch hour for Max to appear. The first day, butterflies danced in her stomach. Every time a shadow appeared, she would look up from a book she was pretending to read. On the second day, butterflies turned to irritation. Maybe his earnestness had been all a game. But it was a game, then what was the prize? She regretted not exchanging numbers, so she could give him a piece of her mind. He had gotten her hopes up, allowed her to see a possible future. She now felt stupid for indulging in romantic pipe dreams. On the third day as she sat seething, two women walked by engrossed in conversation. When the taller one said Max's name, Shana looked up.

"I still can't believe it. He was such a sweet young man. A little weird, but always respectful."

"Excuse me," Shana said as she stood up quickly and both women turned around in unison to stare at her. "Are you talking about Max," Shana realized she didn't even know his last name. Her mind dashed through her memory, searching for his image, which was right at the front door of her thoughts.

"Yes, that's Max Waters," the older of the two woman said once Shana described him. She reminded Shana of someone's kindly grandmother with her bifocals, gray hair in a bun and makeup applied haphazardly. "It's so sad what happened to him? Were you a friend?"

"Well, we just met recently and he seemed nice," Shana offered. "What happened to him?"

The other woman who had remained quiet, finally spoke. Her voice was shaky as she began, overcome with emotion. "He was only doing the right thing and it got him killed." Hearing that Max was dead made Shana gasp and blink back tears. "An older woman's purse was stolen on the train and Max took off after the hoodlum. He was caught later that day and according to him, they fought and during the fight, Max fell on some broken glass, which severed some nerves in his back and leg. He bled out."

"He died?" Shana said to no one in particular.

"Everyone loved him at work, even though he could be a bit odd at times, but in a nice way."

The two ladies and Shana spoke for a few more minutes. They hugged and said goodbye. Still distraught, she sat down on the same bench she had shared with Max, trying to process what she had just heard. She felt bad for thinking he had ditched her, only to find out he had died bravely.

It seemed pointless to her now that she had met this great guy, one time, and the effect he had on her had been amazing. Her heart had traveled farther than their initial meeting. Her co-workers had commented that there was something different about her. Even though she shrugged off their observations, she felt it. It was hope. It was that innocence of believing that good things were going to happen. Even though their encounter had been brief. It had been meaningful. They had flirted innocently. Their conversation had been different and had left her hungry for more. She had seen something in him she had been searching for. And now, just like that, it was gone. It made no sense. It saddened her, but at the same time, she felt lucky for the brief time they had shared. It had proven to her that there were still men out there willing to have a conversation and treat a lady like a lady. Before heading back to work, Shana said a silent prayer for Max and slowly walked back to her office. It was a beautiful day. The kind of day you just want to linger outside a few extra minutes because it feels as if something special could happen at any moment.

A KILLER REVIEW

Myles Banks banged his closed black fists against the wooden table in a dive bar, *The Last Shot*, in downtown Washington, DC. The counter shook and almost buckled from the unexpected assault. His steely stare remained on the flat screen television playing behind the bar. All eyes in the restaurant turned to him. Either something was about to go down, or they could get back to their boring conversations, drinks and trying to discreetly check their cell phones for more interesting social media updates. A few of the patrons already had 911 on speed dial, especially for occasions like this, and they were ready to press *Record*. The expectation of violence is always present, even in an atmosphere of merriment. It is the new American reality. You are not safe anywhere. Any time. Any place. Expect the unexpected is the survivor's motto. Never allow yourself to get too comfortable. Comfort can cause your death.

Shante Combs had destroyed his career before the public had even read the first chapter of his book. She had distorted his life's work, and now, she was capitalizing on his misfortune. Maybe if she had done it to someone else, he would be able to appreciate the ruthless annihilation of another person's career on social media. But it was his balls which had been surgically removed. They were dangling all over the internet for public fodder and ridicule. Her scathing, some said hilarious review of his novel should win some kind of literary review award. It had gone viral after a few bloggers posted it and other trolls began to meme her review. Suddenly, it was trending all over social media. Even the late-night talk shows had joined in to assassinate his career. Along with his publisher, Myles Banks watched helplessly as the monster machine of social media ripped him apart, ran over him without an ounce of remorse and left him for dead. No one cared that behind all the mockery was an actual human being. It's easy to forget sometimes that your anonymous words are actually hurting someone. There is someone behind the computer screen or cell phone reading all this nasty, hurtful stuff. A mob mentality takes hold and people who are usually kind or pretend to be kind, become these vicious animals, just to be accepted by faceless asshole strangers who would walk right by them on the street, without sharing a word or a smile. It would make for an interesting book, but the only thing on Myles Banks' mind was exacting revenge. He didn't know how yet, but he was a writer. He planned to unleash the full depravity of his imagination on Shante Combs. That bitch would woe the day she fucked with him and lived to write and profit on his good name.

"One more shot of tequila for the road," Myles held up his empty shot glass for the bartender. His fingers were sweaty and the glass almost slipped from between them.

The bartender stared at him, unsure if he should refuse him one last drink. It wasn't his responsibility to police a grown ass man. But he didn't want to hear about some kid being run over on the news by this drunken fool. His conscience needed a reprieve from guilt.

"Last one buddy. Looks like you've had a rough day." Russo placed the tequila shot in front of the unshaven, yet vaguely familiar black man.

"You have no fucking idea. Ever had the world in your hands one day, and then the next—it's all gone?"

Russo gave the angry man a nod of his head. He stared at him with empathy. Something he had perfected over the years as a bartender. It gave the appearance of caring, and folks felt more generous with tips. He was sure that the man's anger had something to do with the overly processed black woman on *Ellen*. A few times, he thought that the angry customer would have marched behind the bar and smashed the television into the hundreds of bottles of liquor lining the shelves. He had been wrong so far, but he kept his huge fingers curled around the knob of his baseball bat, just in case. He was an ex-hockey player, wrestler, bodyguard turned bartender. Violence was in his DNA. Besides, he was itching for a good fight. It made him feel alive and it was a chance to relive his glory days as a bruiser.

"I can relate, brother." Russo leaned into the counter, his brown hair dangling loosely around his face. His tattooed arms seemed too small for his body. His teeth were a bit too perfect for someone who had been in countless fights. It had been his only dalliance into any sort of reconstructive surgery. Women don't mind a man being rugged, but you cannot look like you've taken a beaten, it doesn't project strength. One thing women hate more in a man than being broke, is a man who looks like he's gotten his ass kicked.

Brother. Through bloodshot eyes, Myles stared at the man who reminded him of Thor and smirked. If he hadn't been so drunk, he would have challenged the assertion of this supposed *brotherhood.* White men like him probably have a few black friends, listened to some rap music and had tasted black pussy, so their demeanor and language becomes gentrified. He could deal with only one enemy at a time. Shante Combs was the only thing on his mind. Everyone else would have to get in line.

"That bitch stole my life," Myles said as he stared at a smiling Shante being interviewed by Ellen. She had come out twerking to *Back 2 Back* by Drake. Ellen joined in and the crowd went nuts. It was great television, but not for Myles. If his life was a cartoon show, smoke would be coming out his ears right now.

"You know her?" Russo was mildly interested now. He turned his gaze to a table in the middle of the bar as he waited for a response. There were a few young college students blowing off some steam and getting a tad loud. They were usually harmless, but he could sense they were on the verge of getting rowdy. He would have to step in soon to diffuse it.

"Never met her. I plan on having a conversation with her real *soon,*" Myles said ominously. The face staring back at him in the mirror behind the bar didn't look like the man whom *Essence, Kirkus Reviews,* and *Publishers Weekly* had anointed as the next big thing in literature. He had been anointed as the lovechild of Anaïs Nin and James Baldwin. He had been stamped, approved and trotted out for worldwide success. And then, that fucking review came out two weeks before the release of his first novel.

"Hopefully, it's not tonight. You might do something you regret forever."

"Not if I don't get caught."

Russo stared at the man at the bar. His eyes were bloodshot. He was tall, at least six-two. He hadn't shaved in a few days and was in need of a haircut. There was an edge to him, a Jekyll and Hyde sort of vibe that gave him the creeps. Once he cleaned himself up, Russo was sure that he would look like a gentleman and wooer of women. But right now, he was plain scary.

"I hope the cops don't come around here asking questions," Russo joked.

There was that *look* again from him. It made Russo squeeze the bat handle under the bar just a bit tighter. Then just like that, a smile. It unnerved him. Without even thinking about it, Russo poured him another drink and walked away to talk to the increasingly loud patrons, who were now on the table dancing to the latest hit by Rihanna, *Bitch Better Have My Money.*

Myles spun around in his seat, drink in hand, and watched the stocky bartender lumber over to the noisy table. His handsome face didn't match his physique. It threw him off for a minute. He wasn't that drunk, or maybe he was. Commercials were on and he needed to drain the python. The floor beneath him felt like he was on a wave surfing and would drown at any second. He stood still for a few seconds to get his bearings and then strode confidently to the bathroom, ignoring the ruckus around him.

This is where she belonged, Shante Combs thought to herself as she twerked her way onto *Ellen.* This was her moment to shine, and she had every intention of milking her fifteen minutes of fame and turning it into something beyond being flushed down the twenty-four-hour news cycle. What she lacked in movie star looks, she more than made up for it by being cunning and being able to smell the next opportunity like a silent fart in a room of non-farters.

The viral review happened quite by accident. Before she knew it, she had become the latest internet sensation. Being a social media sensation is cool, but the trick is being able to turn your surprise notoriety into cold, green cash. The *I ain't got time for that* lady from a few months ago had been able to do a few commercials and public appearances. Shante had bigger plans as she twerked her behind off, her short, thick frame levitating inches from the floor. She even showed Ellen a few moves that only the sistas knew how to do. Shante flashed her thousand-watt phony ass Shaquille O'Neal smile at the camera, and imagined all of America falling in love with her at that moment.

Dancing next to the white lesbian goddess of daytime television was a stroke of dumb, stupid luck. People with actual talent and deserving of the spotlight who are actually creating something, weren't as lucky as Shante Combs. She had stumbled on to the brightest stage in America and had every intention of keeping it trained on her, no matter what she had to do or say to keep America in love with her. Nothing was off-limits. Opportunity doesn't care if you're deserving or smart. When it presents itself to you—you have to be ready to take complete advantage of its kindness. Anyone who doesn't is a fool. Shante Combs was many things, but a fool wasn't one of them.

"I love your outfit," Ellen said as she innocently flirted with Shante. They were seated now after a raucous twerking battle. The producers had to calm the audience down or else Shante would have had them running a Soul Train line on stage. The last thing they wanted was for some of their older audience members to break a hip on live television. Someone catches a cold in your house these days and next thing you know, they are suing you for your life savings.

"I wore it just for you, Ellen," Shante flirted right back. If America's favorite lesbian wanted some chocolate, then Shante had no problem giving her a taste of the goodies, for a price of course.

Before Ellen could deliver one of her famous one-liners, Shante stood up and twirled around for the audience, as if she were a runway model. She was wearing a body hugging purple dress that made her ass pop back and her breasts lean forward. It was a minor miracle that the whole damn thing hadn't come apart as she twerked for America. Her stomach was more sucked in than a woman taking a selfie to post on Facebook. Getting beautiful can be an ugly business. Purple open-toed high heels with matching polish adorned her small feet. Her weave was believably real, even though you knew it was fake. Not too long. Not too short. When you saw it, you might question its authenticity, but it was a question not worth asking because it created just enough doubt.

Shante knew, without a doubt, she was slaying it and couldn't wait to get back to her hotel room, exhale out of her dress and watch the show. If she was lucky, while out in California, she might even meet a man. She was pretty enough, but she never felt that way, especially when she went out with her girlfriends. Men would flock to them, fawning, as if their brains had turned to oatmeal. They would stampede past her like she was invisible. The only time they spoke to her was to get information or if they were inebriated, only then would they somehow see the woman she really was. Maybe being five feet five and a buck sixty was too much for most men to handle. Maybe she had too many degrees, made too much money and always spoke her mind. Maybe you should smile more and talk less, her friends had advised her. Men love to feel like they are in control, even when they are not. When you get them hooked, then you can let him know who's in charge. There were too many rules to follow. Too many games to play. It was after another bad date, she had stayed up late into the evening, speed reading a free copy of Myles Banks' book. His publisher had sent her an ARC (advanced reader copy) because Amazon had recognized her as one of their most prolific reviewers. She had no idea who he was, but her mood was already foul after another date from hell and she began to read and drown her anger over a few glasses of red wine. Reading that book was like pouring gasoline on her broken heart. That's when she wrote the now infamous viral review.

"With us today is social media sensation, Shante Combs. Any relation to Puffy, or is it P. Diddy, or is it back to Sean?"

"Thanks for having me on today, Ellen. If Puffy and I were related everyone would know about it by now. As you can tell, I have no problem speaking my mind."

"Talking about speaking your mind, remind me never to make you mad or else you might come and heckle me."

The crowd roared with laughter. All of them had a copy of the review along with other goodies from the show. Shante had been paid to sign every laminated review, as if it were a real book.

"Well, Ellen, it's like this, I was only venting and didn't expect any of this to happen. I was just being a woman and speaking my mind."

Shante played to the crowd, and the audience was eating it up like biscuits dripping in gravy. She made sure to angle her head, so the camera could capture her earrings, which she had designed herself. It was a silver hook painted in rainbow colors. The idea came to her on a cruise with her girlfriends to St. Lucia a few years ago. Business had picked up since she went viral, and hopefully being on Ellen this week, and Wendy Williams the following week would send her sales through the roof. She was on her way to being famous.

"What exactly set you off, girl? My audience wants to know. And I'm sure writers out there want to know also, so they can stay on your good side. By the way those earrings are the *business*. Where are they from?"

The sound of cash registers were ringing in Shante's ears as she opened her mouth. "Ellen, I made them myself. They are available in every color. I can even custom make any color you want. My website is www.bossshante.com." Without missing a beat, Shante helped Ellen to put on a pair of turquoise earrings, her favorite color. You can practically find out anything you want to know about someone on the internet these days. Privacy is a fallacy. The crowd clapped its approval and the interview continued.

"These are beautiful."

"Thank you."

"Have you ever heard from Mr. Banks?"

"Not directly. Someone from his publishing house called one day asking me to recant my review. They even tried getting Amazon to take it down. Everyone knows how much Amazon cares about writers, but for once, they did the right thing."

"I read your review about five times. It's quite literally, genius. But is it more an attack on the book or the writer? It sounded *really* personal, as if you were getting back at an ex-boyfriend."

"Interesting you mentioned that, Ellen. It was cathartic. In a way I was striking back at all the men who take women like me for granted. They don't see us. They only see the chick with the perfect little butt, long hair and weighing less than what any full-grown woman should ever weigh." The crowd broke into a tremendous applause. Some women were whooping and hollering. Shante had struck a nerve. "The expectations placed upon women are outrageous," she continued. "From the books, movies, magazines and commercials, the unreasonable expectations we are forced to endure is ridiculous. So, when I read Mr. Banks' book about an average woman who undergoes plastic surgery to catch her man—it infuriated me. He made it seem as if she wasn't good enough. It sends the wrong message to young girls and women, who are already dealing with body issues."

"Let me play devil's advocate, Shante. I wish I had a devil costume on right now, but isn't that the job of a writer to push the boundaries and make you think?"

Shante had watched enough reality television and Maury Povich to know that it didn't take much for an audience to turn on you. One minute they love you, and the next, everyone wants your scalp. The irony wasn't lost on her. She wondered briefly if Myles Banks was watching her shine on his dime. It gave her a devilish thrill to imagine him watching her and there was not a goddamn thing he could do about it.

"I could say it's your job to entertain, Ellen. But would you come out here in front of millions of people and make fun of certain people?" Before Ellen could respond, Shante answered her own question. "No—you wouldn't because to profit from the pain of someone is to lose your soul."

The crowd cheered. The name Shante Combs was trending again on social media, this time ahead of Kanye and the Kardashians. The blogs were lit up and adjectives were being used to describe Shante Combs as a modern-day feminist, a *real* black woman (whatever that means), and things were being set in motion, unbeknownst to her.

In a crowd filled with mostly women, behind glasses too big for his thin long face and frog eyes that gave him an innocent Bambi like look, Garrett Green clapped enthusiastically for the woman he was in love with, Shante Combs. He towered over the other women as he stood up to take pictures of a smiling Shante, to add to the hundreds he already had in his collection, which he had copied from her numerous social media accounts. She was even more beautiful up close. Purple was definitely her color. Watching her twerk when she came out earlier had made Garrett blush, then angry, because two other men with their wives were staring a little too hard at her ass. One of them had even discreetly taken a picture of her. Garrett smiled as he reminisced about following the short, balding fat man to the bathroom during a commercial break. He had waited until the man pulled out his Johnson at the urinal, stood behind him, and pressed a knife against his throat. His Adam's apple bobbed rapidly under the knife.

"It seems we have a problem, my friend." He had calmly informed the elderly man.

"Please don't hurt me. Don't rape me." The elderly man missed the round white target of the urinal and pissed all over his pants and shoes.

"You're not my type old man. You need to drink more water. Your piss looks like Cheetos. Give me your phone."

"My phone?"

"You took a picture of my girlfriend on stage. I need you to delete it."

The bald round patch on top of the older man's head gave Garrett the sudden urge to lick it. He fought the urge, took out the old man's cell phone from his jacket, and handed it to him. His watch beeped again for the fifth time. He needed to take his medication. He would double up later, but for now, he needed this pervert to delete the picture.

"There, it's done. Can I go now?"

"If you ever do that shit again to any woman, I will cut your fucking balls off and flush it down a shit stained toilet bowl. Kapish?"

"Yes. I understand."

"Count to one hundred and then go back to your seat. Make sure you wash your fucking hands. A survey in *Men's Journal* said that over sixty-five percent of men don't wash their hands. Crazy right?"

"What?"

No response was forthcoming. Garrett Green had already slipped out from the bathroom. He was seated and calmly staring at photos of Shante on his cell phone by the time the old pervert had counted to fifty. The show was back from commercial. The old man took his seat in front of Garrett and ignored his wife's questions about what had taken him so long. His hands were still shaking from the encounter.

"I want to thank our social media superstar, Shante Combs, for being our guest today. But I wouldn't be doing my job if I didn't at least ask her to read an excerpt from her famous review."

The crowd applauded again and started to chant her name. It's not a hard name to pronounce, so most of them got it right.

"Shante! Shante! Shante!"

Garrett Green beamed like a happy parent. When you love someone as much as he loved Shante, you are willing to do anything to make them happy.

The audience quieted down and Shante began to read from memory, words that now belonged to her.

"Mr. Myles Banks, if that is your real name, then it's better fiction than what you've written. Men like you who have no idea what makes a woman happy or sad are worse than the politicians who want to play God with our bodies." The audience clapped enthusiastically. Writers like you sit at your laptops with images of a perfect woman dancing naked in your teenage minds and ascribe characteristics to us that *you* think we should have. You don't see us as women, but objects lifted from the pages of *Playboy* and booty shaking videos to be objectified. This is your idea of what a *real* woman should be. Mr. Banks, I am a real woman. I am outside the circle of your perfectly contrived, docile harem of women who you and your publisher seem to think is what the world needs." The crowd was now in a frenzy. Women were high-fiving each other. Shante Combs was speaking for them and to them. Her voice was their voice. They were tired of being overlooked, made to feel less than because they didn't have a Nicki Minaj-Beyoncé-Kim Kardashian butt. The holy triad of Bootylicious women trotted out as American exceptionalism. "If society and Mr. Banks defines a woman by what she sits on and not what's in her brain—then society needs to sit their asses down." By this time the crowd was again chanting her name. Shante was twerking and urging the women in the crowd to do the same. The irony of her words and action was lost on them, as her butt shook to the rhythm of their applause. They were caught up in the moment and the wave of emotion was electric in the audience.

Garrett Green looked around at all the women and felt a sense of pride. He believed he was smiling, but anyone looking at him would be petrified by the glint of evil in his blue eyes. His white skin was translucent, almost beautiful to look at. It didn't fit the sense of evil that permeated his being. He was a chameleon, able to fit into any situation to suit his needs.

Garrett exited the studio, held the door open for an elderly lady and then left quietly. There were things he had to do. He noticed that Shante had a new follower on her Facebook, Twitter, Instagram, Snapchat, and Periscope account. He had quickly done a search of the handle: TIMEISALMOSTUP666. It didn't surprise him to discover who it was. In fact, he had been waiting for it and was already prepared to handle any situation. It was Myles Banks. Garrett Green hailed a cab, which wasn't a problem for a man who looked like him. He needed to get to LAX airport to catch a flight to Washington, DC. He needed to have a talk with Myles Banks, man to man.

The more Shante Combs ran her mouth and twerked her ass on stage, the angrier Myles Banks became. The crowd at the bar by this time had recognized him, and of course, they wanted to take pictures with him to post to their Facebook and Instagram pages. He was already shit-faced and past the point of thinking rationally. Between the alcohol pumping through his veins and hatred for Shante Combs dominating his thoughts, Myles Banks was a man on the edge and capable of doing anything.

"Smile for the camera, Myles," a tall smelly man said to him. He draped his arm around Myles' shoulders, as if they were long lost friends and the flash from the cameras illuminated the bar area, temporarily blinding his vision.

"Enough!" Myles roared.

The crowd stepped back, cell phones in hands, still recording. All of them wanted to be the next social media star at his expense. They wanted him to freak out. Maybe hit someone. Say some dumb shit. Anything that would elevate their social media platform.

"I know my rights, man." Someone from the crowd shouted. Alcohol fuels false confidence. It's the same for weaklings with guns. "This is a public place. You have no expectations of privacy. This is America." Folks love using *this is America*, as if that alone can neutralize any argument.

"Everyone knows their fucking rights," Myles said as he stared bleary-eyed into a dozen or so cell phones recording his image, "but no one has any respect anymore. How would you like it if I put a fucking camera on you and filmed you during the worst time of your life?"

It was the worst thing Myles Banks could say to a group of drunken students raised in the era of confessional television, where pain is exploited for likes and followers and everyone feels entitled to know everything about people they don't know, and could give a shit about. An era of non-talented people believing they have every right to be famous for essentially doing nothing, except talking about themselves and finding ways to exploit their uninteresting lives for fame, and hopefully fortune. Uninteresting facts and stupid acts become fodder for fame. Everyone wants their fifteen minutes. Everyone is a fucking genius. The dilution of the word is circling down the toilet bowl faster than bad food and alcohol regurgitated at two in the morning in a fast food restaurant or dive bar. Everyone is in on the joke that all of this is so fucking ridiculous, but this is what sells in an era of sound bites and status updates replacing real news and human interaction. The world is moving too fast. We are losing the essence of our humanity, but we have spun too far out of control to put the brakes on. So, this is what we have. Everyone's opinion sounds good. Everyone is a fucking expert. But that's just bullshit. Some people just need to shut the fuck up, inhale their polluted oxygen and go about their lives or drop dead. Myles would have said all of these things to the cameras pointed at his face, and if he had, maybe it too would have gone viral. But the twenty second sound bite would make him seem like another angry black man. He wondered in his drunken stupor how President Obama had managed to deftly avoid the trap for eight years. That brother will need some serious anger management once he leaves office.

Russo finally came to Myles' rescue. He had no idea who he was or why he was famous. Even though he was a white male, Russo was in the minority of people who didn't have any social media accounts. It all seemed kind of stupid and desperate to him. He imagined the suicide rate would skyrocket if the internet shuts down for a week, maybe even a day. Human beings won't know what to do with themselves. Even in the sky, thousands of miles away from civilization when he flew from Seattle to Washington, DC, passengers were hooked on their electronic devices. He remembered looking around at them and realizing that he was the lucky and sane one. They probably felt sorry for him, sitting there, lost in thought and just enjoying the moment, looking out into the vast open skies and contemplating life.

"Get back to your fucking seats," he growled at the crowd of social media drunken whores. He then said the magic words. "No more alcohol if you don't." Those words made the crowd disperse and scurry back to their table like well-behaved pets, waiting for their next treat. Russo smiled and turned his attention back to Myles. He was amazed he was still standing and in the morning, he was sure Myles would have a tsunami of a headache. "Let me call you a cab, buddy."

Myles nodded in agreement. Only bad things can happen to an angry black drunk man in a bar. He opted to listen to the quiet voice in his head urging him to go home. One of the students, a pretty Japanese or Chinese young woman with too much makeup, but a nice rack and round black girl ass, was giving him the eye. He can't tell what she is, and he realized maybe that's a bit racist, but in his drunken state, he wasn't sure. But then he thought, how can it be racist, if he didn't say it out loud. He thinks he has found a loophole to jump through the shit hole that is racism. Tomorrow morning, he won't have any recollection of these stupid thoughts. Drunken absolution.

She had trouble smeared all over her blood red lipstick covered lips. His imagination had already surpassed his reality. Right now, he needed to release a ton of stress. He planned to fuck the shit out of her and make her pay for everything Shante Combs had done to him. He held her stare as he exited the bar into the October winter. Like a willing groupie, she followed him into the cab. Without saying a word, he unzipped his pants, his dark erection saluted the night, and her red stained lips covered his erect frustrations. Eyes closed, he never noticed that she was recording their tryst. In the next hour as he slept, his dick, or lack of it, would become the source of more ridicule and memes. White men seeing that there were black men with smaller dicks than theirs, breathed a sigh of relief. It's one less thing they had to worry about when it came to black men taking over the world and stealing their white women. Myles Banks, unknown to him, becomes a hero to the Caucasian male population. He was caught up in a perfect shit storm of circumstance, rabid public interest and everything that was wrong with this country. But for now, he slept naked in his bed, rolled around in his urine and shit-stained bombs that dotted his King-sized bed with brown circles that resembled the game Twister.

Shante sashayed through LAX airport soaking in her social media fame. People recognized her because she was wearing an outfit that demanded attention. A pink track suit from the new Nicki Minaj line, complete with pink sneakers and her line of earrings, of course in pink. She strutted down the corridor as if it was a runway, pulling her roll on pink bag behind her. Shante didn't stop to take pictures or sign autographs. It will devalue your brand her agent had instructed her. People don't value what they can get for free. Today's consumer doesn't care about quality. It's more about what can I get for my buck and keep stretching it, until there's nothing left. The internet is bogged down with people giving away free shit that has no value, especially writers who give away free copies of their books, hoping to expand their audience. Readers these days are hoarders. With a click of their mouse, they gobble up your free book and forget about you. It's on to the next free thing.

There was a long line at Starbucks and waiting wasn't something that famous people like her were supposed to do anymore. Confidently, she strode to the front of the line and placed her order. Coffee addicts in line were too shocked at her brazenness to say a word and barely offered a whisper of protest. Most of the waiting customers were white. No one wanted to be accused of being racist. But there is always one-person willing to speak out against the injustices of a line jumper.

"Excuse me, but there's a line here and you can't just skip to the front of it," a haggard looking middle-aged white woman, who desperately needed her infusion of caffeine told Shante.

Shante whirled around quickly, without acknowledging the woman and smiled at the unsmiling caffeine depleted crowd. If her braids hadn't been in a bun, she would have braid smacked soccer mom right across her botoxed face.

"They don't mind. I just did *The Ellen Show* and I needed my Caramel Macchiato before I lost my mind," Shante offered as an explanation for her rude behavior. Before anyone could respond, she'd already gone. Later that evening, she would be the topic of conversations in many homes about how all black women are rude. All it takes is just one person to fuck up and everyone has to pay the price.

Garrett Green was sitting in the terminal across from the Starbucks kiosk, charging his phone and laptop, sipping on a Coke, and observing Shante. Fame made people feel entitled. They forget they are human beings and have to play by the same rules. Fame doesn't change who you are, it just exposes the character you always had. It amused Garrett how quickly Shante had adapted to being a celebrity. He overheard her earlier on her cell demanding a first-class seat. Customer service informed her that there weren't any seats available. She told them who she was, threatened to unleash a torrent of tweets to her three million followers, who would then retweet it, and before long the airline would be defending themselves against a litany of charges. Of course, she got her way. Just the sniff of bad publicity going viral was enough to bring most companies to their knees, and made them suck and swallow on the imaginary phallic symbol of the angry American consumer.

A few quick clicks on his laptop and he found what he was looking for. It's almost like child's play to find people who don't want to be found. There are data footprints everywhere on the internet. You step into one of them and your prints are cemented there forever. He needed to have a sit-down with Mr. Banks. Either they came to an understanding about Shante, or he would have to silence the writer forever. It would be a shame, his writing had potential, if he could steer clear of following trends, using too much hyperbole and whoring his talent. It's just bad luck that one bad review went viral and killed his chances of having a best seller. Writers by trade have crazy imaginations, but it's not in their nature to act out on their urges. Needless to say, it's easier to mutilate someone on your laptop, than it is to stare them down and take their life. Mayhem only occurs between the pages, but Mr. Banks probably had more incentive than most to want to cause his beloved Shante harm. Garrett was prepared to do any and everything to make sure that that never happened to his beloved future wife.

Across from Garrett Green sat a tired traveler, Larry Clarke. His plane had been delayed two hours. He missed a job interview at Langley in Virginia. His savings had been depleted after being unemployed for over a year and right about now, suicide seemed the only viable way out for him. He was too old for this shit, to start over again and have a snot nose kid young enough to be one of his grandchildren be his fucking boss. This wasn't his life—*but it was.* He was a nobody in a world filled with nobodies, which made him lesser than a nobody. People walked by without giving him a second look. All they saw was an old white man going bald with bad skin wearing a cheap suit. People watching was his favorite past time these days. It's better than anything on Netflix and regular television.

The tall, bugged-eyed white fella sitting across from him, Larry was sure, was up to no good. He just had that look about him that trouble was around the corner. Larry discreetly followed the frogged eyed fella's eyes to the Starbucks across the way, and they landed on a black woman in a pink getup. He wondered what would possess someone to dress like that, but that wasn't any of his business. The world didn't make any sense to him these days. It didn't seem to be made for people like him anymore. Larry was positive he should warn the black woman, or was it African-American woman; it's hard to keep up these days with what one should say or do, so he kept his mouth shut to avoid offending anyone. Simple statements are misconstrued. Aspersions are cast without knowing someone's intent. And besides, after seeing how rude she was to the customers in line, as if she was some kind of celebrity, he didn't need the headache. She wasn't anyone he recognized, maybe she was one of those goddamned, no-talent reality people who were incessantly talking about themselves on those stupid morning talk shows. People talked too damn much, Larry thought to himself. Whatever happened to the real stars? Frank Sinatra. Marilyn Monroe. Katherine Hepburn. Cary Grant. Even that boy, Sidney Poitier wasn't half-bad. All of them dressed conservatively, well except for Marilyn, but she was sexy with class. Today's movie people dressed like they had no home training, walked around half-naked, and claimed that they were expressing themselves. Back in his day, people like that were shunned, until they shaped up and fit into society. Larry sipped on his cold coffee and wondered where all the years had gone. The world had passed him by, and he was too old to try and catch up anymore. Sometimes when you are too tired to care, you just wait for the end to come. It's kind of cathartic, because you no longer have any expectations of life. It's the ultimate freedom.

"Sit back and enjoy your flight. Flight time to Washington, DC is approximately five hours and twenty minutes," a voice over the intercom informed the passengers. "Sit back and relax. We will be coming through the aisles shortly with headsets to purchase. This evening's movie is *The Avengers: Age of Ultron*."

Seated a few rows outside of first class was Garrett Green. He had a clear view of Shante Combs. Restraint was new to him, but he knew if he got too close to her, then everything he had done for the past few months would be for naught. He watched as she bent over to pick up her cell phone on the floor. The roundness of her ass excited him instantly. A sound like a soft crying whimper escaped his lips, and he quickly swallowed what would follow. The pictures on her Facebook page and cell phone didn't do her justice. He had managed to hack into her Android phone and helped himself to a few revealing selfies of her naked body that now adorned his bedroom walls. Everything on her was pink. He preferred the orange thong she had on last week. Against her brown skin, it looked like an orange needing to be peeled by his lips. The imagery made Garrett smile. Soon enough, Shante Combs would find out about everything he had done for her, and she would reciprocate his feelings. His watch beeped again to take his medication. It wasn't necessary. He was doing just fine without it. Love was the only drug he needed.

Shante sipped on a glass of red wine as she watched herself on *Ellen* on the small monitor in front of her. She shrieked out loud as the image of her twerking came across the screen. The sound of her shrieking made Garrett leap from his seat and he walked briskly towards her, but discovered why she shrieked and headed back to his seat. A few drops of wine had spilled on top of the partition attached to the back of the seat. Shante waved over one of the flight attendants over to wipe it for her. The attendant, a tall curvy black woman, who looked like the modern-day reincarnation of Foxy Brown, afro and all, gave Shante attitude with the rolling of the eyes, mumbling under her breath, but she complied because she was a professional. Waiting on asshole passengers without any home training was just another part of her job.

Terri Strawberry swore that if this ratchet bitch pressed the buzzer to request another glass of wine, she would be swallowing more than wine next time. Women like Shante Combs embarrassed her. Terri knew who she was—in fact, they were friends on Facebook, even though they had never ever had an actual conversation.

When the review for *A Woman Knows Her Place* went viral, and Terri realized that it was written by Shante Combs, it didn't really make any sense to her. The only books that this want-to-be ghetto superstar talked about on her page were *Selfish* by Kim K and *How to Be a Bad Bitch* by Amber Rose. All her news and current events came from gossip sites like mediatakeout.com and bossip.com. Reading Shante's updates always made Terri's eyes hurt because of all the misspelled words. But then she read Shante's review of Myles Bank's book that various websites had coined as *A Killer Review*. It was so well-written, it just didn't fit the image she had of Shante. If a writer can have one good book, then maybe she had gotten lucky and written the perfect review.

Somewhere in his Washington, DC apartment, Myles Banks was having another nightmare about the review. The words were jumping off the page and strangling him. No matter where he turned, they followed and tormented him. He couldn't live the rest of his life like this. This had to stop.

Russo after a few searches logged on to the internet and read the review. He now understood Myles Bank's anger. Earlier that evening, at the foot of the barstool, he found a leather bag with a laptop belonging to Myles Banks. A credit card bill had his address on it. Maybe he would deliver it himself, Russo thought. It would be nice to see how a fancy writer lives.

Larry Clarke stepped off the sidewalk right into an oncoming eighteen-wheeler truck. The last thing he saw before his head was squashed under the wheel like an exploding pumpkin was Shante Combs. A jumbo screen flashed an image of her twerking on television, and he realized it was the woman in pink. Just before the truck flattened him, Larry Clarke laughed for the first time in months. The last person he saw before he died was a fucking pop culture personality, a term coined for non-talented people. The universe can give you the middle finger, even on your way out.

"Waitress," Shante snapped her fingers at Terri as if she were at a poetry reading and giving snaps.

Terri's back was turned to Shante as she handed another passenger a cup of coffee. She bent over to pick up a packet of sugar, and made sure she gave Shante a full view of her black ass to kiss.

"I could have your job for that, waitress," Shante stared down Terri when she turned around.

"You don't want any of this—you fake ass want to be reality

star," Terri hissed as she towered over her rude passenger and felt the urge to bitch slap her fake Blac Chyna ass.

The other passengers pretended to be sleeping or reading, but were waiting for something to go down. Their cell phones locked and loaded, just in case.

"Don't be hating because you're just a waitress. You can tell your friends you brought me my wine," Shante smirked.

"You're lucky I need this job. Another time. Another place. You would feel the wrath of this black woman who would love to whoop your trifling ratchet black ass."

Garrett seated a few rows out of first class couldn't hear the heated conversation between the two women, but their body language was clear—it was time to rumble. He was about to get up and intervene. The flight attendant looked like she could handle herself. He wasn't too sure about Shante, his future wife. Luckily before hair could start flying all over the aisles, the captain saved the day, and maybe Shante's ass, by making an announcement about the arrival time.

"Don't let me catch your ass on the streets," Terri taunted Shante as she walked away.

"Just get me my wine, bitch. Save all that mess for when you get back to the projects to hang with your thots."

"That fame drug is just a mirage. It sucks the human right out of you, like fat from your ass. When your fifteen minutes are over, folks will move on to the next hot story. It's like a merry-go-round ride. It's just your turn for a ride, and then what? It's going to kill you to be a nobody again. I'll get your drink, but not because of some bullshit temporary fame. It's my job."

Before Shante could respond, the flight attendant, walked away with her head held high and back as stiff as a dick. Garrett kept his head down as she walked by. He didn't need anyone remembering his face.

Shante sipped on the extra sweet wine and smirked as the flight attendant walked away. That will show that heifer not to mess with me, Shante thought as she took another sip. They would be landing shortly and she couldn't wait to curl up in her own bed and fall asleep. Of course, she would first need to check her emails and all her social media accounts. Things change quickly in cyberspace. If you don't stay ahead of the crowd, you will get trampled or drown under the avalanche of public opinion.

An hour later flight 1520 made a perfect landing into Reagan

National Airport. The crowd cheered wildly. Shante Combs was out of her seat before the plane landed and was ready to deplane as soon as the cabin door opened. Terri knew it was pointless to ask her to sit back down; she smiled and told her to have a great evening as she strutted by her. *You're going to learn today*, Terri Strawberry thought to herself as she said goodbye to the other passengers.

Garrett quickly donned his black jacket, waited for Shante to deplane and hustled after her. Terri stared at the tall white man with frog eyes pushing his way through passengers. Rude people no longer surprised her anymore. She had a two-day layover and planned on getting laid. Her man better be ready to handle and release all her stress. The thought of having a man made her smile. He wasn't someone her friends and family would have chosen for her, but he was a good, hardworking man, and the most important thing, he treated her well. In the end, that's what a woman really wants. All the other stuff is secondary.

Two TSA agents, one man and a woman, waiting at the gate, approached Shante Combs as she disembarked and made her way through the terminal and into the airport.

"Ma'am, please come with us," they informed her sternly. They were flanking her on both sides, just in case she made a run for it. It would be hard to run in those pink high heels she was now wearing. TSA agents have seen everything under the sun, so someone running in heels wouldn't surprise them. Last week an elderly woman on a motor scooter tried engaging them in a high-speed chase as they walked slowly alongside her.

"What? What's wrong?"

"We would prefer to do this in private," the female agent told her.

"Not until you tell me what this is about?"

"We received information about a credible threat."

"Threat? What fucking threat?" Shante's voice got louder. A few people stared as they walked by, thankful that it wasn't them being interrogated. Garrett waited a few feet ahead, watching and knowing exactly what had happened.

The older male agent instantly disliked Shante. He had no patience for people who didn't respect authority. He stared at her through his glasses and one sleepy eye and his hands on his hips. The way he stood projected authority, at least that's what it looked like to him in his bedroom mirror.

"Ma'am, we can do this the easy way or the hard way," Stanley Johnson interrupted the dialogue between his colleague and the potential perp. The sooner you let people know who's in charge, the sooner they shut the fuck up and submit to you.

Shante sized up both agents and tried to decide if they were doing their good cop, bad cop routine. She has watched enough *Law & Order* to know this. She had nothing to hide. But these days you never know. Maybe someone slipped something in her bag while she napped. She was after all a celebrity and there was always someone looking to take down celebrities to push their own agenda. TMZ didn't seem to be around, so Shante relented and went peacefully with the agents.

"That'll teach you not to fuck with people who are serving you drinks and have access to the authorities," a familiar voice hissed into Shante's ear. Terri Strawberry sashayed away without turning around, giving Shante a full view of her ass once again, which hopefully would soon be getting some much needed attention from her boyfriend.

Three hours later after being strip searched and her bags tossed for contraband, Terri's friends released Shante. "They are called flight attendants and not waitresses," Stanley Johnson growled into Shante's ears as they released her. That bitch had gotten her good, Shante thought as she jumped into a cab and headed home. Making a stink about it would only cause her more trouble. The last thing she needed was to have every TSA agent in the country gunning for her whenever she flew. That kind of heat can mess up her money. She was pompous, but not stupid. Money before bullshit.

Incensed at having his plans changed because of some petty female beef, Garrett Green placed his plan on pause to deal with Myles and followed Terri's UBER cab, a gray Escapade, to her apartment building. It struck him as funny the randomness of the act he was about to commit for a woman who didn't even technically know he existed, but he knew everything about her. It's kind of romantic, if you really think about it. You don't even have to be a licensed detective anymore. Social media does it all for you, without even having to leave your home. It wasn't Terri's fault that Shante became a social media sensation who now felt entitled. If the flight attendant had just done what most people did with celebrities, which is to treat them like delicate gods, then he wouldn't be parked across the street from her home about to end her life. Sometimes having principles can get your ass killed.

Killing Terri hadn't been in his plans, but Garrett was sure it's what Shante would have wanted, after the embarrassment of being searched and detained by TSA. What kind of man would he be, if he didn't defend his woman's honor? Maybe later, when they were settled, he would confide in her everything he had done for her. She would be so grateful for all the risks he had taken. The thought of making her happy made Garrett smile. He wasn't sure of how he would enter her building, so he lingered across the street, cap pulled down, waiting. It was a nice neighborhood. Nobody would bother him or call the cops. He looked like he fit in. Half an hour later, he got lucky when a Chinese delivery man rang the doorbell of the apartment building.

"Delivery for Miss Terri," he said. Garrett smiled as he approached the young man. This must be his lucky night. The universe was making up for the snafu with Shante at the airport.

"Hey buddy, I got this. It's for my girlfriend, Terri." Garrett handed the young man a twenty. "Keep the change, buddy," Garrett said as he slipped inside the open front door. He slammed it shut before the delivery man could protest. The extra ten dollars bought his silence and Garrett listened intently as he drove away. He made a mental note of the Chinese restaurant's name, just in case the driver recalled seeing him and had to be dealt with. He scanned the bill and found her apartment number, 13B. The faster he can get this done, the faster he can get back to Shante. She needed him. It's good to feel needed by a woman.

The elevator creaked open. The hallway was empty. Someone on the floor was having Indian food. More than likely they ordered out also. People these days are too busy to cook their own meals. Something has been lost in the fabric of the American family, Garrett thought to himself as he found Terri's apartment. His Mom cooked a meal every evening for him, his brothers and father. They had family time to discuss school and any other problems. It was only after his parents divorced, family time stopped, and he began to act out and get into trouble. His father kept telling him to be responsible for his actions, while his Mom self-medicated herself on her secret booze stash under her bed. It wasn't too long, still a teenager, when Garrett ran away from home, never to return.

"Delivery," Garrett answered after he knocked on the door and Terri asked the obligatory question. He stood in front of the keyhole to obscure her view. Just as she opened her door, the elevator doors slid open. A teenager with headphones on, blasting the latest Adele CD walked by. It was enough to make Garrett want to kill him for playing that insipid song *Hello* that had hypnotized the entire world.

Temporarily distracted, Garrett turned to face Terri. He saw a glimmer of recognition in her eyes, but before she could connect the dots, he forced his way into her apartment. Her food splattered all over the wooden floor. The scent of fried rice and egg rolls reminded him that he hadn't eaten yet. She took off running and screaming towards her bedroom. Garrett stalked her, amused that she was trying to get away. Death had come to claim her and there was nowhere to hide.

She tried to frantically lock the door, but for some reason it wouldn't lock. No one ever thinks they will need the lock on their bedroom door to work. He kicked in the door and it slammed into Terri, sending her flying across the room and onto her bed.

"What do you want?" She screamed at Garrett. She knew his face and it wouldn't dawn on her until his hands were wrapped around her throat who he was. The passenger in 32B. Water no ice.

Her white robe was open. A flash of her pink thong caught his attention and she quickly covered up. It infuriated Garrett that she thought that lowly of him. He didn't need to be a pervert to see a woman naked.

"Don't make this difficult on yourself," he said calmly as he approached her. "I promise I will kill you fast, but only if you don't resist."

Terri's eyes glanced quickly towards the open nightstand drawer on the opposite side of the bed. Garrett noticed and knew what was in there. A woman who lives alone, usually has a weapon stashed somewhere close by, probably a gun or a knife. It would have been better if she kept it under her pillow. Lucky for him, she hadn't thought to do so.

"You might as well try and get it. In about thirty seconds you will be dead."

Terri lunged for the drawer, praying that it was true what people said. In times of crisis, superhuman strength flows through the human body to combat adversity. Her right hand slid into the open drawer. The coldness of the grip against the tip of her fingers gave her hope. Just as quickly her hope was extinguished. The intruder grabbed her by her ankles and dragged her back across the bed. Terri flipped over onto her back, kicking and screaming, but she was unable to break his bear trap grip. There wasn't any time to wonder why this was happening to her. She was completely exposed now. Robe open. No bra. Thong pushed to the side, exposing her vagina. She knew he didn't want to rape her, or else he wouldn't have hidden his face. Was this how her life ended?

He pounced on the bed. She noticed his dirty black boots on her silk red sheets. He was on top of her now. Knees spread across her chest. His crotch was close to her face. She lifted her head, mouth open, to do the only thing that will stop a man in this situation. He had done this before and anticipated her last desperate move to save her life by biting his dick. He punched her squarely in her face. The pain wouldn't register for another few seconds. She would be dead by then.

"You should have just done your fucking job." His hands were wrapped around her throat now. "All you had to do was give her what she wanted. What she was entitled to, but you got your TSA buddies to humiliate her." His hands were strong and crushing her windpipe. Soon she would black out. She pummeled his body, but it was like a feather bouncing off a concrete wall. "Maybe next time you will think twice." He smiled at his own joke and stared into her eyes. He wanted his face to be the last one she saw before she took her last breath.

The last thought Terri had as she went limp was wishing she had slapped the shit out of Shante Combs. All that was left was darkness. She had no more thoughts, no more regrets. Death had welcomed her home.

Garrett stared at her face, beautiful in death. He brushed loose strands of hair away from her face and wanted to kiss her, but he didn't. Even the dead deserve a little bit of respect. He closed her robe to hide her privates when she was finally discovered by the police. Whoever found her shouldn't see her exposed. It's just not right. He slid off the bed and heard the front door close. A man shouted her name. His voice wasn't concerned yet, even though there was Chinese food all over the floor. Garrett reached into the open drawer and pulled out a 9mm gun. He made sure it was loaded because it's been his experience that women overlook things like that. They don't forget their makeup or any other useless things, but something as important as loading a weapon can be overlooked.

Something was off, but Russo couldn't quite place what was wrong. The spilled Chinese food on the floor gave him pause as he called out to Terri. The apartment was too quiet. After a long flight, she was usually blasting Guns N' Roses or Aerosmith. A black chick who loves rock music. It was almost enough to make him fall in love with her during the flight when she told him that. They talked about music throughout the five-hour flight from Seattle to DC. Her smile made him feel special and that everything would always be okay. That was a year ago. He set the leather laptop bag belonging to Myles Banks on the floor and called for Terri again. Maybe she was in the shower. No music. The bathroom door in the hallway was open. The usual flowery scent of her shower gel didn't entice his senses. Something was amiss. He removed his gun from its holster and approached her bedroom. He exhaled when he saw on the bed, fast asleep. Watching her sleep always relaxed him. The way she softly snored made him laugh. He approached the bed and holstered his gun. He called her name softly and sat next to her. He leaned down to kiss her lips. They were cold. She was not breathing. He searched her body for any wounds, nothing. His mind was racing. This made no sense as he cradled her in his arms, tears stinging his eyes. He closed his eyes, inhaled her scent and reminisced about their first conversation on the flight from Seattle to DC. He had fallen in love with her in less than five hours, but didn't want to admit it. Love was not supposed to happen that fast. It's the kind of stuff you saw in movies, but he was proof that love isn't about the length of time spent together, but simply based on circumstance and opportunity. He never heard Garrett's footsteps approaching the bed or heard the click of the gun. The music of his memories was playing in his mind. There was a bright flash of noise, and then nothing. His life ended in mid-tear.

Garrett stepped back to admire his handiwork. He wasn't worried about getting caught. The only person that might recognize him was the Chinese delivery man. Immigrants tended to mind their business. They didn't come to America to get killed over somebody else's problems. So, he was pretty sure the delivery man would keep his mouth shut. Before leaving he made sure he hadn't dropped anything. He didn't want to be one of those stupid killers or burglars who somehow forget their wallet at the scene of the crime.

It would be a few days before their bodies were found. He would be long gone by that time. Garrett stopped in his tracks when he approached the front door and stared down at the monographed black lettering of the leather laptop bag. MYLES A. BANKS. It seemed too good to be true. Was this a setup or just pure dumb luck? Six degrees of separation. He bent down and fondled the lettering with his fingertips. How did the stewardess' boyfriend end up with the bag of a famous writer? He opened the bag and inside was a laptop, a copy of *Animal Farm* by George Orwell and a nametag with his phone number and address. Garrett thumbed through the novel while munching on an egg roll that was on the floor. He vaguely remembered hearing about *Animal Farm*, but never read it. Gun magazines were more his reading style. Don't get cocky, he reminded himself as he quickly packed up the leather bag, placed it on his shoulder and exited the apartment. Next stop was Shante's hotel room. It was time she met her secret angel. Maybe he could kill two birds with one stone and prove to her that he was the man of her dreams.

The hot water felt good on her skin. *Hotline Bling* by Drake was on repeat. It was her jam. That fine ass light skin motherfucker could go from 0 to 100 on her pussy any day of the week. Just before stepping in the shower, she received a call from a reporter at *Rolling Stone* magazine, wanting to do a story on her. It might even garner the cover, he had said. The story would be about the explosion of viral videos and how most consumers watched television shows in this age of social media. The centerpiece of the story would of course be her. It would give her a chance to reach a whole new audience and expand her brand. Excited at the prospect of being interviewed and photographed, Shante had insisted that the reporter come to her hotel room, when he told her that he was on his way out of town and would not be back for another two weeks. Media moves at the speed of light. She knew two weeks would be too long. She was hot now, and she had to capitalize on her moment in the spotlight. The social media generation is a fickle bunch. Love you in the morning and by lunchtime, you're old news. It flattered her ego that the reporter, Garrett Green, had watched her interview on *Ellen* and a few other television spots she had done. He would be there in an hour. Keep it simple, he had told her. Let America see you as a real person and not a cookie cutter celebrity. *You're special* he had said before hanging up. His heartfelt words had made her blush as she continued to sing along to *Hotline Bling*.

"Hello, Myles Banks? Is this Myles Banks the famous writer?"

"Who is this? How did you get this fucking number?"

Myles' face was buried under a pillow, hoping the phone call was a dream and he could get back to sleeping. Snippets of the evening flashed in his mind, but he wasn't sure if it really happened, or maybe his imagination was playing tricks on him.

"Wow, Myles Banks," Garrett did his best to sound like a groupie. "My name is Garrett Green, and I found your laptop bag at *The Last Shot*. I knew I had to get it back to you. We writers have to stick together. Right, Mr. Banks?"

Myles groaned as he sat up in bed, naked. There was a stench in the air that he rather not remember where it came from. He looked around the pile of clothes on the floor and then walked around his apartment searching for his bag. "Shit!" he screamed into his cell phone. In his drunken stupor, he had forgotten his bag at the bar.

"Don't worry, Mr. Banks. Your bag is safe. I will kick some serious ass if anyone tries to take this bag away from me."

"I appreciate that. Where can I meet you to get it back?"

"You can meet me at The Jefferson on 16th Street NW."

"Okay. I've stayed there before. Beautiful place."

"In an hour?"

"Sounds good."

"Looking forward to meeting you and returning your bag, Mr. Banks."

"Thanks kid."

Garrett pulled into a garage two blocks away from the hotel after hanging up his cell phone. Two blocks was a safe distance, not too far or too close, if everything went as planned. He walked briskly to the hotel. A homeless man begged him for fifty cents. He wondered why he set his sight so low. That's the problem with the homeless; they don't know how to exploit their situation for maximum sympathy. He continued walking without breaking stride. He had gone over every variable in his plan and it excited him that the finish line was near. He could finally reveal himself to Shante as the man behind the curtain. Her reaction might be shock at first, but he fully expected her to appreciate all the sacrifices he had made, all in the name of love. Women say men don't know how to plan and show their appreciation. Garrett knew he would be the perfect boyfriend. He had been planning and preparing for a life with Shante. He smiled as he entered the elevator and pressed her floor. It was time to put his plan in motion.

Feeling refreshed after a nice hot shower, Shante put on a sexy black negligee under her fluffy white robe. Both felt good against her skin. It reminded her of how long it had been since a man touched her. Dildos can only do so much. They can't whisper nasty things in your ears and pin you down in bed as you are having an orgasm. A dildo was built for pleasure, but it can't interpret a woman's moods and desires. A man, even at his worst, has a better chance satisfying that need, even when it seems like they don't have a fucking clue.

Shante popped open the complimentary bottle of champagne and flipped to her favorite show, *Keeping Up with the Kardashians*. Kim was her mentor. She had studied her career the same way Kobe had studied and copied Michael. If you're going to steal, you might as well steal from the best. The public looks at Kim Kardashian as a selfie porn queen without any talent because all she does is exploit her body for fame and fortune. Talent doesn't keep you at the top. Talent is the least desirable commodity in today's entertainment world. It's good if you have it and nice to put down on your resume, but at the end of the day, creating a buzz is what sells. Who has more talent Jill Scott or Kim K? It's a ridiculous question to ask, but who does America and the world care about? Nobody does it better than KK.

A knock at the door distracted Shante's attention from her show. Someone always seemed to either text, call or knock on your door when you're about to relax and watch your favorite show. It's like they know what you're about to do and will do anything to stop you from enjoying yourself. As she walked away, she heard Kim telling Kanye, "when you really want something, you just have to go get it. Getting to the top isn't always easy. Sometimes it's downright ugly, but winners like us understand it's the price of fame and we will do *anything* to get it."

"Who is it?" Shante asked as she peeped through the peephole.

"It's me, Garrett Green. We spoke earlier about the *Rolling Stone* interview."

She couldn't really see his face. He was too tall, but she could see that he was wearing a brownish suit with a laptop bag on his shoulder, and another bag in his right hand. Shante closed her robe and opened the door. She stared up at the tall, thin white man with glasses, big eyes and shaggy blonde hair. He kind of reminded her of Shaggy from the Scooby Doo cartoon series. His smile wasn't much of a smile. It seemed practiced, as if he didn't know how to convey it properly. Under normal circumstances, she would never let a stranger into her hotel room, but he was dressed properly, credentialed, wearing glasses and white.

"Thank you for coming over, Mr. Green."

"Call me, Garrett."

"Okay, Garrett. You can call me Shante."

Garrett stepped into her hotel room and gave her his jacket to hang up. He made sure that Myles Banks' monogrammed name on the laptop bag faced inward. Garrett looked around the room. It was a standard hotel room, king-sized bed, flat screen television, a small couch, and a table with a chair.

"You mind if I set up over there," he pointed to the table."

"Yeah, that's fine."

"Did you expect any of this? Being on television, people wanting your autograph and being interviewed for *Rolling Stone*? It's a lot to take in, I would imagine. You're a star," Garrett continued to stroke Shante's massive ego. "If you play this right, you could get your own reality television show."

Shante's eyes opened wide and she blushed. "You really think so? It does feel natural, as if this is what I was born to do."

Garrett placed his camera on a tripod, pointed it at the bed where Shante was sitting down. The red light came on and started to record. He could tell she was warming up to him. It was his first time being this close to her. His hands trembled slightly as he pulled out a recorder to tape his fake interview. He didn't want to appear too nervous. Nervous, strange men frighten women. The scent of her perfume calmed him down as he inhaled her and it aroused him. Luckily his back was to her, and by the time he turned around, his erection had faded.

"When opportunity knocks you have to kick the door in," Garrett stared at her on the bed, sipping champagne. She was even more beautiful, now that he could see her up close, instead of through a pair of binoculars. He wanted to open her robe, see what she had on underneath. Maybe she was naked. Her brown skin reminded him of honey. He swallowed hard and imagined her taste sliding down his throat. It had been too long since he had made love to a woman. He was saving himself for Shante. She deserved the best and he wanted to give it to her.

"I plan on doing whatever it takes to get my celebrity on. If Kim and Amber can do it, then so can I."

"You can do anything you want, Shante. I believe in you."

"That's sweet of you, Garrett."

Garrett stared at her intently and then smiled. This time it was genuine. "So, tell me about Shante Combs." He turned the recorder and camera on and took a seat. He listened as she rambled on and kept on sipping on his glass of champagne. Her body relaxed. A sliver of her cleavage was revealed. Underneath her robe, he noticed the lacey black material. It must be something new. She hadn't worn it before in her apartment. Women only buy a new negligee to make them feel sexy or for a new man. The idea of another man touching his Shante made Garrett clench his fists, and if Shante hadn't turned her face, she would have seen the storm brewing in his eyes. By the time she turned back, his affable demeanor had returned.

"So how do you feel about being a celebrity?"

"I like being on television. I just did *The Ellen Show*."

"Yes, I saw that. You were a natural," Garrett gushed like a love-struck boyfriend. "And when you started twerking, I stood up in my seat and cheered."

He realized he had said too much and hoped she didn't fully comprehend what he said.

"Wait. Were you in the audience?"

Without missing a beat, Garrett responded, "I was at a bar with a few guys and we stood up to cheer you on. It was beautiful. Nicki, Rihanna and Beyoncé have nothing on you. When Ellen tried to twerk, it was hilarious."

The look on Shante's face told Garrett he had reeled her in. A few well-placed compliments can melt away the ice and allow you to get close to someone. It cuts through the red tape of conversation and gifts. He knew Shante was an attention whore. Always posting pictures of herself on Facebook and Instagram in bathing suits and every new outfit she bought. She craved the attention of her followers. If one photo didn't garner enough likes, she would delete it and quickly replace it with something more risqué. A woman like that isn't too hard to figure out and find her weak points of vanity.

"That was so much fun. The traffic on my Facebook page doubled after that. I have Wendy Williams next and my agent is trying to get me on Oprah. It's crazy. Can you believe it?" She took another swallow of champagne and raised her hands in triumph. "All of this because of some damn review that went viral."

"It was a very cutting review. You let that writer have it and you didn't hold anything back."

Garrett said as he stood up and Shante averted his eyes. Her red lipstick stained the glass. He wanted to trace his fingertip around it. Let the color seep into his skin and lick his finger. The thought made him shiver slightly, but not enough for her to notice.

"It was just some dumb review I wrote. I was shocked when the other blogs picked it up."

"It was a masterpiece," Garrett couldn't help himself from proudly saying.

"I could have done better, but I was hung over when I posted it."

The muscles in Garrett's jaw tightened. He tried to smile, to keep it light.

"That review was perfect." His voice was low, almost threatening.

Three glasses of champagne had dulled her senses, lowered her inhibitions.

"It's the kind of stuff that amateur writers write and think it's literary fiction. You're acting as if someone gave you a bad review," Shante said jokingly.

"You are. I wrote the review you're telling the world that you wrote. It's my words that made you famous."

"You what?" Shante's eyes opened wide and the energy in the room shifted. "How could you write something I wrote on my computer, genius?"

Garrett towered over her now and for the first time, she noticed how intense he was. She shrank back onto the bed, raised her feet up and the rest of the champagne spilled onto the sheet.

"It didn't take much effort to hack into your computer. I sent you a fake link about those reality bimbos and when you clicked on it, you downloaded my spyware into your laptop."

"What? Spyware? I don't know what the fuck is going on, but you need to get the fuck out my room now—sicko pervert!"

"After everything I've done for you," Garrett sat on the bed, with his back facing Shante. "If it wasn't for me you wouldn't be on television and the toast of social media. I did that. I gave you everything you have now. I deleted that pathetic review you wrote. It was littered with a ton of misspellings and improper grammar usage. I stayed up all night, rewriting it, while watching you sleep on video. Everything I've done is for you. I love you, Shante." Garrett turned his head to face her and stretched his hand out towards her, but she recoiled.

"Leave now and I won't scream for security," she threatened him.

"Shante, I won't hurt you—unless you make me. Close your robe. I want to see you naked when you're ready," he said as he stared up at the ceiling calmly. "I love this bed. It's so soft." He rolled over just in time to see Shante scampering off the bed and making a run for the door. Garrett leaped off the bed and was quite fast and agile for a tall man. Before Shante could make it to the door, he grabbed her in a headlock with his left hand, whipped his gun out and pressed it against her right temple. "Before you can finish screaming you will be dead," he warned her. She was gasping for breath, but nodded her head. A gun pressed against your temple will make you see things clearly. She had allowed a lunatic into her hotel room. He was either going to rape or kill her, unless she calmed down and found a way to get on his good side. "Now that you're calm and-." A knock at the door interrupted his thoughts. "Keep quiet," he whispered in her ear. "You make one sound and *boom.*" Shante flinched but managed to nod her head vigorously.

"Who is it?" Garrett asked. He already knew who was at the door. Myles Banks might be many things, an asshole even, but at least he was a prompt asshole.

"It's Myles Banks. We spoke earlier on the phone. You found my laptop bag at the bar."

"Oh God," Shante said, barely above a whisper, "It's him." Two men, who had been stalking her, one unknown to her, were now in the same place. *This can't be happening,* she thought. *It's like a bad reality show meeting an even worse campy horror movie.*

"This is all for you," Garrett mouthed to her. He turned her around and they were now face to face. "You will see how much I love you."

"Hold on Mr. Banks. I'm in the bathroom. Give me a minute," Garrett shouted as he ushered Shante away from the door and back to the bed. "Now, please be quiet and sit here like a good girl while I deal with Mr. Banks." There was a glint of evil in his eyes as he spoke. It reminded her of everything she was scared of embodied in one person. "I will explain everything after Mr. Banks has paid for all the vile things he said about you. The same way I took care of the stewardess at the airport."

A puzzled look crossed Shante's face, then a look of horror as she covered her mouth. She didn't have to ask him what he did. It was written all over his sick, crazy face. There was another knock at the door, this time more incessant and impatient. Myles Banks wasn't used to being made to wait in a hotel corridor. Garrett pointed the gun directly between Shante's eyes, smiled, then walked briskly towards the door, with his right hand behind his back.

The hotel door swung open and one of the most intimidating white men that Myles had laid eyes on filled the door frame. He briefly wondered if this was good idea, but he needed to get his laptop bag back. He had notes on his laptop for his next novel which he hoped to get published, once this whole Shante Combs hatchet job blew over. He found it a bit off putting that the frog eyed man didn't extend his hand for a greeting as he entered the room, but he didn't let it bother him. This should take no longer than five minutes.

"I appreciate you returning my bag," Myles said casually as he walked ahead of the stranger. "Maybe you would like an autograph," he laughed, but it wasn't an enthusiastic laugh. He was not used to making small talk.

"I don't need an autograph. I will tell you what I need, Mr. Banks."

Before Myles could respond, he stared straight ahead and saw a familiar face on the bed. At first, the shock of seeing her didn't register who he was staring at. Then it dawned on him.

"What the fuck is going on here?" He turned around angrily to face the man known as Garrett Green. "You better explain this shi-"

"It's quite simple, Mr. Banks," Garrett pointed the gun at his face. Shocked, Myles put his hands up and backed up closer to the bed. "I'm sure you know Shante Combs. You've been sending her harassing text and email messages. You've basically been stalking her, and it ends today. I cannot have you traumatizing my future wife. You owe her an apology."

Speechless, Myles stared at Garrett and then Shante. His mind was whirling, trying to assess the situation. They didn't seem to be in cahoots. The bitch who ruined his career body language told him she was scared of the maniac with the gun. For some reason there was a camera pointed at all three of them. Maybe they were having sex, but it didn't seem likely. To make matters worse, the annoying voice of Kim Kardashian was on the television blabbering about selfies. It was the first time Myles had ever heard her speak.

"Listen, fella."

"I've given you respect by calling you Mr. Banks. Please, do the same."

"Okay," Myles exhaled to calm himself, "Mr. Green."

"Garrett is fine. Mr. Green is my dad. May the Devil rest his soul, "Garrett smiled, as if he was reminiscing."

"Okay—Garrett. Not sure what's going on here—and I don't really care or want to know. I'm not sure if you know, but this bitch-"

Before Myles could continue, Garrett slammed the butt of the gun against the right side of his face. The blow caught Myles by surprise and he staggered backwards, but didn't go down. Blood trickled from his cheek.

"Don't insult the lady."

Even though Shante knew this guy was sick and had already killed someone in her name, it made her feel good that he was sticking up for her. Black men didn't stick up for their women anymore. They were too busy chasing snow bunnies and assimilating. Having a crazy, bug-eyed white man fight for her wasn't the worst thing in the world.

Myles regained his composure and his angry stare bored into the man waving a gun at his face. It had been a rough two weeks. Being the target of ridicule on social media. Being shunned by his contemporaries like Dickey, K'wan and Mosley hurt him the most. All three writers had unfriended him on Facebook and blocked him on Instagram and Twitter. And this stupid bitch had gotten famous by making a mockery of his work. It had gotten so ridiculous that publishing companies were now in a bidding war to publish her fucking memoir. What memoir! Her memoir should be a meme on toilet paper to wipe his black ass and flush down the fucking toilet. He was trying to remain calm, but the injustices perpetrated against him were spiking his blood pressure. Every time you try to get ahead, someone tries to steal your light and bury you in darkness. And now, of all things, he had an insane white man pointing a gun at him, demanding a fucking apology to someone he just wanted to smack around—until she apologized for fucking up his life. Myles Banks had had enough. They were not in Florida, but he made up his mind to stand his ground.

"She's no fucking lady. And there's no way I'm apologizing for shit," Myles growled as he stared down Garrett.

His heart was beating too fast for him to hear all his words. All he saw was the gun pointed directly at his forehead, a serene smile on the maniac's face and somewhere in the background; he heard Shante Combs screaming. Momentarily distracted by her screams, Garrett turned to look at her, while still pointing the gun at Myles. It was now or never. Myles lunged at a surprised Garrett and both men toppled to the floor. The gun fell on the carpet, a few feet away. Myles landed on top of Garrett, and he didn't need much incentive to start pummeling his face with both fists. His hands felt like the size of boxing gloves and blood was streaming from Garrett's face, but he hadn't made a sound or tried to defend himself. The next two blows broke his nose and the sickening sound of broken teeth meeting a black fist echoed throughout the room.

"That'll teach you not to fuck with someone you don't know," Myles screamed down at Garrett's bloodied and broken face. He was breathing hard. This was the most exercise he's had in weeks and he was sweating profusely through his blue shirt and jacket. Before he could get up and look for the gun, the full force of Garrett's knee connected with his crotch, toppling Myles over as he screamed in pain and reached for his balls. Both men felt like they had been run over by a truck. The pain made Myles roll over a few times, until he was on his back, next to the bed and Garrett was now standing over him.

"You're a dead man," Garrett screamed as he stomped his right foot into Myles' stomach as his eyes frantically searched for his gun.

Myles turned his face towards the bed and his right hand stretched under the bed. His fingers curled around the trigger of the gun. He whipped it out and pointed it at a surprised Garrett.

"You don't have the balls to shoot me. You're just a fucking writer who writes about shit you know nothing about," Garrett taunted him.

He lifted his foot to stomp on Myles again, but he heard the crackle of a gunshot and grabbed his throat. Blood was spilling from his mouth and over his two hands clasped around his neck. He spun around looking for Shante and stretched a bloody hand towards her. He tried to speak, but the words wouldn't come, only more blood. He knew he was about to die. This is not how he planned it. He wanted Myles to be his traveling company on this journey to hell. His feet got tangled with Myles', who was still on the floor and Garrett toppled forward like a sawed-off tree. The dresser broke his fall as his forehead crashed into the edge of it. A sickening sound of bone meeting wood made both Shante and Myles grimace in pain. Garrett tumbled to the floor, face up, next to Myles. His eyes were open and vacant of life.

Myles staggered to his feet with the gun in his right hand. Shante was in the middle of the bed, scared and not saying anything. For a second, he felt sympathy for her, but then he remembered what she had done to him. A fleeting thought crossed his mind as he stared at her, and she read his thoughts, but common decency prevailed on him and he tossed the gun on the bed.

"I didn't mean to kill him," he said into the camera. The camera was still recording. "It was either me or him. It's all your fucking fault," Myles turned to Shante and screamed at her. He slumped over and sat down in the chair next to the camera. He leaned forward and buried his face in his palms.

"I'm sorry. I never meant for any of this to happen. That sicko hacked my email, rewrote my review and posted it online."

Myles looked up at Shante. "You didn't write it?" He said incredulously. "So why the fuck did you take credit for it, making money off my misery and doing all these damn television shows?"

"I couldn't turn down the opportunity," Shante responded honestly. "It fell into my lap and I had to get everything I could out of it. You would have done the same thing."

"No. I would have never done that. You're despicable." He rose to his feet, unsure of what he would do next. In front of him was the source of all his troubles and the solution was a bullet away.

Shante had been around a few unstable men before. She knew when they had lost touch with reality and reasoning with them was pointless. It was either him or her. Just as he lunged forward to reach for the gun, she did the same thing. She was quicker than him and it was closer to her. An ex-boyfriend taught her how to shoot for protection, even though he was the one she needed protection from. She reached for it with both hands and then toppled backwards against the headboard as she pulled the trigger. All three shots found its mark, and Myles fell forward onto the bed, motionless. Shante kept the gun trained on him, just in case, but it wasn't necessary. The writer known as Myles Banks had written his last word.

Two dead men in her hotel room. The smoking gun in her hand. Would the cops believe her? Would the press and social media crucify her? Shante stared directly into the camera and started to cry. A few minutes later the police broke down the door and entered the room. Shante reached for Officer Wells, a strapping rookie cop with movie star looks. When the leaked video went viral on social media the following week, Officer Wells became an overnight celebrity. The image of Shante wrapped in his arms as he carried her to the gurney made women swoon. He had to take a leave of absence because his precinct was flooded with false calls in hopes that Officer Wells would come to the rescue.

The media and social media vilified Garrett Green. Lost in his vilification was credit for writing the review and having the camera turned on in Shante's hotel room. His story didn't fit the narrative, so he was soon a footnote and forgotten.

Myles Banks, *A Woman Knows Her Place* skyrocketed to the top of Best Sellers list. Amazon and Barnes & Noble couldn't keep up with the demand. It turned out that his book was satire on the role of how women are treated in today's society. Women groups were calling him a modern-day feminist. The tagline for the upcoming movie was *a bad review can get you killed.* Without the review, the book wouldn't have gone viral. Myles Banks would have been just another excellent writer the public never heard about.

Two dead men in a hotel room became an afterthought, an anecdote in the Shante Combs story. Andy Warhol had it wrong. In the social media age, fifteen minutes of fame can be extended past the point of being necessary. Keep feeding the public what they want, bit by bit, and few months of fame becomes the new criteria for fifteen minutes. You build your brand from fifteen minutes and it can sustain you for a lifetime. It's the legacy of The Kardashian clan and Shante Combs was making sure to follow the blueprint laid out by her mentor.

"So, what's next for you, Shante," Oprah asked the reviewer turned reality and social media superstar.

Weaved down to her ass after losing thirty pounds and a few minor physical enhancements, the new Shante Combs stared into the camera and said, "maybe I will write a book, Oprah. It doesn't seem that hard. Look what I did for what's his name." The audience lapped it up like trained seals and Shante gave her practiced coy smile. In a few months, she would be forgotten and replaced with the next media sensation of the moment shoved in front of America to love and then rip apart. But for now, she was a star, whatever that meant these days, without any discernible talent, except the good luck of going viral in a cyber-world that's not real, but inhabited by millions of voyeurs looking for their fifteen minutes of fame, by any means necessary.

WE LOVE OUR CHILDREN TOO

G eraldine Banton had been a fighter all her life. Against her father's wishes, she had left home at nineteen and emigrated from St. Lucia to New York in the sixties while everyone else was either going to England or the Caribbean. She had a plan for her future. College. Marriage. Kids. She worked two jobs, sometimes three, while attending college and graduated from NYU with a degree in Finance. Four years later, she was married. A year after that, her angel, Lucien was born. When Lucien was four, her husband was killed by a mugger on his way home from work. Lucien became her life. Nothing else mattered except to make sure he had everything a child could need and more. She became his mother and father. She was the one who taught him how to tie a tie. She was the one who told him about sex and taught him how to drive. She was the one he came home crying to in high school when that stupid girl broke his heart. She never told him, but a few days after, she went down to the record store where the stupid girl worked and gave her a piece of her mind. And through everything, no son could have made a mother prouder than Geraldine was of her son. When he graduated from her alma mater, she screamed, stomped and cried when his name was announced. Every sacrifice had been worth it. She only wished his father had lived to see his son grow into a man and claim his place in the world.

"You are embarrassing me, Mama," he had said. She hugged him tightly as he laughed with his friends. But the tone in his voice told her he didn't mind at all.

"No mother could ask for a better son," she had whispered in his ear as tears continued to flow. "And no son could ask for a better mom," he had whispered back. He dabbed her eyes with the corner of his fingertips. Then lifted her into his arms as all of his friends cheered her on as they captured their special moment on their cellphones. If Geraldine could have somehow known it would be the last time she would see her son alive, she would have held on to him with all the love a mother feels for her child. She would have moved heaven and earth to keep him safe. But life operates on its own schedule. Foresight only deepens our guilt and leaves us with a sense of displacement and yearning for closure that will never come.

The August heat had settled into the earth, but the air was still humid by the time Geraldine drove home and pulled into her driveway on DeReimer Avenue in the Bronx. The streetlights hadn't come on as yet, so the streets still had children riding their bikes and teenagers milling around on their phones and getting into mischief. She had lived on the same block for thirty years and had known many of the families. But over the years, most had moved away after retiring and others had passed on. Geraldine avoided a crack in the pavement and remembered a time when the front tire of Lucien's bicycle had stuck in it and he went flying over the handlebar. His elbows and knees were bruised, but he hadn't cried in front of his friends. That was him, always tough and never showing any weakness. It was how she raised him to be. A single woman raising a black son cannot raise him to be weak. She has to instill in him a sense of compassion, but also an edge as sharp as a sword, so the world would not exploit his believed deficiency. No one had shown her how to do this. Back in her day there wasn't any self-help books, Oprah or Iyanla Vanzant on how to raise a black boy in America. She recalled the lessons her father had taught her brothers as boys and applied his teachings to her son. It had been good enough for her family, so it was good enough for her son. She closed the front door and was greeted by the silence of the house. It made her sad that no one was there waiting for her. Maybe now she would join one of those dating sites. The thought made her laugh as she dropped her purse on the couch and went into the kitchen to make a cup of cinnamon tea.

A few hours later, unsure if she was dreaming or awake, Geraldine turned on the lamp next to her bed and reached for her vibrating cellphone. Her alarm clock displayed fifteen minutes after three. By the time she answered, the call had disconnected. Then the house phone rang and it echoed throughout the quiet house. Fully awake now, Geraldine ran downstairs to the living room, already knowing, her life would never be the same.

The stranger's voice on the other end of the phone said her full name, but she didn't respond. Geraldine gripped the handle of the phone so tightly, her fingers ached. The monotone voice said her name again. It wasn't his first time making a phone call like this, so he knew that at this time of the morning, mothers know a phone call only carries bad news from the police. He spoke slowly, trying to put himself in her shoes, even though he couldn't and delivered the news that every parent dreads to hear. News he had delivered too often and always left him depressed days after. Detective Warren Staples had listened to the anguished screams of many mothers and fathers over his twenty years in the NYPD, but the sound he heard that morning from Geraldine Banton would stay with him for the rest of his life. It's the sound he would sometimes hear in his quiet moments as he sipped coffee on his front porch and he could still see her, slumped to the floor, defeated. The grandkids would be running around and his thoughts would find their way to that evening and everything that came after. But for now, he had a job to do, so he holstered his feelings and continued delivering the bad news.

Shot.

Dead.

Lucien.

Tragic.

Geraldine heard the words coming through the phone from the policeman's mouth. It felt like she was trying to put together a jigsaw puzzle to understand the full picture of what he was saying. Her body slumped to the floor, still clutching the phone to her ear. This had to be a mistake. She could still hear his laughter echoing in her ears at his graduation earlier. A laughter like that, so filled with life, just cannot be extinguished, never to be heard again. *This had to be a mistake.*

The world had changed when Geraldine stepped out of her home and jumped into the police cruiser that Detective Staples had dispatched to her home. He had instinctively known that she would be unable to drive. There was no need to compound a tragedy with another avoidable tragedy.

The cold air in the morgue clung to Geraldine's skin like death as she followed the Medical Examiner down a dark hallway. There was no preparing for something like this. This happened to other people. You saw it in the movies and on television. It wasn't real, until it happened to you.

"You don't have to view the body now," the young medical examiner told her before entering the room. "We have a photograph."

"I need to see my son."

The tone of her voice told the M.E. he would not be able to deter her. He stepped aside and directed her to the covered body of her son on the gurney. It was only his second week on the job and even though this was something Justin Monroe had trained for, the reality of the job was vastly different from working in a lab. Here was a mother about to view her dead son, and he was sure she was hoping that somehow a mistake had been made. That's why she wanted to see the body and not just a photograph. He slowly pulled down the white sheet covering the young man's face and then stood aside, hands clasped in front of him and waited for the inevitable.

Geraldine had prepared herself for what she believed would happen, but seeing her beautiful baby boy's eyes closed with three bullets in his chest made her stagger backwards. A few hours ago he was alive and looking forward to a bright future, now, he was a crime statistic, another black male's potential cut short. The M.E., standing behind her had been quick enough to catch Geraldine and help her to stand upright. She reached hesitantly to touch his face. It still felt like him, as if he were sleeping and would wake up at any second. Geraldine leaned over and rested her face against her son's chest where one of the bullets had stolen his life. "Wake up, baby. Mama is here now. Wake up, please," she whispered into his chest. Justin Monroe bowed his head in an effort to give her some privacy. The heart wrenching words touched a chord in him as he fought back his own memories. He wondered how many more times he would see this exact scene playing out and would he ever become desensitized to the grief of death. A month later, after seeing numerous gunshot wounds, M.E. Justin Monroe quit and started driving Uber.

The best that Geraldine could gather over the next few days was that Lucien was driving home when he was pulled over for running a red light. According to the Officer who shot her son, his partner backed the account, Lucien, unprovoked, became belligerent as they questioned him and asked him to exit the vehicle to take a sobriety test. Her son didn't drink, not even beer, so Geraldine was already suspicious of the two officers' account that was relayed to her by Detective Staples. According to the police officers, Lucien was told multiple times to adhere to their instructions, but at some point during the exchange between the officers and her son, they felt threatened and one of them had drawn his weapon and killed her son in self-defense. According to the NYPD, the bodycam had somehow malfunctioned minutes before the incident. An investigation into why it malfunctioned was being launched in a separate unit in the department. When the autopsy was performed on the deceased, as expected by his mother and friends, his blood alcohol level was zero.

"How do you explain this?" Geraldine asked Detective Staples. "Your detectives told a story that I knew to be untrue and now it's proven to be so. "You have children, Detective Staples?" Geraldine glanced at the family portrait on the wall behind of him, "What would you think if this was your child?"

"As a parent I would be outraged because it seems as if something went tragically wrong. But as a police officer, I have to believe that the policeman in question followed protocol."

"It's quite convenient that the methods put in place by your department have failed to work, once again."

Detective Staples winced visibly at the accusation. The lack of a video from either the dash cam or the bodycam was troubling. It wasn't an indication of guilt or innocence, but the optics, given the climate of police altercations with black motorists, left the department in an untenable position. The woman standing before him had seemingly aged twenty years in the last few days since he last saw her. Her no nonsense posture and stern brown eyes behind her glasses made him think of his own wife. Mothers protect their children, and when they no longer can, they make sure that their memory isn't sullied.

"I understand your anger, but please wait for the investigation to be completed. Tensions are already high and any speculation could only further enflame it."

"You seem like a nice man, Detective Staples. I am sure other nice, well-meaning policemen like yourself told the mothers of Tamir Rice, Michael Brown, Eric Garner, Walter Scott, Freddie Gray, Alton Sterling, Terence Crutcher, Chandra Weaver and Sandra Bland to wait for justice. They are still waiting. Of the cases I just mentioned, how many officers were convicted? The law of averages tell you that at least one of them should have been convicted. How many went to jail?"

Detective Staples pursed his lips. He exhaled deeply and looked around his tiny office as if an answer would magically materialize.

He stared at a picture of his son, a college graduate this year and knew what his reaction would have been if the roles were reversed. Every police department knew the answer to that question Lucien Banton's mom was asking. He feared sometimes if he dug too deeply, the answers would disturb him greatly and make him question everything he believed in as an officer. But looking away from what appeared to be a systemic problem was only passing the buck to the next generation of police officers.

"Life is filled with loss. You just have to make your loss count for something. I intend on doing just that." There was something ominous in her voice that made the hair on his arms stand up. It wasn't exactly a threat, but the resolute belief of a mother that her son's life wouldn't end on a dirty New York street in a pool of his own blood.

The predictable uproar of a police cover-up soon followed. It was answered by an even more predictable response from the NYPD. Everyone called for calm, a few lone voices wanted street justice. Memories of the violence that had taken place in Ferguson and across the country was still raw in the minds of the minority communities. Geraldine stopped watching the news, reading the newspapers and answering her doorbell. Everyone seemingly wanted something from her grief. It made people selfish. She didn't know who to trust. She didn't know who had an ulterior motive to use her son's death as a platform to elevate their agenda.

The next few days were a blur for Geraldine. She was the pillar of strength on the outside for friends and family, but every night, in the quiet of her home, she shed tears for everything she had lost and for a future her son would never see. All that hard work, the sacrifices, the dreams deferred, and grandchildren she would never play with. He was the light at the end of the tunnel. Her reason for being. For no reason that made a single drop of sense, it was over, just like that. She alternated between sadness, grief, anger and a feeling that others have felt, *when will this ever end.*

She stood stoic, lost in a memory of her son as his casket was lowered into the earth. It struck a chord with Detective Staples to see the contrast of inconsolable mourners in the midst of this uproar. He was parked across the street on his day off as a civilian. He wanted to show his respect and express his condolences to Ms. Banton. A cop showing up at the funeral of a young black man killed by another officer would probably only make matters worse. He watched for a few more minutes and as he drove away, he caught the eye of a young black man dressed in a black suit. The young man's eyes reflected the thoughts of his community. Detective Staples felt vulnerable without his uniform and gun. His thoughts were interrupted by his vibrating cellphone. *All hell is about to break loose. Banton case. Get your ass in here!* Detective Staples stepped on the gas and hightailed it to his precinct.

At the same time Detective Staples had received the urgent text, the young man in the black suit was watching a video on TMZ. It was recorded by an immigrant taxi driver from Ethiopia, who had been fast asleep in his taxi, about twenty feet away. He had held on to the video, fearful of reprisal from the authorities. But his wife had convinced him to release it to the media because the truth had to be told, no matter the consequences. The amateur video spread like wildfire across social media. The young man ran back to Geraldine, who was alone at the gravesite and showed her the video. The tears she had been holding back, surged forward as she watched the final, painful moments of her son's life.

The clarity of the video left no doubt about what happened to her son. Geraldine watched, holding her breath as the video played between her trembling hands. It looked like a routine traffic stop. Lucien pulled over under a street lamp and remained in his car, waiting for the officer to approach him. The street was empty of pedestrians, which was unusual for any street in New York. It was an ominous sign of things to come.

The approaching officer asked for his license and registration which Lucien handed to him through the window. The license fell on the ground and instead of picking it up himself, the officer ordered Lucien out the vehicle to do it. Geraldine watched with her hand on her chest, praying for a different outcome than the one that had already been delivered. The officer stepped away from Lucien, hand on his gun as Lucien picked up his license and handed him his license and registration. Everything else that followed happened so fast, that Geraldine forgot to breathe as she watched. The officer walked away and Lucien followed. The officer, his hand already on his gun, turned around to see an approaching Lucien and in a panic, opened fire. Lucien grabbed his chest, and said with a shocked, surprised expression displayed on his face, "I was coming to take the sobriety test." He then fell heavily to the filthy street and the camera zoomed in on his face. Geraldine watched as her son breathed heavily, then sighed and stared off into the night sky. She wondered what his last thoughts were. Was he thinking about a future he would never see? Was he wondering how could a traffic stop go so horribly wrong? Geraldine heard the other officer shouting at the officer who had pulled his weapon—*what the fuck did you do?* The officers then looked in the direction of the camera and before they could get to it, the vehicle sped off.

The video was an explosion of violence needed to send an already volatile situation and city into a frenzy. Within hours, groups of young, angry people armed with signs gathered at City Hall and various police stations to voice their distrust of an establishment that historically over policed their neighborhoods. It wouldn't take much for both sides to step over the line and all hell to break loose. Another innocent life might be lost, be it protestor or policeman; another family would be grieving.

Fifteen year-old Rebecca Parsons sat on her bed and watched the disturbing video on her cellphone like almost everyone in America. Her father, Richard Parsons had been home for the past few days and said he was on vacation. A horrified Rebecca watched in shock as her father shot Lucien Banton and the panic that ensued between him and the other officer. The man on camera wasn't the father she knew at home, who was always in control and fun to be around. She watched the video for the next few hours, trying to find the reason why her father would shoot an unarmed man. Maybe he was scared and in fear for his life? But aren't police officers trained to deal with fear and not overreact? Should someone lose their life because an officer overreacted? There was no way her father would deliberately kill an innocent person. He must have had a reason.

Friends from school were blowing up her phone with texts. Most were supportive, a few were vile memes of her dad. She knew what would happen if she went on social media. Trolls were probably waiting with bated breath and fingers on their keyboards for her to respond and defend her father. Defending him would only stoke this blazing fire, remaining quiet would look weak, but social media can devour you once the machinery gets rolling.

Rebecca tiptoed down the long hallway adorned with family portraits. On the way downstairs, she stopped and stared at one of them taken with her father. Everyone said she looked like her dad, even though she didn't see it, but now she did. They had the same shade of sky blue eyes and blonde hair the color of sand. She was tall for her age and everyone said she should be playing basketball.

It made her sweat too much and that always embarrassed her. Halfway down the stairs she could already hear the loud voice of Bill O'Reilly on Fox discussing the case. There were rumors circulating that he had sexually harassed a few women, but her dad had said over dinner, that powerful men like him don't have to do things like that, so it was obviously a media witch hunt. Her mom had kept quiet because arguing with her father was always futile. He loved a good argument, but enjoyed winning even more her mother always said. Rebecca stood behind her father for a few minutes and watched the show with him. He seemed unaware of her presence and barely moved, except to bring the Corona to his lips and then back down to the armrest.

"I didn't see you standing there, sweetie." He lowered the volume of the television and she sat down next to him.

"Why didn't you tell me what happened, daddy? It's all over the internet and my friends are texting me about it and calling you names."

"It will be okay, sweetie. I didn't do anything wrong. I was only doing my job."

"Couldn't you maybe have warned him to step back or just shoot to injure him?"

Richard Parsons stared at his daughter waiting intently for an answer. He stroked his week old beard and realized he hadn't taken a shower in two days. The questions his daughter was now asking him were questions he had asked himself. He had no good answers, except the obvious one.

"Honey, these thing are complicated. Sometimes as an officer, you have to make a split life and death decision. It's either me or them." He knew how it sounded, but he was too stressed and too tired to care.

"But he was unarmed, daddy," Rebecca said carefully in a low tone.

"But he could have been armed?"

"But he wasn't. He was only following your instructions and now he's dead. His mother is grieving. The city is angry. What's going to happen to us, daddy?"

Richard Parsons didn't have any answers, so he turned back to the television hoping that O'Reilly's commentary would instill him with the necessary confidence. A few minutes later he fell asleep and the nightmare he had been having for the past few days played again in his mind.

Geraldine Banton knew that Officer Parsons would probably be charged and stand trial for her son's death. She also knew it would be done just to appease the public, but in the end, she knew that he would be found innocent. Juries find it difficult to convict officers, even when the evidence is on videotape. They want to give officers the benefit of the doubt at every turn, sometimes looking for explanations when they are none to be had, except the obvious ones. Geraldine knew the Mayor would call for calm. He would say that the system had worked and all the citizens of New York City would have to accept the verdict of the courts. In a few weeks, people would go back to their lives. The politicians on television would find another ambulance to case. The uproar on social media would calm down because frankly it's hard to sustain that kind of anger for a long time, unless it directly affects you, few people can. But for mothers like Geraldine Banton, every breath they take is in remembrance of a child lost. All the hopes and dreams for the future suddenly comes to an end. Without warning, their life is over and you as the parent are still here and left with questions that will never be answered.

Within hours after TMZ aired the damning cellphone video, the character assassination of Lucien Banton was in full effect. Excerpts from some of his social media commentary about police brutality and supporting Black Lives Matter were posted. The intent of the leaked posts were obvious. Another post had him dressed in street clothes surrounded by a few other guys who looked like gang members. The headline blared: NOT A CHOIR BOY. The picture was from a play Lucien had participated in years ago, but nowhere in the article was that mentioned. Geraldine was savvy enough to understand that once these stories get out into the public arena that the forces behind them mean business. They would not stop until her son had been reduced to a statistic and people who once supported him would have cause to doubt his character. You put out enough false claims against anyone, and eventually, added together, it can resemble the truth because of any stereotypes or preconceived notions that people already have. Her son had worked too hard; she had sacrificed too much for it to end like this. An *eye for an eye* her Pastor had raged during his Sunday service while looking at her. The tension of the city had infiltrated the church. She prayed for guidance. Officer Parsons was probably praying to the same God for an acquittal. Whose prayers would he answer this time?

There was only one thing Geraldine could do. She went down into her basement, searched through boxes of memories she had forgotten about and found what she was looking for next to a picture of her late husband holding Lucien in his arms. His face was filled with joy and pride as he beamed at the bundle in his arms. Geraldine traced her fingertip over her husband's face and for a moment, she thought she could feel his presence comforting her. He had only bought the gun to protect their home. A string of robberies had left the entire neighborhood on edge, but the robberies had mysteriously stopped and the gun had been in the basement all these years. She shoved it in her purse, looked around her home at all the memories, turned off the lights and headed out the door.

The knock on his front door had been so soft at first, that Richard Parsons wasn't sure he had heard it. He stood up too fast and always toppled over. The television was on a Geico commercial as he walked to the door. His wife hadn't made it home from work as yet, and he assumed that his daughter was upstairs on her cellphone as she usually is. He was dressed in jeans, a Bruce Springsteen t-shirt with a black hoodie. Before he opened the door, Richard tossed the hoodie onto the hook behind the door and opened the door.

The glare of the afternoon sun beamed down directly into his eyes, momentarily blinding him as he focused on the short, black woman standing on the first step, two steps beneath him. The Brooklyn neighborhood was still busy with activity. A few houses down, he could hear the local boys playing football and he knew before long, an alarm would be triggered when the football landed on a car. Richard Parsons had a quizzical look on his face, unsure what she wanted. He didn't get too many black people knocking on his door in his neighborhood. He was wary of strangers and always cautious when opening his door, but as he stood in his doorway, he didn't sense any immediate danger.

"Yes, how I can help you?" Richard Parsons squinted at the black woman at his front door as he shielded his eyes.

Geraldine was a woman of few words. She always got to the point and didn't permit any room for ambiguity. When disciplining Lucien as a child, her approach had been the same. No debate. You did as you were told or suffered the consequences. It had served her well throughout her life. She saw no reason why it should be any different this time.

"You murdered my son."

It was a statement free of question and uncertainty. It was to the point and didn't require any further explanations of what she already believed. As Geraldine spoke the words, she reached into her purse and pointed her husband's old revolver at Richard Parsons. Her aim was steady and true. The lessons from her husband flooded back to her as she took aim. *Don't point a gun at anyone, unless you're willing to take a life*, he had cautioned her. Geraldine Banton was ready to take the life of Richard Parsons. *An eye for eye* as her Pastor had railed during Sunday service.

Maybe he should have expected the knock at his door from a parent whose child had been killed. He would have probably done the same thing if the circumstances were reversed. Richard Parsons thought of his daughter, his only child as he stared into the round, dark muzzle of the revolver. Without turning around, he closed the front door behind him and waited. He didn't recall seeing her on television. Up until that moment, he hadn't really wondered about her and what she might be going through. His concern had been for his family, himself and his job. But as she stood there now, pointing a gun at him, he wondered how could he not have thought of her. Anguish lined her dark face. Behind her glasses he could see the eyes of a woman torn by grief and lack of sleep. She couldn't be more than five-foot-four and about one hundred fifty pounds. Small patches of gray were sprinkled throughout her hair. Richard Parson knew better than to underestimate anyone, especially a woman who had lost a child and was pointing a gun at him.

"It was a terrible accident," he said as he stood at the top of his stairs. None of his neighbors were paying attention, but it was just a matter of time before someone saw the scene playing out in his front yard. "I am sorry for your loss." He didn't know her name or else he would have said it.

"My name is Geraldine Banton, mother of Lucien Banton. You should at least know the name of the man you murdered, Officer Parson."

He wanted to tell her it wasn't murder, but he knew it would only antagonize her further. She hadn't come all this way to hear him offer explanations. It should have been obvious to him, but it dawned on him that she had come to kill him.

"You didn't have to kill my son. He was only doing as you told him, and for that you shot him. How do you sleep at night, Officer Parsons?"

"It was an accident, Ms. Banton. A very tragic accident which I will regret for the rest of my life."

"At least you will have the rest of your life. My son's life is over. He will never get the chance to get married, have children and grow into an old man. You took all of that away from him and me. Do you understand what you've done?" Geraldine's voice tinged with anguish, but her tone remained steady as the gun remained pointed at his face.

The commotion in Richard Parson's front yard had been noticed by some neighbors. The older ones stayed inside, but peeked from behind curtains. The younger ones, fearless because such is the stupidity of youth and wanting social media fame because of a viral video, came closer with cellphone cameras pointed and doing the job of the news media. Geraldine was oblivious to the gathering crowd. She wanted an answer that would make sense as to why her son was dead. She needed some sort of justification besides the obvious reason.

If her son had a gun pointed at the officer, she could have understood.

If her son was high on drugs and charging the officer, she would have understood.

If he had been disrespectful and belligerent, even that would not have been a plausible reason for his death, but it would have been something. Instead she had nothing. When someone loses their life, there has to be a reason why a good person no longer walks this earth.

Rebecca Parsons heard voices outside her bedroom window. Confused at the gathering crowd below her, she could only see the outstretched arms of a woman with her hands clasped around a gun. She instantly knew who it was. Just moments before walking over to the window, her mind had wandered to Ms. Banton, and now here she was, at her home, pointing a gun at her father.

Richard Parsons knew it would be only minutes before his front yard and street were buzzing with police activity. Whenever that happened, even though it should instill confidence that a situation was under control, it couldn't be further from the truth. Instead, the buzz of police activity and more guns, only served to make these kinds of situations more volatile and unpredictable. Innocent people get hurt. He wasn't concerned for his safety, he was concerned about his daughter. As long as Rebecca stayed inside, she would be safe.

"Why did you kill my son, Officer Parsons?"

Richard Parsons stared out at the growing crowd, cellphone cameras pointed at him and he wondered if any of them had bothered to even call the police. They were more interested in internet fame than his safety, or even theirs.

"If I had to do it over again, maybe I would have done something differently. I don't know what, just something. I only did what I was trained to do, Ms. Banton."

"The NYPD trained you to kill and not disarm?"

He could feel the invisible lens of the cellphone cameras stretching forward to record his words. Words which would be damning to hear. It's one thing to believe something, but when you hear a certain policy articulated, it can be a gut punch.

So he gave her the diplomatic answer. "The NYPD trains us to defend ourselves."

"But there wasn't anything to defend, Officer Parsons. My son was unarmed and complying with your orders. What were you defending?"

The first police vehicle with sirens blaring pulled into his front yard, followed by three others. Geraldine was ordered to drop her weapon and back away with her arms in the air. She had arrived prepared for this scenario and didn't bother turning around to acknowledge the command. The second her son took his last breath, her life was over. Her greatest fear in the world had been realized. Being surrounded by police officers with loud sirens and guns pointed at her did not scare her. She was prepared for the outcome and had made her peace with herself and God. She had prayed for forgiveness, but was ready to die without it.

"I...we couldn't have known what the suspect had in mind. My only thought I had was being in fear for my life."

"You had the gun. You had the power. I don't understand how you could be in fear for your life with an unarmed person. Doesn't your training teach you how to defuse potential volatile situations like that without causing death? You didn't have to murder my son."

It was the second time she had said the word, murder. He had never considered his action to be murder, but self-defense. Murder in his mind was premeditated. His action was immediate, without thought to anything else except self-preservation. He knew what she wanted to hear. He knew what all the protestors thought. It wasn't who he was, yet he wondered for a brief moment, if Lucien Banton had been a white male, would he have been so quick to pull the trigger? Would his fear have caused him to react so decisively?

He looked around his neighborhood, all the faces of his neighbors were white. The only time most of them probably saw a black face was on the train or random faces walking down the street. The only black people he came in contact with were the ones he arrested. Could that experience make him more likely to view Lucien Banton as a suspect, instead of just a person being stopped? Every time he closed his eyes, he could see the shocked expression on the young man's face as he slumped to the street, clutching his chest. *"Why did you shoot me?"* He had asked. Richard Parsons had watched, stunned and in shock at how terribly wrong everything had gone in a few seconds. Amazing how you try to live your life the right way for thirty-eight years and in thirty seconds of a video that goes viral, you become public enemy number one. Some people called him a hero, and others called him a racist. It's not a word he had ever associated with himself. It didn't fit. To admit something so vile about himself would be to acknowledge he had failed as an officer to protect and serve all citizens, regardless of race.

Rebecca had stood on the inside of the front door and knew her father wouldn't allow her to come outside. So she had gone around the back and was now standing in the crowd of onlookers. She looked out of place. She was the only one without a cellphone recording the exchange in her front yard.

"If my son were white would you have shot him?"

Some of the onlookers were broadcasting the riveting scene on Facebook Live. A few of the networks like CNN and MSNBC had picked up the feed and were commenting on it. The scene was now playing in bars, on work computers, commuters on the trains, buses, and people walking down the street. Geraldine was oblivious to being the *news* right now. All she wanted was some kind of justice for her son. An admittance of guilt from his killer.

"I didn't consider his race. Everything happened so fast."

"When was the last time a police officer shot and killed a white motorist?"

"I don't know the answer to that question."

"Just the fact that you don't know, doesn't that tell you something?"

"I know you want justice for your son, Ms. Banton, but this isn't the way to get it."

"How do you suggest I get justice, Officer Parsons? Through the courts? I think both of us know that won't happen. Police officers don't value brown lives. The courts, like politicians, only care about getting elected for another term. One less black man in this world is viewed as a victory to people like you."

Rebecca had slowly made her way through the crowd and was in the front now. She dashed forward to run to her father's side as he shouted at her to stay put, but it was too late. Lucien's mother had moved back a few feet and was now on the grass and her father was on the bottom step. Without even thinking, as most teenagers do, she was now between her dad and the revolver pointed directly at him. It was now trained on her. Richard Parsons looked in horror as his worst nightmare was being played out in front of him. The officers behind her and on both sides ordered Geraldine to drop her weapon, but she had the upper hand now.

"Don't come any closer," she ordered him. If you do, then your daughter will pay for your sins."

Richard Parsons remained about two feet away from his daughter. So close, yet so far. A bullet would travel faster than him if he attempted to do anything heroic.

"Don't hurt my baby. She's all I have."

"My son was all I had, Officer Parsons and you took him away. Maybe you need to feel the same pain I am feeling now, so you can fully comprehend what you've done."

Before her dad could defend himself, Rebecca spoke up. "Please, Ms. Banton, my dad is a good man. Whatever he did, I am sure he did it to protect himself. He didn't mean to kill your son. It was an accident."

"The innocence and stupidity of youth," Geraldine smiled. Her words were without malice. The young blonde girl with blue eyes obviously loved her father. No child should ever be punished or questioned for loving a parent. She saw the best in her father, but he had been at his worst when he murdered her son. She kept the gun trained on Rebecca now. The clouds above were beginning to darken. A thunderstorm was fast approaching. "This time when I ask you the question again, keep in mind what you have to lose," her eyes flickered briefly towards Rebecca, "and what I have to lose, is nothing." Richard Parsons nodded and understood the implicit meaning of what she was saying. "Why did you murder my son? He was unarmed and no threat to you. Were you scared because he was a black male?"

Richard Parsons nodded his head.

"That's not an answer. I need you to answer my question, Officer Parsons."

"Yes. I was scared and in fear for my life because he was black."

"Good. I just want your honesty. If my son were white, would he still be alive today?"

The sound of police radios crackled all around them. The crowd was hushed, hanging on to the exchange between Geraldine Banton and Officer Richard Parsons. Televisions and cellphones were tuned in to the drama. Work everywhere had come to a standstill.

"I don't know. I just don't know."

"You must know, Officer Parsons. You already admitted to being fearful because he was black, so it would stand to reason, if he were white, you would not be as fearful and therefore not as quick to pull the trigger. Isn't that a fair assumption?"

"Yes, that's a reasonable assumption, if you think your life isn't in danger."

"Don't get cute with me, Officer Parsons. I don't think your daughter wants to pay the price for you being cute."

Richard Parsons stared at the woman standing a few feet away. He had seen that look before. She had resigned herself to the outcome of the situation she had initiated. Her son had been her life. Any life after him was just a hollow existence. She wanted him to give her answers he hadn't fully come to terms with himself.

"What did my son do to make you an officer of the law scared for his life?"

"I'm not sure what you mean."

"Did he pull a gun on you? Seem high on marijuana? Did he antagonize you? Was my son in any way, that you can now recall, disrespectful of you as a man or as an officer?"

Richard Parsons sighed and the last words of Lucien Banton played in his mind again. *Why did you shoot me?* He knew the networks had probably already picked up the story and his image was all over the television sets of Americans. His professional life was over. There was no way he would ever work as an officer in New York or anywhere else. He was radioactive. His only concern now was making sure Rebecca remained unharmed. "No. Your son did not do anything that warranted him being killed. He should still be alive."

Tears now streamed freely down Geraldine's face. She had heard what she came for from her son's killer. In the distance, lightning crackled across the darkening skies. The noise startled Geraldine and the revolver still clasped between both hands was now pointed directly at the young girl's chest. Somewhere an order was given and the thunderous sounds of many gunshots filled the air. Onlookers ducked for cover. Richard Parsons sprinted for his daughter and covered her body. Geraldine wobbled unsteadily. The gun fell to the grass and Geraldine Banton fell to her knees, eyes skyward, searching the sky for something that wasn't there.

Rebecca Parsons shook off her dad and ran towards Geraldine. She kneeled down in front of her and cradled her head in her arms. Death was only a few minutes away for Geraldine. Her spirit was already traveling, on its way to meet her son. She struggled to find the words as she looked at the white hands of the daughter against her dark skin. The image was beautiful and filled her suddenly with sadness and joy.

"You were safe. I wasn't-"

"I know. You just wanted the truth."

Geraldine nodded.

"I'm sorry for everything. Your son didn't deserve to die."

She nodded again and squeezed the young girl's hand. Maybe something like this is what's needed to jumpstart the conversation and stop the genocide of police officers killing black men. Maybe the death of her son will have some meaning and the way police departments do business will be reevaluated. It was a lot to hope for, but it was all Geraldine had to hold on to, as death rode on the evening wind to claim soul. Just as suddenly as the dark clouds had arrived, they disappeared. The sun pushed its way through and covered Geraldine in its warmth. She closed her eyes for the last time as the memory of a young Lucien smiling at her made her smile.

Paperbacks available @ www.deanjeanpierre.com & KINDLE

Also by Dean Jéan-Pierre

Woman Worship 4
Rage
The Killer In You
Orgasms for Lunch (E-book)
Birthday Girl Dessert (E-book)
A Killer Review (E-book)
I Didn't Mean to Kill My Neighbor (E-book)
Crave
The Randomness of Everything
Don't Mess With Eva
The Killing Club of Ex-Girlfriends
Kiss Me Softly
Woman Worship 3
Insatiable (1-2)
Assume The Position
Woman Worship 2
Stiff (E-book)
Moist
Aural Sex (Poetry CD)
Cum For Me
Woman Worship
The Pussy Whispers

www.deanjeanpierre.com

www.ingramcontent.com/pod-product-compliance
Lightning Source LLC
Chambersburg PA
CBHW020405210626
46816CB00006BB/2127